He had a thin face fram  hair, looking like a dandy his long black cape and t spilling over his collar.

He carried a doctor's ba opened with one hand, all without taking his eyes off us as he took something from it, something long and curved.

Then he smiled and drew the dagger from its sheath, and it gleamed wickedly in the dark.

"Stay close, Élise," whispered Mother. "Everything's going to be all right."

I believed her because I was an eight-year-old girl and of course I believed my mother. But also because having seen her with the wolf, I had good reason to believe her.

Even so, fear nibbled at my insides.

"What is your business, monsieur?" she called levelly.

He made no answer.

"Very well. Then we shall return to where we came from," said Mother loudly, taking my hand and about to depart.

At the alley entrance a shadow flickered and a second figure appeared in the orange glow of the lantern. It was a lamplighter; we could tell by the pole he carried. Even so, Mother stopped.

"Monsieur," she called to the lamplighter cautiously, "I wonder if I might ask you to call off this gentleman bothering us?"

The lamplighter said nothing, going instead to where the lamp burned and raising his pole. Mama started, "Monsieur . . ." and I wondered why the man would be trying to light a lamp that was already lit and realized too late that the pole had a hook on the end—the hook that they used for dousing the flame of the candle inside.

"Monsieur . . ."

The entrance was plunged into darkness.

ASSASSIN'S
CREED®
UNITY

OLIVER BOWDEN

ACE BOOKS, NEW YORK

THE BERKLEY PUBLISHING GROUP
Published by the Penguin Group
Penguin Group (USA) LLC
375 Hudson Street, New York, New York 10014

USA • Canada • UK • Ireland • Australia • New Zealand • India • South Africa • China

penguin.com

A Penguin Random House Company

ASSASSIN'S CREED® UNITY

An Ace Book / published by arrangement with Penguin Books, Ltd.

Ace Books are published by The Berkley Publishing Group.
ACE and the "A" design are trademarks of Penguin Group (USA) LLC.

For information, address: The Berkley Publishing Group,
a division of Penguin Group (USA) LLC,
375 Hudson Street, New York, New York 10014.

ISBN: 978-0-425-27973-1

PUBLISHING HISTORY
Ace premium edition / December 2014

PRINTED IN THE UNITED STATES OF AMERICA

10 9 8 7 6 5 4 3 2 1

Interior text design by Kristin del Rosario.

ASSASSIN'S
C R E E D ®
U N I T Y

12 SEPTEMBER 1794

On my desk lies her journal, open to the first page. It was all I could read before a flood tide of emotion took my breath away and the text before me was splintered by the diamonds in my eyes. Tears had coursed down my cheeks as thoughts of her returned to me: the impish child, racing through the hallways of the great Palace of Versailles; the firebrand I came to know and love in adulthood, tresses of red hair across her shoulders, eyes intense beneath dark and lustrous lashes. She had the balance of the expert dancer and the master swordsman. She was as comfortable gliding across the floor of the palace beneath the desirous eye of every man in the room as she was in combat.

But behind those eyes lay secrets. Secrets I was about

to discover. I pick up her journal once again, wanting to place my palm and fingertips to the page, caress the words, feeling that on this page lies part of her very soul.

I begin to read.

9 APRIL 1778

i

My name is Élise de la Serre. My father is François, my mother Julie, and we live in Versailles: glittering, beautiful Versailles, where neat buildings and grand châteaus reside in the shadow of the great palace, with its lime-tree avenues, its shimmering lakes and fountains, its exquisitely tended topiary.

We are nobles. The lucky ones. The privileged. For proof we need only take the fifteen-mile road into Paris. It is a road lit by overhanging oil lamps, because in Versailles we use oil lamps, but in Paris the poor use tallow candles, and the smoke from the tallow factories hangs over the city like a death shroud, dirtying the skin and choking the lungs. Dressed in rags, their backs hunched either with the weight of their physical burden or of mental sorrow, the poor people of Paris creep through streets that never seem to get light. The streets stream with open sewers, where mud and human effluent flow freely, coating the legs of those who carry our sedan chairs as we pass through, staring wide-eyed out the windows.

Later we take gilded carriages back to Versailles and pass figures in the fields, shrouded in mist like ghosts. These barefooted peasants tend noble land and starve if the crop is bad, virtual slaves of the landowners. At home I listen to my parents' tales of how they must stay awake to swish sticks at frogs whose croaking keeps landowners awake; how they must eat grass to stay alive; how the nobles are exempt from paying taxes, excused from military service and spared the indignity of the *corvée*, a day's unpaid labor working on the roads.

My parents say Queen Marie Antoinette roams the hallways, ballrooms and vestibules of the palace dreaming up new ways to spend her dress allowance while her husband King Louis XVI lounges on his *lit de justice*, passing laws that enrich the lives of nobles at the expense of the poor and starving. They talk darkly of how these actions might foment revolution.

My father had certain "associates." His advisers, Messieurs Chretien Lafrenière, Charles Gabriel Sivert, and Madame Levesque. "The Crows," I called them, with their long black coats, dark felt hats and eyes that never smiled.

"Have we not learned the lessons of the Croquants?" says my mother.

Mother had told me about the Croquants, of course. Those peasant revolutionaries of two centuries ago.

"It would appear not, Julie," Father replies.

There is an expression to describe the moment you

suddenly understand something that had previously been a mystery to you. It is the moment when "the penny drops."

As a small child, it never occurred to me to wonder why I learned history, not etiquette, manners and poise; I didn't question why Mother joined Father and the Crows after dinner, her voice raised in disagreement to debate with as much force as they ever did; I never wondered why she didn't ride sidesaddle, nor why she never needed a groom to steady her mount, and I never wondered why she had so little time for fashion or court gossip. Not once did I think to ask why my mother was not like other mothers.

Not until the penny dropped.

ii

She was beautiful, of course, and always well dressed though she had no time for the manner of finery worn by the women at court, of whom she would purse her lips and talk disapprovingly. According to her they were obsessed with looks, status, with *things*.

"They wouldn't know an idea if it hit them between the eyes, Élise. Promise me you'll never end up like them."

Intrigued and wanting to know more about how I should never end up, I used my vantage point at the hem of Mother's skirt to spy on these hated women. What I saw were overpowdered gossips who pretended they were devoted to their husbands even as their eyes roamed the room over the rims of their fans, looking for unsuspecting lovers to snare. Unseen, I would glimpse behind the powdered mask, when the scornful laughter dried on their lips and the mocking look died in their eyes. I'd see them for what they really were, which was frightened. Frightened of falling out of favor. Of slipping down the society ladder.

Mother was not like that. For one thing she couldn't have cared less about gossip. And I never saw her with a fan, and she hated powder, and she had no time whatsoever for charcoal beauty spots and alabaster skin, her sole concession to fashion being shoes. Otherwise, what attention she gave her comportment was for one reason and one reason only: to maintain decorum.

And she was absolutely devoted to my father. She stood by him—at his side, though, never behind him—she supported him, was unswervingly loyal to him, backing him in public even though behind closed doors they would debate and I would hear her cooling his temper.

It's been a long time, though, since I last heard her debating with Father.

They say she may die tonight.

10 April 1778

She survived the night.

I sat by her bedside, held her hand and spoke to her. For a while I had been under the delusion that it was me comforting her, until the moment she turned her head and gazed at me with milky but soul-searching eyes, and it became apparent that the opposite was true.

There were times last night when I gazed out of the window to see Arno in the yard below, envying how he could be so oblivious to the heartache just feet away from him. He knows she's ill, of course, but consumption is commonplace, death at the doctor's knee an everyday occurrence, even here in Versailles. And he is not a de la Serre. He is our ward, and thus not privy to our deepest, darkest secrets, nor our private anguish. Moreover, he has barely known any other state of affairs. For most of his time here. To Arno, Mother is a remote figure attended to on the upper floors of the château; to him she is defined purely by her illness.

Instead, my father and I share our turmoil via hidden glances. Outwardly we take pains to appear as normal, our mourning mitigated by two years of grim diagnosis. Our grief is another secret hidden from our ward.

ii

We're getting closer to the moment that the penny dropped. And thinking about the first incident, the first time I really began to wonder about my parents, and specifically Mother, I imagine it like a signpost along the road toward my destiny.

It happened at the convent. I was just five when I first entered it, and my memories of it are far from fully formed. Just impressions, really: long rows of beds; a distinct but slightly disconnected memory of glancing outside a window crowned with frost and seeing the tops of the trees rising above billowing skirts of mist; and . . . the Mother Superior.

Bent over and bitter, the Mother Superior was known for her cruelty. She'd wander the corridors of the convent with her cane across her palms as though presenting it to a banquet. In her office it was laid across her desk. Back then we'd talk of it being "your turn," and for a while it was mine, when she hated my attempts at happiness, begrudged the fact that I was swift to laughter and would always call my happy smile a smirk. The cane, she said, would wipe that smirk off my face.

Mother Superior was right about that. It did. For a while.

And then one day Mother and Father arrived to see the Mother Superior on what matter I have no idea, and I was called to the office at their request. There I found my parents turned in their seats to greet me, Mother Superior standing from behind her desk, the usual look of undisguised contempt upon her face, a frank assessment of my many shortcomings only just dry on her lips.

If it had been Mother alone to see me, I should not have been so formal. I would have run to her and hoped I might slip into the folds of her dress and into another world out of that horrible place. But it was both of them, and my father was my king. It was he who dictated what modes of politeness we abided by; he who had insisted I was placed in the convent in the first place. So I approached and curtsied and waited to be addressed.

My mother snatched up my hand. How she even saw what was there I have no idea, since it was by my side, but somehow she'd caught a glimpse of the marks left by the cane.

"What are these?" she demanded of the Mother Superior, holding my hand toward her.

I had never seen the Mother Superior look anything less than composed. But now I would say that she paled. In an instant my mother had transformed from proper and polite, just what was expected of a guest of the

Mother Superior, to an instrument of potential anger.
We all felt it. Mother Superior the most.

She stammered a little. "As I was saying, Élise is a
willful girl and disruptive."

"So she's caned?" demanded my mother, her anger
rising.

Mother Superior squared her shoulders. "How else
do you expect me to keep order?"

Mother snatched up the cane. "I expect you to be
able to keep order. Do you think this makes you strong?"
She slapped the cane to the table. Mother Superior
jumped and swallowed and her eyes darted to my father,
who was keeping watch with an odd, unreadable expression, as though these were events that did not require
his participation. "Well, then you are sorely mistaken,"
added Mother. "It makes you weak."

She stood, glaring at the Mother Superior, and made
her jump again as she slapped the cane to the desk a second time. Then she took my hand. "Come along, Élise."

We left, and from then on I have had tutors to teach
me schoolwork.

I knew one thing as we bustled out of the convent
and into our carriage for a silent ride home. As Mother
and Father bristled with things left unsaid, I knew that
ladies did not behave the way my mother had just done.
Not normal ladies, anyway.

Another clue. This happened a year or so later, at a
birthday party for a spoiled daughter in a neighboring
château. Other girls my age played with dolls, setting
them up to take tea, only a tea for dolls, where there was

no real tea or cake, just little girls pretending to feed tea and cake to dolls, which to me, even then, seemed stupid.

Not far away the boys were playing with toy soldiers, so I stood to join them, oblivious to the shocked silence that fell over the gathering.

My nursemaid Ruth dragged me away. "You play with dolls, Élise," she said, firmly but nervously, her eyes darting as she shrank beneath the disapproving stare of other nursemaids. I did as I was told, sinking to my haunches and affecting interest in the pretend tea and cake, and with the embarrassing interruption over, the lawn returned to its natural state: boys playing with toy soldiers, the girls with their dolls, nursemaids watching us both, and not far away a gaggle of mothers, highborn ladies who gossiped on wrought-iron lawn chairs.

I looked at the gossiping ladies and saw them with Mother's eyes. I saw my own path from girl on the grass to gossiping lady, and with a rush of absolute certainty realized I didn't want that. I didn't want to be like those mothers. I wanted to be like my own mother, who had excused herself from the gaggle of gossips and could be seen in the distance, alone, at the water's edge, her individuality plain for all to see.

iii

I have had a note from Mr. Weatherall. Writing in his native English, he tells me that he wishes to see Mother and asks that I meet him in the library at midnight to escort him to her room. He urges me not to tell Father.

Yet another secret I must keep. Sometimes I feel like one of those poor wretches we see in Paris, hunched over beneath the weight of expectations forced upon me.

I am only ten years old.

11 APRIL 1778

i

At midnight, I pulled on a gown, took a candle and crept downstairs to the library, where I waited for Mr. Weatherall.

He had let himself into the château, moving like a mystery, the dogs undisturbed, and when he entered the library so quietly that I barely even heard the door open and close, he crossed the floor in a few strides, snatched his wig from his head—the accursed thing, he hated it— and grasped my shoulders.

"They say she is fading fast," he said, and needed it to be hearsay.

"She is," I told him, dropping my gaze.

His eyes closed, and though he was not at all old—in his mid-thirties, the same age as Mother and Father— the years were etched upon his face.

"Mr. Weatherall and I were once very close," Mother had said before. She'd smiled as she said it. I fancy that she blushed.

ii

It was a freezing-cold day in February the first time I met Mr. Weatherall. That winter was the first of the really cruel winters, but while in Paris the River Seine had flooded and frozen, and the poverty-stricken were dying in the streets, things were very different in Versailles. By the time we awoke, the staff had made up the fires that roared in the grates, and we ate steaming breakfast and wrapped up warm in furs, our hands kept warm by muffs as we took morning and afternoon strolls in the grounds.

That particular day the sun was shining although it did nothing to offset the bone-chilling cold. A crust of ice sparkled prettily on a thick layer of snow, and it was so hard that Scratch, our Irish wolfhound, was able to walk upon it without his paws sinking in. He'd taken a few tentative steps, then on realizing his good fortune, given a joyous bark and dashed off ahead while Mother and I made our way across the grounds and to the trees at the perimeter of the south lawn.

Holding her hand, I glanced over my shoulder as we walked. Far away our château shone in the reflection of sun and snow, its windows winking, then, as we stepped out of the sun and into the trees, it became indistinct, as though shaded by pencils. We were farther out than usual, I realized, no longer within reach of its shelter.

"Do not be alarmed if you see a gentleman in the shadows," said Mother, bending to me slightly. Her voice was quiet. I clutched her hand a little tighter at the very idea and she laughed. "Our presence here is no coincidence."

I was six years old then and had no idea that a lady meeting a man in such circumstances might have "implications." As far as I was concerned, it was simply my mother meeting a man, and of no greater significance than her talking to Emanuel, our gardener, or passing the time of day with Jean, our coachman.

Frost confers stillness on the world. In the trees it was even quieter than on the snow-covered lawn and we were absorbed by an absolute tranquility as we took a narrow path into the depth of the wood.

"Mr. Weatherall likes to play a game," said my mother, her voice hushed in honor of the peace. "He might like to surprise us, and one should always be aware of what surprises lie in store. We take into account our surroundings and cast our expectations accordingly. Do you see tracks?"

The snow around us was untouched. "No, Mama."

"Good. Then we can be sure of our radius. Now, where might a man hide in such conditions?"

"Behind a tree?"

"Good, good—but what about here?" She indicated overhead and I craned my neck to gaze into the canopy of branches above, the frost twinkling in shards of sunlight.

"Observe everywhere, always." Mother smiled. "Use your eyes to see, don't incline your head if at all possible. Don't show to others where your attention is directed. In life you will have opponents, and those opponents will attempt to read you for clues as to your intentions. Maintain your advantage by making them guess."

"Will our visitor be high in a tree, Mama?" I asked.

She chuckled. "No. As a matter of fact, I have seen him. Do you see him Élise?"

We had stopped. I gazed at the trees in front of us. "No, Mama."

"Show yourself, Freddie," called Mother, and sure enough, a few yards ahead of us a gray-bearded man stepped from behind a tree, swept his tricorn from his head and gave us an exaggerated bow.

The men of Versailles were a certain way. They looked down their noses at anybody not like them. They had what I thought of as "Versailles smiles," hoisted halfway between bemused and bored, as though constantly on the verge of delivering the witty quip by which, it seemed, all men of court were judged.

This man was not a man of Versailles, the beard alone saw to that. And though he was smiling, it was not a Versailles smile; instead, it was soft but serious, the face of a man who thought before he spoke and made his words count.

"You cast a shadow, Freddie." Mother smiled as he stepped forward, kissed her proffered hand then did the same to me, bowing again.

"The shadow?" he said, and his voice was rough, uncultured, the voice of a seaman or soldier. "Oh, bloody hell, I must be losing my touch."

"I hope not, Freddie," laughed Mother. "Élise, meet Mr. Weatherall, an Englishman. An associate of mine. Freddie, meet Élise."

An associate? Like the Crows? No, he was nothing like them. Instead of glaring at me, he took my hand, bowed and kissed it. "Charmed, mademoiselle," he rasped, his English accent mangling the word "mademoiselle" in a way that I couldn't help but find charming.

Mother fixed me with a serious expression. "Mr. Weatherall is our confidant and protector, Élise. A man to whom you may always turn when in need of help."

I looked at her, feeling a little startled. "But what about Father?"

"Father loves us both dearly, and would gladly give his life for us, but men as important as your father need shielding from their domestic responsibilities. This is why we have Mr. Weatherall, Élise—that your Father need not be troubled by those matters concerning his womenfolk." An even more significant look came into her eyes. "Your father need not be troubled, Élise, do you understand?"

"Yes, Mama."

Mr. Weatherall was nodding. "I am here to serve, mademoiselle," he said to me.

"Thank you, monsieur." I curtsied.

Scratch had arrived, greeting Mr. Weatherall excitedly, the two of them evidently old friends.

"Can we talk, Julie?" said the protector, replacing his tricorn and indicating that the two of them might walk together.

I stayed some steps behind, hearing brief snatches and disjointed snippets of their hushed conversation. I heard "Grand Master" and "King," but they were just words, the kind I was used to hearing from behind the doors of the château. It's only in the years since then that they've taken on a much greater resonance.

And then it happened.

Looking back I can't remember the sequence of events. I remember seeing Mother and Mr. Weatherall tense at the same time as Scratch bristled and growled. Then my mother wheeled. My gaze went in the direction of her eyes and I saw it there, a wolf standing in the undergrowth to my left, a black-and-gray wolf standing absolutely still in the trees, regarding me with hungry eyes.

Something appeared from within Mother's muff, a silver blade, and in two quick strides she had crossed to me, had swept me up and away and deposited me behind her so that I clung to her skirts as she faced the wolf, her blade outstretched.

Across the way Mr. Weatherall held a straining, growling, hackles-risen Scratch by the scruff of his neck, and I noticed that his other hand reached for the hilt of a sword that hung at his side.

"Wait," commanded Mother. An upraised hand stopped Mr. Weatherall in his tracks. "I don't think this wolf will attack."

"I'm not so sure, Julie," warned Mr. Weatherall. "That is an exceptionally hungry-looking wolf you got there."

The wolf stared at my mother. She looked right back, talking to us at the same time. "There's nothing for him to eat in the hills; it's desperation that has brought him to our grounds. But I think this wolf knows that by attacking us, he makes an enemy of us. Far better for it to retreat in the face of implacable strength and forage elsewhere."

Mr. Weatherall gave a short laugh. "Why am I getting the whiff of a parable here?"

"Because, Freddie"—Mother smiled—"there is a parable here."

The wolf stared for a few moments more, never taking its eyes from Mother, until at last it dipped its head, turned and slowly trotted away. We watched it disappear into the tress and my mother stood down, her blade replaced in her muff. I looked at Mr. Weatherall; his jacket was once again buttoned and there was no sign of his sword.

And I came one step closer to the penny dropping.

iii

I showed Mr. Weatherall to her room and he asked that he see her alone, assuring me that he could see himself out. Curious, I peered through the keyhole and saw him take a seat by her side, reach for her hand and bow his head. Moments later I thought I heard the sound of him weeping.

12 APRIL 1778

i

I gaze from my window and remember last summer, when in moments of play with Arno I ascended from my cares and enjoyed blissful days of being a little girl again, running with him through the hedge maze in the grounds of the palace, squabbling over dessert, little knowing that the respite from worry would be so temporary.

Every morning I dig my nails into my palms and ask, "Is she awake?" and Ruth, knowing I really mean, "Is she alive?" reassures me that Mother has survived the night.

But it won't be long now.

ii

So. The moment that the penny dropped. It draws nearer. But first, another signpost.

The Carrolls arrived in the spring of the year I first met Mr. Weatherall. What a gorgeous spring it was. The snows had melted to reveal lush carpets of perfectly trimmed lawn beneath, returning Versailles to its natural state of immaculate perfection. Surrounded by the perfectly cut topiary of our grounds, we could barely hear the hum of the town, while away to our right the slopes of the palace were visible, wide stone steps leading to the columns of its vast frontage. Quite the splendor in which to entertain the Carrolls from Mayfair in London, England. Mr. Carroll and Father spent hours in the drawing room, apparently deep in conversation and occasionally visited by the Crows, while Mother and I were tasked with entertaining Madame Carroll and her daughter, May, who lost no time at all telling me that she was ten and that because I was only six, that made her much better than me.

We invited them for a walk and wrapped up against a slight morning chill soon to be burned away by the sun: Mother and I, Madame Carroll and May.

Mother and Madame Carroll walked some steps in front of us. Mother, I noticed, wore her muff, and I wondered if the blade was secreted within. I had asked about it, of course, after the incident with the wolf.

"Mama, why do you keep a knife in your muff?"

"Why, Élise, in case of threats from the marauding

wolves, of course." And with a wry smile she added, "Wolves of the four-legged and two-legged variety. And anyway, the blade helps the muff keep its shape."

But then, as was quickly becoming customary, she made me promise to keep it as one of our *vérités cachées*. Mr. Weatherall was a *vérité cachée*. Which meant that when Mr. Weatherall had given me a sword lesson, that became a *vérité cachée* as well.

Secrets by any other name.

May and I walked a polite distance behind our mothers. The hems of our skirts brushed the lawn so that from a distance we would appear to be gliding across the grounds, four ladies in perfect transport.

"How old are you, smell-bag?" whispered May to me, though as I've said, she had already established our ages. Twice, in fact.

"Don't call me smell-bag," I said primly.

"Sorry, smell-bag, but tell me again how old you are."

"I'm six," I told her.

She gave a six-is-a-terrible-age-to-be chortle, like she herself had never been six. "Well, I am ten," she said haughtily. (And as an aside, May Carroll said everything haughtily. In fact, unless I say otherwise, just assume she said it haughtily.)

"I know you are ten," I hissed, fondly imagining sticking out a foot and watching her sprawl to the gravel of the driveway.

"Just so you don't forget," she said, and I pictured little bits of gravel sticking to her bawling face as she picked herself up from the ground. What was it Mr. Weatherall had told me? The bigger they are, the harder they fall.

(And now I have reached the age of ten I wonder if I am arrogant like her. Do I have that mocking tone when I talk to those younger or lower in status than I? According to Mr. Weatherall I'm overconfident, which I suppose is a nice way of saying "arrogant," and maybe that's why May and I rubbed up against each other the way we did, because deep down we were actually quite similar.)

As we took our turn around the grounds, the words spoken by the ladies ahead of us reached our ears as Madame Carroll said, "Obviously we have concerns with the direction your Order appears to want to take."

"You have *concerns*?" said Mother.

"Indeed. Concerns about the intentions of your husband's associates. And as we both know, it is our duty to ensure our husbands do the right thing. Perhaps, if you don't mind my saying, your husband is giving certain factions leave to dictate his policies?"

"Indeed, there are high-ranking members who favor, shall we say, more *extreme* measures regarding the changing of the old order."

"This concerns us in England."

My mother chortled. "Of course it does. In England you refuse to accept change of any kind."

Madame Carroll bridled. "Not at all. Your reading of our national character lacks subtlety. But I'm beginning to get a feel for where your own loyalties lie, Madame de la Serre. You yourself are petitioning for change?"

"If change be for the better."

"Then do I need to report that your loyalties lie with your husband's advisers? Has my errand been in vain?"

"Not quite, Madame. How comforting it is to know that I enjoy the support of my English colleagues in opposing drastic measures. But I cannot claim to share your ultimate goal. While it's true there are forces pushing for violent overthrow, and while it's true that my husband believes in God-appointed monarchy, indeed, that his ideals for the future encompass no change at all, I myself tread a middle line. A third way, if you like. Perhaps it won't surprise you to learn that I consider my belief to be the more moderate of the three."

They walked on some steps and Madame Carroll nodded, thinking.

Into the silence my mother said, "I'm sorry if you don't feel our goals are aligned, Madame Carroll. My apologies if that makes me a somewhat unreliable confidante."

The other woman nodded. "I see. Well, if I were you, Madame de la Serre, I would use my influence with both sides in order to propose your middle line."

"On that issue I shouldn't like to say, but be assured your journey has not been in vain. My respect for you and your branch of the Order remains a steadfast as I hope it does in return. From me you can rely on two things: firstly that I will abide by my own principles, and secondly that I will not allow my husband to be swayed by his advisers."

"Then you have given me what I want."

"Very good. It is some consolation, I hope."

Behind, May inclined her head to me. "Have your parents told you of your destiny?"

"No. What do you mean, 'destiny'?"

She put a hand to her mouth, pretending to have said too much. "They will do, perhaps, when you turn ten years old. Just as they did me. How old are you, by the way?"

"I am six." I sighed.

"Well, perhaps they will tell you when you are ten, as they did me."

In the end, of course, my parents' hand was forced, and they had to tell me my "destiny" much earlier, because two years later, in the autumn of 1775, when I had just turned eight years old, Mother and I went shopping for shoes.

iii

As well as the château in Versailles, we had a sizable villa in the city, and whenever we were there, Mother liked to go shopping.

As I have said, while she was contemptuous of most fashions, detesting fans and wigs, conforming to the very minimum of flamboyance when it came to her gowns, there was one thing about which she was fastidious.

Shoes. As I've said, she loved shoes. She bought silk pairs from Christian in Paris, where we would go, regular as clockwork, once every two weeks, because it was her one extravagance, she said, and mine too, since we always came away with a pair of shoes for me as well as her.

Christian was located in one of Paris's more salubrious streets, far away from our villa on the Île Saint-Louis. But still, everything is relative and I found myself holding my breath as we were helped out of the comfortable and fragrant-smelling interior of our carriage and into the noisy, surging street, where the sound was of shouting and horses' hooves and a constant rumbling of carriage wheels. The sound of Paris.

Above us women leaned from windows across folded arms and watched the world go by. Lining the street were stalls that sold fruit and fabrics, barrows piled high with goods manned by shouting men and women in aprons who immediately called to us. "Madame! Mademoiselle!"

My eyes were drawn to the shadows at the edges of the street, where I saw blank faces in the gloom, and I fancied I saw starvation and desperation in those eyes as they watched us reproachfully, hungrily.

"Come along now, Élise," said Mother, and I picked up my skirts just as she did and trod daintily over the mud and excrement beneath our feet and we were ushered into Christian's by the owner.

The door slammed behind us, the outside world denied. A shop boy busied himself at our feet with a towel, and in moments it was as though we had never made that perilous crossing, those few feet between our carriage and the door of one of Paris's most exclusive shoe shops.

Christian wore a white wig tied back with a black ribbon, a justaucorps and white breeches. He was a perfect approximation of half nobleman, half footman, which was how he saw himself on the social ladder. He was fond of saying that it was in his power to make women feel beautiful, which was the greatest power a man possessed. And yet to him Mother remained an enigma, as though she was the one customer upon whom his power did not quite work. It didn't, and I knew why. It was because other women simply saw the shoes as tributes to their own vanity, whereas Mother adored them as things of beauty.

Christian, however, hadn't yet reached that conclusion, so every visit was marked by him barking up the wrong tree.

"Look, Madame," he said, presenting to her a pair of slippers adorned with buckles. "Every single lady through that door goes weak at the knees at the mere sight of this exquisite new creation, yet only Madame de la Serre has ankles pretty enough to do them justice."

"Too frivolous, Christian." My mother smiled and with an imperious wave of the hand swept past him to other shelves. I cast an eye at the shop boy, who returned my look with an unreadable gaze, and followed.

She chose briskly. She made her choices with a certainty that Christian remained bewildered by her. I, her constant companion, saw the difference in her as she chose her shoes. A lightness. A smile she cast in my direction as she slipped on yet another shoe and admired her beautiful ankles in the mirror to the accompanying gasps and bleats of Christian—every shoe an exquisite work of art in progress, my mother's foot the final flourish in order to make them complete.

We made our choices, Mother arranged for payment and delivery and we left, Christian helping us out onto the street where . . .

There was no sign of Jean, our coachman. No sign of our carriage at all.

"Madame?" said Christian, face creased with concern. I felt her stiffen, saw the tilt of her chin as her eyes roamed the street around us.

"There's nothing to worry about, Christian," she assured him, breezily. "Our carriage is a little late, that is all. We shall enjoy the sights and sounds of Paris as we await its return here."

It was beginning to get dark and there was a chill in the air, which had thickened with the first of the evening fog.

"That is quite out of the question, Madame, you cannot wait on the street," said an aghast Christian.

She looked at him with a half smile. "To protect my sensibilities, Christian?"

"It is dangerous," he protested, and leaned forward to whisper with his face twisted into a slightly disgusted expression, "*and the people.*"

"Yes, Christian," she said, as though letting him into a secret, "just people. Now please, go back inside. Your next customer values her exclusive time with Paris's most attentive shoe salesman as highly as I do, and would no doubt be most put out having to share her time with two strays awaiting their negligent coachman."

Knowing my mother as a woman who rarely changed her mind, and knowing she was right about the next customer, Christian bowed acquiescence, bid us *au revoir* and returned to the shop, leaving us alone on the street, where the barrows were being removed, where people dissolved into shapes moving within the murky fog.

I gripped her hand. "Mama?"

"Don't concern yourself, Élise," she said raising her chin. "We shall hire a carriage to return us to Versailles."

"Not to the villa here in Paris, Mama?"

"No," she said, thinking, chewing her lip a little, "I think I should prefer that we return to Versailles."

She was tense and watchful as she began to lead us along the street, incongruous in our long skirts and bonnets. From her purse she took a compact to check her rouge and we stopped to gaze in the window of a shop.

Still as we walked she used the opportunity to teach me. "Make your face impassive, Élise, and do not show your true feelings, especially if they are nerves. Don't appear to hurry. Maintain your calm exterior. Maintain control."

The streets were thinning out now. "At the square they have carriages for hire, and we shall be there in a few moments. First, though, I have something I need to tell you. When I tell you, you must not react, you must not turn your head. Do you understand?"

"Yes, Mama."

"Good. We are being followed. He has been following us since Christian's. A man in a tall felt hat and cloak."

"Why? Why is the man following us?"

"Now that, Élise, is a very good question, and that is something I intend to find out. Just keep walking."

We stopped to look into another shop window. "I do believe our shadow has disappeared," she said thoughtfully.

"Then that's a good thing," I replied, with all the naivety of my unburdened eight-year-old self.

There was concern on her face. "No, my darling, it's

not a good thing. I liked him where I could see him. Now I have to wonder if he really has gone or, as seems more likely, he's sped on ahead to cut us off before we can reach the square. He will expect us to use the main road. We shall fox him, Élise, by taking another route."

Taking my hand she led us off the street, first onto a narrower highway, then into a long alleyway, dark apart from a lit lantern at each end.

We were halfway along when the figure stepped out of the fog in front of us. Disturbed mist billowed along the slick walls on either side of the narrow alley. And I knew Mother had made a mistake.

iv

He had a thin face framed by a spill of almost pure white hair, looking like a dandyish but down-at-the-heel doctor in his long black cape and tall shabby hat, the ruff of a shirt spilling over his collar.

He carried a doctor's bag that he placed to the ground and opened with one hand, all without taking his eyes off us as he took something from it, something long and curved.

Then he smiled and drew the dagger from its sheath, and it gleamed wickedly in the dark.

"Stay close, Élise," whispered Mother. "Everything's going to be all right."

I believed her because I was an eight-year-old girl and of course I believed my mother. But also because having seen her with the wolf, I had good reason to believe her.

Even so, fear nibbled at my insides.

"What is your business, monsieur?" she called levelly.

He made no answer.

"Very well. Then we shall return to where we came from," said Mother loudly, taking my hand and about to depart.

At the alley entrance a shadow flickered and a second figure appeared in the orange glow of the lantern. It was a lamplighter; we could tell by the pole he carried. Even so, Mother stopped.

"Monsieur," she called to the lamplighter cautiously, "I wonder if I might ask you to call off this gentleman bothering us?"

The lamplighter said nothing, going instead to where the lamp burned and raising his pole. Mama started, "Monsieur . . ." and I wondered why the man would be trying to light a lamp that was already lit and realized too late that the pole had a hook on the end—the hook that they used for dousing the flame of the candle inside.

"Monsieur . . ."

The entrance was plunged into darkness. We heard him drop his pole with a clatter and as ours eyes adjusted I could see him reach into his coat to bring something out. Another dagger. Now he, too, moved forward a step.

Mother's head swung from the lamplighter to the doctor.

"What is your business, monsieur?" she asked the doctor.

In reply the doctor brought his other arm to bear. With a snicking sound a second blade appeared from his wrist.

"Assassin," she said with a smile as he moved in. The lamplighter was close now too—close enough for us to see the harsh set of his mouth and his narrowed eyes. Mother jerked her head in the other direction and saw the doctor, both blades held at his side. Still he smiled. He was enjoying this—or trying to make it look as though he was.

Either way, Mother was as immune to his malevolence as she was to the charms of Christian, and her next move was as graceful as a dance step. Her heels clip-clopped on the stone as she kicked out one foot, bent and drew a boot knife, all in the blink of an eye.

One second we were a defenseless woman and her child trapped in a darkened passageway, the next we were not: she was a woman brandishing a knife to protect her child. A woman, who by the way she'd drawn her weapon and the way she was now poised, knew exactly what to do with the knife.

The doctor's eyes flickered. The lamplighter stopped. Both given pause for thought.

She held her knife in her right hand, and I knew something was amiss because she was left-handed, and presented her shoulder to the doctor.

The doctor moved forward. At the same time my mother passed her knife from her right hand to her left, and her skirts pooled as she dipped and with her right hand outflung for balance slashed her left across the front of the doctor, whose justaucorps opened just as neatly as though cut by a tailor, the fabric instantly soaked with blood.

He was cut but not badly wounded. His eyes widened and he lurched backward, evidently stunned by the skill of Mother's attack. For all his sinister act, he looked frightened, and amid my own fear I felt something else: pride and awe. Never before had I felt so protected.

Still, though he had faltered he stood his ground, and as his eyes flicked to behind us, Mother twisted too late to prevent the lamplighter's grabbing me from behind, a choking arm around my neck.

"Lay down your knife, or . . ." was what the lamplighter started to say.

But never finished, because half a second later, he was dead.

Her speed took him by surprise—not just the speed with which she moved but the speed of her decision, that if she allowed the lamplighter to take me hostage, then all was lost. And it gave her the advantage as she swung into him, finding the space between my body and his, leading with her elbow, which with a yell she jabbed into his throat.

He made a sound like *boak* and I felt his grip give, then saw the flash of a blade as Mother pressed home her advantage and drove her boot knife deep into his stomach, shoving him up against the alley wall and with a small grunt of effort driving the blade upward, then stepping smartly away as the front of his shirt darkened with blood and bulged with his spilling guts as he slid to the floor.

Mother straightened to face a second attack from the doctor, but all we saw of him was his cloak as he turned and ran, leaving the alley and running for the street.

She grabbed my arm. "Come along, Élise, before you get blood on your shoes."

V
———

There was blood on Mother's coat. Apart from that there was no way of telling she'd recently seen combat.

Not long after we arrived home messages were sent and the Crows bustled in with a great clacking of walking canes, huffing and puffing and talking loudly of punishing "those responsible." Meanwhile, the staff fussed, put their hands to their throats and gossiped around corners, and Father's face was ashen and I noticed how he seemed compelled to keep embracing us, holding us both a little too tightly and a little too long and breaking away with eyes that shone with tears.

Only Mother seemed unruffled. She had the poise and authority of one who has acquitted herself well. Rightly so. Thanks to her, we had survived the attack. I wondered, did she feel as secretly thrilled as I did?

I would be asked to give my account of events, she had warned me in the hired carriage on the way back to our château. In this regard I should follow her lead, support everything she said, say nothing to contradict her.

And so I listened as she told versions of her story, first to Olivier, our head butler, then to my father when he arrived, and lastly to the Crows when they bustled in. And though her stories acquired greater detail in the telling, answering all questions fired at her, they all lacked one very important detail. The doctor.

"You saw no hidden blade?" she was asked.

"I saw nothing to identify my attackers as Assassins," she replied, "thus I can't assume it was the work of Assassins."

"Common street robbers are not so organized as this man seems to have been. You can't think it a coincidence that your carriage was missing. Perhaps Jean will turn up drunk but perhaps not. Perhaps he will turn up dead. No, Madame, this has none of the hallmarks of an opportunistic crime. This was a planned attack on your person, an act of aggression by our enemies."

Eyes would flick to me. Eventually I was asked to leave the room, which I did, finding a seat in the hallway outside, listening to the voices from the chamber as they bounced off marble floors and to my ears.

"Grand Master, you must realize this was the work of Assassins."

(Although to my ears, it was the work of "assassins" and so I sat there thinking, *Of course it was the work of assassins, you stupid man. Or "would-be assassins" at least.*)

"Like my wife, I would rather not leap to any false conclusions," replied Father.

"Yet you've posted extra guards."

"Of course I have, man. I can't be too careful."

"I think you know in your heart, Grand Master."

My father's voice rose. "And what if I do? What would you have me do?"

"Why, take action at once, of course."

"And would that be action to avenge my wife's honor or action to overthrow the king?"

"Either would send a message to our adversaries."

Later, the news arrived that Jean had been discovered with his throat cut. I went cold, as though somebody had opened a window. I cried. Not just for Jean but, shamefully, for myself as well. And I watched and listened as a shock descended on the house and there were tears to be heard from below stairs and the voices of the Crows were once more raised, this time in vindication.

Again they were silenced by Father. When I looked out the windows, I could see men with muskets in the grounds. Around us, everybody was jumpy. Father came to embrace me time and time again—until I got so fed up I began wriggling away.

vi

"Élise, there's something we have to tell you."

And this is the moment you've been waiting for, dear reader of this journal, whoever you are—the moment when the penny finally dropped, when I finally understood why I had been asked to keep so many *vérités cachées*, when I discovered why my father's associates called him Grand Master, and when I realized what they meant by Templar and why "assassin" actually meant "Assassin."

They had called me into Father's office and requested that chairs be gathered by the fire before asking the staff to withdraw completely. Father stood while Mother sat forward, her hands on her knees, comforting me with her eyes. I was reminded of once when I had a splinter and Mother held me and comforted me and hushed my tears while Father gripped my finger and removed the splinter.

"Élise," he began, "what we are about to say was to have waited until your tenth birthday. But events today have no doubt raised many questions in your mind, and your mother believes you are ready to be told, so . . . here we are."

I looked at Mother, who reached to take my hand, bathing me in a comforting smile.

Father cleared his throat.

This was it. Whatever dim ideas I'd formed about my future were about to change.

"Élise," he said, "you will one day become the French head of a secret international order that is centuries old. You, Élise de la Serre, will be a Templar Grand Master."

"Templar Grand Master?" I said, looking from Father to Mother.

"Yes."

"Of France?" I said.

"Yes. Presently, I hold that position. Your mother also holds a high rank within the Order. The gentlemen and Madame Levesque who visit, they too are Knights of the Order and, like us, they are committed to preserving its tenets."

I listened, not really understanding but wondering why, if all these knights were committed to the same thing, they spent every meeting shouting at one another.

"What are Templars?" I asked instead.

My father indicated himself and Mother, then extended his hand to include me in the circle. "We all are. We are Templars. We are members of a centuries-old secret order committed to making the world a better place."

I liked the sound of that. I liked the sound of making the world a better place. "How do you do it, Papa?"

He smiled. "Ah, now, that is a very good question, Élise. Like any other large, ancient organization there are differing opinions on how best to achieve our ends. There are those who think we should violently oppose those who oppose us. Others who believe in peacefully spreading our beliefs."

"And what are they, monsieur?"

He shrugged. "Our motto is, 'May the father of understanding guide us.' You see, what we Templars know is that despite exhortations otherwise, the people don't want real freedom and true responsibility because these things are too great a burden to bear, and only the very strongest minds can do so.

"We believe people are good but easily led toward wickedness, laziness and corruption, that they require good leaders to follow, leaders who will not exploit their negative characteristics but instead seek to celebrate the positive ones. We believe peace can be maintained this way."

I could literally feel my horizons expand as he spoke. "Do you hope to guide the people of France that way, Father?" I asked him.

"Yes, Élise, yes we do."

"How?"

"Well, let me ask you—how do *you* think?"

My mind went blank. How did I think? It felt like the most difficult question I had ever been asked. I had no idea. He looked at me kindly yet I knew he expected an answer. I looked toward Mother, who squeezed my hand encouragingly, imploringly with her eyes, and I found my beliefs in words I myself had heard her speak to Mr. Weatherall and to Madame Carroll.

I said, "Monsieur, I think our present monarch is

corrupted beyond redemption, that his rule has poisoned the well of France and that in order for the people's faith to be restored in the monarchy, King Louis needs to be set aside."

My answer caught him off guard and he looked startled, casting a quizzical look at Mother, who shrugged as though to say, *Nothing to do with me*, even though they were her words I was parroting.

"I see," he said. "Well, your mother is no doubt pleased to hear your espouse such views, Élise, for in this matter she and I are not in full agreement. Like you she believes in change. Myself, I know that that monarch is appointed by God and I believe that a corrupt monarch can be persuaded to see the error of his ways."

Another quizzical look and a shrug and I moved quickly on. "But there are other Templars, Papa?"

He nodded. "Across the world, yes. There are those who serve the Order. Those who are sympathetic to our aims. However, as you and your mother discovered today, we have enemies, too. Just as we are an ancient order hoping to shape the world in our image, so there is an opposing order, one with as many adherents sensitive to their own aims. Where we hope to unburden the good-thinking people of the responsibility of choice and be their guardians, this opposing order invites chaos and gambles on anarchy by insisting man should think for himself. They advocate casting aside traditional ways of thinking that have done so much to guide humanity for thousands of years in favor of a different kind of freedom. They are known as Assassins. We believe it was Assassins who attacked you today."

"But, monsieur, I heard you say you weren't sure . . ."

"I said that purely in order to quench the warlike thirst of some of the more vocal members of our Order. It can only be Assassins who attacked you, Élise. Only they would be so bold as to kill Jean and send a man to kill the wife of the Grand Master. No doubt they hope to destabilize us. On this occasion they failed. We must make sure that if they try again, they fail again."

I nodded. "Yes, Father."

He glanced at Mother. "Now, I expect your mother's defensive actions today came as a surprise to you?"

They hadn't. That "secret" encounter with the wolf had seen to that.

"Yes, monsieur," I said, catching Mother's eye.

"These are skills that all Templars must have. One day you will lead us. But before that you will be initiated as a Templar, and before that you will learn the ways of our Order. Starting tomorrow you will begin to learn combat."

Again I caught Mother's eye. I had already begun to learn combat. I had been learning combat for over a year now.

"I realize this may be a lot to take in, Élise," continued Father as my mother colored slightly. "Perhaps you saw your life as being similar to other girls of your age. I can only hope the fact that it will be so different is not a source of anxiety for you. I can only hope you embrace the potential you have to fulfill your destiny."

I'd always thought I wasn't like the other girls. Now I knew for sure.

vii

The following morning Ruth dressed me for a walk in the grounds. She fussed and tutted and mumbled under her breath that I shouldn't be taking such risks after what had happened yesterday, how we only just escaped the evil man who had attacked us; and how Mother and I might be lying dead in that alleyway but for the mysterious gentleman who had been passing, who saw off the robber.

So that was what the staff had been told. Lots of lies, lots of secrets. It thrilled me to know that I was one of only two people—well three, I suppose, if you counted the doctor—who knew the full truth of what had happened yesterday, one of a select number who knew it was Mother who had dealt with the attack, not some mystery man—and one of the select few who knew the full extent of the family business, not to mention my own part in it.

I had awakened that morning with sunshine in my life. At last all those *vérités cachées* I'd been asked to keep made sense. At last I knew why it was that our family seemed so different from the others, why I myself had never fitted in with the other children. It was because my destiny lay along a different path from theirs, and always had.

And best of all, "Your mother shall be your tutor in all things," Father had said with a warm smile at Mother, who in turn had reflected his love to me. With a smile he stopped himself. "Well, perhaps not in *all* things. Perhaps in matters of beliefs, you would be better advised to heed the words of your father the Grand Master."

"François," Mother had chided, "the child shall make up her own mind. The conclusions she reaches shall be her own."

"My love, why do I have the distinct impression that for Élise, today's events are not the surprise they might have been?"

"What do you think we ladies talk about in our perambulations, François?"

"Shoes?"

"Well, yes," she conceded, "we do indeed talk about shoes, but what else?"

He understood, shaking his head, wondering how he could have been so blind as to miss what had been happening right under his nose.

"Did she know about the Order before today?" he asked her.

"Not as such," she said, "though I daresay she was prepared for the revelation."

"And weapons?"

"She has had a little training, yes."

Father indicated for me to stand. "Let's see if you have learned your *en garde*, Élise," he said, adopting the position himself, his right arm outstretched and forefinger pointed like a blade.

I did I was as I was told. Father shot an impressed look at my mother and studied my posture, walking around me as I bathed in the glow of his approval. "Right-handed like her father"—he chuckled—"not a lefty like her mother."

I bounced slightly on my knees, checking my balance, and my father smiled once more. "Do I detect the hand of a certain Englishman in our daughter's training, Julie?"

"Mr. Weatherall has been helping me in filling Élise's extracurricular hours, yes," she agreed airily.

"I see. I had thought we were seeing a little more of him than usual at the château. Tell me, does he still hold a torch for you?"

"François, you embarrass me," chided Mother.

(At the time I had no idea what they meant, of course. But I do now. Seeing Mr. Weatherall the other night, a broken man. Oh, I do now.)

Father's face became serious. "Julie, you know I trust you in all things and if you have been tutoring the child, then I support you in that, too, and if what she's already had helped Élise keep a cool head during yesterday's attack, then it's been more than justified. But Élise will be Grand Master one day. She will follow in my footsteps. In matters of combat and tactics she may be your protégé, Julie, but in matters of belief, she must be mine. Is that understood?"

"Yes, François." Mother smiled sweetly. "Yes, that is understood."

A look passed between Mother and me. An unspoken *vérité cachée*.

viii

And so, having escaped Ruth's unnecessary concern, I arrived in the reception hall ready for my walk with Mother.

"You will take Scratch, and the guards, please, Julie," Father told her in a tone of voice that brooked no argument.

"Of course," she said, and indicated one of the men who lurked in the shadows of the reception hall, our whole house feeling a little more crowded all of a sudden.

He came forward. It was Mr. Weatherall. For a second he and Father regarded one another carefully, before Mr. Weatherall bowed deeply and the two shook hands.

"François and I have told Élise what lies in store for her," said my mother.

Mr. Weatherall's eyes slid from my father's face to mine and he nodded before bowing deeply again, extending his palm to kiss the back of my hand, as though I were a princess.

"And how does that make you feel, young Élise, knowing that one day you will lead the Templars?"

"Very grand, monsieur," I said.

"I'll bet it does," he said.

"François has correctly guessed that Élise has been receiving a little training," said Mother.

Mr. Weatherall turned his attention back to Father. "Of course," he said, "and I trust my tutelage has not given the Grand Master offense?"

"As I explained last night, I trust my wife implicitly concerning such matters. I know that with you, Freddie, they are in good hands."

Just then Olivier approached, maintaining a distance until he was ushered forward to whisper in his master's ear. Father nodded and addressed Mother.

"I must take my leave, my dear," said Father. "Our 'friends' are here to visit."

The Crows, of course. They had returned for a morning of shouting. And it was funny how knowing what I did cast my father in a new light. He wasn't just my father anymore. Not just my mother's husband. But a busy man. A man of responsibility, whose attention was constantly required. A man whose decisions changed lives. The Crows were entering as we left, politely greeting Mother and Mr. Weatherall, crowding into the reception hall, which was suddenly very busy and alive with more talk of avenging yesterdays' attack, seeing to it that Jean had not died in vain.

Eventually we stepped outside, the three of us, and walked for some way before Mr. Weatherall spoke. "So, Élise, how do you *really* feel knowing your destiny?" asked Mr. Weatherall.

"As I said with Father," I told him.

"Not a little apprehensive, then, petal? All that responsibility to come?"

"Mr. Weatherall feels you too young to know your destiny," explained Mother.

"Not at all. I look forward to finding what the future holds, monsieur," I replied.

He nodded, as if that was good enough for him.

"And I like that I get to do more sword fighting, monsieur," I added. "With no secrecy now."

"Exactly! We shall work on your *riposte* and your *envelopment* and you may show off your skills to your father. I think he'll be surprised, Élise, what an accomplished swordswoman you already are. Perhaps one day you shall be a better swordsman and than either your mother or your father."

"Oh, I doubt that, monsieur."

"Freddie, please don't put strange ideas into the girl's head." Mother nudged me and whispered, "Though I think he may be right, Élise, just between you and me."

Mr. Weatherall became serious. "Now. Are we going to talk about what went on yesterday?"

"An attempt on our lives, Freddie . . ."

"I only wish I had been there . . ."

"No matter that you were not, Freddie, we remain unharmed and barely even traumatized by the incident. Élise acquitted herself perfectly, and . . ."

"You were the lioness protecting her young, eh?"

"I did what I had to do. It is a matter of regret that one of the men escaped."

Mr. Weatherall stopped. "*One* of the men? What? There was *more* than one?"

She gave him meaningful eyes. "Oh yes. There was another man, the more dangerous of the two. He used a hidden blade."

His mouth formed an O. "So it really was the work of Assassins?"

"I have my doubts."

"Oh yeah? Why?"

"He ran, Freddie. Have you ever known an Assassin to run?"

"They are merely human and you are a formidable opponent. I think I should have been tempted to run myself in his shoes. You're a right devil with that boot knife." He glanced back at me with a wink.

Mother glowed. "You may be assured your flattery does not go unappreciated, Freddie. But this man, there was something about him that wasn't quite right. He was all . . . *show*. He was an Assassin, the hidden blade was proof of that. But I wonder, was he a *true* Assassin?"

"We need to find him, ask him."

"Indeed we do."

"Tell me, what did he look like?"

Mother gave him a description of the doctor.

". . . and there is something else."

"Yes?"

She led us to the hedges. Last night as we escaped the alley she had scooped up the doctor's bag to take with us on the carriage ride home. Before arriving back at the château, she had me run and hide it, and she handed it to Mr. Weatherall now.

"He left this, did he?"

"Indeed. He used it to carry a blade but there's nothing else inside."

"Nothing to identify him?"

"There is something . . . Open it. See the label inside?"

"The bag was made in England," said Mr. Weatherall, surprised. "An English Assassin?"

Mother nodded. "Possibly. Very possibly. Do you not think it plausible that the English might want me dead? I made it plain to Madame Carroll that I favored a change of monarchy."

"But also that you oppose bloodshed."

"Quite. And Madame Carroll seemed to think that was enough for her Order. Perhaps not, though."

Mr. Weatherall shook his head. "I can't see it myself.

I mean, putting my own national loyalty to one side, I can't see what's in it for them. They see you as a moderating influence on the Order as a whole. Killing you risks destabilizing that."

"Perhaps it's a risk they were willing to take. Either way an English-made doctor's bag is the only clue we have as to the identity of the Assassin."

Mr. Weatherall nodded. "We will find him, Madame," he told her. "You can be sure of that."

That, of course, was three years ago. And of the doctor there has been no sight or sound since. The attempt on our lives has disappeared into history, like paupers swallowed up by the Paris fog.

13 April 1778

i

I want her to get better. I want there to be a day when the sun shines and her maids enter to open her drapes only to find her sitting up in bed, "feeling quite revived," and I want the sun that floods through her drapes to crowd its way into the hallways of our darkened home and chase away the grief-ridden shadows lurking there, touch Father, restore him and bring him back to me. I want to hear songs and laughter from the kitchen again. I want an end to this contained sadness and I want my smile to be real, no longer masking a hurt that churns inside.

And more than all of that I want my mother back. My mother, my teacher, my mentor. I don't just want her, I need her. Every moment of every day I wonder what life would be like without her and have no idea, no conception of life without her.

I want her to get better.

ii

And then, later that year, I met Arno.

12 SEPTEMBER 1794

Our relationship was forged in the fire of death—my father's death.

For how long did we have a normal, conventional relationship? Half an hour? I was at the Palace of Versailles with my father, who had business there. He'd asked me to wait as he attended to what he had to do, and while I sat with my legs dangling, watching the highborn members of the court pass to and fro, who should appear but Élise de la Serre.

Her smile I would come to love later, her red hair nothing special to me then, and the beauty over which my adult eyes would later linger was invisible to my young eyes. After all, I was only eight, and eight-year-old boys, well, they don't have much time for eight-year-old girls, not unless that eight-year-old girl is something very special. And so it was with Élise. There was something *different* about her. She was a girl. But even in the first seconds of meeting her I knew she wasn't like any other girl I'd met before.

Chase me. Her favorite game. How many times did we play it as children and as adults? In a way we never stopped.

On the mirrored surfaces of the palace's marble floors we ran—through legs, along corridors, past columns and pillars. Even to me now the palace is huge, its ceilings impossibly tall, its halls stretching almost as far as the eye can see, huge arched windows looking out to the stone steps and sweeping grounds beyond.

But to me then? To me then it was impossibly vast. And yet, even though it was this vast, strange place, and even though with each step I took I went farther away from my father's instructions, I still couldn't resist the lure of my new playmate. The girls I had met weren't like this. They stood with their heels together and their lips pursed in disdain at all things boylike; they walked a few steps behind like Russian-doll versions of their mothers; they didn't run giggling through the halls of the Palace of Versailles ignoring any protests that came their way, just running for the joy of running and the love of play. I wonder, had I already fallen in love?

And then, just as I started to worry that I would never find my way back to Father, my concerns became irrelevant. A shout had gone up. There was the sound of rushing feet. I saw soldiers with muskets and, quite by chance, came upon the spot where he had met his killer and I knelt to him as he breathed his last.

When at last I looked up from his lifeless body it was to see my savior, my new guardian: François de la Serre.

14 APRIL 1778

i

He came to see me today.

"Élise, your father is here," said Ruth. Like everyone else her demeanor changed when my father was around, and she curtsied and withdrew, leaving us alone.

"Hello, Élise," he said stiffly from the door. I remembered that evening years ago when Mother and I had returned from Paris, survivors of a terrible attack in an alleyway, and how he had been unable to stop taking us in his arms. He'd embraced me so much that by the end of the night I'd been wriggling away from him just to get some air. Now, as he stood there looking more like a governor than a father, I would have given anything for one of those embraces.

He turned and paced, hands clasped behind his back.

He stopped, gazing from the window but not really see-ing the lawns beyond, and I watched his blurred face in the reflection of the glass as without turning, he said, "I wanted to see how you were."

"I'm fine, thank you, Papa."

There was a pause. My fingers worked at the fabric of my smock. He cleared his throat. "You do a fine job of disguising your feelings, Élise; it is qualities such as these that you will one day call upon as Grand Master. Just as your strength comforts our household it will one day be of benefit to the Order."

"Yes, Father."

Again he cleared his throat. "Even so, I want you to know that in private or when you and I should find our-selves alone, that . . . that it's okay *not* to be fine."

"Then I will admit I am suffering, Father."

His head dropped. His eyes were dark circles in the reflection of the glass. I knew why he found it difficult to look at me. It was because I reminded him of her. I reminded him of his dying wife.

"I, too, am suffering, Élise. Your mother means the world to us both."

And if there was a moment in which he might have turned from the window, crossed the room, gathered me in his arms and allowed us to share our pain, then that was it.

But he didn't.

And if there was a moment when I might have asked him why, if he knew my pain, did he spend so much of his time with Arno and not with me, then that was it.

But I didn't.

Little else was said before he left. Sometime later I heard that he left to go hunting—with Arno.

The physician arrives soon. He never brings good news.

ii

In my mind's eye I revisit another meeting, two years before, when I was summoned to Father's study for an audience with him and Mother, who unusually for her wore a look of concern. I knew that there were serious matters they wanted to discuss when Olivier was asked to withdraw, the door closed and Father bade me take a seat.

"Your mother tells me that your training is progressing well, Élise," he said.

I nodded enthusiastically, looking from one to the other. "Yes, Father. Mr. Weatherall says I'm going to be a bloody good sword fighter."

Father looked taken aback. "I see. One of Weatherall's British expressions, no doubt. Well, I'm pleased to hear it. Obviously you take after your mother."

"You're no slouch with a blade yourself, François," said Mother, with a hint of a smile.

"You've reminded me it's a while since we dueled."

"I'll take that as a challenge, shall I?"

He looked at her and for a moment the serious business was forgotten. I was forgotten. For a second it was just Mother and Father in the room, being playful and flirting with one another.

And then, just as quickly as the moment had begun, it ended and the attention returned to me.

"You are well on your way to becoming a Templar, Élise."

"When shall I be inducted, Papa?" I asked him.

"Your schooling will be finished at the Maison Royale in Saint-Cyr, then you will become a fully fledged member of the Order and you will train to take my place."

I nodded.

"First, though, there is something we have to tell you." He looked at Mother, their faces serious now. "It's about Arno . . ."

iii

Arno was by then my best friend, and I suppose the person I loved the most after my parents. Poor Ruth. She'd had to abandon any lasting hope she might have had that I would settle down to girlhood and begin taking an interest in those same girly things adored by others my age. With Arno on the estate not only did I have a playmate whenever I wanted one, but a *boy* playmate. Her dreams lay in ruins.

I suppose, looking back, I had taken advantage of him rather. An orphan, he had come to us adrift in need of direction and I, of course, as much a novice Templar as a selfish little girl, had made him "mine." We were friends, and of the same age, but even so my role was one of older sister and it was a role I had taken to with great gusto. I loved besting him in pretend sword fights. During Mr. Weatherall's training sessions I was a craven novice prone to mistakes and, as he was often pointing out, leading with my heart and not my head, but in play fights with Arno my novice skills made me a dazzling, spinning master. At other games—skipping, hopscotch, shuttlecock—we were evenly matched. But I always won at sword fighting.

When the weather was fine we roamed the grounds of the estate, spying on Emanuel and other grounds staff, skimming stones on the lake. When it rained we stayed indoors and played backgammon, marbles or jacks. We spun hoops through the great corridors of the ground floor and roamed the floors above, hiding from house-maids, running giggling when they shooed us away.

And that was how I spent my days: in the morning I was tutored, groomed for my adult life of leading the French Templars; the afternoon was when I let go those responsi-bilities and instead of being an adult-in-waiting became a child again. Even then, though I never would have articu-lated it as such, I knew that Arno represented my escape.

And of course nobody had failed to notice how close Arno and I had become.

"Well, I've never seen you so happy," said Ruth resignedly.

"You're certainly very fond of your new playmate, aren't you, Élise?" from my mother.

(Now—now as I watch Arno sparring with my father in the yard and hear that they've gone hunting together, I wonder, was my mother just a tiny bit jealous that I had a significant other in my life? Now I know how she might have felt.)

Yet it had never occurred to me that my friendship with Arno might be a cause for concern. Not until that very moment when I stood before them in the chamber and they told me they had something to say about him.

iv

"Arno is of Assassin descent," said my father.

And a little bit of my world shook.

"But . . ." I began, and tried to reconcile two pictures in my mind: one of Arno in his shiny-buckle shoes, waistcoat and jacket, running through the hallways of the château steering his hoop with his stick. The other of the Assassin doctor in the alleyway, his hat tall in the fog. "Assassins are our enemy."

Mother and Father shared a glance. "Their aims are opposed to ours, it's true," he said.

My mind was racing. "But . . . But does this mean Arno will want to kill me?"

Mother moved forward to comfort me. "No, my dear, no, it doesn't mean that at all. Arno is still your friend. Though his father, Charles Dorian, was an Assassin, Arno himself knew nothing of his destiny. No doubt he would have been told, in time, perhaps on his tenth birthday as we were planning to do with you. But as it stands, he entered this house unaware of what the future had in store for him."

"He is not an Assassin then. Simply the son of an Assassin."

Again they looked to one another. "He will have certain innate characteristics, Élise. In many ways Arno is, *was* and always will be an Assassin. It is just that he doesn't know it."

"But if he doesn't know it, then we shall never be enemies?"

"That is quite correct," said Father. "In fact we believe his nature might be overcome by nurture."

"François . . ." said Mother warningly.

"What do you mean, Father?" I asked, my eyes darting from him to her, noting the discomfort in her expression.

"I mean that you have a certain influence over him, do you not?" said Father.

I felt myself coloring. Was it so obvious?

"Perhaps, Father . . ."

"He looks up to you, Élise, and why not? It is gratifying to see. Most encouraging."

"François . . ." Mother said again, but he stopped her with an upraised hand. "Please, my darling, leave this to me."

My eyes darted.

"There is no reason why you, as Arno's friend and playmate, can't begin to educate him in our ways."

"Indoctrinate him, François?" A flash of anger from my mother.

"Guide him, my dear."

"Guide him in a manner that goes against his nature?"

"How do we know? Perhaps Élise is right that he is not an Assassin until he's made one. Perhaps we can save him from the clutches of his people."

"The Assassins don't know he's here?" I asked.

"We don't believe so."

"Then there's no reason he need be found out."

"That's quite right, Élise."

"Then he needn't be . . . anything."

A look of confusion crossed Father's face. "I'm sorry, my dear, I don't quite follow."

What I wanted to say was, *Leave him out of this.* Let Arno be for me, nothing to do with the way we see the world, the way we want to shape the world. Let the bit of my life I share with Arno be free of all that.

"Quite," agreed Mother.

He pursed his lips, not especially liking this wall of resistance thrown up by his womenfolk. "He is my ward. A child of this house. He will be brought up according to the doctrines of the house. To put it bluntly, Élise, we need to get to him before the Assassins do."

"We have no reason to fear that the Assassins will ever discover his existence."

"We cannot be sure. If the Assassins reach him, they will bring him into the Order. He would not be able to resist."

"If he would not be able to resist, then how can it be right to steer him otherwise?" I pleaded, though my reasons for doing so were more personal than based on beliefs. "How can it be right for us to go against what fate has in store for him?"

Father fixed me with a hard look. "Do you want Arno to be your enemy?"

"No," I said, impassioned.

"Then the best way to be sure of that is to bring him round to our way of thinking."

"Yes, François, but not now," interrupted Mother. "Not just yet. Not when the children are so young."

He looked from one protesting face to the other and appeared to soften. "You two," he said with a smile. "Very well. Do as you wish for the time being. We shall review the situation later."

I shot a grateful look at my mother.

What will I do without her?

v

She fell ill soon after that and was confined to her rooms, which stayed darkened day and night, that part of the house out of bounds to all but her lady's maid, Justine, my father and I, and three nurses who were hired to look after her, who were all called Marie.

To the rest of the house, she began to cease to exist. My morning routine stayed the same, spent with my governor, then in the woods at the edge of our grounds, learning sword fighting with Mr. Weatherall. I no longer whiled afternoons away with Arno; instead, I spent them at my mother's bedside, clasping her hand as the Maries fussed around us.

I watched as he began to gravitate toward my father. I watched my father find comfort away from the stress of Mother's illness in being Arno's guardian. My father and I were both trying to cope with the gradual loss of Mother, both finding different ways to do it. The laughter in my life gradually faded away.

I used to have a dream. Only it wasn't a dream because I was awake. I suppose you'd have to say a fantasy. In the fantasy I was sitting on the throne. I know how it may sound, but after all, if you can't admit it to your journal, when can you admit it? I am sitting on the throne before my assembled subjects, who in the daydream have no identity but I suppose must be Templars. They are assembled before me, the Grand Master. And you know it's not a particularly serious daydream because I'm sitting before them as a ten-year-old girl, the throne way too big for me, my legs sticking out and my arms not even long enough to reach over the arms of the chair. I am the least monarchlike monarch you can possibly imagine, but it's a daydream and that's the way daydreams go sometimes. What's important about this daydream isn't that I turn myself into a king, nor that I have brought my ascendance to Grand Master forward by decades. What's significant about it for me, and what I cling to, is that sitting at either side of me are my mother and father.

Each day that she grows a little weaker and closer to death, and each day that he gravitates closer toward Arno, the impression of them at my side becomes more and more indistinct.

15 APRIL 1778

"There's something I have to tell you, Élise, before I go."

She took my hand and her grip was so frail. My shoulders shook as I began to sob. "No, please, Mother, no . . ."

"Hush child, be strong. Be strong for me. I am being taken from you and you must see that as a test of your strength. You must accept it is God's purpose and see it as a test of your strength. You must be strong, not only for yourself, but also for your father. My passing makes him vulnerable to the raised voices of the Order. You must be a voice in his other ear, Élise. You must press for the third way."

"I can't."

"You can. And one day you will be the Grand Master,

and you must lead the Order abiding by your own principles. The principles in which you believe."

"They are yours, Mother."

She dropped my hand and reached to stroke my cheek. Her eyes were cloudy and the smile floated on her face. "They are principles founded on compassion, Élise, and you have so much of that. So much of it. You know, I'm so proud of you. I couldn't have hoped for a more wonderful daughter. In you, I see the best of your father and the best of me. I couldn't have asked for more, Élise, and know now that I will die happy—happy to have known you and honored to have witnessed the birth of your greatness."

"No, Mother, please, no."

The words were spoken, spoken between sobs that wracked my body. My hands gripped her upper arm through the sheets. Her so-thin upper arm through the sheets. As though by holding it I might prevent her soul departing. Her red hair was spread across the pillow. Her eyes fluttered. "Please call your father, if you would," she said in a voice that was too weak and too soft, as though the life was slipping out of her. I rushed to the door, flung it open, called for one of the Maries to fetch Father, slammed the door shut again and returned to her side, but the end was coming quickly now, and as death settled over her she looked at me with watering eyes and the fondest smile I have ever seen.

"Please look after each other," she said. "I love you both so very much."

18 APRIL 1778

i

I have frozen. I wander rooms, breathing the fusty smell I had come to associate with her illness and know that we will have to open the drapes and fresh air will banish the scent but not wanting that because it will mean she is gone and I can't accept that.

When she was ill I wanted her back to full health. Now she is dead I just want her here. I just want her in the house.

This morning I watched from my window as three carriages arrived on the gravel outside and valets lowered steps and began to load them with trunks. Shortly afterward the three Maries appeared and began giving each other kisses good-bye. They wore black and dabbed their eyes and of course they grieved for Mother but it was a temporary grief by necessity, because their work here was over, payment made, and they would go to tend to other dying women and feel the same passing sadness when that next appointment came to an end.

I tried not to think of their departure as being in indecent haste. I tried not to resent their leaving me alone with my grief. They were hardly alone in not knowing my depth of feeling. Mother had made Father promise not to observe the usual mourning rituals, and so the drapes of the lower floors stayed open and the furniture was not cloaked in black. There were newer members of staff who had only known Mother briefly, or never met her at all. The Mother I remembered was beautiful and graceful and protective, but to them she was remote. She wasn't really a person. She was a weak lady in bed, and a lot of households had one of those. Even more than the Maries their mourning was nothing more than a brief pang of sadness.

And so the household carried on almost as though nothing had happened, just a few of us truly grieving, the few who had known and loved Mother as she was. When I caught Justine's eye I could see in her a reflection of my own deep pain. She had been the only member of staff allowed in Mother's rooms during the sickness.

"Oh, mademoiselle," she said, and as her shoulders began to heave I took her hand and thanked her for everything she'd done, assuring her that Mother had been so grateful for her care. She curtsied, thanked me for my comfort and left.

We were like two survivors of a great battle sharing memories with our eyes. She, I and Father were the only three remaining in the château who had tended to Mother as she lay dying.

It has been two days since she died and though Father had held me at her bedside on the night of her passing, I haven't seen him since. Ruth told me that he has remained in his rooms, weeping, but that very soon he will find the strength to emerge and that I shouldn't worry for him; I should think of myself. She clasped me to her, pulling me into her bosom and rubbing my back as though trying to wind me.

"Let it out, child," she whispered. "Don't keep it all inside." But I wiggled away, thanking her, telling her that will be all, a bit haughty, the way I imagine May Carroll speaks to her maid.

There's nothing to let out, is the problem. I feel nothing.

Unable to stand the upper floors any longer, I left to wander the château, passing through the hallways like a ghost.

"Élise . . ." Arno lurked at one end of a hallway with his hat held in his hand and his cheeks red as though having just been running. "I'm sorry to hear about your mother, Élise."

"Thank you, Arno," I said. The corridor seemed too long between us. He was hopping from one foot to another. "It was expected, not at all a shock, and though of course I'm grieving, I'm grateful I was able to be with her until the end."

He nodded sympathetically, not really understanding, and I could see why because everything in his world remained unchanged. To him a lady he barely knew, who had lived in a part of the house he wasn't allowed to visit, had died, and that made people that he cared for sad. But that was it.

"Perhaps we could play later," I said, "after our lessons," and he brightened.

He was probably missing Father, I reasoned, watching him go.

ii

I spent the morning with the governor and met Arno again at the door as he entered to begin his own lessons. Out timetables were ordered so that Arno should be with the governor while I trained with Mr. Weatherall, so that he would never see me sword fighting. (Perhaps in his own journal one day he will talk of signposts toward that moment when the penny dropped. "It never occurred to me to question why she was so adept at sword fighting . . .") I left by a rear door and walked along the line of the topiary until I came to the woodland at the bottom and took the path to where Mr. Weatherall sat on a stump waiting for me. He had used to sit with his legs crossed and the tails of his jacket arranged over the stump, cutting quite a dash, and where before he had bounded from it to greet me, the light dancing in his eyes, a smile never far from his lips, now his head was bowed as though he had the weight of the world on his shoulders. Beside him on the seat was a box about a foot and a half long, a hand wide.

"You have been told," I said.

His eyes were heavy. His bottom lip trembled a little and for a horrible moment I wondered what I would do if Mr. Weatherall were to cry.

"How are you taking it?"

"It was expected," I said, "not at all a shock, and though of course I'm grieving, I'm grateful I was able to be with her until the end."

He handed me the box. "It's with a heavy heart I give you this, Élise." His voice was gruff. "She hoped to give it to you herself."

I took the box and weighed the dark wood in my hands, knowing already what was inside. Sure enough a short sword lay within. Its sheath was soft brown leather with white stitching along the sides, and the belt a leather strap designed for tying at the waist. The blade of the sword took the light; the steel was new, its handle bound tight with stained leather. There by the hilt was an inscription. "May the father of understanding be your guide. Love, Mother."

"It was always to have been your going-away present, Élise," he said flatly, glancing away into the woods and discreetly pushing the ball of his thumb into his eyes. "You're to use it for practice."

"Thank you," I told him and he shrugged. I wished I could move forward to a time when the sword thrilled me. For now I felt nothing.

There was a long pause. There wasn't going to be any training today, I realized. Neither of us had the heart for it.

After a while, he said, "Did she say anything of me? At the end, I mean."

I only just managed to hide my startled look, seeing

something in his eyes I recognized as a cross between desperation and hope. I'd known his feeling for her was strong, but until that moment I hadn't realized quite how strong.

"She asked me to tell you that in her heart was love for you, and that she was eternally grateful for everything you had done for her."

He nodded. "Thank you, Élise, that's a great comfort," he said, and turning, wiped tears from his eyes.

iii

Later, I was summoned to see Father and the two of us sat on a *chaise longue* in his darkened study, he with his arms around me, holding me tight. He had shaved, and outwardly was the same as he always was, but his words emerged slow and forced and brandy clouded his breath.

"I can tell you're being strong, Élise," he said, "stronger than I am."

Inside us both was a hollow ache. I found myself almost envying his ability to touch the source of his pain.

"It was expected," I said, but was unable to finish because my shoulders shook, and I gripped him with hands that trembled, allowing myself to be enveloped by him.

"Let it out, Élise," he said, and began to stroke my hair.

And I did. I let it out. And at last I began to cry.

12 SEPTEMBER 1794

Guilt-stricken, I laid down her journal, overwhelmed by the pain that poured off the page. Horribly aware of my own contribution to her misery.

Élise is right. The Madame's death hardly even gave me pause for thought. To the selfish young boy I was, it was just something that prevented François and Élise from playing with me. An inconvenience that meant that until things returned to normal—and Élise was right, because of the house opting not to mourn, things did seem to get back to normal more quickly—I had to make my own entertainment.

That, to my shame, is all the Madame's death meant to me.

But I was only a little boy, just ten.

Ah, but so was Élise, just ten. And yet so far ahead of

me in intelligence. She writes of our time with the governor, but how he must have groaned when it was my turn to be taught. He must have packed away Élise's textbooks and reached for my more elementary versions with a heavy heart.

And yet, in growing so quickly—and, as I now realize, in being "groomed" to grow so quickly—Élise was forced to live with a burden. Or so it seems to me reading these pages. The little girl I knew was just a little girl, full of fun and mischief and yes, like a sister, inventing all the best games, being handy with the excuses when we were caught out of bounds or stealing food from the kitchen or in doing whatever other japes she had planned for the day.

Little wonder, then, that when Élise was sent to the Maison Royale de Saint-Louis school at Saint-Cyr in order to complete her education she ran into trouble. Neither of those two opposing sides of her personality were suitable for school life, and predictably she hated the Maison Royale. Hated it. Though it was just under thirty kilometers away from Versailles, she might as well have been in a different country for all the distance she felt between her new life and her old. In her letters she referred to it as *Le Palais de la Misère*. Visits home were restricted to three weeks in the summer and a few days at Christmas, while the rest of her year was spent submitting to the regimes of the Maison Royale. Élise was not one for regimes. Not unless they suited her. The regime of learning sword with Mr. Weatherall was a very "Élise" kind of regime; the regime of school, on the other hand, was a very "not Élise" kind of regime. She hated the restrictions of school life. She hated having to learn "accomplishments" such as embroidery and music. So in her journal there is entry after entry of Élise in trouble at school. The entries themselves become repetitive. Years and years of unhappiness and frustration.

The way things worked at the school was that the girls were split into groups, each with a head pupil. Of course Élise had clashed with the head of her group, Valerie, and the two had fought. At times, I read with a hand to my mouth, not sure whether to laugh at Élise's daring or be shocked by it, they *literally* fought.

Time and time again, Élise was brought before the hated headmistress, Madame Levene, asked to explain herself, then punished.

And time and time again she would respond with insolence and her insolence would make the situation worse and the severity of the punishments was increased. And the more the punishments were increased the more rebellious Élise became, and the more rebellious Élise became the more she was brought before the headmistress and the more insolent she was and the more the punishments were increased . . .

I'd known she was often in trouble, of course, because although we rarely saw each other during this period—snatched glimpses through the windows of the tutor's window during her all-too-brief holidays, the odd regretful wave—we corresponded regularly. I, an orphan, had never been sent letters before, and the novelty of receiving them from Élise never faded. And of course she wrote of her hatred for school, but the correspondence lacked the detail of her journal, from which pulsed the scorn and contempt Élise felt for other pupils, for the teachers and for the hated headmistress, Madame Levene. Even a huge fireworks display to celebrate the school's centenary in 1786 could do nothing to lift her spirits. The king had apparently stood on the terraces at Versailles to enjoy the huge display, but even so it was not enough to cheer Élise. Instead, her journal was filled with a sense of injustice and of Élise at odds with the world around her—page after page and year after year of my love failing to see the vicious circle into which she was locked. Page after page of her failing to realize that what she was doing wasn't rebelling. It was mourning.

And reading on, I began to discover that there was something else she had withheld from me . . .

8 SEPTEMBER 1787

My father came to see me today. I was called to Madame
Levene's office for an audience with him and had been
looking forward to seeing him, but of course the witchy
old headmistress remained cackling in the room, such
were the rules of *Le Palais de la Misère*, and so the visit was
conducted as though for an audience. With the window
behind her offering a sweeping view of the school grounds
that even I had to admit was stunning, she sat with her
hands clasped on the desk in front of her, watching with a
thin smile as Father and I sat in chairs on the other side of
the desk, the awkward Father and his rebellious daughter.

"I had rather hoped the path to complete your education would be a graceful canter rather than a limp, Élise,"
he said with a sigh.

He looked old and tired and I could imagine the

chattering Crows at his shoulder, constantly badgering him—*do this, do that*—while to add to his woe his errant daughter was the subject of irate letters home, Madame Levene detailing my shortcomings at great length.

"For France, life continues to be hard, Élise," he explained. "Two years ago there was a drought and the worst harvest anyone can remember. The king authorized the building of a wall around Paris. He has tried to increase taxes but the *parlement* in Paris supported the nobles who defied him. Our stout and resolute king panicked, withdrew the taxes and there were demonstrations of celebration. Soldiers ordered to fire into the demonstrators refused to do so . . ."

"The nobles defied the king?" I said with a raised eyebrow.

He nodded. "Indeed. Who would've thought it? Perhaps they hope that the man on the street will be grateful, pass a vote of thanks and return home."

"You don't think so?"

"I fear not, Élise. I fear that once the workingman has the bit between his teeth, once he has a taste for the power—the potential power of the mob—then he will not be content merely with the withdrawal of some new tax laws. I think we may find a lifetime of frustration flooding out of these people, Élise. When they threw fireworks and stones at the *Palais de Justice* I don't think they were supporting noblemen. And when they burned effigies of the Vicomte de Calonne I don't think they were supporting noblemen then either."

"They burned effigies? Of the controller-general of finances?"

Father nodded. "Indeed they did. He has been forced to leave the country. Other ministers have followed. There will be unrest, Élise, you mark my words."

I said nothing.

"Which brings us to the matter of your behavior here at school," he said. "You're a senior now. A lady. And you should be behaving like one."

I thought about that and how wearing the seniors' uniform of the Maison Royale didn't make me feel like a woman. All it did was make me feel like a pretend-lady. When I felt like a real woman was after school, when I discarded the hated bone-stiff dress, unpinned my hair and let it drop to where it met my newly acquired bosom. When I gazed into the looking glass and saw my mother staring back at me.

"You're writing to Arno," he said, as though wanting to try a different approach.

"You're not reading my letters, are you?"

He rolled his eyes. "No, Élise, I am not reading your letters. For God's sake, what do you think of me?"

My own eyes dropped. "I'm sorry, Father."

"So busy rebelling against any available authority you've forgotten your true friends, is that it?"

At her desk Madame Levene was nodding sagely, feeling vindicated.

"I'm sorry, Father," I repeated, ignoring her.

"The fact remains that you have been writing to Arno and—going purely on what he has told me—you have done nothing to fulfill the terms of our agreement."

He cast a significant look toward the headmistress, eyebrows ever so slightly raised.

"What agreement would that be, Father?" I asked innocently, the devil in me.

With another brief nod in the direction of our audience, he added meaningfully, "The *agreement* we made before you left for Saint-Cyr, Élise, when you assured me you would be doing your utmost to convince Arno of his suitability for *adoption* into our family."

"I'm sorry, Father, I'm still not quite sure what you mean."

His brow darkened. Then with a deep breath he turned to the headmistress. "I wonder, Madame, if I might speak to my daughter alone."

"I'm afraid that runs contrary to the policies of the academy, monsieur." She smiled sweetly. "Parents or guardians needing to see pupils in private must provide a request in writing."

"I know, but . . ."

"I'm sorry, monsieur," she insisted.

He drummed his fingers on the leg of his breeches. "Élise, please don't be difficult. You know exactly what I mean. Before you came away to school we agreed that the time was right to *adopt* Arno into our *family*." He gave me a meaningful look.

"But he is a member of another family," I said, as though butter wouldn't melt in my mouth.

"Please do not play games with me, Élise."

Madame Levene gave a harrumph. "We are well used to that at the Maison Royale, monsieur."

"Thank you, Madame Levene," said Father irritably. But when he returned his attention to me our eyes met, and some of the frostiness between us evaporated in the face of Madame Levene's unwelcome presence, the corners of his mouth even twitching as he suppressed a smile. In response I gave him my most beatific, innocent look. His eyes grew affectionate as we shared the moment.

He was more measured when he spoke. "Élise, I'm quite certain that I don't need to remind you of the terms of our agreement. Simply to say that if you continue to fail to abide by them, then I shall have to take matters into my own hands."

We both stole a look at Madame Levene, who sat with her hands clasped on the desk in front of her, trying her level best not to look confused but failing miserably. It was the moment I came closest to simply bursting out laughing.

"You mean you will attempt to persuade him of his suitability, Father?"

He became serious, catching me in his gaze. "I will."

"Even though by doing that, you would lose me Arno's trust?"

"It's a risk I would have to take, Élise," replied Father. "Unless you do as you have agreed to do."

And what I had agreed to do was indoctrinate Arno. Bring him into the fold. My heart grew heavy at the thought—the thought of somehow *losing* Arno. Yet it was do that or have Father do it himself. I imagined Arno, furious, confronting me at some unspecified point in the future—*"Why did you never tell me?"*—and couldn't bear the thought.

"I will do as we agreed, Father."

"Thank you."

We turned our attention to Madame Levene, who scowled at Father.

"And make sure your behavior improves," he added quickly before slapping his hand to his thighs, which I knew from years of experience meant that our meeting was over.

The headmistress's scowl deepened as instead of admonishing me further, Father stood and gathered me in his arms, almost surprising me with the force of his emotion.

There and then I decided that, for him, I would improve. I would do right by him. Be the daughter he deserved.

8 JANUARY 1788

When I look back to the diary entry of 8 September 1787, it's to wince with shame at having written, "I would do right by him. Be the daughter he deserved," only to do . . .

. . . absolutely nothing of the sort.

Not only had I neglected to persuade Arno of the joys of converting to the Templar cause (a situation at least partly informed by me disloyally wondering if in fact there *were* any joys in converting to the Templar cause), my behavior at the Maison Royale had failed to improve.

It had really failed to improve.

It had got a lot worse.

Why, only yesterday Madame Levene called me into her office, the third time in as many weeks. How many times had I made the trip across the years? Hundreds?

For insolence, fighting, sneaking out at night (oh, how I loved to sneak out at night, just me and the dew), for drinking, for being disruptive, for scruffiness or for my particular favorite, "persistent bad behavior."

There was nobody who knew the route to Madame Levene's office as well as I did. There can't have been a beggar alive who had held out their palm more than I had. And I had learned to anticipate the swish of the cane. Even welcome it. Not to blink when the cane left its brand upon my skin.

It was just as I expected this time, more repercussions from a fight with Valerie, who as well as being our group leader was also the star drama pupil when it came to productions by Racine and Corneille. Take my advice, dear reader, and never pick an actress as an adversary. They are so terribly dramatic about everything. Or, as Mr. Weatherall would say, "Such bloody drama queens!"

True, this particular disagreement had ended with Valerie in receipt of a black eye and a bloody nose. It had happened while I was supposedly on probation for an act of minor revolt at dinner the month before, which is nothing worth going into here. The point was that the headmistress claimed to be at the end of her tether. She had had "quite enough of you, Élise de la Serre. Quite enough young lady."

And there was, of course, the usual talk of expulsion. Except, this time, I was pretty sure it was more than just talk. I was pretty sure that when Madame Levene told me she planned to send a strongly worded letter home requesting my father's attention at once in order that my future at the Maison Royale should be discussed, this was no longer a series of idle threats and that her mind was indeed at the end of its tether.

But still I didn't care.

No, I mean, I *don't* care. Do your worst, Levene; do your worst, Father. There's no circle of hell to which you can consign me worse than the one in which I already find myself.

"I have been sent a letter from Versailles," she said. "Your father is sending an emissary to deal with you."

I had been gazing out of the window, my eyes traveling past the walls of the Maison Royale to the outside, where I longed to be. Now, however, I switched to looking at Madame Levene, her pinched, pruny face, her eyes like stones behind her spectacles. "An emissary?"

"Yes. And from what I read in the letter, this emissary has been given the task of *beating* some sense into you."

I thought to myself, *An emissary? My father was sending an emissary. He wasn't even coming himself, he was sending an emissary.* Perhaps he planned to isolate me, I thought, suddenly realizing how horrific I found the idea. My father, one of only three people in the world I truly loved and trusted, simply shutting me out. I'd been wrong. There was another circle of hell into which I could be cast.

Madame Levene gloated. "Yes. It appears that your father is too busy to attend to this matter himself. He must send an emissary in his place. Perhaps, Élise, you are not as important to him as you might imagine."

I looked hard at the gloating face of the headmistress and for a brief second imagined myself diving across the desk and wiping the smirk off her face myself, but I was already fomenting other plans.

"The emissary wishes to see you alone," she said.

"I expect you shall listen outside the door."

Her lips thinned. Those stony eyes glittered. "I will enjoy knowing that your impertinence has come with a price, Mademoiselle de la Serre, you can be sure of that."

21 JANUARY 1788

And so the day came when the emissary was due to arrive. I had stayed out of trouble the week prior to his arrival. According to the other girls I was quieter than usual. Some were asking when the "old Élise" would return; the usual suspects were crowing that I had finally been tamed. We'd see.

Actually, what I was doing was readying myself, mentally and physically. The emissary would be expecting meek acquiescence. He would be expecting a frightened teenager, terrified of expulsion and happy to take any other punishment. The emissary was expecting tears and contrition. He wasn't going to get that.

I was summoned to the office, told to wait, and wait I did. With my hands grasping my purse in which I had secreted a horseshoe "borrowed" from above the dormitory door. It had never brought me any luck. Now was its chance.

From the vestibule outside I heard two voices, Madame Levene with her obsequious, ingratiating welcome to Father's emissary, telling him that "the miscreant awaits her just deserts in my office, monsieur," and then the deeper, growling voice of the emissary as he replied, "Thank you, Madame."

With a gasp I recognized the voice, and still had my hand to my mouth in shock as the door opened and in came Mr. Weatherall.

He closed the door behind him and I threw myself at him, knocking the breath out of him with the force of my emotion, shoulders wracked with sobs that came before I had a chance to stop them. My shoulders heaved as I wept into his chest and I tell you this—I've never ever been as pleased see anyone in my life as I was at that moment.

We stayed like that for some time, with me silently sobbing into my protector until at last I was able to gain control of myself and he held me at arm's length to gaze into my eyes, then, first putting his finger to his lips and moving in front of the keyhole.

Over his shoulder he said loudly, "You may well cry, mademoiselle, for your father is too furious with you to attend to the matter himself. So full of emotion that he has asked me, your governor"—he winked—"to administer your punishment in his place. But first, you shall write to him a letter of abject apology. And when that is done I shall administer your punishment, which you may expect to be the most severe you have ever experienced."

He ushered me to a school desk in one corner of the office, out of view from the keyhole, where I perched with writing paper, quill and pen just in case the head-mistress should find an excuse to walk in on us. Then he pulled up a chair, put his elbows to the surface of the desk and, whispering, we began to talk.

"I'm pleased to see you," I told him.

He chortled softly. "Can't say I'm surprised. After all, you were expecting to have seven shades of shit knocked out of you."

"Actually," I said, opening my purse to reveal the horseshoe inside, "it was the other way around."

He frowned. Not the reaction I wanted. "And what then, Élise?" he whispered crossly, his forefinger jabbing the top of the desk for emphasis. "You would have been expelled from the Maison Royale. Your education—delayed. Your induction—delayed. Your ascendance to Grand Master—delayed. Exactly what would that path have achieved, eh?"

"I really don't care," I said.

"You don't care, eh? You don't care about your father anymore?"

"You know damn well I care about Father."

He sneered at my cursing. "And I know damn well you care about your mother, too. And the family name, come to that. So why are you so intent on dragging it through the mud? Why are you seeing to it that you never get as far as Grand Master?"

"It is my *destiny* to be Grand Master," I replied, real-izing with an uncomfortable twinge that I reminded myself of May Carroll.

"A destiny can change, child."

"I'm not a child anymore," I reminded him. "I am twenty years old."

His expression saddened. "You'll always be a child to me, Élise. Don't forget I can remember the little girl learning sword fighting in the woods. Most able pupil I ever had, but also the most impulsive. Bit too full of herself." He looked sideways at me. "You been keeping up your sword fighting?"

I scoffed. "In here? How would I manage that?"

Sarcastically, he pretended to think. "Oh, let's see. Um, how about by keeping a low profile so your every move wasn't watched. So you could sneak away every now and then instead of always being the center of attention. The sword given to you by your mother was for exactly that purpose."

I felt guilty. "Well, no. As you know I haven't been doing that."

"And so your skills have been neglected."

"Then why send me away to a school where that was bound to happen?"

"Point is, it wasn't *bound* to happen. You shouldn't have let it happen. You're to be a Grand Master."

"Well, that could change, according to you," I retorted, feeling like I'd won the point.

He didn't miss a beat. "And it *will* change if you don't knuckle down and mend your ways. That lot you call the Crows—Messieurs Lafrenière, Le Peletier, Sivert, and Madame Levesque—are just dying to see you slip up. You think it's all cozy in the Order, do you? That they're all strewing flowers ahead of your coronation as their 'right-ful queen,' like in the history books? Nothing could be further from the truth. Every single one of them would like to end the reign of de la Serre and make it so their family name carries the title Grand Master. Every single one of them is looking for reasons to depose your father and snatch the title for himself. Their policies differ from those of your father, remember? He hangs on to their confidence by a thread. Having an errant daughter is the last thing he bloody needs. Besides . . ."

"What?"

He glanced to the door. No doubt Madame Levene had her ear pressed hard against it, and it was for her benefit that Mr. Weatherall said loudly, "And just you make sure you use your very best handwriting, made-moiselle."

Quietening, he leaned closer toward me. "You remember the two men who attacked you, no doubt?"

"How could I forget?"

"Well," continued Mr. Weatherall, "I promised your mother I'd find the fella who wore the doctor outfit, and I think I have."

I gave him a look.

"Yeah, all right," he admitted, "so it's taken me a while. But I've found him is the important thing."

Faces so close they were almost touching. I could smell wine on his breath.

"Who is he?" I asked.

"His name is Ruddock, and he is indeed an Assassin, or *was*, at least."

He went on, "Seems that he was excommunicated from the Order. Been trying to get back in ever since."

"Why was he excommunicated?"

"Bringing the Order into disrepute. Likes a wager by the sounds of things. Only he's not the lucky sort. He's up to his eyes in debt by all accounts."

"Could it be he hoped to kill Mother as a means of gaining favor with his Order?"

Mr. Weatherall shot me an impressed look. "Could well be the case though I can't help but think it'd be a bit of half-witted strategy for him. Could be that killing your mother would have brought him even greater disgrace. He'd have no way of knowing." He shook his head. "Wait to see if the assassination is viewed in a favorable light and only then claim credit for it, maybe. But no, I can't see it. To me this sounds as though he was offering his services to the highest bidder, trying to clear those gambling debts. I reckon our friend Ruddock was working as a sword for hire."

"So the Assassins were not the ones behind the attempt?"

"Not necessarily."

"Have you told the Crows?"

He shook his head.

"Why not?"

He looked evasive. "Your mother had certain . . . *suspicions* concerning the Crows."

"What sort of suspicions?"

"Do you remember a certain François Thomas Germain?"

"I'm not sure I do."

"Fierce-looking guy. He would have been around when you were a child. François Thomas Germain was your father's lieutenant. He had some dodgy ideas and your father turfed him out of the Order. He's dead now. But your mother always wondered if Messieurs Lafrenière, Le Peletier, Sivert, and Madame Levesque might have had sympathies with him."

I started, unable to believe what I was hearing. "You can't believe my father's advisers would plot to kill Mother?"

True, I'd always hated the Crows, but then again I'd always hated Madame Levene, and I couldn't imagine her plotting my murder. The idea was too far-fetched.

Mr. Weatherall continued. "Your mother's death would have suited their ends. The Crows might well have been your father's advisers in name, but after Germain got the boot it was your mother who had his ear above all others, including them. With her out of the way . . ."

"But she is 'out of the way.' She's dead, and my father has remained true to his policies."

"It's impossible to say what goes on, Élise. Maybe he's proven less pliable than expected."

"No, it still doesn't make sense to me," I said, shaking my head.

"Things don't always make sense, love. The Assassins trying to kill your mother didn't make sense, but everyone was keen to believe it. No, for the time being

I'm staying suspicious unless I have evidence otherwise, and if it's all the same to you, I'm playing it safe until we know either way."

Inside me was a strangely hollow feeling, a sense that a curtain had been drawn back to expose uncertainties behind. There might be people within our own organization who wished us wrong. I had to find out—I had to find out either way.

"What about Father?"

"What of him?"

"You haven't told him your suspicions?"

With his eyes fixed on the top of the desk, he shook his head.

"Why?"

"Well, firstly because they are just suspicions, and as you've pointed out, pretty wild ones at that. If they're not true—which they're most likely not—I look like a bloody idiot; if they are, then all I've done is alert them and while they're busy laughing it off because I don't have a shred of proof, they're making plans to do away with me. And also . . ."

"What?"

"I have not been acquitting myself well since your mother died, Élise," he admitted. "Reverting to old ways, you might say, and in the process burning what bridges I had built with my fellow Templars. There are some similarities between me and Mr. Ruddock."

"I see. And that's why I can smell wine on your breath, is it?"

"We all cope in our own way, child."

"She's been gone almost ten years, Mr. Weatherall."

He gave a short mirthless laugh. "Mourn too much for your tastes, do I? Well, I could say the same of you, pissing away the last of your education, making enemies when you should be forging connections and contacts. Don't you be sneering at the likes of me, Élise. Not until your own house is in order."

I frowned. "We need to know who was behind that attempt."

"Which is what I'm doing."

"How?"

"This bloke Ruddock is hiding out in London. We have contacts in London. The Carrolls, if you recall. I've already sent word ahead of my arrival."

Never was I more certain of anything. "I'm coming with you."

He looked at me peevishly. "No you're bloody well not, you're staying here and finishing your schooling. For crying out loud, girl, what on earth would your father say?"

"How about we tell him I'm to pay an educational visit to London in order to improve my English?"

The protector jabbed his finger on the desk. "No. How about we do nothing of the sort? How about you stay here?"

I shook my head. "No, I'm coming with you. This man has haunted my nightmares for years, Mr. Weatherall." I fixed him with my best imploring look. "I have some ghosts I need to lay to rest."

He rolled his eyes. "Pull the other one. You forget

how well I know you. More likely you want the excitement, and you want to get away from this place."

"Well, okay," I said, "but come on, Mr. Weatherall. Do you know how difficult it is to have the likes of Valerie sneering at me and not tell them that one day, when she's pushing out children for the drunken son of a marquis, I will be head of the Templars? This stage of my life cannot end soon enough for me. I'm desperate for the next stage to start."

"You'll just have to wait."

"I've only got a year to go," I pushed.

"They call it finishing for a reason. You can't finish unless you finish."

"I won't even be away that long."

"No. And anyway, even—*even*—if I agreed, you'd never get her out there to say yes."

"We could forge letters," I insisted. "Anything she writes to Father, you could intercept. I take it you *have* been intercepting the letters . . ."

"Of course I have. Why do you think I'm here and not him? But he's going to find out sooner or later. At some point, Élise, one way or another, your lies will be exposed."

"It'll be too late then."

He bulged with fresh anger, his skin reddening against the white of his whiskers. "This—this is exactly what I'm talking about. You're so full of yourself you've forgotten your responsibilities. It's making you reckless and the more reckless you are the more you endanger your family's position. I wish I'd never bloody told you now. I thought I could talk some sense into you."

I looked at him, an idea forming, and then in a display of acting that would have impressed Valerie, pretended to decide he was right and that I was sorry and all the other stuff he wanted to see in my face.

He nodded and cast his voice toward the door. "Right, at last, you're finished. This letter I shall take home to your father, accompanied by the news that I gave you six strokes of the cane."

I shook my head and held up desperate fingers.

He blanched. "What I mean is, *twelve* strokes of the cane."

I shook my head furiously. Held out fingers again.

"I mean ten strokes of the cane."

Pretend-wiping my brow, I called out, "Oh no, monsieur, not ten strokes."

"Now, is this the cane used to punish you girls?"

He had moved over to Madame Levene's desk, which was in sight of the keyhole, and picked the cane from its pride of place across her desk. At the same time he used the cover of his back and sleight of hand to pluck a cushion from her chair and skim it across the floor to me.

It was all very smooth. Like we did it every day. What a team we made. I picked up the cushion and laid it across the desk as he walked over with a cane, and once more we were out of sight of the keyhole.

"Right," he said loudly, for the benefit of Madame Levene, with a wink at me. I stood to one side while he gave the cushion ten smart whacks, making suitable ouch noises after each one. And after all, when it came to authentic pain noises, who knew better than I? I could imagine Madame Levene cursing as all the action happened out of sight, no doubt planning to rearrange the furniture as soon as possible.

When it was over and I'd summoned thoughts of Mother to make myself cry, and we'd replaced the cushion and cane, we opened the door. Madame Levene was standing in the vestibule some distance away. I arranged my face to look like a person who had recently been punished, gave her a baleful look with my red-rimmed eyes and, with my head down and resisting the temptation to give Mr. Weatherall a good-bye wink, I scuttled off as if to lick my wounds.

In fact I had a little thinking to do.

23 JANUARY 1788

Let's see. How did this start? That's right—with Judith Poulou saying that Madame Levene had a lover.

That was all Judith had said, one night after lights out, that Madame Levene had "a lover in the woods" and the other girls had mainly scoffed at the idea. But not me. I'd remembered a night some time ago when, just after supper, I'd spied the dreaded headmistress from a dormitory window, wrapping herself in a shawl as she hurried down the steps away from the schoolhouse, then melted into the darkness beyond.

There'd been something about the way she behaved that made me think she wasn't just planning to take the air. The way she looked from left to right. The way she headed toward the path that led in the direction of the sports fields and, yes, maybe, the woods at the perimeter.

It had taken me two nights of keeping watch, but last night I saw her again. Just as before, she left the schoolhouse, and with the same furtive air, although not furtive enough to detect a window opening in the schoolhouse above, and me climbing from it, clambering down the trellis to the ground and setting off in pursuit.

At last I was putting my training into action. I became like a wraith in the night, keeping her just in sight, silently tracking her as she used the light of the moon to navigate her way along the lawn and to the perimeter of the sports fields.

They were an open expanse and I scowled for a moment—then did what my mother and Mr. Weatherall had always taught me to do. I assessed the situation. Madame Levene with the light of the moon behind her— her old bespectacled eyes versus my young ones. I decided to stay behind her, keeping her in the distance, so that she was little more than a shadow ahead of me. I saw the moonlight glint on her spectacles as she turned to check she wasn't being followed, and I froze, became part of the night, prayed my calculations had been correct.

They were. The witch kept on going until she reached the tree line and was swallowed up by the harsh shapes of tree trunks and undergrowth. I sped up and followed her, finding the same path she'd taken, that cut through the woods, and becoming a ghost. The route reminding me of years spent taking a similar track to see Mr. Weatherall. A track that used to end with my protector perched waiting on his tree stump, smiling, unburdened, then, by the weight of my mother's death.

I'd never smelled wine on his breath back then.

I banished the memory as ahead of us I saw the small groundskeeper's lodge and realized where she was heading. I drew to a halt and from my position behind a tree watched as she knocked gently and the door was opened. I heard her say, "I couldn't wait to see you," and there was the distinct sound of a kiss—*a kiss*—and then she disappeared inside, the door closing behind her.

So this was her lover in the woods. Jacques, the groundskeeper, of whom I knew little other than what I'd seen as he attended to his duties in the middle distance. One thing I did know was that he was younger than Madame Levene. What a dark horse she was.

I returned, knowing the rumors were true. And, unfortunately for her, not only was I the one in possession of that information, but I was not above using it to get what I wanted from her. Indeed, that was precisely what I intended to do.

25 JANUARY 1788

Just after lunch, Judith came to see me. The very same
Judith from whom I'd heard the rumor about Madame
Levene's love. Neither one of my enemies nor my admir-
ers, Judith face was impassive as she delivered the news
that the headmistress wanted to see me in her office
right away in order to talk about the theft of a horseshoe
from the dormitory door.

I made my face grave as if to say, "Oh God, not again.
When will this torture ever end?" when in fact I couldn't
have been more thrilled. Madame Levene was playing
right into my hands. Handed to me on a plate was a golden
opportunity to give her the good news that I knew all
about her lover, *Jacques*, because while she thought she
was going to cane me for stealing the dormitory's lucky
horseshoe, in actual fact I'd be leaving not with the usual

smarting palm and a seething sense of injustice, but a letter for my father. A letter in which Madame Levene informed him that his daughter Élise was to be leaving for individual English tuition in . . . *guess*.

If all went to plan, that was.

At her door I knocked smartly, entered, then, with my shoulders flung back and my chin inclined, strode across her office to where she sat before the window and dropped the horseshoe on her desk.

There was a moment of silence. Those beady eyes fixed on the unwelcome bit of rusted iron on her desk, then rose to meet mine, but instead of the usual look of disdain and barely masked hatred, there was something else there—some unreadable emotion I'd never seen in her before.

"Ah," she said, a slight tremor in her voice, "very good. You have returned the stolen horseshoe."

"That's what you wanted to see me about, wasn't it?" I said carefully, less sure of myself all of a sudden.

"That was what I told Judith I wanted to see you about, yes." She reached beneath her desk and I heard the sound of a drawer scraping open, and she added, "But there was another reason."

I felt a chill, hardly dared ask, "And what was that, Madame?"

"This," she said, placing something on the desk in front of her.

It was my journal. I felt my eyes widen. Was suddenly short of breath. My fists flexing.

"You . . ." I tried, but could not finish. "You . . ."

She leveled a trembling bony finger at me and her eyes blazed as her voice rose, her anger matching mine.

"Don't play the victim with me, young lady. Not after what I've read." The pointing finger jabbed at the cover of my journal—a cover that I knew so well, that looked *odd* and out of place on the headmistress's desk—a cover under which were my most private thoughts, ripped from their hiding place under my mattress. Pored over by most hated enemy.

My temper began to rise. I fought to control my breathing and my shoulders rose and fell, fists still clenching and unclenching.

"How . . . how much did you read?" I managed.

"Enough to know you were planning to blackmail me," she said tersely. "No more, no less."

Even in the heat of my anger I couldn't miss the irony. We were both caught—hoisted halfway between shame at our own actions and outrage at what had been done to us. Myself, I felt a potent brew of fury, guilt and sheer hatred, and in my mind formed the image of me diving across the desk at her, hands fixing around her neck as her eyes bulged behind her round spectacles . . .

Instead, I simply stared at her, barely able to comprehend what was happening.

"How could you?"

"Because I saw you, Élise de la Serre. I saw you creeping around outside the cottage the other night. I saw you spying on me and Jacques. And so I thought, not unreasonably, that your journal might illuminate me as to your intentions. Do you deny that you intended to blackmail me, de la Serre?" Her color rose. "*Blackmail* the headmistress of the school?"

But our fury was at cross-purposes.

"Reading my journal is unforgivable," I raged.

Her voice rose. "What you planned to do was unforgivable. *Blackmail*." She spat the word as though she couldn't quite believe it. As though she had never even encountered the concept before.

I bridled. "I meant you no harm. It was a means to an end."

"I daresay you relished the prospect of it, Élise de la Serre." She brandished my journal. "I've read exactly what you think of me. Your hatred—no, worse, your *contempt*—for me pours off every page."

I shrugged. "Does that surprise you? After all, don't *you* hate *me*?"

"Oh, you stupid girl," she raged, "of course I don't *hate* you. I'm your headmistress. I want what's best for you. And, for your information, I don't listen at doors either."

I gave her a doubtful look. "You seemed gleeful enough when it came to the thought of my impending punishment."

Her eyes dropped. "In the heat of the moment we all say things we shouldn't, and I regretted that remark. But the fact is, while you're by no means my favorite person in the world, I'm your headmistress. Your guardian. And you, in particular, came to me a damaged girl, fresh from the loss of her mother. You, in particular, needed special attention. Oh, yes, my attempts to help have taken the form of a battle of wills, and I suppose that's hardly surprising, and, yes, I suppose the fact you think I hate you is to be expected—or was, when you were younger and first arrived here. But you're a young lady now, Élise, you should know better. I read no more of your journal than I needed to in order to establish your guilt, but I read enough to know that your future lies in a different direction from that of the majority of the pupils here, and for that I'm pleased. Nobody with your spirit should settle down to a life of domesticity."

I started, hardly able to believe what I was hearing, and she soaked it up before continuing, her voice softer. "And now we find ourselves at a difficult juncture, for we have both done something terrible and we both have something the other wants. From you I want silence about what you saw; from me you want a letter to your father." She passed the journal across the table to me. "I'm going to give you your letter. I'm going to lie for you. I'm going to tell him that you will be spending part of your final year in London so that you can do what it is you need to do, and when you have exorcised whatever it is that compels you to go, I trust it will be a different Élise de la Serre who returns to me. One who has held on to the spirit of the little girl but abandoned the hot-headed juvenile."

The letter would be with me by the afternoon, she said, and I stood to leave, feeling mollified, shame making my head heavy. As I reached the door she stopped me. "One more thing, Élise. Jacques isn't my lover. He's my son."

I don't think Mother would be very proud of me just now.

7 FEBRUARY 1788

i

I am a long way from Saint-Cyr now. And after a fairly tumultuous last two days I write this entry in . . .

Well, no. Let's not give anything away just yet. Let's go back to when I took my carriage away from the dreaded *Le Palais de la Misère*, when there was no backward glance, no friends to bid me *bon voyage* and certainly no Madame Levene standing at the window waving her handkerchief good-bye. There was just me in a carriage and my trunk lashed to the top.

"We're here," the coachman said when we arrived at the docks in Calais. It was late and the sea was a dark, undulating shimmer beyond the cobbles of the harbor and the bobbing mast of moored ships. Above us were squawking gulls and around us were the people of the docks, staggering from tavern to tavern, the night in full swing, a rowdy hubbub in the air. My coachman took disapproving looks left and right, then stood on the footboard to free my trunk before laying it on the cobbles of the dockside. He opened my door and his eyes boggled. I was not the same girl he'd picked up.

Why? Because during the journey I'd changed. Off had come the accursed dress and I now wore breeches, a shirt, waistcoat and justaucorps. I'd cast aside the dreaded bonnet, unpinned my hair and tied it back. And now, as I stepped out of the carriage, I plonked my tricorn on my head, bent to my trunk and opened it, all under the speechless gaze of the coachman. My trunk full of the clothes I hated and trinkets I planned to throw away anyway. All I needed was in my satchel—that and the short sword that I pulled from the trunk's depths and tied around my waist, allowing my satchel to fall over it so it was hidden.

"You can keep the trunk, if you like," I said. From my waistcoat I took a small leather purse and proffered coins.

"Who's here to escort you, then?" he said, pocketing them as he looked around, scowling at the nighttime revelers making the way along the dockside.

"Nobody."

He looked askance at me. "Is this some kind of joke?"

"No, why would it be?"

"You can't be roaming the docks on your own at this hour."

I dropped another coin into his palm. He looked at it.

"No," he said firmly, "I can't allow it, I'm afraid."

I dropped another coin into his palm.

"All right, then," he acquiesced. "On your own head be it. Just steer clear of the taverns and stay near the lantern light. Watch the docks, they're high and uneven, and many an unfortunate has fallen off them from getting too close for a peek over the edge. And don't catch anybody's eye. Oh, and whatever you do, keep that purse hidden."

I smiled sweetly, knowing I intended to take all of his advice apart from the bit about the taverns because the taverns were exactly where I wanted to be. I watched the carriage draw away, then headed straight to the nearest one.

The first one I came to had no name, but hanging above a set of windows set high was a wooden sign on which was a pair of crudely drawn antlers, so let's call it the Antlers. As I stood on the cobbles gathering the courage to go inside, the door opened, allowing out a blast of warm air, exuberant piano and the stink of ale, as well as a man and woman, rosy-cheeked and unsteady on their feet, each holding the other up. In the instant of the open door I got a glimpse of the tavern inside and it was like staring into a furnace before the door shut quickly and it was quiet on the dockside once more, the noise from inside the Antlers reduced to a background babble.

I braced myself. *All right, Élise. You wanted to get away from that prim and proper school, the rules and regulations you hated. On the other side of that door lies the exact opposite to school. The question is, Are you really as tough as you think you are?*

(The answer, I was about to find out, was no.)

Entering was like walking into a new world fashioned

entirely from smoke and noise. The sound of raucous laughter, squawking birds, the piano and drunken singing assaulted my ears.

It was a small room, with a balcony at one end and birdcages hanging from beams, and it was heaving with drinkers. Men lounged at tables or on the floor and the balcony seemed to heave with people craning over to heckle revelers below. I stayed by the door, lingering in the shadows. Drinkers nearby eyed me with interest, and I heard a wolf whistle cut through the din, then caught the eye of a servingwoman in an apron, who turned from setting down two jugs of ale on a table, the ale thankfully arresting the attention of the men sitting there.

"I'm looking for the captain of a ship leaving for London in the morning," I said, loudly.

She wiped her hands on her apron and rolled her eyes. "Any particular captain? Any particular ship?"

I shook my head. It didn't matter.

She nodded, looking me up and down. "See that table at the back there." I squinted through the ropes of smoke and capering bodies to a table in the far corner. "Go up back, speak to the one they call the Middle Man. Tell him Selene sent you."

I looked harder, seeing three men sitting with their backs to the far wall, curtains of smoke giving them the look of ghosts, like returning spirit-drinkers, cursed to haunt the tavern forevermore.

"Which one is the Middle Man?" I asked Selene.

She smirked as she moved off. "He's the one in the middle."

Feeling exposed I began to make my way toward the

Middle Man and his two friends. Faces were upturned as I threaded through tables.

"Now that's a very fetching little one to be in a place like this," I heard, as well as a couple of other, more near-the-knuckle suggestions that modesty forbids me sharing. Thank God for the smoke and gloom and noise and the overall state of drunkenness that hung over the place. It meant that only those nearest to me paid me any interest.

I came to the three spirit-men and stood before the table where they sat facing the room with tankards close at hand, dragging their gaze away from the festivities and to me. Whereas others had leered or pulled faces or made lewd, drunken suggestions, they simply stared appraisingly. The Middle Man, smaller than his two companions, gazed past me and I turned in time to catch a glimpse of the grinning servingwoman as she slid away.

Uh-oh. All of a sudden I was conscious of how far away I was from the door. Here in the depths of the tavern it was even darker. The drinkers behind me seemed to have closed in on me. The flames from a fire flickered on the walls and the faces of the three men watching me. I thought of my mother's advice, wondered what Mr. Weatherall would say. Stay impassive but watchful. Assess the situation. (And ignore that nagging feeling that you should have done all that *before* entering the tavern.)

"And what's a fine-dressed young woman doing all by herself in a place like this?" said the man in the middle. Unsmiling, he fished a long-stemmed pipe from his breast pocket and fitted it into a gap between his crooked, blackened teeth, chomping on it with pink gums.

"I was told you might be able to help me find the captain of a ship," I said.

"And what might you be wanting a captain for?"

"For passage to London."

"To London?"

"Yes," I said.

"You mean to Dover?"

I felt my color rise, swallowed my stupidity. "Of course," I said.

The Middle Man's eyes danced with amusement. "And you need a captain for this trip, do you?"

"Quite."

"Well, why don't you just take the packet?"

The out-of-depth feeling had returned. "The packet?"

The Middle Man suppressed a smirk. "Never mind, girl. Where you from?"

Somebody jostled me rudely from behind. I shoved back with my shoulder and heard a drunk rebound to a nearby table, spilling drinks and being roundly cursed for his pains before folding to the floor.

"From Paris," I told the Middle Man.

"Paris, eh?" He took the pipe from his mouth and a rope of drool dropped to the tabletop as he used it as a pointer. "From one of the more salubrious areas of town, though, I'll be bound, just to look at you, I mean."

I said nothing.

The pipe was returned. The pink gums chomped down. "What's your name, girl?"

"Élise," I told him.

"No second name?"

I made a noncommittal sound.

"Could it be that I might recognize your surname?"

"I value my privacy, that's all."

He nodded some more. "Well," he said, "I think I can find you a captain to speak to. Matter of fact me and my friends were just on our way to meet this particular gentleman for an ale or two. Why don't you join us?"

He made as if to stand . . .

This was all wrong. I tensed, aware of the clamor around me, jostled by drinkers and yet, somehow, completely isolated, then gave a small bow without taking my eyes from theirs. "I thank you for your time, gentlemen, but I've had second thoughts."

The Middle Man looked taken aback and his lips cracked in a smile, revealing more graveyard teeth. This was what a minnow saw—seconds before it was devoured by a shark.

"Second thoughts, eh?" he said with a sidelong look left and right at his two bigger companions. "How do you mean? Like you've decided you don't want to go to London no more? Or is it that me and my friends don't look sufficiently seafaring for your liking?"

"Something like that," I said, and pretended not to notice the man on his left push back his chair as though ready to leave his seat, and the man on the other flank lean forward almost imperceptibly.

"You're suspicious of us, is that it?"

"Might be," I agreed, with jutted chin. I folded my arms across my chest and used it as an opportunity to bring my right hand closer to the hilt of my sword.

"And why might that be?" he asked.

"Well, you haven't asked me how much I can afford, for a start."

Now his lips cracked in a smile. "Oh, you'll be earning your berth to London."

I pretended not to understand what he meant. "Well, that's quite all right, and I thank you for your time, but I shall take care of my own passage."

Now he laughed openly. "Taking care of your passage was what we had in mind."

Again I let it wash over me. "I shall take my leave, messieurs," I said, bowing slightly, making to turn and push my way back through the throng.

"No, you won't," said the Middle Man, and with a wave of his hand he set his two dogs upon me.

They stood, hands on their swords at their waists. I stepped back and to the side, drawing my own sword and brandishing it at the first, a movement that stopped them both in their tracks.

"Ooh," said one, and the two of them began to laugh. That rattled me. For a second I had no idea how to react as the Middle Man reached into his clothes and produced a curved dagger, and the second man wiped the smile off his face and came forward.

I tried to ward him off with the sword but I wasn't assertive enough and there were too many people around. What should have been a confident warning slash across the face was ineffective.

"You're to use it for practice."

But I hadn't. In almost ten years of schooling I'd barely practiced my sword fighting at all, and though I had on occasion, when the dormitory around me was quiet, taken the presentation box from its hiding place, opened it to inspect the steel anew, running my fingers over the inscription on the blade, I had rarely taken it to a private place in order to work on my drills. Just enough to prevent my skills calcifying completely, not enough to prevent them rusting.

And either that or my inexperience, or more likely a combination of the two, meant that I was woefully unprepared to take on these three men. And when it came it wasn't some dazzling swordplay that sent me sprawling to the wet and stinking sawdust-strewn boards of the tavern, but a two-handed push from the first of the thugs to reach me. He'd seen what I hadn't. Behind me lay the same drunken man who had recoiled off me earlier, and as I skated back a step and my ankles met him I lost my balance, fell and in the next instant was lying on top of him.

"Monsieur," I said, hoping that somehow my desperation would penetrate the veil of alcohol, but his eyes were glassy and his face wet with drink. In the next second I was screaming with pain as the heel of a boot landed on the back of my hand, grinding the flesh and making me let go of the sword. Another foot kicked my beloved sword away, and I rolled and tried to get to my feet but hands grabbed me and pulled me up. My desperate eyes went from the crowds who shrunk away, most laughing as they enjoyed the show, to the prone, drunken man and then to my short sword, which was now beneath the table, out of harm's way. I kicked and writhed. Before me was the Middle Man, brandishing his curved knife, lips pulled back in a mirthless grin, teeth still chomped around the stem of the pipe. I heard a door open behind, felt a sudden rush of chill wind, and then I was being dragged out into the night.

It had all happened so quickly. One moment I was in the heaving tavern, the next in an almost empty yard, just me, the Middle Man and his two thugs. They shoved me to the ground and I stayed there a second, snarling and catching my breath, trying to show them a brave face but inside, thinking, *Stupid—stupid, inexperienced, arrogant little girl.*

What the hell had I been thinking?

The yard opened out to the dockside at the front of the Antlers, where just a few yards away people passed by ignorant or oblivious to my plight, while not far away was a small carriage. The Middle Man jumped up to it now, one of his thugs grabbing me roughly by the shoulders while the other dragged open the door. I caught a glimpse of another girl inside, younger than me, maybe fifteen or sixteen, who had long blond hair down to her shoulders, and wore a ragged brown smock dress, the dress of a peasant girl. Her eyes were wide and frightened and her mouth open in an appeal I didn't hear over the sound of my own screaming and shouting. The thug carried me easily, but as he tried to swing me into the carriage, my feet found purchase on the side and, knees bent, I shoved myself off, forcing him backward into the yard and making him curse. I used the force of our momentum to my advantage, twisting around again so that this time he lost his footing and we both tumbled to the dirt.

Our dance was greeted with a gale of laughter from the Middle Man atop the carriage as well as the thug holding the door, and behind their merriment I could hear the sobbing of the girl and knew that if the thugs managed to bundle me into the carriage, then we were both lost.

And then the back door to the tavern opened, cutting off their the laugher with a gust of noise and heat and smoke, and a figure staggered out, already reaching into his breeches.

It was the same drunken man. He stood with his legs apart, about to relieve himself on the wall of the tavern, craning back over his shoulder.

"Everything all right over there?" he croaked, head lolling as he returned to the serious business of undoing the buttons of his breeches.

"No, monsieur," I started, but thug grabbed me and held my mouth, muffling my cry. I wriggled and tried to bite, to no avail. Sitting in the driver's seat still, the Middle Man gazed down upon us all: me, pinned to the ground and gagged by the first thug; the drunk man still fiddling with his breeches; the second thug awaiting his instructions with an upturned face. The Middle Man drew a finger across his throat.

I increased my efforts to get free, shouting into the hand clamped over my mouth and ignoring the pain of his elbows and knees as I writhed on the ground, hoping somehow to wriggle free or at least make enough noise to attract the drunkard's attention.

Casting a look toward the yard entrance, the thug drew his sword silently and moved up on the oblivious drunkard. I saw the girl in the carriage. She had moved across the seats and was peeking out. *Shout out, warn him.* I wanted to scream but couldn't and so settled for gnashing my teeth instead, trying to nip the flesh of the sweaty hand across my mouth. For a second our eyes met and I tried to urge her simply with the power of my gaze, blinking furiously and widening my eyes and swiveling them over to the drunk man who stood concentrating on his breeches, death just a foot or so away.

But she couldn't do anything. She was too scared. Too scared to shout out and too scared to move, and the drunk man was going to die and the thugs were going to bundle us in the carriage and into a ship, then . . . well, put it this way, I was going to wish I was back at the school.

The blade rose. But then, something happened—the drunk man wheeled around, faster than I would have thought possible, and in his hands was my short sword, which flashed, tasting blood for the first time as he swept it flat across the thug's throat, which opened, spraying crimson mist into the yard.

For maybe half a second the only reaction was shock and the only noise the wet sound of lifeblood leaving the thug. Then with a roar of anger and defiance the second thug took his knee off my neck and leapt at the drunkard.

I'd allowed myself to believe that the drunkenness was an act, and that he was in fact an expert swordsman *pretending* to be drunk. But no, I realized, as he stood there, swaying from side to side and trying to focus on the advancing henchman. Though he might well have been an expert swordsman, he was certainly drunk. Enraged, the second thug charged him, wielding his sword. It wasn't pretty; even though he was in his cups, my savior seemed to dodge him easily, striking backhand with my short sword, catching the thug on the arm and eliciting a scream of pain.

From above me I heard, "Ha!" and looked up in time to see the Middle Man shake the reins. For him the battle was over and he didn't want to leave empty-handed. As the carriage lurched toward the entrance, with its passenger door swinging, I sprang to my feet and sprinted after it, reaching inside just as we came to the narrow entrance.

I had one chance. One moment. "Grab my hand," I screamed and thank God she was more decisive than she had been before. With desperate, frightened eyes, her cry a guttural shout, she lunged across the seats and grabbed my outstretched hand. I flung myself backward and dragged her out of the carriage door just as it skittered through the yard entrance and was gone, clacking away along the cobbles of the dockside. From my left came a shout. It was the remaining thug. I saw his mouth drop open in the shock of abandonment.

The drunken swordsman made him pay for his moment of outrage. He ran him through where he stood and my sword tasted blood for the second time tonight.

Mr. Weatherall had once made me promise never to name my sword. Now, as I watched the henchman slide off the blood-dripping blade and crumple dead to the dirt, I understood why.

ii

"Thank you, monsieur," I called into the silence that descended over the yard in the wake of the battle.

The drunken swordsman looked at me. He had long hair tied back, high cheekbones and faraway eyes.

"May we know your name, monsieur?" I called across the yard.

We might have been meeting at a civilized social function but for the two bodies sprawled on the dirt—that and the fact that he held a sword stained red with blood. He moved as though to hand my sword back to me, realized it needed cleaning, looked for somewhere to wipe it, then, finding nothing, settled for the body of the nearest thug. When that was done he raised a finger, said, "Excuse me," turned and vomited against the wall of the Antlers.

The blond girl and I looked at one another. That finger was still held up as the drunkard coughed up the last of his vomit, spat out a final mouthful then turned and gathered himself before sweeping off an imaginary hat, making an exaggerated bow and introducing himself. "My name is Captain Byron Jackson. At your service."

"Captain?"

"Yes—as I was trying to tell you in the tavern before you so rudely shoved me away."

I bristled. "I did no such thing. You were very rude. You pushed into me. You were drunk."

"Correction, I *am* drunk. And maybe also rude. However, there's no disguising the fact that though drunk and rude, I was also trying to help you. Or the very least keep you from the grasp of these reprobates."

"Well, you didn't manage that."

"Yes, I did," he said, offended, then seemed to think. "Eventually, I did. And on that note, we had better leave before these bodies are discovered by the soldiers. You desire passage to Dover, is that right?"

He saw me hesitate and waved an arm at the two

bodies. "Surely I've proved my suitability as an escort. I promise you, mademoiselle, that despite appearances to the contrary, my drunkenness and perhaps a certain uncouth manner, I fly with the angels. Just that my wings are a little singed is all."

"Why should I trust you?"

"You don't have to trust me." He shrugged. "No skin off my nose who you trust. Go back in there, and you can get the packet."

"The packet?" I repeated, irritated. "What is this *packet*?"

"The packet is any ship carrying mail or freight to Dover. Virtually every man in there is a packetman, and they'll be in the process of drinking up because the tides and winds are ripe for a crossing tonight. So by all means go back in there, flash your coin and you can secure yourself passage. Who knows? You might even get lucky and find yourself in the company of other fine lady travelers such as yourself." He pulled a face. "You might not, of course . . ."

"And what's in it for you if I come with you?"

He scratched the back of his neck, looking amused. "A lonely merchant would be very glad of the company for the crossing."

"As long as the lonely merchant didn't get any ideas."

"Such as?"

"Such as the ways in which he might pass the time."

He gave a hurt look. "I can assure you the thought never crossed my mind."

"And you, of course would never consider telling an untruth?"

"Absolutely not."

"Such as claiming to be a merchant when you are in fact a smuggler."

He threw up his hands. "Oh, that's just dandy. She's never heard of the packet and thinks you can sail straight to London, but makes me for a smuggler."

"So you *are* a smuggler?"

"Look, do you want passage or not?"

I thought about that for a moment or so.

"Yes," I said, and stepped forward to retrieve my sword.

"Tell me, what is the inscription near the hilt?" he asked, handing it over. "I would of course read it myself but for the fact that I'm drunk."

"Are you sure it's not that you cannot read?" I said teasingly.

"Oh, woe. Truly my lady has been fooled by my rough manners. What can I do to convince her that I really am a gentleman?"

"Well, you could try behaving like one," I said.

I took the proffered sword and with it held loosely in my palm I read the inscription on the hilt—"May the father of understanding guide you. Love, Mother"—and then before he could say anything, I brought the point of the sword to his neck and pressed it into the flesh of his throat.

"And on her life if you do anything to harm me, then I will run you through," I snarled.

He tensed, held out his arms, looked along the blade at me with eyes that were laughing a little too much for my liking. "I promise, mademoiselle. Tempting though it would be to touch a creature quite so exquisite as yourself, I shall be sure to keep my hands to myself. And anyway," he said, looking over my shoulder, "what about your friend?"

"My name is Helene," she said, as she came forward. Her voice trembled. "I am indebted to the mademoiselle for my life. I belong to her now."

"What?"

I dropped the sword and turned to face her. "No you aren't. No you don't. You must find your people."

"I have no people. I am yours, mademoiselle," she said, and I had never seen a face so earnest.

"I think that settles that," said Byron Jackson from behind me. I looked from him then back to her, lost for words.

And with that I had acquired a lady's maid and a captain.

iii

Byron Jackson, it turned out, was indeed a smuggler. An Englishman posing as a Frenchman, he piled his small ship, the *Granny Smith*, with tea, sugar and whatever else was taxed heavily by his government, sailed it to along England's east coast, then by means he would only describe as "magic" smuggled it past the customs houses.

Helene, meanwhile, was a peasant girl who had watched both her mother and father die, and so traveled to Calais in the hope of finding her last remaining living relative, her uncle Jean. She hoped to find a new life with him; instead, he sold her to the Middle Man. And, of course, the Middle Man would want his money back and Uncle Jean would have spent the money within a day or so of receiving it, so there would be trouble involving Helene if she stayed. So I let her be indebted to me, and we made a fellowship of three as we set off from Calais earlier.

And now I can hear the sounds of supper being laid. Our gracious host, the captain of the *Granny Smith*, has promised us a hearty repast. He has enough food, he says, for the whole of the two-day crossing.

8 FEBRUARY 1788

i

"If she's to be your lady's maid, she needs to learn some manners," Byron Jackson had remarked at dinner last night.

Which, when you considered that he drank constantly from his flask of wine, ate with his mouth open and his elbows propped on the table, was a statement burdened with a staggering degree of hypocrisy.

I looked at Helene. She'd torn off a piece of crust, dipped it in her soup and was about to shove the whole dripping hunk into her mouth, but had stopped and was now regarding us from under her hair, as though we were talking in a strange, foreign language.

"She's fine as she is," I said, mentally thumbing my nose at Madame Levene, my father, the Crows and every servant in our house at Versailles, all of whom would have been repulsed by my new friend's table manners.

"She might be fine for having her supper on board a smuggling vessel," said Byron cheerfully, "but she won't be fine when you're trying to pass her off as your lady's maid in London during this 'secret assignation' of yours."

I shot him an irritated look. "It's not a secret assignation."

He grinned. "You could have fooled me. Either way, you're going to need to teach her how to behave in public. For a start she needs to begin addressing you as mademoiselle. She needs to know the basics of etiquette and decorum."

"Yes, all right, thank you, Byron," I said primly. "I don't need you to tell me about table manners. I shall teach her myself."

"As you please, mademoiselle," he said, and grinned. He did that a lot. Both the sarcastically referring to me as "mademoiselle" and the grinning.

When supper was over, Byron took his flask of wine and some animal skins above deck and left us to prepare for bed. I wondered what he was doing up there, what he was thinking.

We sailed through the next day. Byron tethered the wheel with rope and he and I sparred, my neglected sword fighting skills beginning to return as I danced across the boards and our steel met. I could tell he was impressed. He laughed and smiled and gave me encouragement. A more handsome sparring partner than Mr. Weatherall, though perhaps a little less disciplined.

That night we ate again. Helene retired to her berth in the cramped conditions we called our cabin belowdecks while Byron left to man the wheel. Only this time, I reached for an animal skin of my own.

"Have you ever used your sword in anger before?" he said when I joined him on the upper deck. He sat steering with his feet and drinking from his leather flask of wine.

"By anger you mean . . ."

"Well, let's start with, have you ever killed anyone?"

"No."

"I'd be the first, eh, if I tried to touch you without your permission?"

"Exactly."

"Well, I shall just have to make sure that I have your permission, then, shan't I?"

I felt myself go warm despite the chill on the deck.

"Okay. So have you ever crossed swords with an opponent?"

The moon-dappled sea sucked at the hull but otherwise the night was almost totally still, like we were the only two people left alive.

"Of course."

"An opponent who meant you harm?"

"No," I admitted.

"Fair enough. Have you drawn your sword in order to protect yourself?"

"Indeed I have."

"How many times?"

"Once."

"And that was the one time, was it? Back there in the tavern?"

I pursed my lips. "Yes."

"Didn't go so well for you, did it?"

"No."

"And why was that, do you think?"

"I know why it was, thank you," I said primly. "I don't need telling by the likes of you."

"Go on, humor me."

"Because I hesitated."

He nodded thoughtfully, swigged from his flask, then handed it to me. I gulped down a mouthful, feeling the alcohol spread warmly through my body. I wasn't stupid. I knew that the first step to gaining a lady's permission to get into her bed was to get her drunk. But it was cold and he was agreeable company, if a little frustrating and . . . Oh, and nothing. I just drank.

"I hesitated."

"That's right. What should you have done?"

"Look, I don't need . . ."

"Don't you? But you were almost carried away back there. You know what they would have done to you after taking you from that yard. You wouldn't be above deck sipping wine with the captain. You'd have spent the voyage belowdecks, on your back, amusing the crew. Every member of the crew. And when you arrived at Dover, broken, mentally and physically, they would have sold you like cattle. Both of you. You and Helene. All of that but for my presence in the tavern. And you still don't think I have a right to tell you where you went wrong?"

"I went wrong going in the tavern in the bloody first place," I said.

He arched an eyebrow. "Been to England before, have you?" he asked.

"No, but it was an Englishman who taught me my sword skills."

He chortled. "And what he'd tell you if he were here is that your hesitancy almost cost you your life. A short sword is not a warning weapon. It is a doing weapon. If you draw it, use it. Don't just wave it around." He lowered his eyes, took a long thoughtful draught from his leather flask and passed it back to me. "There are plenty of reasons to kill a man: duty, honor, vengeance. All of them might give you pause for thought. And a reason for guilty reflection afterward. But self-protection or protection of another, killing in the name of protection, that is one reason you should never have to worry about."

ii

The following day Helene and I bid good-bye to Byron Jackson on the beach at Dover. He had much work to do, he said, in order to bypass the customs houses, so Helene and I would have to manage alone. He accepted the coins I gave him with a gracious bow and we went on our way.

As we took the path away from the beach, I turned to see him watching us go, waved and was pleased to see him wave back. And then he turned and was gone, and we took the steps toward the cliff top, the Dover lighthouse as our guide.

Though I'd been told the carriage ride to London could be hazardous thanks to highwaymen, our journey passed without incident and we arrived to find London a very similar city to the Paris I had left behind, with a blanket of dark fog hovering above the rooftops and a menacing River Thames crowded with traffic. The same stink of smoke and excrement and wet horse.

In a cab, I said to the driver in perfect English, "Excuse me, monsieur, but could you please be transporting myself and my companion to the home of the Carrolls in Mayfair."

"Whatchootalkinabaht?" He peered at us through the hinged communication hatch. Rather than try again I simply passed him the piece of paper. Then, when we were moving, Helene and I pulled the blinds and took turns hanging on to the communication hatch as we changed. I retrieved my by-now rather creased and careworn dress from the bottom of my satchel and instantly regretted not taking the time to fold it more carefully. Meanwhile, Helene discarded her peasant's dress in favor of my breeches, shirt and waistcoat—not much of an improvement considering the dirt I'd managed to accrue over the last three days, but it would have to do.

Finally we were dropped off at the home of the Carrolls in Mayfair, where the driver opened the door and gave us the now-familiar boggle eyes as two differently dressed girls materialized before his very eyes. He offered to knock and introduce us but I dismissed him with a gold coin.

And then, as we stood with the two colonnades of the entrance on either side, my new lady's maid and I, we took a deep breath, hearing approaching footsteps before the door was opened by a round-faced man in a coat, who smelled faintly of silver polish.

I introduced us and he nodded, recognizing my name, it seemed, then led us through an opulent reception hall to a carpeted hallway, where he asked us to wait outside what appeared to be a dining room, the sound of polite chatter and civilized clinking of cutlery emanating from within.

With the door ajar I heard him say, "My lady, you have a visitor. A Mademoiselle de la Serre from Versailles is here to see you."

There was a moment of shocked silence. Outside in the hallway I caught Helene's eye and wondered if I looked as worried as she did.

Then the butler reappeared, bidding us, "Come in," and we entered to see the occupants seated at the dining-room table having just enjoyed a hearty meal: Mr. and Mrs. Carroll, whose mouths were in the process of dropping open; May Carroll, who clapped her hands together with sarcastic delight and crowed, "Oh, it's smell-bag," and the mood I was in, I could just as easily have stepped over and given her a slap for her troubles; and Mr. Weatherall, who was already rising to his feet, his face reddening, roaring, "What the bloody hell do you think you're doing here?"

11 FEBRUARY 1788

My protector gave me a couple of days to settle in before coming to see me this morning. In the meantime I've borrowed clothes from May Carroll, who was at pains to tell me that the dresses lent to me were "old" and "rather out of fashion" and not really the sort of thing she'd be wearing this season—but would be "fine for you, smell-bag."

"If you call me that one more time, I'll kill you," I said.

"I beg your pardon?" she said.

"Oh, it's nothing. Thank you for the dresses." And I meant it. Fortunately, I have inherited my mother's disdain for fashion so although the out-of-fashion dresses were evidently designed to irritate me, they did nothing of the sort.

What irritates me is May Carroll.

Helene, meanwhile, has been braving below-stairs life, finding that the servants are even more snooty than the aristocrats above. And, it has to be said, hasn't been doing an awfully good job when it's come to masquerading as my lady's maid, performing strange, random curtsies while shooting constant, terrified glances my way. We'd have to work on Helene, there was no doubt about that. At least the Carrolls were so arrogant and pleased with themselves that they simply assumed Helene was "very French" and put her naivety down to that.

Then Mr. Weatherall knocked.

"Are you decent?" I heard him say.

"Yes, monsieur, I am decent," I replied, and the protector entered—and then immediately shielded his eyes.

"Bloody hell, girl, you said you were decent," he rasped.

"I *am* decent," I protested.

"What do you mean? You're wearing a nightdress."

"Yes, but I am decent."

He shook his head behind his hand. "No, look, in England, when we say, 'Are you decent?' it means 'Have you got your clothes on?'"

May Carroll's nightdresses were hardly revealing, but even so I had no wish to scandalize Mr. Weatherall, so he withdrew and some moments later we tried again. In he came, pulling up a chair while I perched on the end of the bed. The last time I'd seen him was the night of our arrival, when he'd gone a shade of beetroot as Helene and I entered the dining room, both of us looking like—what was the expression Madame Carroll had used?—"like something the cat had dragged in" and I had quickly spun a story about having been held up by highwaymen on the road between Dover and London.

I had cast my eyes around the table seeing faces that I had first laid eyes on over a decade ago. Madame Carroll looked no different, the same for her husband. The two of them wearing the usual bemused smile so beloved of the English upper classes. May Carroll, though, had grown— and if anything looked even more tiresomely haughty than she had when we had first met in Versailles.

Mr. Weatherall, meanwhile, was forced to pretend that he was aware of my upcoming arrival, masking his obvious surprise as concern for my well-being. The Carrolls had worn a selection of bemused looks and asked a number of searching questions, but he and I had bluffed with enough confidence to avoid being ejected there and then.

To be honest, I thought we'd made a good team.

"What the bloody hell do you think you're playing at?" he said now.

I fixed him with a look. "You know what I'm playing at."

"For crying out loud, Élise, your father is going to have me killed for this. I'm not exactly his favorite person as it is. I'm going to wake up with a blade at my throat."

"Everything has been smoothed over with Father," I told him.

"And Madame Levene?"

I swallowed, not really wanting to think about Madame Levene if I could help it. "That too."

He cast me a sidelong glance. "I don't want to know, do I?"

"No," I assured him. "You don't want to know."

He frowned. "Well, now you're here, we have to . . ."

"You can forget any thoughts you have of sending me home."

"Oh, I'd love to send you home if I could—if I didn't think that by sending you home, your father would want to know why, and I'd get in even deeper trouble. And if the Carrolls didn't have plans for you . . ."

I bridled. "*Plans* for me? I'm not their serf. I am Élise de la Serre, daughter of the Grand Master, a future Grand Master myself. They have no authority over *me*."

He rolled his eyes. "Oh, get over yourself, child. You're here in London as their guest. Not only that, you're hoping to benefit from their contacts in order to find Ruddock. If you didn't want them to have authority over you, then maybe it would have been best not have placed yourself in this position." I began to protest, but he held up a hand to stop me. "Look, being a Grand Master isn't just about swordplay and behaving like Charlie Big Potatoes. It's about diplomacy and statesmanship. Your mother knew that. Your father knows that and it's about time you learned it too."

I sighed. "What then? What do I have to do?"

"They want you to insinuate yourself into a household here in London. You and your maid."

"They want me to—what?—myself?"

"Insinuate. Infiltrate."

"They want me to spy?"

He scratched his snow-white beard uncomfortably. "In a manner of speaking. They want you to pose as someone else in order to gain entry into the household."

"Which is spying."

"Well . . . yeah."

I thought, and decided that despite everything, I quite liked the idea of it. "Is it dangerous?"

"You'd like that, would you?"

"It's better than the Maison Royale. When am I to find out the details of my mission?"

"Knowing this lot, when they're good and ready. In the meantime I suggest you spend some time licking that so-called lady's maid of yours into shape. At this moment in time she's neither useful nor ornamental." He looked at me. "Quite what you did to inspire such loyalty I don't suppose I'll ever know."

"Perhaps best you don't know," I told him.

"Which reminds me. Something else while on the subject."

"What is that, monsieur?"

He cleared his throat, stared at his shoes, worked at his fingernails. "Well, it's the crossing. This captain you found to bring you across."

I felt myself redden. "Yes?"

"What nationality was he?"

"English, monsieur, like you."

"Right." He nodded. "Right." He cleared his throat again, took a deep breath and raised his head to look me in the eye. "The crossing from Calais to Dover takes nothing like two days, Élise. It's more like a couple of hours if you're lucky—nine, ten at the outside if you're not. Why do you think he kept you out there for two days?"

"I'm quite sure I couldn't possibly say, monsieur," I said primly.

He nodded. "You're a beautiful girl, Élise. God knows

you're as beautiful as your mother ever was and let me tell you that every head turned when she walked into the room. You're going to meet more than your fair share of rogues."

"I'm aware of that, monsieur."

"Arno awaits your return, no doubt, in Versailles."

"Exactly, monsieur."

I hoped so.

He stood to go. "So exactly what did you do for two days on the English Channel, Élise?"

"Swordplay, monsieur," I said. "We practiced our swordplay."

20 MARCH 1788

The Carrolls—that little cabal of Monsieur, Madame and May—have promised to help find Ruddock, and, according to Mr. Weatherall, this puts a network of spies and informants at our disposal. "If he remains in London, then he'll be found, Élise, you can be sure of that." But, of course, they want me to accomplish this task.

Of course I should be nervous about the assignment ahead, but poor Mr. Weatherall was nervous enough, constantly fretting at his whiskers and worrying aloud at every turn. There wasn't enough anxiety for us both.

And anyway, he was right to assume I found the idea exciting. There's no point in denying it, I do. And after all, can you blame me? Ten years of the drab and hateful school. Ten years of wanting to reach out and take a destiny that remained just inches away from my finger-tips. Ten years, in other words, of frustration and long-ing. I was ready.

Over a month has passed, of course. I had to write a letter which was then sent to Carroll associates in France, who sealed it and forwarded it to an address here in London. While we waited for a reply, I helped Helene with her reading and taught her English, and in doing so, polished my own skills.

"Will this be dangerous?" Helene asked me one after-noon, using English as we took a turn around the grounds.

"It will, Helene. You should remain here until I return, maybe try to find employment at another house."

She switched to French, saying shyly, "You're not get-ting rid of me that easily, mademoiselle."

"It's not that I want to get rid of you, Helene. You're wonderful company and who wouldn't want a friend who is so warm and generous of spirit. It's just that I feel the debt is paid. I have no need of a maid nor want the responsibility of one."

"What about a friend, mademoiselle? Perhaps I can be your friend?"

Helene was the opposite of me. Where I let my mouth get me into trouble she was more reticent and days would pass when she'd barely say more than a word or two; while I was demonstrative, as quick to laughter as I was to temper, she kept her own counsel and rarely betrayed her emotions. And I know what you're thinking. The same as Mr. Weatherall was thinking. That I could learn a thing or two from Helene. Perhaps that's why I relented, just as I had when I first met her, and on several occasions since. I allowed her to stay with me and wondered why God has seen fit to favor me with this angel.

As well as spending time with Helene, not to mention avoiding either of the conceited Carroll ladies, I have been spending my time by practicing sparring with Mr. Weatherall, who . . .

Well, there's no getting round it—he's slowed down. He is not the swordsman he used to be. He's not as fast as he used to be. Not as clear-eyed. Was it age? After all, some fourteen years had passed since I first met Mr. Weatherall, so undoubtedly there was that to consider. But also . . . At mealtime I watch him reach for the carafe of wine before the serving staff can get there, which doesn't go unnoticed by our guests, going by the way May Carroll looks down her nose at him. Their distaste make me feel very protective of him. I tell myself he still mourns Mother.

"Perhaps a little less wine tonight, Mr. Weatherall," I joked during one session, when he bent to pick his wooden sparring sword from the grass at our feet.

"Oh, it's not the booze that's making me look bad. It's you. You underestimate your own skills, Élise."

Maybe. Maybe not.

I also spent time writing to Father, reassuring him that my studies were continuing, and that I had "knuckled down." When it came to writing to Arno I paused guiltily as I found my thoughts returning to my charming smuggler Byron Jackson. For a moment I considered telling Arno—and then reconsidered. It would break his heart. It would change everything. And why do that? Why do that when the upshot of "liaison" with Byron had not, as you might expect, taken my heart away from Arno. Rather it had made my affection for him even stronger, my gut feeling that he is "the one" merely confirmed.

All right, Élise, I decided, take that tryst and keep it secret—keep it to within the pages of this journal and instead of allowing it to be a destructive thing, something that pulls you and Arno apart, make it positive. Make it something that brings you together.

And so, though the letter I wrote to Arno was by necessity not exactly the most honest account of my present situation, there was one major truth among the fabrication and that was that I loved him. Never before had I written a letter of such affection to him. True, though the sentiments were born of infidelity (and that guilt my soul would just have to bear) they were true, and when I signed off by telling Arno I hoped to see him soon—in the next couple of months or so—I had never written words more true in my life.

So what if my reasons for wanting to see him were selfish? That I see him as an escape from my everyday responsibilities, a ray of sunlight in the dark of my destiny? Does it matter when my only desire is to bring him happiness?

I have been called. Helene informs me that a letter has arrived, which means it's time for me to squeeze into a dress, go downstairs and find out what lies in store for me.

12 SEPTEMBER 1794

Though I still kept in contact with François de la Serre, who was something of a surrogate father to me, by the time of Élise's visit to London I had moved away from the de la Serre estate to digs in the village, where I spent my days and nights drinking, playing cards against the likes of Victor and Hugo and . . . yes, entertaining women, too.

So if she were here, I could tell her that I, too, had strayed during the early years of our adulthood. Betrothed though we were, sweethearts in name at least, we were rarely actually together—snatched moments during the holidays was all we had—and she was not alone in wanting, as she put it, "liaisons."

Like her my infidelities (because, yes, sorry, Élise, there was more than one, the ladies of Versailles village being as accommodating as they were fetching) did nothing to tempt me away from her.

There are those men who think it's their right to sow their wild oats while their beloved stays virtuous, but I'm not one of those. I'm not a hypocrite. I try not to be, at least.

2 APRIL 1788

i

The day began with a panic.

"We don't think you would have a lady's maid," said Monsieur Carroll.

The terrible trio stood in the reception hall of their house in Mayfair, regarding Helene and me as we prepared to leave for our secret mission.

"That's quite all right with me," I said, and though I did of course have to still a flutter of nerves at the thought of going alone, I would at least have the advantage of not needing to worry about Helene.

"No," said Mr. Weatherall, coming forward. He shook his head emphatically. "She can invent a story about the family finding fortune. I don't want her to go in there alone. It's bad enough I can't go with her."

Madame Carroll looked doubtful. "It's one more thing she needs to remember. One more thing she needs to deal with."

"Mrs. Carroll," growled Mr. Weatherall, "with the greatest respect, that's a right lot of nonsense. The role of a noble lady is one young Élise has been playing her entire life. She'll be fine."

Helene and I stood patiently as our future was decided for us. Different in almost every other way, what she and I had in common was that other people decided our destinies for us. We were used to it.

And when they had finished our belongings were strapped to the roof of a carriage, and a coachman, an associate of the Carrolls we were assured could be trusted, took us across town to Bloomsbury, and an address at Queen Square.

ii

"It used to be called Queen Anne's Square," the coachman had told us. "It's just Queen Square now."

He'd accompanied Helene and me to the top of the steps and pulled the bell. As we waited I glanced around at the square, seeing two neat rows of white mansions, side by side, very English. There were fields to the north and nearby a church. Children played in the highway, darting in front of carts and carriages, the street alive with life.

We heard footsteps, then a great scraping of bolts. I

tried to look confident. I tried to look like the person I was supposed to be.

Which was?

"Miss Yvonne Albertine and her lady's maid, Helene," announced the coachman to the butler who opened the door, "to see Miss Jennifer Scott."

In contrast to the life and noise behind us, the house radiated dark and foreboding, and I fought a strong sense of not wanting to go in there.

"Mademoiselle Scott is expecting you, mademoiselle," said the expressionless butler, motioning to us to enter.

We walked into a large entrance hall, which was dark with wood paneling and closed doors leading to rooms off the hall. The only light came from windows on a landing above and the house was quiet, almost deathly quiet. For a second or so I struggled to think what it was the atmosphere reminded me of, then I remembered: it was like our château in Versailles in the days after Mother had died. That same sense of time standing still, of life carried out in whispers and silent footsteps.

I had been warned it would be like this: that Mademoiselle Jennifer Scott, a spinster in her mid-seventies, was somewhat . . . *odd*. That she had an aversion to people, and not just strangers or any specific type of person, but *people*. She maintained a skeleton staff at her house on Queen Square and for some reason—some reason the Carrolls had yet to reveal to me—she was very important to the English Templars.

Our coachman was excused, then Helene was whisked away, perhaps to go and stand awkwardly in a corner of the kitchen and be gawked at by the staff, the poor thing; and then when it was just the butler and me left, I was led to the drawing room.

We entered a large room with drawn curtains. Tall potted plants had been placed in front of the windows, deliberately, I presumed, to limit people looking in or out. Again, it was dingy and dark in the room. Sitting in front of a bumbling fire was the lady of the house, Mademoiselle Jennifer Scott.

"Miss Albertine to see you, my lady," he said, and left without getting a reply, closing the door softly behind him, leaving me alone with this strange lady who doesn't like people.

What else did I know about her? Her father was the pirate Assassin Edward Kenway and her brother the renowned Templar Grand Master Haytham Kenway. I assumed it was their portraits on one wall, two similar-looking gentlemen, one wearing the robes of an Assassin and another in a military uniform that I took to be Haytham. She herself had spent years on the Continent, a victim of the strife between Assassin and Templar. Though no one seemed to know exactly what had happened to her, there was no doubt she had been scarred by her experiences.

The door closed behind me and I was alone in the room with her. I stood there for some moments, watching her as she sat staring into the flames with her chin in her hand, preoccupied. I was just wondering whether I should clear my throat to get her attention or if perhaps I should simply approach and introduce myself, when the fire came to my rescue. It crackled and popped, startling her so that she appeared to realize where she was, lifting her chin slowly from her hand and looking at me over the rims of her spectacles.

I was told that she had once been a beauty and truly the ghost of that beauty lingered around her, in features that remained exquisite and dark hair that was slightly unkempt and streaked with thick gray, like a witch. Her eyes were flinty, intelligent and appraising. I stood obediently and let her study me.

"Come forward, child," she said at last, and indicated the chair opposite.

I took a seat and again was subject to a long stare.

"Your name is Yvonne Albertine?"

"Yes, Mademoiselle Scott."

"You may call me Jennifer."

"Thank you, Mademoiselle Jennifer."

She pursed her lips. "No, just Jennifer."

"As you wish."

"I knew your grandmother and your father," she said, and waved her hand. "Well, I didn't really 'know' them as such, but I met them once in a château near Troyes in your home country."

I nodded. The Carrolls had warned me that Jennifer Scott was likely to be suspicious and might try to test me. Here it came, no doubt.

"Your father's name?" prompted Mademoiselle Scott, as though having trouble recalling it.

"Lucio," I told her.

She raised a finger. "That's right. That's right. And your grandmother?"

"Monica."

"Of course, of course. Good people. And how are they now?"

"Passed, I am sad to say. Grandmother some years ago; Father in the middle of last year. This visit—the reason I'm here—was one of his final wishes, that I should come to see you."

"Oh yes?"

"I fear that things ended badly between my father and Mr. Kenway, my lady."

Her face remained impassive. "Remind me, child."

"My father wounded your brother."

"Of course, of course." She nodded. "He stuck a sword in Haytham, didn't he? How could I ever forget?"

You didn't forget.

I smiled sadly. "It was perhaps his biggest regret. He said that shortly before your brother lost consciousness he insisted on leniency for himself and Grandmother."

She nodded into her chest, hands grasped. "I remember, I remember. Terrible business."

"My father regretted it, even at the moment of death."

She smiled. "What a shame he was not able to make the journey to tell me this himself. I would have reassured him that he need have nothing to worry about. Many's the time I wanted to stab Haytham myself."

She stared into the jumping flames, her voice drifting as she was claimed by her memories. "Little squirt. I should have killed him when we were kids."

"You can't mean that . . ."

She chuckled wryly. "No, I don't suppose I can. I don't suppose what happened was Haytham's fault. Not all of it anyway." She took a deep breath, fumbled for a walking cane that rested by the arm of her chair and stood.

"Come, you must be tired after your journey from Dover. I shall show you to your room. I'm afraid to say that I am not one for socializing, and especially not when it comes to my evening meal, so you shall have to dine alone, but perhaps tomorrow we can walk the grounds, make each other's acquaintance?"

I stood and curtsied. "I would like that very much," I said.

She gave me another look as we left for the bedchambers on the floor above. "You look very much like your father, you know," she said.

"Thank you, my lady."

iii

Later when I had eaten, a meal that I took alone, waited upon by Helene, I retired to my bedchamber in order for me to prepare for bed.

The truth was that I hated being fussed over by Helene. I had long ago drawn the line at allowing her to dress and undress me, but she said she had to do something, just to make all those hours she spent listening to boring gossip below stairs worthwhile, so I allowed her to lay out my clothes and fetch me a bowl of warm water for washing. In the evening I let her brush my hair, something I'd come to quite enjoy.

"How's everything going, my lady?" she asked, doing it now, speaking in French but still in a lowered voice.

"Everything is going well, I think. Did you happen to speak to Mademoiselle Scott at all?"

"No, my lady, I saw her in passing and that was all."

"Well, you didn't miss much. She's certainly an odd character."

"A fine kettle of fish?"

That was one of Mr. Weatherall's expressions. We grinned at each other in the mirror.

"Yes," I said, "she certainly is a fine kettle of fish."

"Am I allowed to know what it is that Mr. and Mrs. Carroll want with her?"

I sighed. "Even if I knew, it would be best that you don't."

"You don't know?"

"Not yet. Which reminds me, what is the time?"

"Just coming up for ten, Mademoiselle Élise."

I shot her a look, hissing, "It's *Mademoiselle Yvonne*."

She blushed. "I'm sorry, Mademoiselle Yvonne."

"Just don't do that again."

"Sorry, Mademoiselle Yvonne."

"And now, I must ask you to leave me."

iv

When she had gone, I went to my trunk stored beneath the bed, pulled it out, knelt and flicked the locks. Helene had emptied it but she wasn't aware of the false bottom. Beneath a fabric tab was a hidden catch and when I clicked it the panel came away to reveal the contents.

Among them was a spyglass and a small signaling

device. I fitted the candle to the signal, took the spyglass and went to the window, where I opened the curtains just wide enough to look out into Queen Square.

He was across the road. Looking for all the world like a cab driver awaiting a fare, Mr. Weatherall sat atop a two-wheeled carriage, the lower half of his face covered with a scarf. I gave the predetermined signal. He used his hand to mask the carriage light, giving his reply, then, with a glance left and right, unwound the head-scarf. I brought the spyglass to my eye, so that I was able to see him clearly, and read his lips as he said, "Hello, Élise," then brought a spyglass to his own eye.

"Hello," I mouthed in return.

Thus we had our silent conversation.

"How is it going?"

"I am in."

"Good."

"Please be careful, Élise," he said, and if it was possible to inject real concern and emotion into a silent conversation held in the dead of night, Mr. Weatherall managed it then.

"I will be," I said. Then I withdrew to sleep and to puzzle over my purpose in this strange place.

6 APRIL 1788

i

Much time has passed and there is much to tell you about the events of the last few days. My sword has tasted blood for the second time, only this time it was wielded by me. And I have discovered something—something which, reading my journal back, I really should have known all along.

But let's begin at the beginning.

"I wonder if I might be seeing Miss Scott this morning for breakfast?" I'd asked a footman on the morning of our first full day. His eyes darted, then he exited wordlessly, leaving me alone with the fusty smell of the dining room and a stomach that churned, as it seemed to every morning. The long, empty breakfast table stretched out before me.

Mr. Smith, the butler, materialized in the footman's place, closing the door behind him then gliding to where I sat with my breakfast.

"I am sorry, mademoiselle," he said with a short bow, "but Miss Scott is taking breakfast in her room this morning as is occasionally her custom, especially when she is feeling a little under the weather."

"Under the weather?"

He smiled thinly. "An expression meaning not altogether fit and well. She asks that you make yourself at home and hopefully she will join you at some point later today in order to continue making your acquaintance."

"I should like that very much," I said.

We waited, Helene and I. We spent the morning wandering around the mansion, like two people conducting an unusually detailed viewing. There was no sign of Mademoiselle Scott. In the second half of the morning we retired to the drawing room where the years of sewing at the Maison Royale were at last put into practice. There was no still no sign of our host.

And, further, not a peep during the afternoon when Helene and I took a walk around the grounds. She failed to make an appearance at dinner, too, and once again I dined alone.

My annoyance began to grow. When I thought of the risks I had taken getting here—the ugly scenes with Madame Levene, the deception of my father and Arno . . . My purpose for being here was to find Ruddock, not to spend days struggling to look competent at sewing and being a virtual prisoner of my host—and still no nearer to knowing exactly what I was supposed to be doing here.

I retired, then later, at eleven o'clock, signaled Mr. Weatherall again.

This time I mouthed to him, "I'm coming out," and watched his face register panic as he frantically mouthed back, "No, no," but I had already disappeared from the casement, and of course he knew me too well. If I said I was coming out, then I was coming out.

I pulled an overcoat over my nightdress, slipped my feet into slippers, then crept down to the front door. Very, very quietly, I drew back the bolts, then let myself out and darted across the road to his carriage.

"You're taking a big risk, child," he said crossly. But still, I was pleased to see, unable to hide his pleasure at seeing me.

"I haven't seen her all day," I told him quickly.

"Really?"

"No, and I've had to spend the entire day wandering around, like a particularly disinterested peacock. Perhaps if I knew what I was supposed to be doing there, then I might have been able to get on with it, complete my mission and leave that awful place." I looked at him. "It's bloody torture, in there, Mr. Weatherall."

He nodded, suppressing a grin at my use of his English curse word. "All right, Élise. Well, as it happens they told me today. You're to recover letters."

"What sort of letters?"

"The writing sort. Letters written by Haytham Kenway to Jennifer Scott before his death."

I looked at him. "Is that it?"

"Isn't that enough? Jennifer Scott is the daughter of an Assassin. The letters were written to her by a high-ranking Templar. The Carrolls want to know what they say."

"Seems like a fairly roundabout way of finding out."

"A previous agent placed on the house staff failed to come up with the goods. All he managed to establish was that wherever the letters were stored it wasn't in some obvious and easy-to-reach place. Miss Scott isn't keeping them in a pretty bow in a writing bureau some-where. She's hidden them."

"And in the meantime?"

"Ruddock, you mean? The Carrolls tell me that their people are making inquiries."

"They assured us they were making inquiries weeks ago."

"These things don't happen quickly."

"They're happening too slowly for my liking."

"Élise . . ." he warned.

"It's all right, I won't do anything stupid."

"Good," he said. "You're in a dangerous enough posi-tion as it is. Don't do anything else to make it worse."

I gave him a peck on the cheek, stepped out of the carriage and dashed back across the road. Letting myself quietly in, I stood for a second, getting my breath— then realized I was not alone.

He stepped out of the gloom, his face in the shadows. Mr. Smith, the butler. "Miss Albertine?" he said quizzi-cally, head on one side, eyes flashing in the dark, and for a second I forgot that I was Yvonne Albertine of Troyes.

"Oh, Mr. Smith," I spluttered, gathering my overcoat around me. "You startled me. I was just . . ."

"It's just Smith," he corrected me. "Not *Mr.* Smith."

"I'm sorry, Smith, I . . ." I turned and indicated the door. ". . . I just needed some air."

"Your window not sufficient, miss?" he said agreeably, though his face remained in the shadows.

I fought a little wave of irritation, my inner May Carroll outraged that I should be interrogated by a *mere butler.*

"I wanted more air than that," I said, rather weakly.

"Well, that's quite all right, of course. But you see, when Miss Scott was just a girl, this house was the scene of an attack during which her father was killed."

I knew this but nodded anyway as he continued. "The family had soldiers on duty and guard dogs, too, but the raiders still managed to gain entrance. The house was badly burned during the attack. Since her return, the mistress has insisted that doors are barred at all hours. While you are, of course, quite welcome to leave the house at any time"—he gave a short mirthless smile—"I must insist that a member of staff be present to ensure the bolts are thrown after your exit and return."

I smiled. "Of course. I quite understand. It won't happen again."

"Thank you. That would be much appreciated." His eyes roamed my clothes, leaving me in no doubt that he considered my garb a little "unusual," then he stepped aside, one hand gesturing to the stairs.

I left, cursing my own stupidity. Mr. Weatherall was right. I should never have taken such a stupid risk.

ii

The next day was the same. Well, not *exactly* the same, just maddeningly similar. Once again I breakfasted alone; once more I was told that she would see me at some point today and asked to remain in the vicinity of the house. There was more wandering of corridors, more clumsy sewing, more small talk, not to mention a thrilling turn around the grounds.

There was at least one aspect to our perambulations that had changed for the better. My route was a little more purposeful than before. I found myself wondering where Jennifer might hide the letters. One of the doors off the reception hall led to a games room, and I took the opportunity for a quick inspection of the wood panels inside, wondering if any of them might slide away to reveal a secret compartment beneath. To be honest I needed a more thorough look through the entire house, but it was huge, the letters could be in any one of two dozen rooms and after my scare of last night I wasn't keen on creeping around after dark. No, my best chance of recovering the letters was getting to know Jennifer.

But how could I do that if she wasn't even leaving her room?

iii

The same thing happened on the third day. I won't go into it. Just more sewing, small talk, and, "Oh, I think we'll take the air, Helene, don't you?"

"I don't like it," mouthed Mr. Weatherall when we liaised that night.

It was difficult to communicate via signals and reading lips, but it would have to do. He wasn't keen on my sneaking out and, after my encounter with Smith the other night, neither was I.

"What do you mean?"

"I mean they could be checking out your cover story."

And if they did, would my cover story stand up? Only the Carrolls knew that. I was as much at their mercy as I was a prisoner of Jennifer Scott.

And then, on the fourth day—at last!—Jennifer Scott emerged from her room. I should meet her by the stables, I was told. The two of us were to take the promenade at Rotten Row in Hyde Park.

When we arrived we joined other midday promenaders. These were men and women who walked together under slightly unnecessary parasols wrapped up against the chill. The walkers waved to carriages and were awarded with imperious waves in return, while those on horseback waved to the walkers and the carriage riders, and every man, woman and child was resplendent in their best finery, waving, walking, smiling, more waving . . .

All apart from Miss Jennifer Scott, who, though she had dressed up for the occasion and wore a stately dress, peered distastefully out at Hyde Park from behind a veil of her gray-streaked hair.

"Was this the kind of thing you hoped to see when you came to London, Yvonne?" she asked, with a dismissive hand at the wavers, smilers and small children buttoned into suits. "Idiots whose horizons barely stretch beyond the walls of the park?"

I suppressed a smile, thinking that she and my mother would have got along. "It was you I hoped to see, Mademoiselle Scott."

"And why was that again?"

"Because of my father. His dying wish, remember?"

She pursed her lips. "I may seem old to you, Miss Albertine, but I can assure you I'm not so old that I forget things like that."

"Forgive me, I meant no offense."

That dismissive hand again. "None taken. In fact, unless I indicate otherwise, assume that no offense has been taken. I do not offend easily, Miss Albertine, of that you may be certain."

I could well believe it.

"Tell me, what happened to your father and grandmother after they left us that day?" she asked.

I steeled myself and told the story I had learned. "After your brother was merciful my father and grandmother settled just outside Troyes. It was they who taught me English, Spanish and Italian. Their skills in language and translation became much in demand and they made a good living from the services they offered."

I paused, searching her face for signs of disbelief. Thanks to my years of woe at the Maison Royale I could just about pass in the languages if she decided to test me.

"Enough to afford servants?" she asked.

"We were fortunate in that regard," I said and in my mind I tried to reconcile the image of the two "language experts" being able to afford a household full of staff, and found that I couldn't.

Even so, if she had her doubts, then she kept them hidden behind those gray, half-lidded eyes.

"What of your mother?"

"A local girl. Alas, I never knew her. Shortly after they were married she gave birth to me—but died in childbirth."

"And what now? With both your grandmother and your father dead, what will you do when you leave here?"

"I shall return to Troyes and continue their work."

There was a long pause. I waved at promenaders.

"I wonder," I said at last, "was Mr. Kenway in contact with you before his death? Did he write to you, perhaps?"

She gazed from the window but I realized she was looking at her own reflection. I held my breath.

"He was struck down by his own son, you know," she said a little distantly.

"I see."

"Haytham was an expert fighter, like his father," she said. "Do you know how our father died?"

"Smith mentioned it," I replied, then added quickly as she shot me a look, "by way of explaining the security-conscious nature of the household."

"Indeed. Well, Edward—our father—was struck down by our attackers. Of course the first fight you lose is the one that kills you, and nobody can win every fight, and he was an older man by then. But notwithstanding those facts he had the skills and experience to defeat two other swordsmen. I believe he lost the fight because of an injury he'd sustained years before. It slowed him down. Likewise, Haytham lost a fight against his own son, and I have often wondered why. Was he, like Edward, handicapped by an injury? Was that injury the sword your father pushed into him? Or perhaps Haytham had another sort of handicap? Perhaps Haytham had simply decided that now was his time, and that dying at the hands of his son might be a noble thing to do. Haytham was a Templar, you see. The Grand Master of the Thirteen Colonies, no less. But I know something that very few people know about Haytham. Those who have read his journals, perhaps; those who have read his letters . . ."

The letters. I felt my heart hammering in my chest. The clip-clopping of the horses and the incessant chatter from the promenaders outside seemed to fade into the background as I asked, "What was that, Jennifer? What did you know of him?"

"His *doubts*, my child. His doubts. Haytham had been the subject of indoctrination by his mentor, Reginald Birch, and to all intents and purposes that indoctrination had worked. After all, he ended his life a Templar. Yet he could not help but question what he knew. It was in his nature to do that. And though it's unlikely that he ever had answers to his questions, the very fact that he had them was enough. Do you have beliefs, Yvonne?"

"Doubtless I have inherited the values of my parents," I replied.

"Indeed, I expect your manners are impeccable and that you are endlessly considerate of your fellow man . . ."

"I try to be," I said.

"How about in more universal issues, Yvonne? Take

matters in your home country, for example. Where do your sympathies lie?"

"I daresay the situation is more complex than a simple allotment of sympathy, Mademoiselle Scott."

She arched an eyebrow. "A very sensible answer, my dear. You strike me as one who is not a born follower."

"I like to feel I know my own mind."

"I'm sure you do. But tell me, in a little more detail this time, what do you make of the situation in your home country?"

"I have never given the matter much thought, mademoiselle," I protested, not wanting to give myself away.

"Please, humor me. Give the matter some thought now."

I thought of home. Of my father, who so fervently believed in a monarch appointed by God, and that every man should know his place; the Crows, who wanted to depose the king altogether. And Mother, who believed in a third way.

"I believe that reform of some kind is needed," I told Jennifer.

"You do?"

I paused. "I *think* I do."

She nodded. "Good, good. It is good to have doubts. My brother had doubts. He put them into his letters."

The letters again. Not sure where this was going, I said, "It sounds as though he was a wise man as well as a merciful one."

She chortled. "Oh, he had his faults. But at heart, yes, I think he was a wise man, a good man. Come"—she tapped the ceiling of the carriage with a handle of her cane—"let us return. It is almost time for lunch."

I was close now, I thought, as we returned to Queen Square. "I have something I want to show you before we dine," she said as we drove, and I wondered, could it be the letters?

At the square the coachman helped us down, but then, instead of accompanying us up the steps to the front door, returned to the driver's seat, shook the reins and was gone, clip-clopping away into a curtain of fine mist that swirled around the wheels of his vehicle.

Then we walked to the door, where Jennifer pulled the bell once, then with two more quick jerks.

And maybe I being paranoid, but . . .

The coachman's leaving like that. The bellpull. On edge now I kept the smile on my face as bolts were drawn back, the door opened, Jennifer greeting Smith with just the faintest nod before stepping inside.

The front door shut. The soft hum of the square was banished. The now-familiar sense of imprisonment washed over me, except this time mixed with a genuine fear, a sense that things were not right. Where was Helene? I wondered.

"Perhaps you would be so kind as to let Helene know I have returned, please, Smith?" I asked the butler.

In return, he inclined his head the usual way, and with a smile said, "Certainly, mademoiselle."

But did not move.

I looked inquiringly at Jennifer. I wanted for things to be normal. For her to chivvy along the butler, but she didn't. She looked at me, said, "Come, I wish to show you the games room, for it was in there that my father died."

"Certainly, mademoiselle," I said, with a sideways look at Smith as we moved over to the wood-paneled door, closed as usual.

"Though I think you've seen the games room, haven't you?" she said.

"During the last four days I have had ample opportunity to view your beautiful property, mademoiselle," I told her.

She paused with her hand on the door handle, then looked at me. "Four days has given us the time we needed, too, Yvonne . . ."

I didn't like that emphasis. I *really* didn't like that emphasis.

She opened the door and ushered me inside.

The drapes were shut. The only light came from candles placed along ledges and mantelpieces, giving the room a flickering orange glow as though in preparation for some sinister religious ceremony. The billiards table had been covered and moved to one side, leaving the floor bare apart from two wooden kitchen chairs facing each other in the middle of the room. Also there was a footman who stood with his gloved hands clasped in front of him. Mills, I think his name was. Usually Mills smiled, bowed and was as unfailingly polite and decorous as a member of staff should be to a visiting noblewoman from France. Now, however, he simply stared, his face expressionless. Cruel, even.

Jennifer was continuing, "The four days gave us the time we needed to send a man to France in order to verify your story."

Smith had stepped in behind us and stood by the door.

I was trapped. How ironic that having spent the last few days moaning about being trapped, now I really was.

"Madame," I said, sounding more flustered than I wanted to, "I must be honest and say I find this whole situation as confusing as I do uncomfortable. If this is perhaps some practical joke or English custom of which I am unaware, I would ask you please to explain yourself."

My eyes went to the hard face of Mills, the footman, to the two chairs and then back to Jennifer. Her face was impassive. I yearned for Mr. Weatherall. For my mother. My father. Arno. I don't think I have ever felt quite so afraid and alone as I did at that moment.

"Do you want to know what our man discovered there?" said Jennifer. She had ignored my question.

"Madame . . ." I said in an insistent voice, but still she took no notice.

"He discovered that Monica and Lucio Albertine had indeed been making a living from their language skills, but not enough to afford staff. There was no local girl either. No local girl, no wedding and no children. Certainly not an Yvonne Albertine. Mother and son had lived in modest circumstances on the edge of Troyes—right up until the day they were murdered just four weeks ago."

iv

I caught my breath.

"No." The word was out of me before I had a chance to stop it.

"Yes. I'm afraid so. Your friends the Templars cut their throats as they slept."

"No," I repeated, my anguish as much for myself—for my fraud laid bare—as it was for poor Monica and Lucio Albertine.

"If you'll excuse me a minute," said Jennifer and departed, leaving me under the gaze of Smith and Mills. She returned.

"It's the letters you want, isn't it? You all but told me on Rotten Row. Why do your Templar masters want my brother's letters, I wonder?"

My thoughts were a jumble. Options raced across my brain: confess, brazen it out, make a break for it, be indignant, break down and cry . . .

"I'm quite sure I don't know what you're talking about, mademoiselle," I pleaded.

"Oh I'm quite sure you do, Élise de la Serre."

Oh God. How did she know that?

But then I had my answer as in response to a signal from Jennifer, Smith opened the door and another footman entered. He was manhandling Helene into the room.

She was dumped into one of the wooden chairs, where she sat and regarded me with exhausted, beseeching eyes.

"I'm sorry," she said. "They told me you were in danger."

"Indeed," said Jennifer, "and neither did we lie, because in fact you are both in danger."

v

"Now tell me, what does your Order want with the letters?"

I looked from her to the footmen and knew the situation was hopeless.

"I'm sorry, Jennifer," I told her. "I truly am. You're right, I am an imposter in your home, and you're right that I hoped to lay my hands on the letters from your brother . . ."

"To *take* them from me," she corrected tautly.

I hung my head. "Yes. Yes, to take them from you."

She brought two hands to the handle of her cane and leaned toward me. Her hair had fallen over her glasses but the one eye I could see blazed with fury.

"My father, Edward Kenway, was an Assassin, Élise de la Serre," she said. "Templar agents attacked my house and killed him in the very room in which you now sit. They kidnapped me, delivering me into a life that even in my most fetid nightmares I could never have imagined for myself. A living nightmare that continued for years. I'll be honest with you, Élise de la Serre, I'm not best disposed toward Templars, and certainly not Templar spies. What do you suppose is the Assassin punishment for spies, Élise de la Serre?"

"I don't know, mademoiselle," I implored, "but please don't hurt Helene. Me if it pleases you but please not her. She has done nothing. She is an innocent in all of this."

But now Jennifer gave a short, barked laugh. "An innocent? Then I can sympathize with her plight because I, too, was an innocent once.

"Do you think I deserved everything that happened to me? Kidnapped and kept a prisoner? Used as a whore. Do you think that I, an innocent, deserved to be treated in such a way? Do you think that I, an innocent, deserve to live out the rest of my years in loneliness and darkness, terrified of demons that come in the night?

"No, I don't suppose you do. But you see, innocence is not the shield you wish it to be, not when it comes to the eternal battle between Templar and Assassin. Innocents die in this battle you seem so eager to join, Élise de la Serre. Women and children who know nothing of Assassins and Templars. Innocence dies and innocents die— that is what happens in a war, Élise, and the conflict between Templars and Assassins is no different."

"This isn't you," I said at last.

"What on earth can you mean, child?"

"I mean you won't kill us."

She pulled a face. "Why not? An eye for an eye. Men of your stripe slaughtered Monica and Lucio, and they were innocents, too, were they not?"

I nodded.

She straightened. Her knuckles whitened as her fingers flexed on the ivory handle of her cane and watching her gaze off into space reminded me of when we'd first met, when she'd sat staring into the fire. The painful thing was that in our short time together I'd come to like and admire Jennifer Scott. I didn't want her to be capable of hurting us. I thought she was better than that.

And she was.

"The truth is, I hate the bloody lot of you," she said at last, exhaling the words at the end of a long sigh as though she'd waited years to say them. "I'm sick of you all. Tell that to your Templar friends when I send you and your lady's maid . . ." She stopped and pointed the cane toward Helene. "She's not really a lady's maid, is she?"

"No, mademoiselle," I agreed and looked over at Helene. "She thinks she owes me a debt."

Jennifer rolled her eyes. "And now you owe her a debt."

I nodded gravely. "Yes—yes, I do."

She looked at me. "You know, I see good in you, Élise. I see doubts and questions and I think those are positive qualities, and because of that I've come to a decision. I'm going to let you have the letters you seek."

"I no longer want them, mademoiselle," I told her tearfully. "Not at any price."

"What makes you think you have a choice?" she said. "These letters are what your colleagues in the Templars want and they shall have them, on the condition, firstly, that they leave me out of their battles in future—that they *leave me alone*—and, secondly, that they read them. They read what my brother has to say about how Templar and Assassin can work together, then maybe, just maybe, act upon them."

She waved a hand at Smith, who nodded and moved over to panels inset into the wall.

She smiled at me. "You'd wondered about those panels, hadn't you, I know you had."

I avoided her eye. Meantime, Mills had moved to the wall panels, triggered a switch so that one of them slid back and taken two cigar boxes from a compartment. Returning to stand beside his mistress, he opened the top one to show me what was inside: a sheaf of letters tied with a black ribbon.

Without even looking, she indicated them. "Here it is, the sum total of Haytham's correspondence from America. I want you to read the letters. Don't worry, you won't be eavesdropping on any private family matters. We were never close, my brother and I. But what you will find is my brother expanding upon his personal philosophies. And you may—if I have read you correctly, Élise de la Serre—find in them a reason to alter your own thinking. Perhaps take that mode of thinking into your role as a Templar Grand Master."

She passed the first box back to Mills, then opened the second. Inside was a silver necklace. On it hung a pendant inset with sparkling red jewels in the shape of a Templar cross.

"He sent me this, too," she explained. "A gift. But I have no desire for it. It should go to a Templar. Perhaps one like you."

"I can't accept this."

"You have no choice," she repeated. "Take them—take them both. Do what you can to bring an end to this fruitless war."

I looked at her and, though I didn't want to break the spell or change her mind, couldn't help but ask, "Why are you doing this?"

"Because there has been enough blood spilled," she said, turning smartly away as though she could no longer bear to look at me—as though she was ashamed of the mercy she felt in her soul and wished she were strong enough to have me killed.

And then, with a gesture, she ordered her men to carry Helene away, telling me, when I looked like I might protest, "She will be looked after.

"Helene didn't want to talk because she was protecting you," Jennifer continued. "You should be proud to inspire such loyalty in your followers, Élise. Perhaps you can use those gifts to inspire your Templar associates in other ways. We shall see. These letters are not given lightly. I can only hope that you read them and take note of the contents."

She gave me two hours with them. It was enough time to read them and form questions of my own. To know that there was another way. A third way.

vi

Jennifer did not bid us good-bye. Instead, we were shown out of a rear entrance and into the stable yard, where a carriage had been asked to wait. Mills loaded us inside and we left without another word.

The coach rattled and shook. The horses snorted and their bridles jangled as we made our way across London and toward Mayfair. In my lap I carried the box, inside it Haytham's letters and the necklace I had been given by Jennifer. I held them tight, knowing that they provided the key to future dreams of peace. I owed it to Jennifer to see that they fell into the right hands.

By my side Helene sat silent and badly shaken. I reached for her, fingertips stroking the back of her hand as I tried to reassure her that everything was going to be all right.

"Sorry I got you into this," I said. "I'm so sorry, Helene."

"You didn't get me into anything, mademoiselle, remember? You tried to talk me out of coming."

I gave a mirthless chuckle. "I expect you wish you'd done as I'd asked now."

She gazed from the glass as the city streets tumbled past us. "No, mademoiselle, not for a second did I wish otherwise. Whatever is my fate it is better than what those men had planned for me in Calais. The one you saved me from."

"In any case, Helene, the debt is paid. When we reach France you must go your own way, as a free woman."

The ghost of a smile stole across her lips. "We shall see about that, mademoiselle," she said. "We shall see."

As the carriage trundled into the tree-lined square at Mayfair I saw activity outside the home of the Carrolls some fifty yards away.

I called to the driver to stop by banging on the ceiling hatch and as the horses complained and stamped, I opened the carriage door and stood on the footboard, shielding my eyes to look toward the distance. There I saw two carriages. The footmen of the Carroll household were milling around. I saw Mr. Carroll standing on the steps of the house, pulling on a pair of gloves. I saw Mr. Weatherall come trotting down the steps, buttoning his jacket. At his side hung his sword.

That was interesting. The footmen were armed, too, and so was Mr. Carroll.

"Wait here," I called to the driver, then peered inside.

"I'll be back soon," I said to Helene softly. And then, picking up my skirts, I hurried to a spot near a set of railings from which I could see the carriages more closely. Mr. Weatherall stood with his back to me. I cupped my hands to my mouth, made our customary owl sound and was relieved when only he turned around, everybody else being too embroiled in their tasks to wonder why they could hear an owl at that time of the early evening.

Mr. Weatherall's eyes searched the square until they found me and he shifted position, drawing his hands across his chest, assuming a casual pose with a hand covering one side of his face. He mouthed to me, "What the hell are you doing here?"

Thank God for our silent conversations.

"Never mind that. Where are you going?"

"They found Ruddock. He's staying at the Boars Head Inn on Fleet Street."

"I need my things," I told him. "My trunk."

He nodded. "I'll fetch it and leave it in one of the stables round back. Don't hang around; we're leaving any moment now."

All my life I've been told I'm beautiful, but I don't think I'd ever really used it until that moment, when I returned to our carriage, fluttered my eyelashes at the coachman and persuaded him to fetch my trunk from the mews.

When he returned I asked him to sit up top while, with a feeling like greeting an old friend, I delved into my trunk. My proper trunk. The trunk of Élise de la Serre rather than Yvonne Albertine. I performed my customary carriage change. Off came the accursed dress. I slapped Helene's hands away as she tried to help. "You're hurt, get some rest!" Then I slipped into my breeches and shirt, pummeled my tricorn into shape and strapped on my sword. I shoved a sheaf of letters into the front of my shirt. Everything else I left in the carriage.

"You're to take this carriage to Dover," I told Helene, opening the door. "You're to go. Meet the tide. Take the first ship back to France. God willing I will meet you there."

"Take this girl to Dover," I called up to the driver.

"Is she sailing to Calais?" he asked, having had the usual reaction to my change of clothes.

"As am I. You're to wait for me there."

"Then she might catch the tide. The road to Dover is full of coaches right now."

"Excellent," I said, and tossed him a coin. "Be sure to look after her and know that if any harm should come to her, I'll come looking for you."

His eyes went to my sword. "I believe you," he said, "don't you worry about that."

"Good." I grinned. "We understand each other."

"Seems like we do."

Right.

I took a deep breath.

I had the letters. I had my sword and a pouch of coins. Everything else went with Helene.

The coachman found me another carriage, and as I climbed in, I watched Helene pull away, silently offering up a prayer for her safe delivery. To my coachman I said, "Fleet Street, please, monsieur, and don't spare the horses."

With a smile he nodded and we were in motion. I slid down the window and looked behind us just in time to see the last of the Carrolls' party board the coaches. Whips split the air. The two carriages moved off. Through the hatch I called, "Monsieur, there are two coaches some distance behind. We must reach Fleet Street ahead of them."

"Yes, mademoiselle," said the driver, unperturbed. He shook the reins. The horses whinnied, their hooves clattered more urgently upon the cobbles and I sat back with my hand gripping the hilt of my sword, and knew that the chase was on.

vii

It wasn't long before we were pulling into the Boars Head Inn on Fleet Street. I tossed coins and gave a grateful wave to the coachman, then, before he had time to open my door, jumped out into the courtyard.

It was full of stagecoaches and horses, ladies and gentlemen directing lackeys who groaned beneath the weight of parcels and trunks. I glanced at the entranceway. There was no sign of the Carrolls. Good. It gave me a chance to find Ruddock. I slipped into the back door, then along a half-dark passage into the tavern itself, darkened, with low, wooden beams. Like the Antlers in Calais, it was alive with the jagged laughter of thirsty travelers, the air thick with smoke. I found a barkeep who stood with his mouth hidden in his jowls, half-asleep and working a towel around a pewter tumbler, eyes far away, as though dreaming of a better place.

"Hello? Monsieur?"

Still he stared. I flicked my fingers, called him even more loudly over the din of the tavern and he came to.

"What?" he growled.

"I'm looking for a man who stays here, a Mr. Ruddock."

He shook his head, and the folds of skin at his neck shuddered as he did so. "Nobody here by that name."

"Perhaps he is using a false name," I said hopefully. "Please, monsieur, it is important that I find him."

He squinted at me with renewed interest. "What does he look like, this Mr. Ruddock of yours?" he asked me.

"He dresses like a doctor, monsieur, at least he did the last time I saw him but one thing he can't change is the distinctive shade of his hair."

"Almost pure white?"

"That's it."

"No, not seen him."

Even in the thick clamor of the inn I could hear it—a disturbance in the courtyard. The sound of carriages arriving. It was the Carrolls.

The innkeeper had seen me notice. His eyes glittered.

"You *have* seen him," I pressed.

"Might have," he said, and with unwavering eyes held out a hand. I crossed his palm with silver

"Upstairs. First room on the left. He's using the name Mowles. Mr. Gerald Mowles. Sounds like you better hurry."

The commotion from outside had increased, and I could only hope they'd take their time assembling and helping Madame Carroll and her hideous daughter out of the carriage before they swept into the Boars Head Inn like minor royalty, giving me plenty of time to . . .

Get upstairs. First door on the left. I caught my breath. I was in the eaves, the slanting beams almost brushing the top of my hat. Even so it was quieter upstairs, the noise from below reduced to a constant background clatter, no hint of the impending invasion.

I took the few moments of calm before the storm to compose myself, raised my hand about to knock, then had second thoughts and instead crouched to peer through the keyhole.

He sat on the bed with one leg pulled up beneath him wearing breeches and a shirt unlaced to show a bony chest tufted with hair beneath. Though he no longer looked like the doctor of that image, there was no mistaking the shock of white hair and the fact that it was definitely him, the man who had populated my nightmares. Funny how this terror of my childhood now looked very unthreatening indeed.

From downstairs came the sound of a minor uproar as the Carrolls burst in. There were raised voices and threats and I heard my friend the innkeeper protesting as they made their presence felt. In moments Ruddock would be aware of what was happening and any element of surprise I had would be lost.

I knocked.

"Enter," he called, which surprised me.

As I came into the room he raised himself to meet me with one hand on his hip, a stance I realized with a puzzled start that was supposed to be provocative. For a second or so we were both confused by the sight of one another: him, posing with his hand on his hip; me, bursting in.

Until at last he spoke in a voice that I was surprised to hear was cultured. "I'm sorry, but you don't look much like a prostitute. I mean, no offense, and you're most attractive, but just not much like a . . . prostitute."

I frowned. "No, monsieur, I am not a prostitute, I am Élise de la Serre, daughter of Julie de la Serre."

He looked at once blank and quizzical.

"You tried to kill us," I explained.

His mouth formed an O.

viii

"Ah," he said, "and you're the grown-up daughter come to take revenge, are you?"

My hand was on the hilt of my sword. From behind I heard the clatter of boots on wooden steps as the Carroll's men made their way upstairs. I slammed the door and threw the bolt.

"No. I'm here to save your life."

"Oh? Really? That's a turnup."

"Count yourself lucky," I said. The footsteps were just outside the door. "Leave."

"But I'm not even dressed properly."

"Leave," I insisted, and pointed at the window. There was a banging on the door that shook in its frame, and Ruddock didn't need telling a third time. He slung one leg over the casement and disappeared, leaving a strong whiff of stale sweat behind, and I heard him skidding down the sloped roof outside. Just then the door splintered and swung open, and Carroll's men burst inside.

There were three of them. I drew my sword and they

drew theirs. Behind them came Mr. Weatherall and the three Carrolls.

"Stop," called Mr. Carroll. "For God's sake, it's Mademoiselle de la Serre."

I stood with my back to the window, the room crowded with people now, swords drawn. From behind I heard a clatter as Ruddock made his way to safety.

"Where is he?" asked Mr. Carroll though not with the urgent tones I might have expected.

"I don't know," I told them. "I came looking for him myself."

At a gesture from Mr. Carroll, the three swordsmen stood down. Carroll looked confused. "I see. You're here looking for Mr. Ruddock. But I thought *we* were the ones supposed to be looking for Mr. Ruddock. Indeed, I was of the understanding that while we were doing that, you would be at the home of Jennifer Scott attending to business there. Very important Templar business, yes?"

"That's exactly what I have been doing," I told him.

"I see. Well, first, why don't you put your sword away, there's a good girl."

"It's because of what I learned from Jennifer Scott that my sword stays unsheathed."

He raised an eyebrow. Madame Carroll curled a lip and May Carroll sneered. Mr. Weatherall shot me a be-careful look.

"I see. Something you were told by Jennifer Scott, the daughter of the Assassin Edward Kenway?"

"Yes," I said. My color rose.

"And do you plan to tell us what this woman, an enemy of the Templars, told you about us?"

"That you arranged for Monica and Lucio to be killed."

Mr. Carroll gave a short, sad shrug. "Ah, well, that is true, I'm afraid. A necessary precaution, in order that the subterfuge should not lack veracity."

"I would never have agreed to take part had I known."

Mr. Carroll spread his hands as though my reaction was a vindication of their actions. The point of my short sword stayed steady. I could run him through—run him through in an instant.

But if I did that, I'd be dead before his body even hit the floor.

"How did you know to come here?" he asked with another look at Mr. Weatherall, knowing, surely, what the truth of it was. I saw Mr. Weatherall's fingers flex, ready to reach for his sword.

"That doesn't matter," I said. "The important thing is that you upheld your end of the bargain."

"Indeed we did," he agreed, "but did you uphold yours?"

"You asked me to recover some letters from Jennifer Scott. It was at great cost to myself and my lady's maid, Helene, but I have managed to do it."

He shared a look with his wife and daughter. "You did?"

"Not only that, but I've read the letters."

His lips turned down as though to say, *Yes? And?*

"I've read the letters and taken note of what Haytham Kenway had to say. And what he had to say involved the worlds of Assassin and Templar ceasing hostilities. Haytham Kenway—a legend among Templars—had a vision for the future of our two Orders and it was that they should work together."

"I see," said Mr. Carroll, nodding. "And that meant something to you, did it?"

"Yes," I said, suddenly sure of it. "Yes. Coming from him it meant something."

He nodded. "Indeed. Indeed. Haytham Kenway was . . . *brave* to put these ideas on paper. Had he been discovered, he would have been tried for treachery by the Order."

"But he may well be right. We can learn from his writings."

Mr. Carroll was nodding. "Quite so, my dear. We can. Indeed, I shall be very interested to see what he had to say. Tell me, do you by any chance have the letters with you?"

"Yes," I said carefully, "yes, I do."

"Oh, jolly good. That's jolly good. Could I by any chance see them, please?"

His hand was held out, palm up. Beyond it a smile that went nowhere near his eyes.

I reached into my shirt, took the sheaf of letters from where they pressed against my breast and handed them to him.

"Thank you," he said, with a smile, his eyes never leaving mine as he passed the letters across to his daughter who took them, a smile spreading across her face. I knew what was going to happen next. I was ready for it. Sure enough, May Carroll tossed the letters on the fire.

"*No,*" I shouted, and sprang forward, but not to the fire as they expected but to the side of Mr. Weatherall, elbowing one of Carroll's minions as I pushed him away. The man gave a cry of pain, brought his sword to bear and the sound of ringing steel was suddenly deafening in the tiny lodging room as our blades met.

At the same time Mr. Weatherall drew his sword and deftly fended off the second of Carroll's men.

"Stop," ordered Mr. Carroll, and the skirmish was over, Mr. Weatherall and I, our backs to the window, faced the three Carroll swordsmen, all five of us breathing heavily, blazing eyes on each other.

With a tight voice, Mr. Carroll said, "Please remember, gentlemen, that Mademoiselle de la Serre and Mr. Weatherall are still our guests."

I didn't feel much like a guest. By my side the fire flared then died, the letters reduced to gray, fluttering sheets of ash. I checked my stance: feet apart, center balanced, breathing steady. My elbows bent and close to the body. I kept the nearest swordsman on point and maintained eye contact while Mr. Weatherall covered another one. The third? Well, he was a floater.

"Why?" I said to Mr. Carroll, without taking my eyes off the nearest swordsman, my partner for this dance. "Why did you burn the letters?"

"Because there can be no truce with the Assassins, Élise."

"Why not?"

With his head slightly on one side and his hands clasped in front of him, he smiled condescendingly. "You don't understand, my dear. Our kind have warred with the Assassins for centuries . . ."

"Exactly," I pressed. "And that is why it should stop."

"Hush, my dear," he said and his patronizing tone was

setting my teeth on edge. "The divisions between our two Orders are too great, the enmity too entrenched. You might as well ask a snake and mongoose to take afternoon tea together. Any truce would be conducted in an atmosphere of mutual distrust and the airing of ancient grievances. Each would suspect the other of plotting to betray them. It would never happen. Yes, we will prevent any attempts to spread the promotion of any such ideas"—he wafted a hand at the fire—"whether they be the writings of Haytham Kenway or the aspirations of a naïve young girl destined to be the French Grand Master one day."

The full impact of what he meant hit me. "Me? You mean to kill me?"

Head on one side, he gave me sad eyes. "It is for the greater good."

I bristled. "But I am a Templar."

He pulled a face. "Well, not quite yet, of course, but I understand your meaning and admit that does affect matters. Just not quite enough. The simple fact is that things must stay as they are. Don't you remember that from when we first met?"

My eyes shifted to May Carroll. Her purse dangling from her gloved fingers, she watched us as though enjoying a night at the theater.

"Oh, I remember our first meeting very well," I told Mr. Carroll. "I remember my mother giving you very short shrift."

"Indeed," he said. "Your mother had progressive tendencies not in line with our own."

"One might almost think you would want her dead," I said.

Mr. Carroll looked confused. "I beg your pardon."

"Perhaps you wanted her dead enough to hire a man to do the job. A disenfranchised Assassin, perhaps?"

He clapped his hands with understanding. "Oh. I see. You mean the recently departed Mr. Ruddock?"

"Exactly."

"And you think we were the ones who hired him? You think we were the ones behind the attempted assassination? And that, presumably, is why you have just helped Mr. Ruddock escape?"

I felt myself color, realizing I had given myself away as Mr. Carroll clapped his hands together.

"Well, weren't you?"

"Much as I hate to disappoint you, my dear, but that particular action was nothing to do with us."

Silently I cursed. If he was telling the truth, then I'd made a mistake letting Ruddock go. They had no reason to kill him.

"So you see our problem, Élise," Mr. Carroll was saying. "For now you are just a young girl with fanciful notions. But you will one day be Grand Master and you have not one but two key principles in opposition to our own. Letting you leave England is out of the question, I'm afraid."

His hand went to the hilt of his sword. I tensed, trying to get a sense of the odds: me and Mr. Weatherall versus three Carroll fighters as well as the three Carrolls themselves.

They were terrible odds.

"May," Mr. Carroll was saying, "would you like to do the honors? You can be blooded at last."

She smiled obsequiously at her father, and I realized that she was the same as me: she'd been trained in swordplay but had yet to kill. I was to be her first. What an honor.

From behind her, Mrs. Carroll proffered a sword, a short sword like my own, custom-built for her size and weight. The light gleamed from an ornate, curved hand-guard, the sword handed to her as though it were some kind of religious artifact, and she turned in order to take it. "Are you ready for this, smell-bag?" she said as she turned.

Oh yes, I was ready. Mr. Weatherall and my mother had always told me that all sword fights begin in the mind and most end with the first blow. It was all about who made the first move.

So I made the first move. I danced forward and rammed the point of my sword through the back of May Carroll's neck and out through her mouth.

First blood was to me. Not exactly the most honorable killing, but at that very moment in time, honor was the last thing on my mind. I was more interested in staying alive.

ix

It was the last thing they expected, to see their daughter impaled on my sword. I saw Mrs. Carroll's eyes widen in disbelief in the half second before she screamed in shock and anguish.

Meanwhile I'd used my forward motion to shoulder-charge Mr. Carroll, yanking my sword from May Carroll's neck and hitting him with such force that he pinwheeled back off balance and splayed into the doorway. May Carroll had sunk, dead before she hit the floor, painting it with her blood; Mrs. Carroll was rooting in her purse but I ignored her. Finding my feet, I crouched and spun in anticipation of an attack from behind.

It came. The swordsman lumbering toward me had a look of startled disbelief plastered across his face, unable to believe the sudden turn of events. I stayed low and met his sword with my blade, fending off his attack and pivoting at the same time, taking his feet from him with an outflung leg so that he crashed to the floor.

There was no time to finish him. By the window Mr. Weatherall was battling but he was struggling. I saw it in his face, a look of impending defeat and confusion, as though he couldn't understand why his two opponents were still standing. Like this had never happened before.

I ran one of his assailants through. The second man pulled away in surprise, finding he suddenly had two opponents rather than one, but with the first swordsman pulling himself to his feet, Mr. Carroll up and reaching for his sword, and Mrs. Carroll at last freeing something from her purse that turned out to be a tiny, three-barrel turnover pistol, I decided I'd pushed my luck far enough.

It was time to go the same way as my friend Mr. Ruddock.

"The window," I shouted, and Mr. Weatherall threw me a look that said, "You must be joking," before I put two hands to his chest and pushed so that he tumbled bottom first out the window and onto the sloped roof outside.

Just as I did there was a crack, the sound of a ball making contact with something soft, and in the window a soft spray of blood, like a red lace sheet suddenly drawn across it, and even as I wondered whether the sound I had heard was the ball hitting me, or if the haze of blood in the window was mine, I hurled myself through the opening, smacked onto the tiles on the other side and slid on my stomach to Mr. Weatherall, who had come to a halt on the lip of the roof.

I saw now that the ball had hit his lower leg, the blood staining his breeches dark. His boots scrabbled on the tiles, which loosened and fell into the yard, accompanied by the sound of shouts and running feet below. There came a cry from above us and a head appeared at the window. I saw the face of Mrs. Carroll contorted with anguish and fury, her need to kill the woman who killed her daughter overriding everything else in her life—including the need to remove herself from the casement so her men could get through and come after us.

Instead, she waved the turnover pistol at us. With a snarl and bared teeth she aimed it at me and surely couldn't miss unless she was jostled from behind . . .

Which was exactly what happened. Her shot was as wild as it was wide, spanging harmlessly off the tiles to our side.

Later, as we raced toward Dover in a horse and carriage, Mr. Weatherall would tell me that it was common for a barrel of a turnover pistol to ignite the other barrels, and that "it could be nasty" for whoever it was doing the firing.

That's precisely what happened to Mrs. Carroll. I

heard a fizzing then a popping sound and the pistol came skidding down the roof toward us while up above Mrs. Carroll screamed as her hand, now a shade of red and black, began to bleed.

I took the opportunity to heave Mr. Weatherall's good leg off the side of the roof. He hung on by his fingertips, screwing his face up in pain but refusing to scream as I manhandled his other leg over then shouted, "Sorry about this," as I clambered over him and, dangling, jumped to the courtyard below.

It was a short drop, but even so it knocked the wind out of us, sweat popping on Mr. Weatherall's face as he chewed back the pain of his shot leg. As he stood I commandeered a horse and carriage, and he limped to take his place beside me.

It all happened in a moment. We thundered out of the courtyard and into Fleet Street. I glanced up and saw faces at the window of the guest room. They would be after us soon, I knew, and I drove the horses as hard as I dared, silently promising them a tasty snack when we reached Dover.

In the end, it took us six hours, and I could at least thank God that there was no sign of the Carrolls behind us on the route. In fact, I didn't see them until we had pushed off Dover beach in a rowing boat, making our way toward the packet, which, we'd been told, was about to weigh anchor.

Our oarsmen grunted as he pulled us closer to the larger vessel, and I watched as two coaches, both bearing the Carroll crest, arrived on the coast road at the top of the beach. We were drawing away, being swallowed up by the ink black sea, with no light of our own, the oarsmen guided by the light of the packet, so they couldn't see us from the shore. But we were able to see them, indistinct but illuminated by their swinging lanterns as they scurried about in search of their quarry.

I couldn't see Mrs. Carroll's face but could imagine the mix of hatred and grief she wore like a mask. Mr. Weatherall, barely awake, his wounded leg hidden beneath travel blankets, watched. He saw me do a discreet *bras d'honneur* and nudged me.

"Even if they could see you, they wouldn't know what you were doing. It's only rude in France. Here, try this." He stuck up two fingers so I did the same.

The hull of the packet was not far away now. I could feel its bulky presence in the night.

"They'll come after you, you know," he said, his chin tucked into his chest. "You killed their daughter."

"Not just that. I've still got their letters."

"The ones that got burned up were a decoy?"

"Some of my letters to Arno."

"Perhaps they'll never find out about that. Either way, they'll come after you."

They had been swallowed up by the night. England was now just a mass of land, the huge, moon-dappled cliffs rising to our left.

"I know," I told him, "but I'll be ready for them."

"Just make sure you are."

9 APRIL 1788

"I need your help."

It was raining. The sort of rain that feels like knives on your skin, that batters your eyelids and pummels at your back. It had plastered my hair to my head and when I spoke the water spouted off my mouth, but at least it disguised the tears and snot as I stood on the steps of the Maison Royale at Saint-Cyr, trying not to fall over from sheer exhaustion, and watched Madame Levene's face pale from the shock of seeing me, as though I were a ghost appearing on the steps of the school in the dead of night.

And standing there, with the carriage behind me, Mr. Weatherall asleep or unconscious inside, and Helene looking anxiously from the window, gaping through the sluicing rain to where I stood on the steps of the school, I wondered if I was doing the right thing.

And for a second, as Madame Levene took in the sight of me, I thought she might simply tell me to go to hell for all the trouble I'd caused and slam the door in my face. And if she did that, then who could blame her?

"I've got nowhere else to go," I said. "Please help me."

And she didn't slam the door in my face. She said, "My dear, of course."

And I dropped into her arms, half-dead with fatigue.

10 APRIL 1788

Was ever a man more brave than Mr. Weatherall? Not once had he shouted out in pain on the journey to Dover, but by the time we boarded the packet he had lost a lot of blood. I met Helene on the packet, the Dover cliffs shrinking in the distance, my time in London becoming a memory already, and we had laid Mr. Weatherall on a section of the deck where we had a little privacy.

Helene knelt to him, placing cool hands to his forehead.

"You're an angel," he said, with a smile up at her, then slipped into unconsciousness.

We bandaged him as best we could, and by the time we reached the shores of Calais he had recovered some of his color. But he was still in pain, and as far as we knew, the ball remained inside his leg, and when we changed his dressings, the wound gleamed at us, showing no signs of healing.

The school had a nurse but Madame Levene had fetched the doctor from Châteaufort, a man experienced in dealing with war wounds.

"It's going to have to come off, ain't it?" Mr. Weatherall had said to him from the bed, five of us crammed into his bedchamber.

The doctor nodded and I felt my tears prick my eyes.

"Don't you worry about it," Mr. Weatherall was saying. "I knew the bloody thing was going to have to come off, right from the second she got me. Sliding on the bloody roof in me own blood, musket ball stuck in me leg, I thought, 'That's it—it's a goner.' Sure enough."

He looked at the doctor and swallowed, a little fear showing on his face at last. "Are you fast?"

The doctor nodded, adding with a slightly proud air, "I can do a leg in forty-four seconds."

Mr. Weatherall looked impressed. "You use a serrated blade?"

"And razor-sharp . . ."

He took a deep, regretful breath. "Then what are we waiting for?" he said. "Let's get it over with."

Jacques and I held Mr. Weatherall, and the doctor was as good as his word, being fast and thorough, even when Mr. Weatherall passed out from the pain. When it was over he wrapped Mr. Weatherall's leg in brown paper and took it away, and the following day returned with a pair of crutches for him.

2 MAY 1788

To keep up appearances, I returned to school, where I was very much a mystery to my classmates, who were told that I had been segregated for disciplinary reasons. For these last few months I would be the most-talked-about pupil at school, subject of more rumors and gossip than I cared to mention: on the grapevine I heard that I had taken up with a gentleman of ill repute (not true), that I had fallen with child (not true) or that I had taken to spending my nights gambling in dockside bars (and, well, yes, I had done that, once or twice).

None of them guessed that I had been trying to track down a man who was once hired to kill me and my mother, that I had returned with an injured Mr. Weatherall and a devoted Helene and that the three of us now lived in the groundskeeper's lodge with Jacques, the illegitimate son of the headmistress.

No, nobody ever guessed that.

I read Haytham Kenway's letters and then, one day, approached Helene, who was sitting on a low stool by the back door of the lodge, a bowl of steaming water between her feet and a basket full of laundry at one side.

"Do you like it here?" I asked her.

She smiled without taking her eyes off her washing. "I think it is a kind of paradise, mademoiselle."

"I'm glad. I'm so glad, because . . . I'm so sorry about what happened to you in London."

She nodded. "Seems I have to keep reminding you of this, but a lot worse would have happened if you hadn't saved me in Calais."

"Yes, I know, but . . . even so."

"It's forgotten, mademoiselle."

Her hands worked a sopping white nightdress, kneading it over and over.

"I was wondering," I said, and cleared my throat. "I'd like to write to Jennifer Scott. There are some things I'd like to discuss with her. But . . . well, I would quite understand if, given what she did to you, you would rather I did not."

When Helene at last took her attention away from her laundry and looked at me, her eyes were shining. "Mademoiselle, I don't think you quite realize what it means to me, the life I have now. You may do what you like. All I care about is what you have given me. And I could never show enough loyalty to repay you for what you've already given me."

"Thank you," I said, and we embraced.

So I did. I wrote to Jennifer Scott. I told her how sorry I was. I "introduced" myself, telling her about my home life, about Arno, my beloved, and how I was supposed to steer him away from the Creed and toward the ways of Templars.

And of course I discussed Haytham's letters and how his words had moved me. I told her that I would do everything I could to help broker peace between our two kinds because she was right, and Haytham was right: there had been too much killing, and it had to stop.

DECEMBER 1788

This evening Mr. Weatherall and I took the cart into Châteaufort, and a house there he called his "drop."

"You're a more agreeable coachman than young Jacques, I must say," he'd said, settling in at my side. "Although I'll say this, he's a cracking horseman. Never needs to use the whip and rarely even touches the reins. Just sits there on the shaft with his feet up, whistling through his teeth, like this . . ."

He whistled in an approximation of his usual coachman. Well, I was no Jacques, and my hands froze on the reins but I enjoyed the scenery as we rode. Winter had begun to bite hard and the fields on either side of the track into town were laced with ice that glimmered beneath a low skirt of early-evening fog. It would be another bad winter, that was for certain, and I wondered how the peasants who worked the fields felt, looking from their windows. My privilege allowed me to see the beauty ushered into the landscape. They would see only hardship.

"What's 'a drop'?" I asked him.

"Aha," he laughed, slapping his gloved hands together, his cold breath clouding around his upturned collar. "Ever seen a dispatch arrive at the lodge? No. That's because they come from here." He pointed up the highway. "A drop is how I can conduct my business without giving away my exact location. The official story is that you're completing your education and I'm whereabouts unknown. That's how I want things to remain for the time being. And to do that I have to route my correspondence through a series of contacts."

"And who are the people you're hoping to hoodwink? The Crows?"

"Could be. Don't know yet, do we? We're still no closer to finding out who hired Ruddock."

There was an awkward moment between us. Almost everything about the trip to London had remained unspoken, but most of all the fact that it had achieved little of real worth. Yes, I now had the letters and had returned a different, more enlightened woman, but the fact was that we'd gone there to find Ruddock and had done nothing of the sort.

Well, we had found him. Only, I had let him go. And the only two pieces of information we had from the experience were that Ruddock no longer dressed like a doctor and that he sometimes went under the alias Gerald Mowles.

"Well, he won't be using that alias again, will he? He'd have to be a bloody idiot to try that again," Mr. Weatherall had grunted, which reduced the pieces of information I had to a single piece of information.

Plus, of course, I had killed May Carroll.

Over the kitchen table at the lodge we had discussed how the Carrolls might respond. For a month or so, Mr. Weatherall had monitored the dispatches and found no mention of the incident.

"I didn't think they'd want to make it official business," Mr. Weatherall had said. "Fact is, they were about to bump off the Grand Master's daughter, herself a Grand Master in waiting. Try explaining that one. No. The Carrolls will want their revenge, but they'll take it the clandestine way. They'll want you, me and maybe even Helene dead. And sooner or later, probably just when we least expect it, someone will pay us a visit."

"We'll be ready for them," I told him. But I remembered the battle in the Boars Head Inn, when Mr. Weatherall had been a shadow of his former self. The drink, the advancing years, a loss of confidence—whatever the reason, he was no longer the great warrior he'd been, even then. And now, of course, he'd lost a leg. I'd been training with him, and while he'd continued coaching me in swordplay, for his own part he had begun to concentrate more on his knife-throwing skills.

We were greeted by the sight of the three castles of Châteaufort, and in the square I climbed down, collected Mr. Weatherall's crutches and helped him down too.

He led us to a shop in one corner of the square.

"A cheese shop?" I said, eyebrows arching.

"Poor Jacques can't stand the smell of it; I have to leave him outside. You coming in?"

I grinned and followed as he bowed his head and removed his hat, stepping inside. He greeted a young girl behind the counter, then moved through to the rear of the shop. Resisting the urge to hold a hand over my mouth, I followed to find him surrounded by wooden shelves on which were wheels of cheese. His nose was raised as he enjoyed the scent of the pungent cheese fumes.

"You smell that?" he asked.

I could hardly miss it. "This is the drop, is it?"

"Indeed it is. If you look beneath that cheese there, you may find some correspondence for us."

It was a single letter that I handed to him. I waited as he read it.

"Right," he said, when he'd finished, folding the letter and tucking it into his greatcoat. "You know how I said that our friend Mr. Ruddock would have to be bloody stupid to use his Gerald Mowles identity again?"

"Yes," I said cautiously, feeling a little tingle of excitement at the same time.

"Well, he is—he's bloody stupid."

JANUARY 1789

It was dark and smoky in the Butchered Cow, as I imagined it always was, and the gloom was oppressive, despite the noise of the place. You know what it reminded me of? The Antlers in Calais. Only the Antlers in Calais removed to the harsh fields and even harsher living conditions of Rouen.

I was right. Winter had bitten hard. Harder than ever.

The smell of ale seemed to hang about the damp boards like mist; it was ingrained in the walls and in the woodwork and the tables at which the drinkers sat stank of it—not that they minded. Some were hunched over their tankards, so low that the brims of their hats were almost touching the tabletops, talking in low voices and whiling the evening away with grumbles and gossip; others were in groups, rattling dice in cups or laughing and joking. They banged their empty tankards on the table and called for more ale, brought to them by the only woman in the room, a smiling barmaid who was as practiced at dispensing ale as she was at dancing out of the way of the men's grabbing hands.

It was into this tavern that I came, escaping a biting wind that whistled and swirled about me as I heaved the door shut and stood for a second on the threshold, stamping the snow off my boots.

I wore robes that almost reached the floor, a hood pulled up to hide my face. The loud chatter in the tavern was suddenly hushed, replaced instead by a low murmur. The brims of hats dipped lower; the men watched as I turned, closed the door, then stood in the shadows for a moment.

I moved across the room, boots clacking on the boards, and to a counter where stood the barkeep, the barmaid and two regulars clutching tankards, one of them regarding the floor, the other watching with flinty eyes and a set mouth.

At the counter I reached to the hood and drew it back to reveal red hair that I shook loose. The barmaid pursed her lips, and almost reflexively her hands went to her hips and her chest wiggled a little.

I looked carefully around the room, letting them know I was not intimidated by my surroundings. The men regarded me back with watchful eyes, no longer studying the tabletops, fascinated and entranced by the new arrival. Some licked their lips and there was much nudging, some sniggers. Ribald remarks were exchanged.

I took it all in, then I turned to give the room my

back, moving up to the counter, where one of the regulars shifted away to let me in. The other one, however, remained where he was, so that he was standing close to me, deliberately looking me up and down.

"Good evening," I said to the barman. "I'm hoping you might be able to help me—I'm looking for a man." I said it loudly enough for the entire tavern to hear.

"Looks like you've come to the right place then," rasped the potato-nosed drinker from by my side, although he said it to the room, which roared with laughter.

I smiled, ignored him. "He goes by the name of Bernard," I added, invoking the name we had learned of from the letter. "He has some information I require. I was told I might find him here."

All eyes turned to a corner of the tavern where the man who must be Bernard sat, his eyes wide.

"Thank you," I said. "Bernard, perhaps we could step outside for a moment in order that we can talk."

Bernard stared but didn't move.

"Come on, Bernard. I won't bite."

Then Potato-Nose stepped away from the counter so that he was in front of me, facing me. His stare grew harder, if such a thing were possible, but his grin was sloppy and he swayed slightly as he stood.

"Now you just wait a minute, girlie," he said with a sneering tone. "Bernard ain't going nowhere, especially not till you tell us what's on your mind."

I frowned a little. Looked him over. "And how are you related to Bernard?" I asked politely.

"Well, it looks like I've just become his guardian," replied Potato-Nose. "Protecting him against a red-haired bint who seems to be getting a bit above herself, if you don't mind my saying so."

There was a chortle from around the tavern.

"My name is Élise de la Serre of Versailles." I smiled. "To be honest, if you don't mind me saying, it's you who's getting above himself."

He snorted. "I doubt that to be the truth. Way I see it, it's soon coming to the end of the road for the likes of you and your kind." He threw the last words over his shoulder, slurring them slightly.

"You would be surprised," I said evenly. "We red-haired bints have a habit of getting the job done. The job in this case being to speak to Bernard. I intend to get it done. So I suggest that you go back to your ale and leave me to my business."

"And what business might that be? Far as I can see, the only business a lady has in a tavern is serving the ale, and I'm afraid that position is already taken." More titters, this time led by the barmaid.

"Or perhaps you have come to entertain us. Is that right, Bernard, have you paid for a singer for the evening?" Potato-Nose licked lips that were already wet. "Or perhaps another kind of entertainment?"

"Look, you're drunk, you're forgetting your manners, so I'll forget you said that on condition you stand aside."

But my voice was steely. The men in the tavern noticed.

Not Potato-Nose, though. He was oblivious to the sudden shift in atmosphere, enjoying himself too much. "Perhaps you are here to entertain us with a dance," he said loudly. "What is it you're hiding under there?" And with that he reached forward to pluck at my robes.

He froze. My hand went to his. My eyes narrowed. Then Potato-Nose was pulling back and snatching a dagger from his belt.

"Well, well," he said loudly, "it looks as though the red-haired bint is carrying a sword." He waved the knife. "Now what you be needing with a sword, mademoiselle?"

I sighed. "Oh, I don't know. In case I need to cut some cheese? Why would it matter to you anyway?"

"I'll take it if you don't mind," he said, "*then* you can be on your way."

Behind him the other customers watched wide-eyed. Some of them began to edge away, sensing that their visitor was unlikely to give up her weapon willingly.

Instead, after a moment of seeming to consider, I reached a hand to my robes. Potato-Nose jabbed threateningly with the dagger but I held my palms out and moved slowly, drawing back the robes.

Below I wore a leather tunic. At my waist was the hilt of my sword. I reached across myself toward it, eyes never leaving those of Potato-Nose.

"Other hand," said Potato-Nose, grinning at his own cleverness, insisting with the knife.

I obliged. With finger and thumb I used my other hand to gently remove the sword by its handle. It slid slowly from the scabbard. All held their breath.

Now, with a sudden movement of my wrist I flicked the sword up and out of the sheath so that one moment it was in my fingers, the next gone.

It happened in the blink of an eye. For a fraction of a

second Potato-Nose gaped at the spot where the sword should have been, then his eyes flicked up in time to see it slice down toward his knife hand.

Which he snatched out of the way, the sword thunking to the wood, where it stuck, vibrating slightly.

A smile of victory had already begun to gather at Potato-Nose's mouth before he realized he had left himself exposed, his knife pointing in the wrong direction, giving me enough room to step forward, twist and smash him across the nose with my forearm.

Blood fountained from his nose, his eyes rolled upward. His knees met the boards as he sank downward, then seemed to wobble as I stepped forward, put my boot to his chest and was about to push him gently backward when I thought better of it, took a step back and kicked him in the face instead.

He dropped face-first and lay still, breathing but out for the count.

There was silence in the tavern as I beckoned Bernard, then retrieved my sword. Bernard was already scrambling obediently over as I sheathed it.

"Don't worry," I told him as he stood some feet away, Adam's apple bobbing. "You're in no danger—unless you're planning on calling me a red-haired bint." I looked at him. "Are you planning on calling me a red-haired bint?"

Bernard, younger, taller and more spindly than Potato-Nose, shook his head vigorously.

"Good, then let's take this outside."

I glanced around to check whether or not there were any more challengers—the customers, owner and barmaid all found something of interest to study at their feet and, satisfied, I ushered Bernard outside.

"Right," I said, once there, "I'm told you may know something about the whereabouts of a friend of mine— he goes by the name of Mowles."

JANUARY 1789

On a hillside overlooking a tiny village outside Rouen, three landworkers wearing leather jerkins laughed and joked, and then, on the count of three, heaved a gallows onto a low wooden platform.

One of the men placed a three-legged stool beneath the gallows, then bent to help his two companions as they went to work hammering in the struts that would keep the gallows in place, the rhythmic knock-knock carried on the wind to where I sat on my horse, a beautiful and calm gelding that I'd called Scratch, in honor of our beloved and long-since-departed wolfhound.

At the bottom of the hill was a village. It was a tiny village, more like a cluster of disconsolate shacks and a tavern that had been scattered around along the perimeter of a brown and muddy square, but it was a village all the same.

A freezing rain had eased to a steady and just-as-freezing drizzle and a fierce, bone-chilling wind had blown up. The villagers waiting in the square wrapped shawls tightly around themselves, clasping shirts at their necks as they awaited the day's entertainment—a hanging. What could be better? Nothing like a good hanging to raise the spirits when the frost had killed the crops and the local landowner was raising his rents and the king in Versailles had new taxes he hoped to enforce.

From a building I guessed was the jailhouse there came a noise, and the frozen spectators turned to see a priest wearing black hat and robes emerge, his voice rich with solemnity as he read from the Bible. Behind him came a jailer, who held a length of rope, the other end of which tied the hands of a man who wore a hood over his head, who staggered and slipped in the mud of the square, blindly shouting protestations in the direction of no one in particular.

"I think there's been some mistake," he was shouting—except he shouted it in English, before remembering to do it in French. Villagers stood watching him as he was led toward the hill, some crossing themselves, some jeering. There was not a gendarme to be seen. No judge or officer of the law. This was what passed for justice out here in the country, it seemed. And they said Paris was uncivilized.

The man, of course, was Ruddock, and looking down the hill upon him, as he was pulled by rope so that he could swing at the end of another one, it was difficult to believe he had ever been an Assassin. No wonder the Creed had washed their hands of him.

I pushed back the hood of my robes, shook my hair free and looked down upon Bernard, who stood gazing up at me with wide, adoring eyes.

"Here they come, mademoiselle," he said, "just as I promised they would."

I dangled a purse into his palm then tweaked it away when he went to grasp it.

"And that's definitely him, is it?" I asked.

"That's him all right, mademoiselle. Man who goes by the name of monsieur Gerald Mowles. They say he tried to swindle an elderly lady out of her money but was caught before he could leave."

"And then sentenced to death."

"That's right, mademoiselle, the villagers sentenced him to death."

I gave a short laugh and looked back to where the grim procession had reached the foot of the hill and was climbing toward the gallows, shaking my head at how low Ruddock had sunk and wondering if it might be better to do the world a favor and let him swing. After all, this was a man who had tried to kill me and my mother. Something Mr. Weatherall had said to me before I left played over in my mind. "If you find him, do me a favor and don't bring him here."

I'd looked sharply at him. "And why would that be, Mr. Weatherall?"

"Well, two reasons. Firstly, because this is our hidey-hole and I don't want it compromised by some bastard who sells his services to the highest bidder."

"And the second reason?"

He shifted uncomfortably and reached to scratch at

the stump of his leg, something he had a habit of doing. "The other reason is that I've been doing a lot of thinking about our Mr. Ruddock. Maybe too much thinking, you might say—than is healthy, I mean. And I suppose I blame him for this." He indicated his leg. "And also because, well, he tried to kill you and Julie, and I've never quite got over that."

I cleared my throat. "Was there ever anything between you and my mother, Mr. Weatherall?"

He smiled and tapped the side of his nose. "A gentleman never tells, young Élise, you should know that."

But he was right. This man had attacked us. Of course I was going to save him from the gallows, but that was because there were things I wanted to know. But what about after that? Did I exact my revenge?

Scrambling toward the gallows was a group of women who formed a disorderly line as Ruddock, still protesting his innocence, was dragged to where the gallows stood silhouetted against the winter-gray skyline.

"What are they doing?" I asked Bernard.

"They're barren women, mademoiselle. They hope that touching the hand of the condemned man will help them conceive."

"You're a superstitious, man, Bernard."

"It's not superstition if I know it to be true, mademoiselle."

I looked at him, wondering what went on his head. How did Bernard and people like him get to be so medieval?

"Did you want to save Monsieur Mowles, mademoiselle?" he asked me.

"Indeed I do."

"Well, you better hurry then. They've started."

What? I swiveled in the saddle in time to see one of the leather jerkins haul the stool away, and Ruddock's body fall and be snapped tight by the noose.

"Mon dieu," I cursed, and set off across the hillside, low in the saddle, hair out straight behind me.

Ruddock jerked and writhed on the rope.

"Gah!" I urged my horse—"Come on, Scratch!"—thundering toward the gallows as Ruddock's dangling legs pumped. I drew my sword.

I dropped the reins and sat upright in the saddle, a matter of yards from the gallows now. I tossed my sword from my right to my left hand, brought the weapon across my body then flung out my right arm. I leaned to the right, dangerously low in the saddle.

His legs gave one last convulsion.

I swept the sword, sliced the rope and at the same time grabbed Ruddock's spasming body with my right arm, heaving it onto the neck of Scratch and hoping to God he could bear the sudden extra weight and that with God's grace and maybe just a little bit of luck, we'd somehow stay on all four legs.

Come on, Scratch.

But the sudden weight was too much for Scratch, whose legs buckled, and we all came crashing to the ground.

In a trice I was on my feet, sword drawn. An enraged villager, deprived of his day's hanging, lumbered out of the small crowd toward me, but I stood, pivoted and kicked, choosing to stun rather than hurt him, and sent him reeling back into the knot of villagers. Collectively they thought twice about trying to stop me, deciding instead to stand and mutter darkly, the women pointing at me—"Oi, you can't do this"—and prodding their men into doing something—and all of them looking pointedly at the priest, who merely looked worried.

Beside me, Scratch had scrambled to his feet. As had Ruddock, who'd immediately set off in a run. Still hooded, panicking, he dashed in the wrong direction, back toward the gallows, his hands tied, the severed noose dancing on his back.

"Watch out," I tried to shout. But with a solid thump he ran into the platform, spinning off with a yell of pain, then falling to the ground, where he lay, coughing and obviously hurt.

I flipped back my robes and sheathed my sword, turned to gather Scratch. Next I caught the eye of a young peasant at the front of the crowd.

"You," I said, "you look like a big strong lad. You can help me with a bit of lifting. *That* barely conscious man on *this* horse, please."

"Oi, you can't . . ." began an older woman nearby, but in a second my sword was at her throat. She looked disdainfully down the blade at me. "You lot think you can do what you want, don't you?" she sneered.

"Really? Then tell me, on whose authority is this man condemned to death? You can all count yourselves lucky I don't report your actions to the gendarmes."

They looked bashful, there was some clearing of throats and the woman at the end of my blade shifted her gaze.

"Now," I said, "I just want some help with some lifting."

My helper did as he was told.

Next, making sure Ruddock was secure, I mounted Scratch. As I pulled him round to leave I caught the eye of the lad who had helped me, gave him a wink—and then was off.

I rode for miles. There were plenty of people abroad, most hurrying home before darkness fell, but they paid me no mind. Perhaps they came to the conclusion that I was a long-suffering wife carrying her drunken husband home from the pub. And if they did come to that conclusion, well, I was certainly long-suffering where Ruddock was concerned.

From the draped body in front of me came the sound of a gurgle so I dismounted, laid my prisoner on the ground, reached for a water bottle and squatted by his side. The stench of him assaulted my nostrils.

"Hello again," I said, when his eyes opened and he gazed glassily at me. "It's Élise de la Serre."

He groaned.

ii

Ruddock tried to pull himself up on his elbows, but he was as weak as a kitten and from my squatting position I easily held him down with the fingertips of one hand, placing the other to the hilt of my sword.

For a moment or so he writhed pathetically; more as though he was having a grown-up-baby tantrum than any concerted effort to escape.

Once he settled, he stared up at me balefully.

"Look, what do you want?" he said with a hurt tone. "I mean, you obviously don't want to kill me; otherwise, you would have done it by now . . ."

Something occurred to him. "Oh no. You haven't been saving my life in order to have the pleasure of killing me yourself, have you? I mean, that would be cruel and unusual. You're not doing that, are you?"

"No," I said, "I'm not doing that. Not yet."

"So what is it you want?"

"I want to know who hired you to kill me and my mother in Paris in '75."

He snorted disbelievingly. "And if I tell you, *then* you'll kill me."

"Try this: if you don't tell me, I'll kill you."

He turned his head to one side. "And what if I don't know?"

"Well, then I'll torture you until you tell me."

"Well, then I'll just say any name until you let me go."

"And then when I find out you lied I'll come after you again, and I've found you twice, Monsieur Ruddock. I'll find you again, then again, if necessary, and again. And you'll never be rid of me, not until I have satisfaction."

"Oh, for crying out loud," he said, "what have I done to deserve this?"

"You tried to kill my mother and me."

"Well, yes," he admitted, "but I didn't succeed, did I?"

"Who hired you?"

"I don't know."

I went up to one knee, drew my sword, held it to his face, the tip of it just under his eyeball.

"Unless you were hired by a ghost, you know who hired you. Now who hired you?"

His eyeballs darted furiously as though trying to get a fix on the point of the blade. "I promise you," he wheedled, "I promise you I don't know."

I jogged the blade slightly. "A man!" he squealed. "A man in a coffeehouse in Paris."

"Which coffeehouse?"

"The Café de Procope."

"And what was his name?"

"He didn't tell me."

I flashed the blade across his right cheek, giving him a cut. He screamed and though inside I flinched, I kept my face blank—cruel, even—the face of someone determined to get what she wants even though I was fighting a sinking feeling inside, a sense that I'd come to the end of a decade-long wild-goose chase.

"I promise. I promise. He was a stranger to me. He didn't tell me, I didn't ask. I took half the money then and was to return for it when the job was done. But, of course, I never went back."

"I think you're telling me the truth," I said. And he was. With a sinking heart I realized he was telling the truth: that thirteen years ago an anonymous man had hired another anonymous man to do a job. And there the story ended.

I had one last bluff up my sleeve, and I stood, keeping the blade where it was.

"Then all that remains is to exact revenge for what you did in '75."

His eyes widened. "Oh for God's sake, you *are* going to kill me."

"Yes," I said.

"I can find out," he said quickly. "I can find out who the man was. Let me find out for you."

I regarded him carefully as though mulling it over, even though the truth was I had no intention of killing him. Not like this. Not in cold blood.

At last I said, "I'll spare your life so that you can do as you say. Know this, though, Ruddock, I want to hear from you within six months—*six months*. You can find me at the de la Serres' Île Saint-Louis estate in Paris. Whether you have learned anything or not, you come to find me or you can spend the rest of your days expecting me to appear from the shadows and slit your throat. Do I make myself clear?"

I sheathed my sword and mounted Scratch. "There's a town two miles in that direction." I pointed. "See you in six months, Ruddock."

I rode away. And I waited until I was out of sight of Ruddock to let my shoulders slump.

Wild-goose chase indeed. All I'd learned was that there was nothing to learn.

Would I ever see Ruddock again? I doubted it. I wasn't sure if my promise to hunt him down was an empty threat or not, but I knew this: like most else in life it was a lot easier said than done.

4 MAY 1789

This morning I woke early, dressed and went to where my trunk was waiting for me by the front door of the lodge. I'd hoped to slip out quietly, but when I crept through to the entrance hall they were all there: Madame Levene and Jacques; Helene and Mr. Weatherall.

Mr. Weatherall held out his hand. I looked at him.

"Your short sword," he prompted. "You can leave it here. I'll take good care of it."

"But then I won't have a . . ."

He'd reached for another sword. He tucked his crutches into his armpits and held it out to me.

"A cutlass," I said, turning it over in my hands.

"Indeed, it is," said Mr. Weatherall. "Lovely fighting weapon. Light and easy to handle, great for close combat."

"It's beautiful," I said.

"Too blinkin' right it's beautiful. It'll stay beautiful if you take good care of it. And no naming it now, you hear?"

"I promise," I said, and stood on tiptoes to kiss him. "Thank you, Mr. Weatherall."

He blushed. "You know, you're a grown woman now, Élise. A grown woman who's saved my life. You can stop calling me Mr. Weatherall. You can call me Freddie."

"You'll always be Mr. Weatherall to me."

"Oh, suit your bloody self," he said, pretending to be exasperated, and used the opportunity to turn and wipe a tear from his eye.

I kissed Madame Levene and thanked her for everything. With gleaming eyes she held me at arm's length, as though wanting to study me. "I asked you to come back from London a changed person, and you did me proud. You went an angry girl, came back a young woman. You are a credit to the Maison Royale."

I brushed aside the proffered hand of Jacques, and instead took him in a hug and gave him a kiss that made him blush and cast a sideways glance at Helene, and in an instant I realized that they had formed a bond.

"He's a lovely lad," I whispered into Helene's ear as I gave her a good-bye kiss, and I'd eat my hat if they weren't together by the time of my next visit.

Talking of which, I put on my hat and took hold of my trunk. Jacques bounded forward to take it from me but I stopped him.

"That's very kind of you, Jacques, but I wish to meet the carriage alone."

And so I did. I took my trunk to the service highway

close to the gates of the Maison Royale. The school build-ing stood on the hillside watching me, and where once upon a time I would have seen malevolence in that stare, now I saw comfort and protection—that I was leaving behind.

It felt as though I'd barely settled into the carriage when we came to the tree-bordered drive of our château, which ahead of me looked like a castle with its turrets and towers, presiding over the gardens that swept away in all directions.

There I was met by Olivier, and once inside greeted by staff, some of whom I knew well—Justine, the sight of her bringing the memories of Mother flooding back—some who were unfamiliar faces to me. When my trunk was installed in my room, I took a tour of the house. I'd returned in the school holidays, of course. It wasn't like this was some great homecoming. But even so, it felt like one. And for the first time in years I climbed the stairs to Mother's rooms and went to her bedchamber.

The fact that it was serviced but otherwise left as it was created a strong, almost overwhelming sense of her presence, as though she might walk in at any moment, find me sitting on the end of her bed and sit down next to me, put an arm around my shoulders. "I'm very proud of you, Élise. We both are."

I stayed like that for a while, with her phantom arm around my shoulders. It wasn't until I felt the tickle of tears on my cheeks that I realized I was crying.

5 MAY 1789

i

In a courtyard of the Hôtel des Menus-Plaisirs in Versailles, the king addressed the 1,614-strong meeting of the Estates General. It was the first time that the representatives of the three Estates—the clergy, the nobility and the common man—had officially met since 1614, and the huge vaulted chamber was full, row upon row of expectant Frenchmen hoping that the king would say something—anything—that would help pull his country from the swamp in which it was apparently mired. Something to point the way forward.

I sat beside my father during the speech and the two of us were positively vibrating with hope before it began, a feeling that soon dissipated as our beloved leader began to drone on—and on, and on—saying nothing of any significance, offering no comfort to the downtrodden third estate, the common man.

Across the way, seated together, were the Crows. Messieurs Lafrenière, Le Peletier, Sivert, and Madame Levesque, wearing scowls that went with the black of their clothes. As I took my seat I caught their eye and gave a short, deferential bow, hiding my true feelings behind a false smile. In return they nodded back with false smiles of their own and I felt their eyes on me, assessing me as I took my seat.

When I pretended to inspect something at my feet I looked at them surreptitiously from beneath my curls. Madame Levesque was whispering something to Sivert and receiving a nod in return.

When the boring speech was over the Estates began shouting at one another. Father and I departed the Salle des États, dismissed our carriage and walked along the Avenue de Paris before taking a footpath that led across to the rear lawns of our château in the village.

We chatted idly as we walked. He asked me about my final year at the Maison Royale but I steered the conversation to less dangerous and lie-filled waters, and so for a while we reminisced about when Mother was alive, and when Arno had joined the household. And then, when we had left the crowds behind and had open fields to one side, the palace watching over us always on the other, he broached the subject—the subject being my failure to bring Arno into the fold.

"Indoctrinate him, you mean," I said, at the mention of the idea.

Father sighed. He was wearing his favorite hat, a black beaver that he now removed, first scratching at the wig below, which irritated him, then passing a hand across his forehead and regarding his palm as though expecting to find it slicked with sweat.

"Do I need to remind you, Élise, that there is the very real possibility the Assassins might reach Arno first? You forget, I have spent a great deal of time with him. I am aware of his abilities. He is . . . gifted. It can only be a matter of time before the Assassins sniff that out too."

"Father, what if I were to bring Arno over to the Order . . ."

He gave a short, mirthless laugh. "Well, then it would be about time."

I plowed on. "You say he's gifted. What if Arno could somehow combine the two creeds? What if he is the one capable of doing that?"

"Your letters," said Father, nodding thoughtfully, "you spoke about this in your letters."

"I've given the matter much thought."

"I can tell. Your ideas, they had a certain youthful idealism, but also they showed a certain . . . maturity."

For that I offered a silent thanks (not to mention an apology) to Haytham Kenway.

"Perhaps it may interest you to know that I have arranged to meet the Assassin Grand Master, Count Mirabeau," continued Father.

"Really?"

He held a finger to his lips. "Yes, really."

"Because you want our two Orders to begin talks?" I asked, whispering now.

"Because I think we may have some common ground on the issue of our country's future."

Perhaps, dear journal, you're wondering if my conversion to the idea of Assassin-Templar unity had anything to do with the fact that I was a Templar and Arno an Assassin?

No, is the answer. Any vision I had for the future was for the good of us all. But if that meant that Arno and I could be together, with no pretense or lies between us, then of course I embraced that, too, but only as a pleasant added benefit. Promise.

ii

Later, in the palace, a ceremony took place—my induction to the Order. My father wore the ceremonial robes of the Grand Master: long flowing, ermine-lined ceremonial cloak and a silk stole draped around his neck, his waistcoat buttoned and the buckles of his shoes polished to a shine.

As he gave me the Templar pin of initiation I gazed into his smiling eyes, and he looked so handsome, so proud.

I had no idea it would be the last time I saw him alive.

But during the initiation there was no sign of the fact that we had argued. Instead of fatigue there was pride in his eyes. There were others there, of course. The dreaded Crows as well as other Knights of the Order, and they smiled weakly and offered insincere congratulations, but the ceremony belonged to the de la Serre family. I felt the spirit of my mother watching over me as they made me a Templar Knight at last, and I vowed to uphold the name of the de la Serres.

iii

And later, at the "private soiree" held to honor my induction, I walked through the party and felt like a changed woman. Yes, perhaps they thought I didn't hear them gossiping behind their fans, telling each other how I spent my days drinking and gambling. They whispered how they pity my father. They made disparaging comments about my clothes.

Their words were water off a duck's back. My mother hated these courtly women and raised me to put no store by what they said. Her lessons served me well. They couldn't hurt me now.

And then I saw him. I saw Arno.

iv

I led him a merry dance, of course, partly for old times' sake and partly so that I could compose myself ahead of meeting him again.

Aha. It seemed that Arno's presence at the party was not officially ratified. Either that or, true to form, he had made an enemy. Knowing him, probably a bit of both. In fact, as I made my way quickly along the corridors, picking up my skirts, weaving between revelers, keeping him just on my tail, it appears that we formed something of a procession.

Of course, it would not do for the newly initiated daughter of the Grand Master to be seen to be participating in, even encouraging, such behavior. (See, Mr. Weatherall? See, Father? I was maturing. I was growing up.) And so I decided to end the chase, ducked into a side room, waited for Arno to appear, dragged him inside and stood facing him at last.

"You seem to have caused quite a commotion," I told him, drinking him in.

"What can I say?" he said. "You were always a bad influence . . ."

"You were a worse one," I told him.

And then we kissed. How it happened I couldn't for certain say. One moment we were reunited friends the next we were reunited lovers.

Our kiss was long, and passionate, and when we eventually broke apart we stared at each other for some moments.

"Are you wearing one of my father's suits?" I teased him.

"Are you wearing a dress?" He retorted. For which he earned a playful smack.

"Don't even start. I feel like a mummy wrapped up in this thing."

"Must be quite an occasion to get you so fancy." He smiled.

"It's not like that. Truth be told it's a lot of ceremony and pontification. Dull as dirt."

Arno grinned. Oh, the old Arno. The old fun come back into my life. It was as though it had been raining and on seeing him the sun had come out—like returning home from far away and at last seeing your front door in the distance. We kissed again and held each other close.

"Well, when you don't invite me to your parties, everyone suffers," he joked.

"I did try, but Father was adamant."

"Your father?"

From the other side of the door came the muted sound of the band, the laughter of revelers making their way back and forth in the corridor outside, heavy footfalls, running feet, guards still in search of Arno. Then suddenly the door shook, thumped from the other side, and a gruff voice called, "Who's in there?"

Arno and I looked at one another, kids again—kids caught pilfering apples or stealing pies from the kitchen. If I could bottle that moment, I would.

Something tells me I'm never going to feel happiness like that again.

v

I bundled Arno out the window, snatched up a goblet, then burst out of the door, affecting an unsteady look. "Oh my. That wasn't the billiard room at all, was it?" I said, gaily.

The soldiers shifted uncomfortably on seeing me. And so they should. After all, this "private soiree" was being held in my honor . . .

"We are pursuing an interloper, Mademoiselle de la Serre. Have you seen him?"

I gave the man a deliberately fuzzy look. "Antelope? No I shouldn't think they can climb stairs, not with those little hooves, and how did they get out of the Royal Menagerie?"

The men shared an uncertain look. "Not an antelope, an interloper. A suspicious person. Have you seen anyone like that?"

By now the guards were anxious and on edge. Sensing their quarry was near, they were irritated by my stalling.

"Oh, there was Madame de Polignac." I dropped my voice to a whisper. "Her hair has a bird in it. I think she stole it from the Royal Menagerie."

Able to control his irritation no longer, another of the guards strode forward. "Please move aside so we may check this room, mademoiselle."

I swayed drunkenly, and perhaps, I hoped, a little provocatively. "You'll only find me, I'm afraid," I beamed at him, giving the full benefit of my smile, not to mention the low-cut neck of my bodice. "I've been searching for the billiard room for almost an hour."

The guard's eye wandered. "We can show you there, mademoiselle," he said with a short bow. "And we'll lock the door to prevent any further misunderstandings."

As the guards accompanied me away, I hoped firstly that Arno would be able to jump down to the courtyard, and secondly that something might happen to distract the guards from actually taking me all the way down to the billiards room.

There is a saying: be careful what you wish for, for you might just get it.

I got the distraction I wanted when I heard a shout: "My God, he's killed Lord de la Serre."

And my whole world changed.

1 JULY 1789

It feels as though France is falling down around my ears. The much-vaunted assembly of Estates General had been given a terrible birth by the king's cure for insomnia masquerading as a speech, and sure enough the whole charade swiftly descended into a parade of bickering and internecine strife, and nothing was achieved.

How? Because prior to the meeting the Third Estate were angry. They were incensed at being the poorest and being charged the most taxes, and they were angry that despite making up the majority of the Estates General, they had fewer votes than the nobility and the clergy.

After the meeting they were even more angry. They were angry that the king hadn't addressed any of their concerns. They were going to do something. The whole country—unless they were stupid or being willfully thick and stubborn—knew that *something* was going to happen.

But I didn't care.

On 17 June, the Third Estate voted to call themselves the National Assembly, an assembly of "the people." There was some support from the other Estates but really this was the common man finding his voice.

I didn't care.

The king tried to stop them by closing the Salle des États meeting room, but that was like trying to shut the stable door when the horse had already bolted. Not to be deterred, they took their assembly to an indoor tennis court instead, and on 20 June, the National Assembly swore an oath. The Tennis Court Oath they called it, which sounds comical, but it wasn't really.

Not when you considered that they were planning to build a new constitution for France.

Not when you considered it spelled the end of the monarchy.

But I didn't care.

By 27 June, the king's nerves were more apparent than ever. As messages of support for the Assembly poured in from Paris and other French cities, the military began to arrive in Paris and Versailles. There was a palpable tension in the air.

And I didn't care about that either.

I should have done, of course. I should have had the strength of character to put my personal troubles behind me. But the fact was, I couldn't.

I couldn't because my father was dead, and grief has

returned to my life like a dark mass living inside me; that awakes with me in the morning, accompanies me through the day, then is restless at night, keeping me from sleep, feeding on my remorse and my regrets.

I had spent so many years being a disappointment to him. The chance to be the daughter he deserved has been snatched away from me.

And yes, I'm aware that our châteaux in Versailles and in Paris slip into neglect, their state mirroring my own state of mind. I'm staying in Paris but letters from Olivier in Versailles arrive twice weekly, increasingly concerned and shrill as he relates details of maids and valets who leave and aren't replaced. But I don't care.

Here on the Paris estate I've banished staff from my rooms and skulk the lower floors at night, not wanting to see another soul. Trays bearing food and correspondence are left outside my door and sometimes I can hear the housemaid whispering with the lady's maid, and I can imagine the kind of things they're saying about me. But I don't care.

I've had letters from Mr. Weatherall. Among other things he wants to know if I've been to see Arno in the Bastille, where he is being held on suspicion of murdering my father, or even if I'm taking steps to protest his innocence.

I should write and tell Mr. Weatherall that the answer is no, because shortly after Father's murder I returned to the Versailles estate, went to his office, and found a letter that had been pushed beneath the door. A letter addressed to Father that read:

Grand Master de la Serre,

*I have learned through my agents that an individ-
ual within our Order plots against you. I beg you be
on your guard at the initiation tonight. Trust no
one. Not even those you call friends. May the father
of understanding guide you,*

L

I wrote to Arno. A letter in which I accused him of
being responsible for my father's death. A letter in which
I told him I never wanted to see again. But I didn't send it.

Instead, my feelings for him festered. In the place of a
childhood friend and latter-day lover came an interloper,
a pathetic orphan who had arrived and stolen my father's
love, then helped to kill him.

Arno is in the Bastille. Good. I hope he rots in there.

4 JULY 1789

It hurt Mr. Weatherall to walk too far. Not only that, but the area of the Maison Royale where they lived, far beyond the school and out of bounds to the pupils, was not exactly the best-kept area of the school; negotiating it with crutches was difficult.

Nevertheless, he loved to walk when we visited. Just me and him. And I wondered if it was because we'd see the odd deer together, watching us from in the trees, or maybe because we would reach a sun-dappled clearing with a tree trunk on which to sit, and it would remind us of the years we had spent training.

We found our way there this morning, and Mr. Weatherall sat with a grateful sigh as he took the weight off his good foot, and sure enough I felt a huge pang of nostalgia for my old life, when my days had been full of swordplay with him and play with Arno. When Mother had been alive.

I missed them. I missed them both so much.

"Arno should have delivered it, the letter?" he asked, after a while.

"No. He should have *given* it to Father. Olivier saw him with a letter."

"So he should and he didn't. And how do you feel about that?"

My voice was quiet. "Betrayed."

"Do you think the letter might have saved your father?"

"I think it might have."

"And is that why you've been so quiet on the small matter of your boyfriend's currently residing in the Bastille?"

I said nothing. Not that there was anything to say. Mr. Weatherall spent a moment with his face upturned to a beam of sunlight that broke the canopy of the trees, the light dancing over his whiskers and the folds of flesh on his closed eyes, drinking in the day with an almost beatific smile. And then, with a short nod to thank me for indulging him in silence, he held out a hand.

"Let me see that letter again."

I dug into my tunic and passed it to him.

"Who is L, do you think?

Mr. Weatherall cocked an eyebrow at me as he handed back the letter. "Who do you think L is?"

"The only 'L' I can think of is our friend, Monsieur Chretien Lafrenière."

"But he's a Crow."

"Would that put paid to the theory that the Crows were conspiring against your mother and father?"

I followed his line of reasoning. "No, it could just mean that some of them were conspiring against my mother and father."

He chuckled, scratched his beard. "That's right. 'An individual,' according to the letter. Only, as far as we know, none have yet made a bid for Grand Master."

"No," I said quietly.

"Well, here's the thing—you're the Grand Master now, Élise."

"They know that."

"Do they? You could have fooled me. Tell me, how many meetings have you had with your advisers?"

I gave him a narrow-eyed look. "I must be allowed to grieve."

"Nobody says different. Just that it's been two months now, Élise. Two months and you've not conducted one bit of Templar business. Not one bit. The Order knows that you're Grand Master in name but you've done nothing to reassure them that the stewardship is in safe hands. If there was a coup—if another knight were to step forward and declare himself Grand Master, well, he wouldn't have much of a challenge on his hands, now, would he?

"Grieving for your father is one thing, but you need to honor him. You're the latest in a line of de la Serres. The first female Grand Master of France. You need to get out there and prove you're worthy of them, not be hanging around your estate moping."

"But my father was murdered. What example would I set if I were to let his murder go unavenged?"

He gave a short laugh. "Well, correct me if I'm wrong but you ain't exactly doing one thing or another at the moment, are you? Best course of action: you take control of the Order and help steer it through the hard times ahead. Second best course of action: you show a bit of de la Serre spirit and let it be known that you're hunting your father's killer—and maybe help flush out this 'individual.' Worst course of action: you sit on your arse moping about your dead mum and dad."

I nodded. "So what do I do?"

"First thing is to contact Lafrenière. Don't mention the letter but do tell him you're keen to take command of the Order. If he is loyal to the family, then he'll hopefully show his hand. Second thing is, I'm going to find you a lieutenant. Someone I know we can trust. Third thing, you should think about going to see Arno as well. You should remember that it wasn't Arno who killed your father. The person who killed your father was the person who killed your father."

8 JULY 1789

A letter has arrived:

My dearest Élise,

Firstly, I must apologize for not having replied to your letters before now. I confess my failure to give you the courtesy of a reply has been mainly out of anger that you deceived your way into my confidences, but on reflection there is much we have in common and in fact I am grateful that you chose to confide in me, and would like to assure you that your apologies are accepted.

I am most gratified that you have taken my brother's writings to heart. Not solely because it justifies my decision to give them to you but because I believe that had he lived, my brother might have gone on to achieve some of his aims, and I hope that you might do so in his stead.

I note that your intended, Arno, can boast an Assassin heritage and the fact that you are in love with him bodes well for a future accord. I do believe you are right in having misgivings over your father's plans to convert Arno, and while I also agree that your misgivings may have their roots in rather more selfish motives, that doesn't necessarily make them the wrong course of action. Equally, if Arno were discovered by the Assassins, the Creed might be persuasive enough to turn Arno. Your beloved might easily become your enemy.

On this note, I have information that may be of use to you. Something that has appeared in what I can only describe as Assassin communiqués. As you can imagine, I would not normally involve myself in such matters; what information on the Creed's activities I receive in passing tends to go no further, as much a function of my own disinterest as any particular discretion. But this particular tidbit may be of importance to you. It involves a high-ranking Assassin named Pierre Bellec, who is currently imprisoned in the Bastille. Bellec has written to say that he has discovered a young man possessing enormous Assassin gifts. The communiqué names this young prisoner as "Arnaud." However, as I'm sure you can imagine, the similarities in the names struck me as *more than coincidental. If nothing it may be some-thing worth your looking into.*

I remain,
Yours truly,
Jennifer Scott

14 July 1789

Paris was in a state of uproar as I made my way through the streets. It had been this way for over two weeks now, ever since twenty thousand of the king's men had arrived in Paris to put down disturbances, as well as threaten Count Mirabeau and his Third Estate deputies. Then, when the king dismissed his finance minister, Jacques Necker, a man who many believed was the savior of the French people, there were more uprisings.

Days ago the Prison de l'Abbaye had been stormed to free the guardsmen imprisoned for refusing to fire on protestors. These days it was said that the common soldier was giving his loyalties to the people, not the king. Already it felt as though the National Assembly—now called the Constituent Assembly—was in charge. They had created their own flag: a "tricolor," which was everywhere. And if ever there was a symbol of the Assembly's fast-growing dominance, that was it.

Since the Abbaye prison revolt the streets in Paris had been thronged with armed men. Thirteen thousand of them had joined a people's militia and they roamed the districts looking for weapons, the call to find arms becoming louder and louder and more intense. This morning, it had reached a crescendo.

In the early hours of the morning the militia had stormed the Hôtel des Invalides and got their hands on muskets, tens of thousands of muskets, by all accounts. But they had no gunpowder, so now they needed gunpowder. Where was there gunpowder?

The Bastille. That's where I was heading. Early morning in a Paris boiling over with repressed fury and vengeance. Not a good place to be.

ii

Looking around as I hurried through the streets, I saw that the crowds, though a mingled-together, rushing, pushing pell-mell of bodies, actually fell into two distinct groups: those intent on preparing for the oncoming trouble, protecting themselves, their families and their possessions, fleeing the trouble because they wished to avoid the conflict or, like me, because they were concerned they might well be the target of the trouble.

And those intent on starting the trouble.

And what distinguished the two groups? Weapons. The carrying of weapons—I saw pitchforks, axes and staffs brandished and held aloft—and the locating of weapons. A whisper had become a shout had become a clamor: where are the muskets? Where are the pistols? Where is the gunpowder? Paris was a tinderbox.

Could all of this been avoided? I wondered. Could we, the Templars, have prevented our beloved country reaching this dreadful impasse, teetering above a precipice of previously unimagined change?

There were shouts—shouts for "freedom!"—mingled with the whinnies and brays of scattering, flustered animals.

Horses snorted as they were driven at dangerous speeds through crowded streets by panicked drivers. Herders tried to take wide-eyed, frightened livestock to safety. The stink of fresh dung was heavy in the air but more than that there was another scent in Paris today. The smell of rebellion. No, not of rebellion, of revolution.

And why was I on the streets, and not helping the staff to board up the windows to the de la Serre estate?

Because of Arno. Because even though I hated Arno, I couldn't stand by—not while he was in danger. The truth was I'd done nothing about the letter from Jennifer Scott. What would Mr. Weatherall, Mother and Father have thought about that? Me, a Templar—no, a Templar Grand Master, no less—knowing full well that one of our own was close to being discovered by the Assassins and doing nothing—not a thing—about it? Skulking around the unpopulated floors of her Paris estate like a lonely old eccentric widow?

I'll say this for rebellion, there's nothing like it to

spur a girl into action, and even though my feelings for Arno hadn't changed—it wasn't as though I'd suddenly stopped hating him for his failure to deliver the letter—I still wanted to get to him before the mob.

I'd hoped that I might arrive before them, but even as I rushed toward Saint-Antoine it became apparent that I was not ahead of a tide of people going in the same direction; rather I was part of it, joining a throng of partisans, militia and tradesmen of all stripes, who brandished weapons and flags as they moved toward that great symbol of the king's tyranny, the Bastille.

I cursed, knowing I was too late, but staying with the crowd, darting between knots of people as I tried, somehow, to get ahead of the pack. With the towers and ramparts of the Bastille visible in the distance, the crowd seemed to slow down all of a sudden and a cry went up. In the street was a cart bristling with muskets, probably liberated from the armory, and there were men and women handing them out to a sea of waving, upstretched hands. The mood was jovial, celebratory, even. There was a sense that this was easy.

I pushed past, through rows of tightly packed bodies, ignoring the curses that came my way. The crowds were less dense on the other side but now I saw a cannon being wheeled along the highway. It was maneuvered by men on foot, some in uniform, some in the garb of the partisans, and for a moment I wondered what was happening until the cry went up: "The Gardes Français have come over!" Sure enough I heard tales of soldiers turning on their commanders; there was talk that men's heads had been mounted on pikes.

Not far away I saw a well-dressed gentleman who overheard the same. He and I shared a quick look and I could see the fear in his eyes. He was thinking the same as I was: was he safe? How far would these revolutionaries go? After all, their cause had been supported by many nobles and members of the other estates, and Mirabeau himself was an aristocrat. But would that mean anything in the upheaval? When it came to revenge, would they discriminate?

The battle at the Bastille began as I came to it. On the approach to the prison I'd heard that a delegation of the Assembly had been invited inside to discuss terms with the governor, de Launay. However, the delegation had been inside for three hours now, eating breakfast, and the crowd outside had become more and more restless. Meanwhile, one of the protestors had climbed from the roof of a perfume shop onto the chains that held the raised drawbridge, had been cutting the chains, and as I rounded the corner and brought the Bastille into view, he finished the job and the drawbridge fell with a great wallop that seemed to reverberate around the entire area.

We all saw it fall onto a man standing below. A man unlucky enough to be in the wrong place at the wrong time, who one moment was standing on the bank of the moat, brandishing a musket and egging on those who were trying to free the drawbridge, and the next moment had disappeared in a mist of blood and tangle of limbs protruding at horrible angles from beneath the drawbridge.

A great cheer went up. This one unfortunate life lost was nothing compared to the victory of opening the drawbridge. In the next instant the crowds began to flood across the open drawbridge and into the outside courtyard of the Bastille.

iii

The reply came. I heard a shout from the battlements and a thunderclap of musket fire was followed by a smoke cloud that rose like a puff of powder from the ramparts.

Below, we dived for cover as musket balls zinged into the stone and cobbles around us, and there were screams. It wasn't enough to disperse the crowds, though. Like poking a wasps' nest with a stick, the gunfire, far from deterring the protestors, had only made them more angry. More determined.

Plus, of course, they had cannons.

"Fire!" came a shout from not far away, and I saw the cannons buck into huge billows of smoke before the balls tore chunks out of the Bastille. Moving forward were more armed men. Muskets held by the attackers bristled above their heads like the spines of a hedgehog.

Militia had taken control of buildings around us, and smoke was pouring from the windows. The governor's house was ablaze, I was told. The smell of gunpowder mingled with the stench of smoke. From the Bastille came another shout and there was a second volley of gunfire and I ducked behind a low stone wall. Around me were more screams.

Meanwhile the crowd had made its way across a second drawbridge and was trying to negotiate a moat.

From behind me planks were produced and used to form a bridge into the inner sanctum of the prison. Soon they would be through.

More shots were fired. The protestors' cannons replied. Stone fell around us.

In there somewhere was Arno. With my sword drawn I joined the protestors flooding through into the inner sanctum.

From above us, the musket fire stopped, the battle won now. I caught a glimpse of the governor, de Launay. He had been arrested and there was talk of taking him to the Hôtel de Ville, the Paris city hall.

For a moment I allowed myself a moment of relief. The Revolution had maintained its head; there was to be no lust for blood.

But I was wrong. A cry went up. Idiotically, de Launay had aimed a kick at a man in the crowd and, incensed, the man had leapt forward and plunged a knife into him. Soldiers attempting to protect him were pushed back by the crowd and de Launay disappeared beneath a seething mass of bodies. I saw blades arcing up and down, plumes of blood making rainbows and heard one long, piercing scream like that of a wounded animal.

Suddenly there was a cheer and a pike rose above the crowd. On it was the head of de Launay, the flesh at his torn neck ragged and bloody, his eyeballs rolled up in their sockets.

The crowd whooped and hollered and looked upon their prize with happy, blood-spattered faces as it bobbed up and down on the pike, paraded back along the planks and drawbridges, over the mangled, forgotten body of the protestor crushed by the drawbridge and out onto the streets of Paris, where the sight of it would inspire further acts of barbarism.

There and then I knew it was the end for us all. For every nobleman and -woman in France it was the end. Whatever our sympathies, even if we'd talked of the need for change, even if we'd agreed that Marie Antoinette's excesses were disgusting and the king both greedy and inadequate, and even if we'd supported the Third Estate and backed the Assembly, it didn't matter, because from this moment on none of us were safe; we were all collaborators or oppressors in the eyes of the mob and they were in charge now.

I heard more screams as more of the Bastille guards were lynched. Next I caught sight of a prisoner, a frail old man who was being lifted down a set of steps leading up to a prison door. And then, with a rush of mixed emotions—gratitude, love and hate among them—I saw Arno high up on the ramparts. He was with another older man, the pair of them running toward the other side of the fortress.

"Arno," I called to him, but he didn't hear. There was too much noise and he was too far away.

I screamed again, "*Arno*," and those nearby turned to look my way, made suspicious by my cultured tones.

Unable to do anything, I watched as the first man came to the edge of the ramparts and jumped.

The jump was a leap of faith. An Assassin leap of faith. So that was Pierre Bellec. Sure enough, Arno hesitated then did the same. Another Assassin leap of faith.

He was one of them now.

iv

I turned and ran. I needed to get home now, send the staff away. Let them get clear before they were caught up in the trouble.

Crowds were moving away from the Bastille and to the city hall. Already I was hearing that the provost of the merchants of Paris, Jacques de Flesselles, had been slaughtered on the steps of the Hôtel de Ville, that his head had been hacked off and was being paraded through the streets.

My stomach churned. Shops and buildings were burning. I heard the sound of smashing glass, saw people running, laden down with stolen goods. For weeks Paris had been hungry. We on our estates and châteaux had eaten well, of course, but the common man had been driven almost to the brink of starvation, and though the militia on the streets had prevented any full-scale looting, they were powerless to do so now.

Away from Saint-Antoine the crowds had thinned and there were carriages and carts in the road, mostly driven by city folk wanting to escape the trouble. They'd hastily shoved their belongings onto whatever mode of transport they could find and were desperately trying to escape. Most were simply ignored by the crowds, but I caught my breath to see a huge, two-horse-drawn carriage, complete with liveried groom at the front, slowly trying to make its way through the streets, knowing straight away that whoever it was inside was asking for trouble.

This one wasn't inconspicuous. As if the simple sight

of this sumptuous carriage wasn't enough to incense the mob, the groom was shouting at bystanders to clear the road, waving at them with his crop as though trying to clear a cloud of insects, all the while being goaded by his red-faced mistress, who peered from the window of the carriage, wafting a lace handkerchief.

Their arrogance and stupidity was astounding, and even I, whose veins ran with aristocratic blood, took a measure of satisfaction when the crowd paid them no mind at all.

Next, though, the mob turned on them. The situation had been inflamed enough and they began to rock the carriage on its springs.

I considered moving forward to help but knew that to do so would be to sign my own death warrant. Instead, I could only watch as the groom was pulled from his imperious perch and the beating began.

He didn't deserve it. Nobody deserved a beating at the hands of a mob because it was indiscriminate and vicious and driven by a collective desire for blood. Even so, he had done nothing to guard against his fate. The whole of Paris knew that the Bastille had fallen. The *Ancien Regime* had been crumbling but in one morning it had fallen completely. To pretend otherwise was madness. Or, in his case, suicide.

The coachman had run. Meanwhile, members of the crowd had clambered on top of the carriage, ripped open trunks and were tossing clothes from the roof as they delved for valuables. The doors were ripped open and a protesting woman dragged out. The crowd laughed as one of the protestors planted a foot on her behind and sent her sprawling to the ground.

From the carriage came a shout of protest. "What is the meaning of this?" and my heart sank a little further to hear the usual tone of aristocratic indignation in his voice. Was he that stupid? Was he too stupid to realize that he and his kind no longer had the right to such a tone of voice? He and his kind were no longer in charge.

I heard his clothes rip as they tore him from the carriage. His wife was sent on her way, screaming down the street, driven by a series of kicks to the backside, and I wondered how she would fare on her own, in a Paris that was topsy-turvy to the one she had known all her life. I doubted she'd last the day.

As I continued on my way my hopes began to sink. It seemed that looters were pouring out of the houses on both sides of the thoroughfare. In the air was the crackle of musket fire and the sound of breaking glass, triumphant cries from those able to get their way, dismayed screams from the unlucky ones.

I was running by now, sword still drawn and ready to face anyone who stood between me and my villa. My heart hammered in my ears. I prayed that the staff had got clear, that the mob had not yet reached our estate. All I could think of was my trunk. Among other things it contained Haytham Kenway's letters and the necklace given to me by Jennifer Scott. Little trinkets I had collected over the years, things that meant something to me.

Arriving at the gates I saw the butler, Pierre, standing

with a case of his own hugged to his chest, his eyes darting to and fro.

"Thank God, mademoiselle," he said, catching sight of
me, and I looked past him, my gaze traveling along the
courtyard up the steps to the front door of the villa.

What I saw was a courtyard strewn with my belongings. The door of the villa stood open and I could see
devastation within. My house had been ransacked.

"The mob were in and out within minutes," said
Pierre breathlessly. "The boards were up and the locks
were bolted, but they captured the gardener Henri and
threatened to kill him unless we opened the doors. We
had no choice, mademoiselle."

I nodded, thinking only of my trunk in my bedchamber, part of me wanting to dash there straightaway,
another part of me needing to put this right.

"You absolutely did the right thing," I assured him.
"What about your personal effects?"

He hefted the case he held. "All in here."

"Even so, it must have been a frightening experience.
You should go. Right now is not a good time to be asso-
ciated with nobility. Make your way to Versailles and we
shall see to it that you receive recompense."

"And what about you, mademoiselle? Won't you come?"

I glanced toward the villa, feeling steely-hearted to
see my family's belongings discarded like rubbish. I recognized a dress that belonged to my mother. So, they
had been to the upper floors and had rampaged through
the bedchambers.

I pointed with my sword. "I'm going in there," I said.

"No, mademoiselle, I can't allow that," said Pierre. "There are still some of the bandits inside, drunk as lords, sifting through the room for more things to steal."

"That's why I'm going in there. To stop them doing that."

"But they're armed, mademoiselle."

"So am I."

"They're drunk and vicious."

"Well, I'm angry and vicious. And that's better." I looked at him. "Now go."

v

He was never really serious about staying. Pierre was a good man, but his loyalty only went so far. He would have resisted the looters—but not *that* much. Perhaps it had been better that I wasn't home when the raiders arrived. There would have been bloodshed. Maybe the wrong people would have lost their lives.

At the front door I drew my pistol. With my elbow I shoved the door wider and crept into the entrance hall.

It was a mess. Overturned tables. Smashed vases. Unwanted booty lying everywhere. Lying on his front close by was a man snoring in a drunken slumber. Slumped in an opposite corner was another one, this one with his chin resting on his chest, an empty bottle of wine in his hand. The door to the wine cellar was open and I approached it carefully, my sword drawn and my pistol raised. I listened but heard nothing, prodded the nearby drunk with my toe and got a loud snore for my troubles. Drunk, yes. Vicious, no. Same for his friend by the door.

Snoring apart, the ground floor was silent. I walked to a stairway that led below stairs and again, I listened, hearing nothing.

Pierre was right; they must have been in and out within moments, looting the wine cellar and the pantry and no doubt looting the silverware from the plate room. My home just another step along the way.

Now for upstairs. I returned to the entrance hall, then took the stairs, heading straight for my bedchamber and finding it in a similar ransacked state to the rest of the house. They'd found the trunk but evidently decided that whatever was inside was worthless, so had settled merely for spreading the contents around the floor. I sheathed my cutlass, holstered my pistol and dropped to my knees, gathering the papers to me, sorting them and replacing them in the trunk. Thank God the necklace had been in the bottom of the trunk— they'd missed it altogether. Carefully I laid the correspondence on top of the trinkets, smoothing out any creased pages, keeping the letters together. When I'd finished I locked the trunk. It would need to go to the Maison Royale for safekeeping, just as soon as I'd cleared and secured my home.

I was numb, I realized as I pulled myself to my feet and sat on the end of the bed to gather my thoughts. All I could think of was closing the doors, crawling into a corner somewhere, avoiding all human contact. Perhaps that was the real reason I'd sent Pierre away. Because the pillaging of my home gave me another reason to mourn, and I wanted to mourn alone.

I stood and went to the landing, peering over the balcony to the entrance hall below. The only noises were the distant sounds of unrest from the street outside, but the light was dimming now; it had begun to get dark outside and I'd need to light some candles. First, though, to rid myself of my unwanted guests.

The one sleeping by the door seemed to rouse a little as I approached the foot of the stairs.

"If you're awake, then I suggest you leave now," I said, and my voice sounded loud in the entrance hall. "And if you're not awake, then I'm going to kick you in the balls until you are."

He tried to lift his head, blinking as though regaining consciousness and trying to remember where he was and how he'd got here. He had one arm trapped beneath himself and he groaned as he rolled to free it.

And then he got up and closed the door.

Just like that. He got up and closed the door.

vi

It took me a second or so to work out the answer. The question being, how did a man who had been lying drunk on my entrance-hall floor stand up, with not a trace of a sway or swagger, and close the door without so much as a fumble or swipe? How did he do that?

The answer was that he wasn't drunk. He never had

been. And what he had beneath him was a pistol that he raised, with an almost casual air, and pointed at me.

Shit.

I swung around in time to see that the second drunk guy had also miraculously sobered up and was on his feet. He too had a pistol that was pointed at me. I was trapped.

"The Carrolls of London say hello," said the first drunk, the older and more barrel-chested of the two, obviously the boss, and I was hit with the blank fact of the inevitable. We knew the Carrolls would come for us, sooner or later. Be ready, we'd said, and maybe we thought we were ready.

"So what are you waiting for then?" I asked.

"The instructions are that you're to suffer before you die," said the boss, evenly and without real malice. "Plus the bounty is for you, a certain Frederick Weatherall and your lady's maid, Helene. We thought that extracting their whereabouts and causing you to suffer might well be combined, a sort of killing-two-birds-with-one-stone arrangement."

I smiled back at him. "You can cause me as much pain as you like, cause me all the pain in the world, I won't tell you."

From behind me, his friend made an *aw* sound, the kind of sound you make when you see a particularly appealing puppy playing with a ball.

The boss inclined his head. "He's laughing because they all say that. Everyone we've ever tortured says it. It's around the time we introduce the hungry rats that they begin to wonder about the wisdom of their words."

I looked theatrically around me, turned back to him and smiled. "I don't see any hungry rats."

"Well, that's because we haven't started yet. It's a long, old process what we have in mind. Madame Carroll was very specific about that."

"She still angry about May, is she?"

"She did say to remind you about May during the process. That's her daughter, I assumed."

"Was, yes."

"And you killed her?"

"Yes."

"Had it coming, did she?"

"I would say she did, yes. She was about to kill me."

"Self-defense then?"

"You might say that. Does knowing that change your mind at all?"

He grinned. The pistol never wavered. "No. It just tells me you're a tricky one and I'll need to watch you. So why don't we start with the sword and the pistol? Drop them both on the floor if you would."

I did as I was told.

"Now step away from them. Turn, face the banister, put your hands on your head and know that while Mr. Hook here is checking you for concealed weapons I'll be covering him with the pistols. I'd like you to remember that Mr. Hook and I are aware of your capabilities, Miss de la Serre. We haven't made the mistake of underestimating you because you're young and female. Isn't that right, Mr. Hook?"

"That's right, Mr. Harvey," said Hook.

"That's reassuring to know," I said, and with a glance

toward Mr. Hook, I did as I was told, moving to the banister, putting my hands to my head.

The light was dim in the entrance hall, and though my two genial killers would have taken that into account, it was still in my favor.

Something else I had in may favor. I had nothing to lose.

Hook was behind me now. He moved my weapons into the middle of the hall before returning, staying a few feet away. "Remove your jacket," he said.

"I beg your pardon."

"You heard the man," said Mr. Harvey. "Remove your jacket."

"I'll have to take my hands off my head."

"Just take off the jacket."

I unbuttoned it, shrugged it to the floor.

In the room, a dense silence. Mr. Hook's eyes roamed. "Untuck your shirt," said Mr. Harvey.

"You're not going to make me . . . ?"

"Just untuck the shirt, gather it at the waist so we can see the waistband."

I did as I was asked.

"Now remove your boots."

I knelt, straightaway thinking I could use a boot as a weapon. But no. As soon as I attacked Hook, Harvey would plug me with the pistol. I needed a different tactic.

With the boots off I stood in my stockinged feet, shirt untucked for inspection.

"Right," said Harvey. "Turn around. Hands back on your head. Remember what I said about having you covered."

I resumed my position facing the banister as Hook

came up behind me. He knelt, his hands reached to my feet and his hands began a journey from the tips of my toes up my breeches. At the top, they lingered . . .

"Hook . . ." warned Harvey.

"Go to be thorough," said Hook, and I could tell from the direction of his voice that he was looking toward Harvey as he said it, which gave me a chance. A tiny chance, but a chance all the same. And I took it.

I jumped, grabbed a banister strut, and in the same movement gripped Hook's neck between my thighs and twisted—I twisted hard, trying to break his neck at the same time as I used him as human shield, but breaking men's necks in a scissor-hold was never a major part of Mr. Weatherall's training and I didn't have the strength to wrench his neck hard enough. Even so, he was now between me and the pistol, which was my first objective. His face reddened, his hands at my thighs trying to free himself as I squeezed, hoping I might be able to exert enough pressure to make him black out.

No such luck. He writhed and pulled and I clung to the banister strut for dear life, feeling my body lengthen and the banister wood begin to give way as he tried to pull away. Harvey, meanwhile, cursed, holstered his pistol and drew a short sword. Over Hook's shoulder I saw him approaching.

With a shout of effort I increased the pressure of my thighs and jerked upward at the same time. The banister splintered and came off in my hands as I flipped upright and for a second was riding Hook like a girl on her daddy's shoulders, looking down upon a suddenly astonished Harvey, the banister strut held high.

It swept down. I plunged it into Harvey's face.

What bits of the banister strut went into what bits of Harvey's face, I couldn't say for sure, and don't particularly want to know.

All I can tell you is that I aimed for an eye, and though the strut was too thick to penetrate the socket, well, it did the job, because one moment he was advancing on us with his short sword ready to attack, and the next he had an eye full of banister strut and was wheeling off, his hands at his face, filling the final seconds of his life with bloodcurdling screams.

With a twist of my hips I brought myself and Hook crashing to the floor. We landed badly but I pulled myself away, throwing myself bodily toward my sword and pistol in the center of the floor. My pistol was primed and ready, but then so was Hook's. All I could do was dive for my gun and pray I reached it before he recovered enough to reach for his.

I got there, whirled onto my back and held it two hands on him—at exactly the same time as he did the same. For the briefest second we both had the drop on one another.

And then the door opened, a voice said, "Élise," and Hook flinched. So I fired.

There was perhaps half a second during which I thought I'd missed Hook entirely, before blood began gushing from his lips, his head dropped and I realized I'd shot him through the mouth.

vii

"It looks like I arrived just in time," Ruddock said later, after we had carried the bodies of Hook and Harvey out through the rear courtyard and into the street, where we left them among the broken crates and barrels and upturned carts that littered the area. Inside we found a bottle of wine in the pantry, lit candles and sat in the housekeeper's study, where we could keep an eye on the back stairs, just in case anybody returned.

I poured us a glass each, pushed one across the table to him. It went without saying that he looked much healthier than he had the last time we met, since he'd been swinging on the end of a rope back then, but even taking that into account, he had recovered a bearing, too. He looked more self-possessed. For the first time since our meeting in '75, I could imagine Ruddock as an Assassin.

"What did they want, your two friends?" he asked.

"To exact revenge on behalf of a third party."

"I see. You've upset someone, have you?"

"Well, obviously."

"Yes, quite. I suspect you do your fair share of upsetting people, do you? As I say, it was lucky I arrived in time."

"Don't flatter yourself. I had it covered," I said, sipping my wine.

"Well, then I'm very pleased to hear it," he said. "Only it looked to me as though it could have gone either way, and that my entrance gave you the element of surprise you needed in order to gain the advantage."

"Don't push your luck, Ruddock," I said.

The truth was that I was amazed to see him at all. But whether he'd taken my threat to hunt him down seriously or he was a more honorable man than I'd taken him for, the fact was he had come. Not just that but he'd come with what you might call "news."

"You've found something?"

"Indeed I have."

"The identity of the man who hired you to kill me and my mother?"

He looked abashed and cleared his throat. "I was only hired to kill your mother, you know. Not you."

I fought a wave of unreality. Sitting in my family's wrecked villa sharing wine with a man who openly admitted trying to kill my mother; who, if all had gone to plan, would no doubt have left me alone and crying over her body

I poured more wine, choosing to drink, not think, because if I thought then maybe I might wonder how I got to be so numb that I could drink with this man, that I could think of Arno and feel no emotion, that I could cheat death and feel nothing.

Ruddock continued. "And the fact is I don't know exactly who it was who hired me, but I do know with whom he was affiliated."

"And who might that be?"

"Have you ever heard of the King of Beggars?"

"No, I can't say that I have—but that is the person with whom your man is affiliated?"

"As far as I can tell, it was the King of Beggars who wanted your mother dead."

That strange wave of unreality again. Hearing it from the man who was hired to carry out the job.

"The question is, why?" I said, taking a gulp of wine.

"Steady on," he said, and reached to touch a hand to my arm. I stopped, the beaker still held to my lips, glaring at his hand until he took it back, abashed.

"Don't touch me again," I said, "*ever.*"

"I'm sorry," he said. His eyes dropped. "I meant no offense. It's just that—you seem to be drinking too swiftly, that's all."

"Haven't you heard the rumors? I'm a drunk of some repute. And I can quite handle my wine, thank you."

"I only want to help, mademoiselle," he said. "It's the least I can do. By saving my life you've given me a new outlook. I am trying to make something of myself now."

"I'm pleased for you. But if I thought that saving your life meant you were going to lecture me about the wine I was drinking, then I wouldn't have bothered."

He nodded. "Again, I'm sorry."

I took another gulp of wine, just to spite him. "Now tell me what you know about the King of Beggars."

"That he is a difficult man to find. The Assassins have tried to kill him in the past."

I cocked an eyebrow. "You were working for a sworn enemy of the Assassins? I take it you'll be keeping that fact quiet?"

He looked ashamed. "Indeed. Those were different, more desperate days, my lady."

I waved it away. "So the Assassins have tried to kill him. Why would that be?"

"He is cruel. He rules over the beggars in the city

who are forced to pay him a tribute. It is said that if the tribute is insufficient, then the King of Beggars has a man who will amputate their limbs, because the good people of Paris are likely to donate more generously to a beggar deprived in such a way."

I fought a wave of disgust. "For that reason Assassin and Templar would *both* want him dead, surely? He is friend to no one." I curled my lip at him. "Or are you saying that only the good-hearted Assassins wanted him dead, while we black-hearted Templars turned a blind eye?"

With a studied look of sadness he said, "Would I be in any position to make moral judgments, my lady? But the fact is that if the Templars do turn a blind eye to his activities, it is because he is one of them."

"Nonsense. We would have nothing to do with such a disgusting man. My father wouldn't have allowed him in the Order."

Ruddock shrugged and spread his hands. "I'm dreadfully sorry if what I'm telling you comes as a shock, my lady. Perhaps you should not take it as a reflection on your entire Order, rather the rogue elements within it. Speaking as something of a 'rogue element' myself . . ."

Rogue elements, I thought. Rogue elements who plotted against my mother. Were these the same people who killed my father? If so, then I was next.

"You want to rejoin the Assassins, do you?" I said, pouring more wine.

He nodded.

I grinned. "Well, look, I've got to say, and you'll have to pardon my rudeness, but you did attempt to kill me once so I think I'm owed a free shot. But if you've got any hopes of rejoining the Assassins, you need to take care of that smell."

"The smell?"

"Yes, Ruddock, the smell. Your smell. You smelled in London, you smelled in Rouen and you smell now. Perhaps a bath might be in order? Some perfume? Now, is that rude?"

He smiled. "Not at all, mademoiselle. I appreciate your candor."

"Why you'd want to rejoin the Assassins is beyond me anyway."

"Begging your pardon, mademoiselle?"

I leaned forward, squinting at him and waggling the beaker of wine at the same time. "I mean I'd think very carefully about that if I were you."

"What can you mean?"

I waved an airy hand. "I mean that you're out of it. *Well* out of it. Free of all that . . ." I waved a hand again. ". . . *stuff*. Assassin, Templar. Pah. They've got enough dogma for ten thousand churches and twice as much misguided belief. For centuries they've done nothing but squabble, and to what end, eh? Mankind carries on regardless. Look at France. My father and his advisers spent years arguing over the 'best' direction for the country and in the end the Revolution went ahead and happened without them anyway. Ha! Where was Mirabeau when they stormed the Bastille? Still taking votes on tennis courts? The Assassins and Templars are like two ticks fighting over control of the cat, an exercise in hubris and futility."

"But, mademoiselle, whatever the eventual outcome,

we have to believe we have the capacity to effect change for the better."

"Only if we're deluded, Ruddock," I said. "Only if we're deluded."

viii

After I had dismissed Ruddock, I decided I would be ready for them if they came, whoever *they* were: looting revolutionaries, agents of the Carrolls, a traitor from my own Order. I would be ready for them.

Luckily there is more than enough wine in the house to fortify me for the wait.

25 July 1789

It was daylight outside when they came. They stole into the courtyard, the noise of their footfalls reaching me where I waited in the darkened, boarded-up hall, a pistol at hand.

I, who had waited, was ready for them. And as they climbed the steps to the door that I had deliberately left ajar, just as I did every day, I reached for the pistol, pulled back the hammer and raised it.

The door creaked. A shadow fell into a rectangle of sunlight on the floorboards and lengthened across the floor as a figure crossed the threshold and came into the gloom of my home.

"Élise," he said, and dimly I realized that it was a long, long time since I had heard another human voice, and how sweet the sound of it was. And what bliss that the voice should belong to him.

Then I remembered that he could have saved my father, and didn't, and that he had fallen in with the Assassins. And, now I came to think of it, perhaps those two facts were connected? And even if they weren't . . .

I lit a lamp, still holding the gun on him, pleased to see him jump slightly as the flame blazed into life. For some moments the two of us simply regarded one another, faces conveying nothing, until he nodded, indicating the pistol.

"That's some welcome."

I softened a little to see his face. Just a little. "One can't be too careful. Not after what happened."

"Élise, I . . ."

"Haven't you done enough to repay my father's kindness?" I said sharply.

"Élise, please. You can't believe I killed Mr. de la Serre. Your father . . . He wasn't the man you thought he was. Neither of our fathers were."

Secrets. How I hated the taste of them. *Vérités cachées.* All my life.

"I know exactly who my father was, Arno. And I know who yours was. I suppose it was inevitable. You an Assassin, me a Templar."

I saw the realization dawn on his face. "You . . . ?"

"Does that shock you? My father always meant for me to follow in his footsteps. Now all I can do is avenge him."

"I swear to you I had nothing to do with his death."

"Oh, but you did . . ."

"No. No. By my life, I swear I didn't . . ."

To hand was the letter. I held it up now.

"Is that . . ." he said, squinting at it.

"A letter intended for my father the day he was murdered. I found it on the floor of his room. Unopened."

I almost felt sorry for Arno, watching the blood drain from his face as it dawned on him what he'd done. After all, he had loved Father too. Yes, I almost felt sorry for him. *Almost.*

Arno's mouth worked up and down. His eyes were wide and staring.

"I didn't know," he said at last.

"Neither did my father," I said simply.

"How could I have known?"

"Just go," I told him. I hated the sound of the sob in my voice. I hated Arno. "Just go."

And he did. And I barred the door behind him, and then took the back stairs down to the housekeeper's study, where I had made my bed. There I opened a bottle of wine. All the better to help me sleep.

20 AUGUST 1789

i

Shaken awake, I blinked blurry bloodshot eyes and tried to focus on the man who stood above my bed, crutches under his armpits. It looked like Mr. Weatherall but it couldn't be Mr. Weatherall because my protector was in Versailles and he couldn't travel, not with his leg the way it was.

And I wasn't in Versailles, I was in Île Saint-Louis in Paris, waiting—waiting for something.

"Right, you," he was saying. "I see you're already dressed. Time to get out of your cot and come with us."

Behind him stood another, much younger man, who lurked uneasily by the door of the housekeeper's study. For a second I thought it was Jacques from Maison Royale, but no, another younger man.

And it *was* him—it was Mr. Weatherall. I shot upright, clasped him by the neck and pulled him to me, sobbing gratefully into his neck, holding him tight.

"Hold up," he said in a strangulated voice. "You're pulling me off my bloody crutches. Just wait a minute, will you?"

I let him go, pulled myself up to my knees. "But we can't go," I said firmly. "I need to be ready, when they come for me."

"When who comes for you?"

I gripped his collars, looked up at him, into that bearded face creased with concern, and didn't want to ever let him go. "The Carrolls sent killers, Mr. Weatherall. They sent two men to kill me for what I did to May Carroll."

His shoulders slumped onto his crutches as he embraced me. "Oh God, child. When?"

"I killed them," I went on, breathlessly. "I killed them both. I put a wooden stake into one of them." I giggled.

He pulled away, looking deep into my eyes, frowning. "And then celebrated with a couple of hundred bottles of wine, by the looks of things."

I shook my head. "No. Only to help me sleep, to help forget that . . . that I've lost Arno, and my father, and what I did to May Carroll, and the two men who came to kill me." I began to sob now, giggling one second, sobbing the next, dimly realizing that this was not normal behavior but unable to stop myself. "I put a stake into one of them."

"Right," he said, then turned to the other man. "Help her to the carriage, carry her if need be. She's not herself."

"I'm fine," I insisted.

"You will be," he said. "This young man here is Jean Burnel. Like you, he's a newly inducted Templar, though unlike you, he isn't Grand Master and he isn't drunk. However, he is loyal to the de la Serre name, and he can help us. But he can't do that until you're on your feet."

"My trunk," I said. "I need my trunk . . ."

ii

That was—well, the truth is, I don't know how long ago that was, and I'm embarrassed to ask. All I know is that since then I've been confined to bed in the grounds-keeper's lodge, perspiring profusely for the first few days, insisting I was going to be okay, getting angry when I was denied a little wine to drink; then after that sleeping a lot, my head clearing enough to understand that I had been in the grip of some dark fugue—a "disorder of the nerves," Mr. Weatherall had said.

iii

At last I was well enough to get out of bed and dress in clothes that had been freshly laundered by Helene, who was indeed an angel, and had indeed formed a strong relationship with Jacques during my absence. Then Mr. Weatherall and I left the lodge one morning and walked in near silence, both of us knowing we were heading for our usual place, and there we stood in the clearing where the sun fell through the branches like a waterfall, and we bathed in it.

"Thank you," I said, when at last we sat, Mr. Weatherall on the stump, me on the soft floor of the copse, absentmindedly picking at the ground and squinting up at him.

"Thank you for what?" he said. That growly voice I loved so much.

"Thank you for saving me."

"Thank you for saving you from yourself, you mean."

"Saving me from myself is still saving me." I smiled.

"If you say so. I had my own difficulties when your mother died. Hit the bottle myself."

I remembered—I remembered the smell of wine on his breath at the Maison Royale.

"There is a traitor within the Order," I said next.

"We thought as much. Lafrenière's letter . . ."

"But now I am more sure. His name is the King of Beggars."

"The King of Beggars?"

"You know him."

He nodded. "I know *of* him. He isn't a Templar."

"That's what I said. Ruddock insists."

Mr. Weatherall's eyes blazed at the mention of Ruddock's name. "Nonsense. Your father would never have allowed it."

"That was exactly what I said, but perhaps Father didn't know."

"Your father knew everything."

"Can the King of Beggars have been inducted since?"

"After your father's murder?"

I nodded. "Perhaps even *because* of my father's murder—as payment for carrying it out, a reward."

"You've got a point there," said Mr. Weatherall. "You say Ruddock was hired by the King of Beggars to kill your mother, maybe to curry favor with the Crows?"

"That's right."

"Well, he failed, didn't he? Perhaps he's been biding his time since, waiting for another opportunity to prove himself. Kills your father, finally gets what he wants—an initiation."

I considered. "Maybe, but it doesn't make an awful lot of sense to me, and I still can't understand why the Crows would want Mother dead. If anything, her third way was a bridge between the two sets of ideals."

"She was too strong for them, Élise. Too much of a threat."

"A threat to whom, Mr. Weatherall? On whose authority is all this happening?"

We shared a look.

"Listen, Élise," he said, pointing, "you need to consolidate. You need to call a special meeting and assert your leadership, let the bloody Order know whose hand is on the tiller, root out whoever it is who's working against you."

I felt myself go cold. "What you're saying is, that it's not just one individual, it's a faction?"

"Why not? In the last month we've seen the reign of a remote and disinterested king overthrown by revolution."

I frowned at him. "And that's what you think I am, do you? A 'remote and disinterested' ruler?"

"I don't think that. But maybe there are others who do."

I agreed. "You're right. I need to rally my supporters around me. I shall host the gathering at the estate in Versailles, beneath portraits of my mother and father."

He raised his eyebrows. "Yeah, all right. Let's not run before we can walk, eh? We need to make sure they'll turn up first. Young Jean Burnel can begin the task of alerting members."

"I need him to sound out Lafrenière as well. What I've learned gives his letter even more credence."

"Yeah, well, you just watch that one."

"How did you recruit Jean Burnel?"

Mr. Weatherall colored a little. "Well, you know, I just did."

"Mr. Weatherall . . ." I pressed.

He shrugged. "All right, well, look, I have my network, as you know, and I happened to know that young Burnel would have jumped at the chance to work closely with the beautiful Élise de la Serre."

I smiled my way through an uneasy, disloyal feeling. "So he's sweet on me?"

"It's the icing on the cake of his loyalty to your family, I'd say, but yes, I suppose he is."

"I see. Perhaps he would make a good match."

He guffawed. "Oh who are you kidding, child? You love Arno."

"Do I?"

"Well, don't you?"

"There's been a lot of hurt."

"Could be that he feels the same way. After all, you kept some pretty big secrets from him. Could be he's got just as much right as you to be feeling like the injured party." He leaned forward. "You ought to start thinking of what you have in common rather than what separates you. You might find the one outweighs the other."

"I don't know," I said, turning my face away. "I don't really know anymore."

5 OCTOBER 1789

i

I have written before that the fall of the Bastille marked the end of the king's rule and though it did in one sense—in the sense that his power had been questioned, tested and failed that test—in name, at least, if not in reality, he remained in charge.

As news of the Bastille's fall began to travel around France, so too did the rumor that the king's army would wreak a terrible revenge on all revolutionaries. Messengers would arrive in villages with the dreadful news that the army was sweeping across the countryside. They pointed to the sunset and said it was a burning village in the distance. Peasants took up arms against an army that never came. They burned tax offices. They fought with local militia sent to quell the disturbance. These disturbances were called the Rural Uprising.

On the back of it, the Assembly passed a law, a "Declaration of the Rights of Man and of the Citizen," to stop nobles demanding taxes, tithes and labor from peasants. The law was drafted by the Marquis de Lafayette, who had helped draft the American Constitution, and it killed noble privilege and made all men equal in the eyes of the law.

It also made the guillotine the official instrument of death of France.

ii

But still, what to do with the king? Officially he still had power of veto. Mirabeau, who had so nearly formed an alliance with my father, argued that the protests should end, and that the king should still rule as he had done before.

In this aim he would have been joined by my father if my father had lived, and when I wondered whether an alliance of Assassin and Templar might have changed things, I found myself sure it would have done, and realized that was why he had been killed.

There were others—chief among them the doctor and scientist, Jean Paul Marat, who, though not a member of the Assembly, had found a voice—who felt that the king's powers should be stripped away from him altogether, that he should be asked to move from Versailles to Paris and there continue purely in an advisory role.

Marat's view was the most radical. As far as I was concerned that was important because not once did I ever hear talk of the king's being deposed, as I had over-heard growing up.

To put it another way: the most passionate revolution-aries in Paris had never proposed anything quite so radi-cal as that suggested by my father's advisers at our estate in Versailles as far back as 1778.

And realizing that sent a chill down my spine as the day of the Templar council approached. The Crows had been invited, of course, although I was going to have to stop using that nickname for them if I was to be their Grand Master. What I should say is that all of my father's close associates and advisers had been requested to attend, as well as representatives of other high-ranking Templar families.

When they were assembled, I would tell them I was in charge now. I would warn them that treachery would not be tolerated and that if my father's killer came from their ranks, then he (or she) would be exposed and pun-ished.

That was the plan. And in private moments I had imagined its happening that way. I had imagined the meeting taking place at our château in Versailles, just as I'd said to Mr. Weatherall that day at Maison Royale.

In the end, however, we'd decided more neutral terri-tory would be preferable and chosen to meet at the Hôtel de Lauzun on the Île Saint-Louis. It was owned by the Marquis de Pimôdan, a Knight of the Order known to be sympathetic to the de la Serres. So not totally neutral. But *more* neutral at least.

Mr. Weatherall demurred, insisting on the need to

maintain a low profile. I'm grateful for that, the way things turned out.

iii

Something had happened that day. These days it felt as though something happened every day but that day—or to be precise, yesterday and today—something bigger than usual had happened, an event for which the wheels were set in motion when, just a few days ago, King Louis and Marie Antoinette drank too much wine at a party held in honor of the Flanders regiment.

The story goes that the royal couple, while making merry, ceremonially trampled on a revolutionary cockade, while others at the party had turned the cockade around to display its white side, considered an antirevolution stance.

So arrogant. So stupid. In their actions the king and his bride reminded me of the noblewoman and her groom on the day the Bastille fell, still clinging to the old ways. And of course the moderates, the likes of Mirabeau and Lafayette, must have been throwing up their hands in disbelief and frustration at the monarch's thoughtlessness, because the king's actions played right into the hands of the radicals. The people were hungry and the king had thrown a banquet. Worse, he had trampled on a symbol of the Revolution.

Marat called for a march on Versailles and thousands of people, mainly women, made the journey from Paris to Versailles. Guards who fired on the protestors were beheaded, and as ever, their heads raised on pikes.

It was the Marquis de Lafayette who convinced the king to speak to the crowd, and his appearance was followed by an appearance by Marie Antoinette, whose bravery in facing the crowd seemed to assuage much of their fury.

After that the king and queen were taken from Versailles to Paris. Their journey took them nine hours, and once in Paris they were installed at the Tuileries Palace. The event had put the city in as much tumult as it had experienced since the fall of the Bastille three months before and the streets were thronged with troops and sansculottes, men, women and children. They filled the Pont Marie as Jean Burnel and I made our way across the bridge, having abandoned our carriage and decided to reach the Hôtel de Lauzun on foot.

"Are you nervous, Élise?" he asked me, face shining with excitement and pride.

"I would ask that you address me as Grand Master, please," I told him.

"I'm sorry."

"And no, I'm not nervous. Leading the Order is my birthright. Those members of the Order in attendance will find in me a renewed passion for leadership. I may be young, I may be a woman, but I intend to be the Grand Master the Order deserves."

I felt him swell with pride on my behalf and I chewed my lip, which was something I did when I was nervous, which I was.

Despite what I'd said to Jean, who was way too much

like an obedient and lovelorn puppy dog for his own good, I was, as Mr. Weatherall would say, "Shaking like a shitting dog."

"I wish I could be there," Mr. Weatherall had said although we'd agreed it best he remained behind. His speech had begun as I presented myself for inspection.

"Whatever you do, don't expect miracles," he'd said. "If you get the advisers and, say, five or six other members of the Order, that will be enough to swing the Order in your direction. And don't forget you've left it a long time to go in there and start demanding your birthright. By all means use the shock of your father's death as a reason for your tardiness but don't expect it to be the medicine that cures all ills. You owe the Order an apology, so you best start off contrite, and don't forget you'll need to fight your corner. You'll be treated with respect but you're young, you're a woman and you've been neglectful. Calls to take you to trial won't be taken seriously but then they won't have been ridiculed either."

I looked at him with wide eyes. "Taken to trial?"

"No. Didn't I just say they wouldn't be taken seriously?"

"Yes, but then after that you said . . ."

"I know what I said after that," he said testily, "and what you have to remember is that for a period of several months you've left the Order without firm leadership— during a time of revolution to boot. And de la Serre or not. Birthright or not. That fact won't be playing well. All you can do is hope."

I was ready to leave.

"Right, are you clear on everything?" he said, leaning

on his crutches to remove fluff from the shoulder of my jacket. I checked my sword and pistol, then shrugged an overcoat on top, hiding my weapons and Templar garb, then pulled my hair back and added a tricorn.

"I think so." I smiled through a deep, nervous breath. "I need to be contrite, not overconfident, grateful for whoever shows their support." I stopped. "How many have pledged their attendance?"

"Young Burnel has had twelve 'ayes' including our friends the Crows. It's the first time I've known a Grand Master to call a meeting in such a fashion so you can depend on there being a few there out of curiosity alone, but then that could work to your advantage."

I stood on tiptoes to give him a kiss, then stepped out into the night, darting across to where the carriage waited, with Jean in the driving seat. Mr. Weatherall had been right about Jean. Yes, he was definitely smitten but he was loyal and he'd worked tirelessly to rally support for the summit. His aim, of course, was to win a place in my favor, become one of my advisers, but that hardly made him alone. I thought of the Crows and remembered their smiles and whispers when I had returned for my induction, the suspicion that now swirled around them, the presence of this King of Beggars.

"Élise . . ." Mr. Weatherall had called from the door.

I turned. Impatiently he motioned me back and I called to Jean to wait, ran back. "Yes?"

He was serious. "Look at me, child, look into these eyes, and remember that you're worthy of this. You're the best warrior I've ever trained. You've got the brains and charm of your mother and father combined. You can do this. You can lead the Order."

For that he got another kiss before I darted off again.

Glancing back at the house to give a final wave I saw Helene and Jacques framed in a window, and at the door of the carriage, I turned, swept my hat off my head and gave them a theatrical bow.

I felt good. Nervous but good. It was time to set things right.

iv

And now Jean Burnel and I made our way through crowds on the Pont Marie and came onto the Île Saint-Louis. I thought of my family's villa, deserted and neglected here on the isle, but put it out of my mind. As we walked, Jean stayed by my side, his hand beneath his coat ready to draw his sword if we were accosted. Meanwhile I kept a hopeful eye out, hoping to see other Knights of the Order in the crowds, also making their way toward the Lauzun.

It seems funny to relate now—and by that I mean funny in an ironic sense—but as we approached the venue there was a part of me that dared to hope for a grand turnout—a huge, historical show of support for the de la Serre name. And though it now seems fanciful to have thought it, especially with the benefit of hindsight, at the time, well . . . why not? My father was a beloved leader. The de la Serres a respected family dynasty. Perhaps an

Order in need of leadership would turn out for me, to honor the legacy of my father's name.

Like everywhere else on the isle the street outside the Lauzun was busy. A large wooden door with a smaller wicket entrance was inset into a high wall overgrown with ivy that surrounded a courtyard. I looked up and down the thoroughfare, seeing dozens and dozens of people, but none who were dressed as we were, on their way here.

Jean looked at me. He'd been quiet since I chastised him and I felt bad about that now, especially when I saw his own nerves and knew they were nerves for me.

"Are you ready, Grand Master?" he said.

"I am, thank you, Jean," I replied.

"Then, please, allow me to knock."

The door was opened by a manservant, elegantly attired in a waistcoat and white gloves. The sight of him, with his embroidered ceremonial sash at his waist, gave me a lift. I was at the right place, at least, and they were ready for me.

Bowing his head, he stepped aside to allow us into the courtyard. There I looked around, seeing boarded-up windows and balconies around a neglected central space littered with dried leaves, overturned plant pots and a number of splintered crates.

In different times a fountain might have been delicately tinkling and the singing of birds providing a lovely end to another civilized day at the Hôtel de Lauzun, but not anymore.

Now there was just Jean and me, the manservant and the Marquis de Pimôdan, who had been standing to one side, attired in his robes and with his hands clasped in front of him, and who now came forward to greet us.

"Pimôdan," I said, warmly. We embraced. I kissed his cheeks and, still encouraged by the sight of our host and his manservant in their Templar garb, allowed myself to believe that my premeeting flutters were for nothing. That everything was going to be all right, even that the apparent quiet was nothing more than a custom of the Order.

But then, as Pimôdan said, "It is an honor, Grand Master," his words sounded hollow and he turned quickly away to lead us across the courtyard and my premeeting flutters returned tenfold.

I glanced at Jean, who pulled a face, unnerved by the situation.

"Are the others assembled, Pimôdan?" I asked, as we made our way to a set of double doors leading into the main building. The manservant opened them and ushered us in.

"The room is ready for you, Grand Master," Pimôdan replied evasively as we stepped over the threshold into a darkened dining room with boarded-up windows and sheets over the furniture.

The manservant closed the double doors, then waited there, allowing Pimôdan to lead us across the floor to a thick, almost ornamental door in the far wall.

"Yes, but which members are in attendance?" I asked. The words were croaky. My throat was dry. He said nothing in response, gripped a large iron ring on the door and turned it. The *chunk* sound it made was like a pistol shot in the room.

"Monsieur Pimôdan . . ." I prompted.

The door opened out onto stone steps leading down, the way lit by flickering torches bolted to the walls. Orange flame danced on rough stone walls.

"Come," said Pimôdan, still ignoring me. He was clutching something, I realized. A crucifix.

And that was it. I'd had enough.

"Stop," I commanded.

Pimôdan was taking another step as though he hadn't heard me, but I whipped back my overcoat, drew my sword and put the point of it to the back his neck. And that stopped him. Behind me Jean Burnel drew his sword.

"Who's down there, Pimôdan?" I demanded to know. "Friend or foe?"

Silence.

"Don't test me, Pimôdan," I growled, prodding his neck. "If I'm mistaken, then I'll offer you my most humble apologies, but until that time I have a feeling that there's something very wrong here, and I want to know why."

Pimôdan's shoulders heaved as he sighed, as though about to throw off the yoke of a huge secret. "It's because there's nobody here, mademoiselle."

I went cold, heard a strange whining noise in my ears as I struggled to understand. "What? *Nobody?*"

"Nobody."

I half turned to Jean Burnel, who stared, unable to believe his own ears. "What about the Marquis de Kilmister?" I said. "Jean-Jacques Calvert and his father? The Marquis de Simonon?"

Pimôdan inclined his neck away from my blade to shake his head slowly.

"Pimôdan?" I insisted, nudging it back. *"Where are my supporters?"*

He spread his hands. "All I know is that there was an attack by sansculottes at the Calvert château this morning," he said. "Both Jean-Jacques and his father perished in a fire. Of the others, I know nothing."

My blood ran cold. To Burnel I said, "A purge. This is a purge." Then to Pimôdan, "And below? Are my killers waiting for me below?"

Now he turned a little in the stairwell. "No, mademoiselle," he said, "there is nothing down there save for some documents in need of your attention."

But as he said it, staring back up at me with wide, craven eyes, he nodded. And it was a crumb of comfort, I suppose, that a last vestige of loyalty remained in this cowardly man, that at least he wasn't going to allow me to descend the steps into a pit of my killers.

I whirled around, bundled Jean Burnel back up the steps, then slammed the door behind us and threw the bolt. The manservant remained by the double doors in the dining room, a look on his face as though he were bemused by the sudden turn of events. As Jean and I rushed across the floor, I drew my pistol and aimed it at the manservant, wishing I could shoot the supercilious look off his face but settling instead for gesturing for him to open the doors.

He did, and we stepped out of the hotel and into the dark courtyard beyond.

The doors closed behind us. Call it a sixth sense but I knew something was wrong immediately, and in the next instant I felt something around my neck.

They were catgut ligatures, dropped with precision

from a balcony above. In my case, not perfect precision: caught by the collar of my coat, the noose didn't tighten straightaway, giving me precious seconds to react, while by my side Jean Burnel's assassin had achieved a flawless drop and in a heartbeat the ligature was cutting into the flesh of his neck.

In his panic, Burnel dropped his sword. His hands scrabbled for the tightening noose around his neck. A snorting noise escaped his nostrils as his face began to color and his eyes boggled. As he was lifted by the neck, his body stretched and the tips of his boots scrabbled at the ground.

I swung for Burnel's ligature with my sword, but at the same time my own attacker pulled sharply to the side and I was yanked away from him, helpless to see his tongue protrude from his mouth, his eyeballs seeming to bulge impossibly as he was hoisted even higher, out of reach. Pulling back on my own ligature, I looked up, saw dark shadows on the balcony above, operating us like two puppeteers.

But I was lucky—*lucky, lucky Élise*—because although the breath was choked out of me my collar was still wedged and it gave me presence of mind enough to swing again with my sword, only this time not at Jean Burnel's ligature—for he was out of reach now, his feet kicking in their death throes—but at my own.

I severed it and crumpled to the ground on my hands and knees, gasping for breath but rolling onto my back at the same time, reaching for my pistol and thumbing back the hammer, aiming it two-handed at the balcony above and firing.

The shot echoed around the courtyard and had an

instant effect, Jean Burnel's body dropping like a sack to the ground as his ligature was released, his face a hideous death mask, and the two figures on the balcony disappearing from view, the attack over—for the time being.

From inside the building I heard shouts and the sound of running feet. Through the glass of the double doors I swear I could see the manservant, standing well back in the shadows, watching me, as I scrambled to my feet, wondering how many there were, counting the two balcony killers, maybe another two or three killers from the cellar. To my left another door burst open and two thugs in the clothes of sansculottes burst out.

Oh. So two more elsewhere in the house as well.

There was the sound of a shot and a pistol ball split the air by the side of my head. There was no time to reload my own gun. No time to do anything but run.

I ran for where a bench was inset into a sidewall, shaded by a courtyard tree. I bounded, hit the bench, and with my leading foot propelled myself upward, finding a low branch and thumping messily against the trunk.

From behind me came a shout and a second pistol shot, and I hugged the tree trunk as the ball embedded itself into the wood between two splayed fingers. *Lucky, Élise, very lucky.* I started to climb. Hands scrabbled at my boot but I kicked out, blindly heading upward in the hope of reaching the top of the wall.

I reached it and stepped across from the tree to the top of the wall. But when I looked down I found myself staring into the grinning faces of two men who'd used the gate and were waiting for me. Grinning up at me with huge "got you" smiles.

They were thinking that they were below me, and that there were other men coming up behind me, and that I was trapped. They were thinking it was all over.

So I did what they least expected. I jumped on them.

I'm not big but I was wearing devilish boots and wielding a sword, and I had the element of surprise on my side. I speared one of them on the way down, impaling him through the face and then, without retrieving my blade, pivoted and delivered a high kick to the throat of the second man. He dropped to his knees with his hands at his neck, already turning purple. I retrieved my sword from the face of the first man—and plunged it into his chest.

There was more shouting from behind. Over my head, faces had appeared at the top of the wall. I took to my heels, pushing my way into the crowd. Behind me were two pursuers doing the same, and I pushed farther on, ignoring the curses of people I shoved, just surging forward. At the bridge I stayed by the low wall.

And then I heard the shout. "A traitor. A traitor to the Revolution. Don't let the redheaded woman escape."

And again, the shout taken up by another of my pursuers. "Get her! Get the redheaded bint."

Another: "A traitor to the Revolution!"

"She spits on the tricolor."

It took a minute or so for the message to spread through the crowd but gradually I saw heads turn to me, people noticing my finer clothes for the first time, their gaze moving pointedly to my hair. My *red* hair.

"*You*," said a man, "it's you." And he shouted, "We have her! We have the traitor!"

Below me on the river was a barge crawling just below the bridge, goods covered with sacking on the foredeck. What goods they were, I didn't know, and could only pray that they were the "soft" kind that might break your fall if you were jumping from a bridge.

In the end, it didn't matter whether they were soft or not. Just as I jumped the enraged citizen made a grab for me, and my jump turned into an evasive move that sent me off course. Flailing, I hit the barge, but the wrong side, the outside, smashing into the hull with a force that drove the breath out of me.

Dimly I realized that the cracking sound I'd heard was my ribs breaking as I slapped into the inky black River Seine.

V

I made it back of course. Once I'd got to the bank, heaved myself out of the river and used the confusion of the king's journey to Paris to "liberate" a horse, I took the debris-littered road in the opposite direction of the crowds, out of Paris and to Versailles, and as I rode I tried to keep as still as possible, mindful of my broken ribs.

My clothes were soaked and my teeth were chattering by the time I got back and slid out of the saddle and onto the doorstep of the groundskeeper's lodge, but whatever the poor shape I was in, all I could think was that I'd let him down. I'd let my father down.

12 SEPTEMBER 1794

Reading, I find myself catching my breath, not just in admiration for her audacity and courage, but because when I follow her journey I realize that I am seeing a mirror image of my own. Mr. Weatherall was right (and thank you, thank you, Mr. Weatherall, for helping her to see that) because we were so much the same, Élise and I.

The difference was, of course, that she got there first. It was Élise who first trained in the ways of her . . . ah, I was going to write her "chosen" Order, but of course there was nothing "chosen" about it, not for Élise. She was born to be a Templar. Groomed for leadership, and if at first she had embraced her destiny, as she surely did, because it gave her a way to escape the life of gossip and fan-wafting she saw at Versailles, then she had come to distrust it as well; she had grown to question the eternal conflict of Assassin and Templar; she had come to ask herself if it was all worth it—if all this killing had achieved anything, or ever would.

As she knew, the man she'd seen me with was Bellec, and I suppose you'd have to say that I fell in with him; that he turned my head, made me aware of certain gifts that were within my grasp. In other words, it was Bellec who made me an Assassin. It was he who had mentored me through my induction into the Assassins, he who set me on a course of hunting down my surrogate father's killer.

Ah yes, Élise. You were not the only one who mourned François de la Serre. You were not the only one who investigated his death. And in that enterprise I had certain advantages: the knowledge of my Order, the "gifts" I had been able to develop under Bellec's tuition, and the fact that I had been there the night François de la Serre had died.

Perhaps I should have waited and allowed you the honor. Perhaps I was as impulsive as you are. Perhaps.

25 APRIL 1790

i

It is six months since I last wrote in my journal. Six months since I took a dive off the Pont Marie on a freezing October night.

For a while of, course, I was bedbound, suffering a fever that came on a few days after my dunk in the Seine and trying to mend a broken rib at the same time. My poor, weakened body was having difficulty doing both those things simultaneously, and for a while, according to Helene anyway, it was a close thing.

I'd had to take her word for it. I'd been absent in mind if not in body, feverish and hallucinating, gabbling strange things in the night, crying out, my emaciated body drenched in freezing sweat.

My memory of that time was waking up one morning and seeing their concerned faces above my bed: Helene,

Jacques and Mr. Weatherall, with Helene saying, "The fever's broken," and a look of relief that passed across them like a wave.

ii

It was some days later when Mr. Weatherall came to my bedchamber and perched himself on the end of my bed. We tended not to stand on ceremony at the lodge. It was one of the reasons I liked it. It made the fact that I *had* to be there, hiding from my enemies, that bit more bearable.

For some time he just sat, and we were silent, the way old friends can be, when silence is not to be feared. From outside drifted the sounds of Helene and Jacques teasing one another, footsteps scampering past the window, Helene laughing and breathless, and we caught each other's eye and shared a knowing smile before Mr. Weatherall's chin dropped back to his chest and he continued picking at his beard, something he had a habit of doing these days.

And then, after a while I said, "What would my father have done, Mr. Weatherall?"

Unexpectedly, he chuckled. "He would have called for help from overseas, child. From England, probably. Tell me, what is the state of your relationship with the English Templars?"

I shot him a withering look. "What else?"

"Well, he would have tried to rally support. And before you say anything, yes, what else do you think I've been doing while you've been in here screaming the place up and sweating for France? I've been trying to rally support."

"And?"

He sighed. "Not much to report. My network is slowly falling silent."

I hugged my knees and felt a twinge of pain from my ribs, still not fully healed. "What do you mean, 'slowly falling silent'?"

"I mean that after months of sending letters and receiving evasive replies, no one wants to know, do they? Nobody will speak to me—*to us*—not even in secret. They say there's a new Grand Master now; that the de la Serre era has come to an end. My correspondents no longer sign their letters. They implore me to burn them once I've read them. Whoever this new leader is, he's got them scared."

"'The de la Serre era has come to an end.' That's what they say?"

"That's what they say, child, yeah, that's about the size of it."

I gave a short, dry laugh. "You know, Mr. Weatherall, I don't know whether to be offended or grateful when people underestimate me. The de la Serre era has not *come to an end*. Tell them that. Tell them that the de la Serre era never comes to an end while I still have breath in my lungs. These conspirators think they're going to get away with it—with killing my father, deposing my family from the Order. *Really?* Then they deserve to die just for their stupidity."

He bristled. "You know what that is? That's revenge talk."

I shrugged. "You call it revenge. I'll call it fighting back. Either way it's not sitting here—as you would say—'on my arse,' hiding out in the grounds of a girls' school, creeping around and hoping that someone will write to our secret drop. I intend to fight back, Mr. Weatherall. Tell that to your contacts."

But Mr. Weatherall could be persuasive. Plus my skills were rusty, my strength depleted—my ribs still hurt for one thing—so I had stayed on at the lodge while he went about his business, writing his letters, trying to rally support for my cause beneath the cloak of subterfuge.

News reaches me that the last of the staff have left the château in Versailles and I yearn to go there, but of course cannot, because it isn't safe, and so I must leave my beloved family home at the mercy of looters.

But I promised Mr. Weatherall I would be patient so I'm being patient. For now.

16 NOVEMBER 1790

Seven months of letter writing and we know this much: my allies and friends are now *former* allies and friends.

The purge is complete. Some turned, some were bribed and the others, the ones who were more resilient and tried to pledge their support, men like Monsieur Le Fanu, well, they were dealt with in other ways. One morning Monsieur Le Fanu was carried feetfirst and naked from a Parisian whorehouse, then left in the street to be gawked at by passersby, and for that dishonor, he was posthumously stripped of his Order status, and his wife and children, who under normal circumstances would have benefited from financial help, left in penury.

Now, Monsieur Le Fanu was a family man, as devoted to his wife, Claire, as a man ever was. Not only would he never have visited a whorehouse, but I doubt he would have known what to do when he got there. Never did a man deserve a fate less than the one bestowed upon Monsieur Le Fanu.

And that was what his loyalty to the name of de la Serre had cost him. It had cost him everything: his life, his reputation and honor, everything.

I knew that any member of the Order who hadn't come into line was going to do so after that, when they knew the potential ignominy of their end. And sure enough, they had.

"I want the wife and children of Monsieur Le Fanu taken care of," I'd said to Mr. Weatherall.

"Madame Le Fanu took her own life and that of the children," Mr. Weatherall told me. "She couldn't live with the disgrace."

I closed my eyes, breathing in and out, trying to control a rage that threatened to boil over. More lives to add to the list.

"Who is he, Mr. Weatherall?" I asked. "Who is this man doing all this?"

"We'll find out, darlin'." He sighed. "Don't you worry about that."

But nothing was done. No doubt my enemies thought that their takeover was complete, that I was no longer dangerous. They were wrong about that.

12 January 1791

My sword skills are back and sharper than ever before, my marksmanship at its most accurate, and I warned Mr. Weatherall that it would be soon—that I would be leaving soon—because I was achieving nothing here; that each day I spent in hiding was a day of the fight-back wasted, and he reacted by trying to persuade me to stay. There was always a reply he was waiting for. One more avenue to explore.

And when that didn't work he reacted by threatening me. Just try leaving and I'd know what it felt like to be resoundingly thrashed with the sweaty armpit end of a crutch. Just try it.

I remain (im)patient.

26 MARCH 1791

i

This morning Mr. Weatherall and Jacques arrived home from the drop at Châteaufort hours after they were due— so late that I'd begun to worry.

For a while we'd been talking about moving the drop. Sooner or later someone would come. According to Mr. Weatherall anyway. The issue of whether to move the drop had become another weapon in the war the two of us constantly waged, the push and pull of should I stay (him: yes) or should I go (me: yes). I was strong now, I was back to full fitness and in private moments I'd seethe with the frustration of inaction; I'd picture my faceless enemies gloating with victory and raising ironic toasts in my name.

"This is the old Élise," Mr. Weatherall had warned. "By which I mean the young Élise. The one who comes sailing over to London and ignites a feud we've yet to live down."

He was right, of course; I wanted to be an older, cooler Élise, a worthy leader. My father never rushed into anything.

But on the other hand, my thoughts would return to the question of *doing something*. After all, where a wiser head might have waited to finish her education like a proper little poppet, the young Élise had sprung into action, taken a carriage to Calais and her life had begun. The fact was that sitting here doing nothing made me feel agitated and angry. It made me feel even *more* angry. And I was already a lot angry.

In the end my hand has been forced by what happened this morning, when Mr. Weatherall had aroused my anxiety by arriving home late from his visit to the drop. I dashed out to the yard to greet him as Jacques drew the cart around.

"What happened to you?" I asked, helping him down.

"Tell you something"—he frowned—"it's bloody lucky that young lad hates the stink of cheese." He said it with an incline of the head toward Jacques.

"Whatever do you mean?"

"Because it was while he was waiting for me outside the fromagerie that something odd happened. Or should I say, he saw something very odd. A young boy hanging around."

We were halfway back to the lodge, where I planned to make Mr. Weatherall a coffee and let him tell me all about it, but now I stopped.

"I beg your pardon?"

"I'm telling you, a little rapscallion, just hanging around."

This rapscallion, it turned out, had indeed been hanging around. Fancy that, I'd said, a young rapscallion hanging around a town square, but Mr. Weatherall had admonished me with a peevish growl.

"Not just *any* rapscallion, but an especially nosy one. He approached young Jacques when Jacques was waiting outside. This boy's asking him questions, questions like, had he seen a man on crutches enter the fromagerie that morning? Jacques is a good lad and he told the boy he hadn't seen a man on crutches at all that day but that he'd keep an eye for him.

"Great, says the rascal, I'll be around, won't be far. Might even be a little coin in it for you if you tell me something useful. This little squirt's no older than ten, Jacques reckons. Where do you suppose he's getting the kind of money he needs to pay an informant?"

I shrugged.

"From whoever is paying him, that's who. The kid's working for the same Templars who plotted against us, or my name's not Freddie Weatherall. They want to find the drop, Élise. They're looking for you, and if they think they've located the drop, they'll be monitoring it from now on."

"Did you speak to the boy?"

"Absolutely not. What do you think I am, some kind of bloody idiot? Soon as Jacques came into the shop and told me what happened we left by the back entrance and took the long route home, making sure we weren't followed."

"And were you?"

He shook his head. "But it's only a matter of time."

"How do you know?" I argued. "There are so many 'ifs.' *If* the rapscallion was working for the Templars and not just looking to rob you or beg for money or just kick one of your crutches away for the fun of it; *if* he's seen enough activity to alert their suspicions; *if* they decide the drop is ours."

"I think they have," he said quietly.

"How can you know?"

"Because of this." He frowned, reached into his jacket and passed me the letter.

ii

Mademoiselle Grand Master,

I remain loyal to you and your father. We must meet in order that I can tell you the truth about the matter of your father's death and events since. Write to me at once.

Lafrenière

My heart thudded. "I must respond," I said quickly.

He shook his head in exasperation. "You'll do no such bloody thing," he snapped. "It's a trap. It's a way of drawing us out. They'll be waiting for us to reply to this. If this is a letter from Lafrenière, then pigs might fly. It's a trap. And if we reply we'll be walking right into it."

"If we reply from here, yes."

He shook his head. "You ain't leaving."

"I have to know," I said, waving the letter.

He scratched his head, trying to think. "You're not going anywhere by yourself."

I gave a short laugh. "Well, who else can accompany me? You?"

And then stopped myself as his head dropped.

"Oh God," I said, quietly. "Oh God, I'm so sorry, Mr. Weatherall. I didn't mean . . ."

He was shaking his head sadly. "No, no, you're right, darlin', you're right. I'm a protector who can't protect."

I came to him, knelt by his chair and put my arms around him.

There was a long pause, silence in the front room of the lodge save for Mr. Weatherall's occasional snuffles.

"I don't want you to go," he said at last.

"I have to," I replied.

"You can't fight them, Élise," he said, pushing tears from his eyes with angry palms. "They're too strong now, too powerful. You can't go up against them alone."

I held him. "I can't keep running either. You know as well as I do that if they've found our drop, then they'll reason we're in the vicinity. They'll draw a circle on a map with the drop at its center and begin to search. And the Maison Royale, where Élise de la Serre finished her education, is as good a place as any to start the search.

"You know as well as I do that we'll have to leave here, you and I. We have to go somewhere else, where we'll make fruitless attempts to rally support and wait for our drop to be discovered before we have to move again. Leaving is not a choice."

He shook his head. "No, Élise. I can think of something. So just you listen here, I'm your adviser, and I advise you that you stay here while we formulate a response to this latest unwelcome development. How does that sound? Does that sound enough like an adviser to advise the idea right out of your head?"

I hated the taste of the lie on my lips when I promised to stay. I wonder if he knew that while the household slept I would creep away.

Indeed, as soon as the ink is dry on this entry, I'll put the journal into my satchel and creep out. It will break his heart. For that I'm so sorry, Mr. Weatherall.

27 MARCH 1791

i

As I crossed silently to the front door on my way out of the lodge, a ghost flitted across the hallway.

I cleared my throat and the ghost stopped, turned and put a hand to her mouth. It was Helene, caught in the act of returning from Jacques's room to her own.

"I'm sorry I startled you," I whispered.

"Oh, mademoiselle."

"Is all that creeping around really necessary?"

She colored. "I couldn't have Mr. Weatherall knowing."

I opened my mouth to argue but stopped, turned to the door instead. "Well, good-bye for a while."

"Where are you going, mademoiselle?"

"Paris. There's something I have to do."

"And you were leaving in the middle of the night, without saying good-bye?"

"I have to, it's . . . Mr. Weatherall. He doesn't want . . ."

She scampered across the boards on her tiptoes, came to me and drew my face to hers, kissing me hard on both cheeks. "Please be careful, Élise. Please come back to us."

It's funny. I embark on a journey supposedly to avenge my family but really the lodge is my family. For a second I considered staying. Wasn't it better to live in exile with those I loved than die in pursuit of revenge?

But no. There was a ball of hate in my gut and I needed to get rid of it.

"I will," I told Helene. "Thank you, Helene. You know . . . You know I think so much of you."

"I do." She smiled, and I turned and left.

ii

What I felt as I rode away from the lodge wasn't happiness, exactly. It was the exhilaration of action and sense of purpose as I spurred Scratch on to Châteaufort.

First, I had a job to do, and arriving in the early hours, I found board and a tavern that was still open, and in there I told anyone who was curious enough to ask that my name was Élise de la Serre, and that I had been living in Versailles but was now bound for Paris.

The next morning I left, and came to Paris, crossing the Pont Marie to the Île Saint-Louis and going . . . home? Sort of. My villa, at least.

What would it look like? I couldn't even recall whether I'd been a diligent caretaker the last time I was there. Arriving, I had my answer. No, I hadn't been a diligent caretaker, just a thirsty one, judging by the many wine bottles lying about the place. I suppressed a shiver, thinking of the dark hours I had spent in this house.

I left the remnants of the past as they were. Next I wrote to Monsieur Lafrenière, a letter in which I asked him to meet at L'Hôtel Voysin in two days' time. When I'd hand-delivered it to the address he'd given me, I returned to the Île Saint-Louis, where I set trip wires, just in case they came to look for me here, and settled in the housekeeper's study to wait.

29 MARCH 1791

i

I made my way to L'Hôtel Voysin in Le Marais, where I had asked to meet Lafrenière. Who would turn up? That was the question. Lafrenière the friend, Lafrenière the traitor? Or somebody else altogether? And if this was a trap, had I walked into it? Or had I done the only possible thing I could if I wanted to avoid a lifetime of hiding from men who wanted me dead?

The courtyard of the L'Hôtel Voysin was dusky gray. The building rose on every side and had once been grand, in looks as aristocratic as those who frequented it, but just as the aristocrats had been laid low by the Revolution—and each day were stripped of further entitlements by the Assembly—so Voysin, too, seemed cowed by the events of the last two years: the windows in which lights would have burned were blacked out, some broken and boarded up. The grounds, which once would have been clipped and tended to by cap-doffing gardeners, had been deserted and left to go to ruin so that ivy climbed the walls unchecked, tendrils of it feeling their way toward the blank first-floor windows. Meanwhile, weeds grew between the cobbles and flagstones of the deserted courtyard, which as I entered echoed to the sound of my boots on stone.

I fought a sense of disquiet, seeing all of those darkened windows looking down on this once-bustling courtyard. Any one of them could have provided a hiding place for an assailant.

"Hello?" I called. "Hello, Monsieur Lafrenière?"

I held my breath, thinking, *This isn't right. This isn't right at all.* Thinking that I was an idiot to arrange to meet here, and that wondering if it might be a trap was hardly the same as being prepared to meet one.

Mr. Weatherall was right. Of course he was, and I'd known it all along myself.

It *was* a trap.

From behind me I heard a sound and turned to see a man emerge from the shadows.

I squinted, flexing my fingers, ready.

"Who are you?" I called.

He darted forward, and I realized it wasn't Lafrenière at the same time as I saw moonlight flash along a blade he brought from his waist.

And maybe I would have cleared my sheath in time. After all, I was fast.

And maybe I wouldn't have cleared my sheath in time. After all, he was fast too.

Either way, it didn't matter. The question was decided by the blade of a third party, a figure who seemingly came from nowhere. I saw what I knew was a hidden blade cut across the darkness and my would-be killer fell, and standing behind him was Arno.

For a second, I could only stand and gawk, because this wasn't Arno as I'd ever seen him before. Not only was he wearing Assassins' robes and a hidden blade, but the boy was gone. In his place, a man.

It took me a moment to recover, and then, just as it struck me that they would never send a lone killer for me, that there would be others, I saw the man looming behind Arno, and all those months of target practice at the lodge counted as I snapped off a shot over his shoulder, gave the killer a third eye and sent him crashing dead to the stone of the courtyard.

ii

Reloading, I said, "What's going on? Where is Monsieur Lafrenière?"

"He's dead," said Arno.

He said it in a tone of voice I didn't quite care for, as though there was a lot more to that story than he was letting on, and I looked sharply at him. *"What?"*

But before Arno could answer there was the sound of a ricochet and a musket ball slapped into a wall nearby, showering us in stone chips. There were snipers in the windows above us.

Arno reached for me, and the part of me that still hated him wanted to wrench away from him, tell him I could manage by myself, thanks, but the words of Mr. Weatherall flashed through my head, the knowledge that whatever else, Arno was here for me, which after all was all that really mattered. And I let him take me.

"I'll explain later," he was calling. "Go!"

And as another volley of musket fire rained down upon us from the windows above, we made a dash for the courtyard gates and hurried out into the grounds.

Ahead of us was the maze, overgrown and untended, but still very much a maze. Arno's robes spread as he ran, his hood dropped back and I gazed upon handsome features, transported back to happier times, before the secrets had threatened to overwhelm us.

"Do you remember that summer at Versailles when we were ten?" I called as we ran.

"I remember getting lost in that damn hedge maze for six hours while you ate my share of the dessert," he replied.

"Then you'd better keep up this time," I called, and despite everything I couldn't help but hear the note of joy in my voice. Only Arno could do this to me. Only Arno could bring this light into my life. And I think if ever there was a moment when I truly "forgave" him—in my heart and in my head—then that was it.

iii

By now we had reached the middle of the maze. Our prize was another killer waiting for us. He readied himself, looking nervously from one to another, and I felt happy for him that he would go to the grave thinking that I had joined with the Assassins. He could meet his maker floating on a cloud of righteousness. In my tale he was the bad man. In his, he was the hero.

I stepped back and let Arno face the duel, taking the opportunity to admire his swordplay. All those years I was learning my own skills, his greatest discipline was our governor's algebra tests. Of the two I was by far the more experienced swordsman.

But he had caught up; he'd caught up fast.

He saw my impressed look and flicked me a smile that would have melted my heart if it needed melting.

We made our way out of the maze and onto the Boulevard, which teemed with people. One thing I'd noticed about the immediate aftermath of the Revolution was that people celebrated more than ever; they lived each day like it was their last.

So it was that the street was alive with actors, tumblers, jugglers and puppeteers all around, and the thoroughfare thick with visitors, some already drunk, some well on their way to being drunk. Most of them with broad smiles plastered across happy faces. I saw plenty of beards and moustaches glistening with ale and wine—men wore them now, to show their support for the Revolution—as well as the distinctive red "liberty caps."

Which was why the three men coming toward us

stuck out like a sore thumb. By my side, Arno felt me tense, about to reach for my sword, but stayed my hand with a gentle grip on my forearm. Anybody else would have lost a finger or two for doing that. Arno I was prepared to forgive.

"Meet me tomorrow for coffee. I'll explain everything then."

30 MARCH 1791

The Place des Vosges, the city's oldest, grandest square, was not far from where I left Arno, and after a night at home, I returned the next day, a mass of nerves, curiosity and barely contained excitement, brimming with the sense that despite the Lafrenière setback, I was getting somewhere. I was moving forward.

I came into the square beneath one of the huge vaulted arcades that formed part of the red brick buildings around its perimeter. Something brought me up short and I stood puzzled for a moment, wondering what was different. After all, the buildings were the same, the ornate pillar still here. But there was something missing.

And then it hit me. The statue in the middle of the square—the equestrian bronze of Louis XIII. It wasn't there anymore. I'd heard that the revolutionaries were melting down the statues. Here was the proof.

Arno was there, in his robes. In the cold light of day, I studied him again, trying to work out where it was that the boy had matured into the man: a firmer, more determined set of the jaw, perhaps? His shoulders were more square, his chin held high, his granite eyes at once fierce and beautiful. Arno had always been a handsome boy. The women of Versailles would remark upon it. The younger girls would blush and giggle into their gloves whenever he passed, the simple fact of his good looks overcoming any misgivings they might normally have had about his social standing as merely our ward. I used to love the warm, superior feeling of knowing, "He's mine."

But now—now there was something almost heroic about him. I felt a twinge of guilt, wondering if by obscuring the true nature of his parentage we'd somehow prevented him reaching his potential before now.

It was joined by another twinge of guilt, this one for Father. If I'd been less selfish and brought Arno over to the fold as I'd once pledged to do, then perhaps this newly minted *man* might now be working in service of our cause rather than the opposition.

But then, as we sat with coffee and some semblance of normal Parisian life carrying on around us, it didn't seem to matter much that I was a Templar and he was an Assassin. If not for the robes of his Creed we might have been two lovers enjoying our morning drink together, and when he smiled it was the smile of the old Arno, the boy I'd grown up and fallen in love with, and for some moments it was tempting to forget it all and bask in that warm bath of nostalgia, let conflict and duty slip away.

"So . . ." I said, at last.

"So."

"It seems you've been busy."

"Tracking down the man who killed your father, yes," he said, averting his eyes, so that again I wondered if there was something he wasn't letting on.

"Best of luck," I told him. "He's killed most of my allies and intimidated the rest into silence. He might as well be a phantom."

"I've seen him."

"What? When?"

"Last night. Just before I found you." He stood. "Come. I'll explain."

As we walked I pressed for more information and Arno related the events of the previous evening. In fact, what he'd seen was a mysterious cloaked figure. There was no name to go with this apparition. Even so, Arno's ability to get so much had been almost uncanny.

"How the devil did you do it?" I pressed.

"I have unique avenues of investigation open to me," he said mysteriously.

I cast him a sideways look and remembered what my father had said about Arno's supposed "gifts." I'd assumed he meant as in "skills," but maybe not. Maybe something else—something so unique the Assassins had managed to sniff it out.

"All right, keep your secrets then. Just tell me where to find him."

"I'm not sure that's a good idea," he protested.

"You don't trust me?"

"You said it yourself. He hunted down your allies and took over your Order. He wants you dead, Élise."

I chortled. "And what? You want to protect me? Is that it?"

"I want to help you." He was serious now. "The Brotherhood has resources, manpower . . ."

"Pity is not a virtue, Arno," I said sharply, "and I don't trust the Assassins."

"Do you trust *me*?" he asked searchingly.

I turned away, not really knowing the answer—no, knowing that I wanted to trust Arno, and in fact was desperate to do so, but knowing he was an Assassin now.

"I haven't changed that much, Élise," he implored. "I'm the same boy who distracted the cook while you stole the jam . . . The same one who helped you over the wall into that dog-infested orchard . . ."

There was something else, too. Another thing to consider. As Mr. Weatherall had pointed out, I was virtually alone: me against them. But what if I had the backing of the Assassins? I didn't have to ask what my father would have done. I already knew he'd been prepared to truce with the Assassins.

I nodded, said, "Take me to your Brotherhood. I'll hear their offer."

He looked awkward. "*Offer* might be a bit strong . . ."

31 MARCH 1791

i

The Assassin Council had turned out to be held in a salon on the Île de la Cité in the shadow of Notre Dame.

"You sure this is a good idea?" I said to Arno as we entered a room surrounded by vaulted stone arches. In one corner was a large wooden door with a steel-ring handle, and standing by it a large, bearded Assassin whose eyes gleamed within the dark depths of his cowl. Without a word he had nodded to Arno, who nodded back, and I had to fight a wave of unreality seeing Arno this way: Arno the man, Arno the Assassin.

"We have a common enemy," said Arno, as the door was opened and we passed through into a corridor lit by burning torches on the walls. "The Council will understand that. Besides, Mirabeau was a friend of your father's, wasn't he?"

I nodded. "Not friends exactly but my father trusted him. Lead on."

First, though, Arno had produced a blindfold from his pocket, insisting I wear it. Just to spite him I counted the steps and the turns, confident I could make my way out of the labyrinth if need be.

When the journey was over I took stock of my new surroundings, sensing I was in a dank underground chamber, similar to the one above, except this one was populated. From around me I heard voices. At first they were difficult to locate and I thought they were coming from galleries above before I realized that the gathered council members were arranged around the walls, their voices rising as though seeping into the stone as they shuffled suspiciously and muttered to themselves.

"Is that . . . ?"

"What's he doing?"

I sensed a figure in front of us, who spoke with a rough and rasping, French-Mr.-Weatherall sort of voice.

"What the hell have you done this time, pisspot?" he said.

My heart hammered, my breathing heavy. What if this infraction was too much? A step too far? What would I hear? More cries of, "Kill the redheaded bint"? It wouldn't be the first time and after all, Arno had allowed me to keep my pistol and sword, but what good would they be if I was blindfolded and facing multiple opponents? Multiple *Assassin* opponents?

But no. Arno had saved me from one trap. He would never deliver me into another. I trusted him. I trusted him as much as I loved him. And when he spoke to address the man who blocked our way, his voice was reassuringly calm and steady, a balm to soothe my nerves.

"The Templars have marked her for death," he said.

"So you brought her *here*?" said the commanding voice doubtfully. This was Bellec, surely?

But Arno had no time to answer. There was another new entrant to the council chamber. Another voice that demanded to know, "Well, who have we here?"

"My name is . . ." I began, but the new arrival had interrupted me.

"Oh, for heaven's sake, take that blindfold off. Ridiculous."

I took it off and faced them, the Assassin Council, who were, just as I'd thought, arranged around the stone walls of this deep and dark inner sanctum, the orange glow of the flames flickering on their robes and their faces unreadable beneath cowls.

My eyes settled on Bellec. Hawk-nosed and suspicious, he stared at me with open contempt, his body language protective of Arno.

The other man I took to be the Grand Master, Honoré Gabriel Riqueti, comte de Mirabeau. As a president of the Assembly he'd been a hero of the Revolution, but these days was a moderate voice compared to others clamoring for more radical change.

I'd heard it said he was mocked for his looks, but though he was a portly, round-faced gentleman, with quite spectacularly bad skin, he had kind, trustworthy eyes and I liked him at once.

I threw my shoulders back. "My name is Élise de la

Serre," I told the room. "My father was François de la Serre, Grand Master of the Templar Order. I've come to ask for your help."

Heads were inclined as the council members began to talk quietly among themselves until the new arrival—Mirabeau, surely—silenced them with a raised finger.

"Continue," he instructed.

Other council members protested—"Must we rehash this debate again?"—but again Mirabeau quietened them.

"We must," he told them, "and we will. If you cannot see the advantage in being owed a favor by François de la Serre's daughter, I despair for our future. Continue, mademoiselle."

"Here we go," spat the man I presumed to be Bellec.

It was to him I addressed my next comments.

"You are not men with whom I would normally parley, monsieur, but my father is dead, as are my allies within the Order. If I must turn to the Assassins for my revenge, so be it."

Bellec snorted. " 'Parley,' my ass. This is a trick to make us lower our guard. We should kill her now and send her head back as a warning."

"Bellec . . ." warned Arno.

"Enough," shouted Mirabeau. "Plainly this discussion is better conducted in private. If you will excuse us, Mademoiselle de la Serre?"

I gave a short bow. "Certainly."

"Arno, perhaps you should accompany her. I'm sure you to have much to talk about."

ii

We left, returning across the bridge and walking the busy thoroughfares until we found ourselves back at the Place des Vosges.

"Well," I said, as we walked, "that went about as well as I expected."

"Give it time. Mirabeau will talk them round."

We walked, and as we did so my thoughts went from Mirabeau, the Grand Master of the Assassins, to the man who had overthrown my own Order.

"Do you really think we can find him?" I asked.

"His luck can't last forever. François Germain believed Lafrenière was . . .

I stopped him. "François Germain?"

"Yes," said Arno, "the silversmith who led me to Lafrenière."

A wave of cold excitement swept through me.

"Arno," I gasped, "François Thomas Germain was my father's lieutenant."

"A Templar?"

"Former. He was cast out when I was younger, something about heretical notions and Jacques de Molay. I'm not entirely sure. But he should be dead. He died years ago."

Germain. Jacques de Molay. I put those thoughts aside to return to later, perhaps with the help of Mr. Weatherall.

"This Germain is remarkably active for a corpse," Arno was saying.

I nodded. "I would very much like to ask him a few questions."

"I would too. His workshop's on rue Saint-Antoine. Not far from here."

With renewed purpose we hurried through a tree-lined passageway that opened out onto a square, bunting hanging above our heads, canopies from the shops and coffeehouses fluttering in a slight summer breeze.

The street bore some of the scars of the unrest still: an overturned cart, a small pile of smashed barrels, a series of scorch marks on the cobbles, and of course there were tricolors hanging overhead, some of which bore the marks of battle.

Otherwise, however, it seemed peaceful, just as it once had been, with people passing to and fro, going about their everyday lives, and for a moment it was difficult to picture its being the site of cataclysmic events that were changing our country.

Arno led us along cobbled streets until we reached a gateway leading into a courtyard. Overlooking it was a grand house in which he said were the workshops. In there we would find the silversmith. Germain.

"There were guards here last time I came," said Arno and stopped, a wary look crossing his face.

"There are none now," I said.

"No. But then again a lot has happened since the last time I was here. Perhaps the guards have been withdrawn."

"Or perhaps something else."

All of a sudden we were hushed and cautious. My

hand went to my sword and I was glad of the feeling of the pistol tucked into my belt.

"Is anybody home?" he called across the empty courtyard.

There was no response. Though there was the noise of the street from behind us, from the foreboding mansion ahead of us came only silence and the unblinking stare of the windows.

The door opened at his touch. With a look at me we made our way inside, only to find the entrance hall deserted. We made our way upstairs, Arno leading us to the workshop. From the sparse look of the place it had recently been abandoned. Inside were most of the accoutrements of a silversmith's trade—at least as far as I could see—but no sign of the silversmith.

We began to look around, cautiously at first, rifling through papers, pulling aside items on shelves, not really sure what we were looking for, just looking, hoping to find some confirmation of the theory that this apparently innocent silversmith was in fact the former high-ranking Templar Germain.

Because if he was, then that meant this apparently innocent silversmith was the man who had targeted my parents and was doing his level best to destroy every other aspect of my life.

My fists clenched at the thought. My heart hardened to think of the pain this man had brought the de la Serre family. Never had the thought of revenge felt more real to me than it did at that moment.

There came a noise from the door. The tiniest of noises—a mere whisper of fabric—it was nevertheless loud enough to alert heightened senses. Arno heard it too, and as one we spun in the direction of the entryway.

"Don't tell me it's a trap," he said.

"It's a trap."

iii

Arno and I exchanged a glance and drew our swords as four grim-faced men filed through the door, took up position to bar our exit, and gazed balefully at us. With their battered hats and scruffy boots, they'd taken care to look like fearsome revolutionaries, unlikely to be challenged in the street, but they had more on their minds than freedom, liberty or . . .

Well, they had death on their minds. They sectioned off, two each for me and Arno. One of the men facing me fixed me with a look, his eyes sunken deep into a high forehead, a red neckscarf tied at his throat. With a knife in one hand he drew a sword from behind his back, twirled it in a brief, dramatic figure-of-eight formation, then held me on point. His companion did similar, offering me the back of his hand raised slightly higher than the flat of his sword. Had they really been revolutionaries, keen to rob or otherwise assault me, then they would have been laughing right now, busy underestimating me in the few brief moments before their swift demise. But they weren't. They were Templar killers. And word had reached their ears that Élise de la Serre was no easy prey; that she would give them a battle.

The one who held his sword high moved forward first,

swinging it in a tactical zigzag toward my midriff at the same time as he shifted his weight onto a leading foot.

The steel rang as I parried his blade to the side and danced a little to my left, correctly anticipating that Red-Scarf would time his own attack simultaneously.

He did, and I was able to meet his sword with a downward sweep of my own, keeping both of the men at bay for at least one moment more, giving them pause for thought, letting them know that what they had been told was right: I was trained; I had been trained by the best. And I was stronger than I had ever been.

From my right I heard the swords of Arno and his two opponents ring out, followed by a scream that wasn't Arno.

Now Flat-Sword made his first mistake, his eyes swiveling to see what fate had befallen his companion, and though it was a momentary lapse of concentration, a half second that his attention was not focused on me, I made him pay for it.

I had him on point, danced forward beneath his guard and struck upward, opening his throat with a flick of the wrist.

Red-Scarf was good. He knew his companion's death gave him a chance and he lurched forward, his sword in a flat, offensive swing that if he'd made contact would have sent me off balance at the very least.

But he didn't. He was just a little too hasty, a little too desperate to take advantage of what he thought was an opening and I had expected his attack from that side, had dropped to one knee and brought my own blade to bear, still sparkling with the fresh blood of Flat-Sword and now embedded beneath Red-Scarf's armpit, between two layers of thick leather armor.

At the same time there came a second squeal from my left and I heard a thud as the fourth body hit the floor and the battle was over, Arno and I the only two left standing.

We caught our breath, shoulders heaving as the final gurgles of our would-be killers dwindled to dry death rasps.

We looked at the corpses, looked back at one another, then mutually decided to resume searching the workshop.

iv

"There's nothing here," I said, after a while.

"He must have known his bluff wouldn't hold up," said Arno.

"So we've lost again."

"Maybe not. Let's keep looking."

He tried a door that wouldn't open and seemed about to leave it before I gave him a grin and kicked it down. What greeted us was another, slightly smaller chamber, this one full of symbols I recognized: Templar crosses wrought in silver, beautifully crafted goblets and carafes.

No doubt about it, this was a Templar meeting place. On a raised dais at one end of the room was an ornate, intricately carved chair where the Grand Master would sit. On either side were chairs for his lieutenants.

In the center of the room was a plinth, inset with crosses, and lying on it was a set of documents that I went to now, snatching them up, the feel of them familiar to me but also strange, as though they were out of place here in a chamber adjacent to a silversmith's workshop and not in the château of the de la Serre family.

One of them was a set of orders. I had seen similar orders before, of course, signed by my father, but this one—this one was signed by Germain. Sealed with a red wax Templar cross.

"It's him. Germain is Grand Master now. How did this happen?"

Arno shook his head, walking toward the window as he spoke. "Son of a bitch. We must tell Mirabeau. As soon as . . ."

He didn't finish his sentence. There was the sound of gunshots from outside, then glass shattering as musket balls zipped through the windows, slapped into the ceiling above us, showering us with plaster stone chippings. We took cover, Arno by the window, me near the door, just as there came another volley of shots.

"Go," he called over. "Get to Mirabeau estate. I'll deal with this."

I nodded, and left, heading to see the Assassin Grand Master, Mirabeau.

v

It was getting dark by the time I reached Mirabeau's villa. Getting there, the first thing to strike me was that scarcity of staff. The house had an odd, silent feel—a feel it took me a moment or so to recognize as how my own house had felt in the wake of Mother's death.

The second thing to strike me—and of course I now know that the two were connected—was the strange behavior of Mirabeau's butler. He had worn an odd expression, as though his features hadn't quite settled on his face; that, and the fact that he didn't accompany me to Mirabeau's bedchamber. I thought back to my arrival at the Boars Head Inn on Fleet Street and realized that it would hardly be the first time someone had mistaken me for a lady of the night, but I didn't think that even the sloppy-faced butler was *that* stupid.

No, there was something amiss. I drew my sword, came silently into the bedchamber. It was in darkness, the curtains drawn. Candles in a candelabra were close to guttering, a fire burned weakly in the grate; on a table was laid out the remnants of what looked like supper, and in the bed was what appeared to be a sleeping Mirabeau.

"Monsieur?" I said.

There was no reply, no response at all from Mirabeau, whose ample chest, which should have been rising and falling with his breathing, remained still.

I went over.

Of course. He was dead.

"Élise, what is this?" Arno's voice from the door startled me, and I whirled around.

A sudden feeling of misplaced guilt welled up within me. "I found him like this. I don't . . ."

He looked at me for a second longer than necessary.

"Of course not. But I must report this to the Council. They'll know . . ."

"No," I snapped. "They don't trust me as it is. I'll be their suspect, first and last."

"You're right," he said, nodding. "Of course you're right."

"What are we going to do?"

"We find out what happened," he said decisively. He turned, studying the wood surround of the entryway just behind him.

"Doesn't look like the door was forced," he said.

"So the killer was expected?"

"A guest, perhaps? Or a servant?"

My mind went to the butler. But if the butler did it, then why was he still here? My guess was that the butler was working in a state of willful ignorance.

Something caught Arno's eye, and he picked it up holding it close to inspect it. At first I took it to be a decorative pin, but he was holding it out, his face serious, something significant about it.

"What is that?" I said, but I knew what it was, of course. I'd been given one at my initiation.

vi

He handed it to me. "It's . . . the weapon that killed your father."

I took it to study, seeing the familiar insignia in the center of the design, then scrutinizing the pin itself. On it was a tiny gutter so that the poison would flow inside the blade, then exit from two tiny openings farther down. Ingenious. Deadly.

And of Templar design. Anybody finding it—one of Mirabeau's Assassin compatriots, for example—would have assumed that the Grand Master had been murdered by a Templar.

Perhaps he would have even assumed that Mirabeau had been murdered by me.

"That's a Templar badge of office," I confirmed to Arno.

He nodded. "You saw no one else when you arrived?"

"Just the butler. He let me in, but he never came upstairs."

He was searching the room now, his gaze moving across the bedchamber as though he was systematically studying each area. With a small exclamation he darted to a cabinet, knelt and reached beneath it, retrieving a wineglass flecked with dried dregs of wine inside.

He sniffed it. "Poison." He recoiled.

"Let me see that," I said, and held it to my nose.

Next I turned my attention to Mirabeau's body, fingertips prying open his eyes to check the pupils, opening his mouth to inspect his tongue, pressing down on the skin.

"Aconite," I said. "Hard to detect, unless you know what you're looking for."

"Popular with Templars, is it?"

"With anyone who wants to get away with murder," I told him, ignoring the insinuation. "It's almost impossible to detect, and the scent and the symptoms resemble natural causes. Useful when you need to get rid of someone without monitoring them."

"And how would one go about acquiring it?"

"It grows easily enough in a garden, but for the symptoms to have come on so suddenly, it must have been processed."

"Or purchased through an apothecary."

"Templar poison, Templar pin . . . It looks damning."

He shot me a significant look that earned him a frown in return. "Bravo, you figured it out," I said witheringly. "My cunning plan was to murder the only Assassin who doesn't want to see me dead, then stand about waiting to be discovered."

"Not the only Assassin."

"You're right. I'm sorry. But you know this wasn't my doing."

"I believe you. The rest of the Brotherhood, though . . ."

"Then let's find the real killer before they get wind of this."

vii

A curious turn of events. Arno had learned from an apothecary that the poison had been acquired by a man who wore Assassins' robes. From there was a trail that Arno followed, and it had led us here, to Sainte-Chappelle on the Île de la Cité.

A storm was brewing by the time we reached the great church, in more ways than one. I could see that Arno was shaken by the idea that there might be a traitor within the Assassin ranks.

Better get used to it, I thought.

"The trail ends here," he said thoughtfully.

"Are you sure?"

He was looking up to where high in the turrets of the great church stood a dark figure. Silhouetted against the skyline, his cloak fluttered in the wind as he gazed down upon us.

"Yes, unfortunately," he said ruefully. I readied myself to go into battle with him once again, but with a hand on mine Arno stopped me.

"No," he said, "I must do this myself."

I rounded on him. "Don't be ridiculous, I'm not letting you do this alone."

"Élise, please. After your father died, the Assassins . . . They gave me a purpose. Something to believe in. To see that betrayed . . . I need to make it right myself. I need to know why."

I could understand. Better than anyone I could understand, and with a kiss I let him go.

"Come back to me," I told him.

viii

I craned my neck to look up to the roof of the church, but saw just stone and the angry sky beyond. The figure had gone. Still I watched, until a few moments later when I saw two figures tussling on a ledge.

My hand went to my mouth. A cry for Arno, which would have been useless anyway, dried in my mouth. In the next instant the two figures were tumbling from the church, hurtling down the front of the building, almost shaded out by the driving rain.

For half a second I thought they were going to hit the ground and die there in front of me but their fall was stopped by an overhang farther down.

From my position below I heard their bodies make impact and their cries of pain. I wondered whether either of them would have survived the fall, then got my answer as they gathered themselves slowly and painfully and continued to fight, slow at first but with increasing ferocity, their hidden blades flashing like lightning strikes in the dark.

Now I could hear them shouting at one another, Arno crying, "For God's sake, Bellec, the new age is upon us. Haven't we grown past this endless conflict?"

Of course, it was Bellec, the Assassins' second-in-command. So—he was the man behind Mirabeau's killing.

"Did everything I teach you bounce off that armor-plated skull?" roared Bellec. "We are fighting for the freedom of the human soul. Leading the revolution against Templar tyranny."

"Funny how short the road is from revolution against tyranny to indiscriminate murder, isn't it?" roared Arno back.

"*Bah*. Stubborn little fuck, aren't you?"

"Ask anyone," retorted Arno, and he leapt forward, his blade making a figure of eight.

Bellec danced back. "Open your eyes," he shouted. "If the Templars want peace, it's only so they can get close enough to put the knife to your throat."

"You're wrong," countered Arno.

"You haven't seen what I have. I've seen Templars put entire villages to the sword, just for the chance of killing one Assassin. Tell me, boy, in your vast experience— what have you seen?"

"I've seen the Grand Master of the Templar Order take in a frightened orphan and raise him as his own son."

"I had hopes for you," screamed Bellec, seething now. "I thought you could think for yourself."

"I can, Bellec. I just don't think like you."

The two of them, still grappling, were framed by a vast stained-glass window of the church. Lashed by the rain, lit and colored from behind, they scuffled for a second, as though teetering on some precipice, as though they might fall one way, off the balcony and down to the slick stone of the church courtyard below, or the other way and into the church itself.

Just a question of which way they were going to fall.

There was a crash, colored glass splintered, robes flapped and tore on shards of glass, then they fell once more, this time into the church. I dashed across the courtyard to a gate, pulling on it and seeing them inside.

"Arno," I called. He stood and shook his head as though to try and clear it, spraying bits of broken glass on the stone floor of the church. Of Bellec there was no sign.

"I'm fine," he called to me, hearing me rattle the gate as I tested it once more, trying to reach him. "Stay there."

And before I could protest he took off and I strained my ears to hear as he ventured deep into the darkness of the church.

Next came the sound of Bellec's voice coming from . . . where, I couldn't see. But somewhere close.

"I should have left you to rot in the Bastille." His voice was a whisper echoed by the damp stone. "Tell me, did you ever really believe in the Creed or were you a Templar-loving traitor from the start?"

He was taunting Arno. Taunting him from the shadows.

"It doesn't have to be this way, Bellec," shouted Arno, looking around, squinting into the dark alcoves and recesses.

The reply came, and once more it was difficult to locate from where. The voice seemed to emanate from the church stone itself.

"You're the one who's making it so. If you just see sense, we could take the Brotherhood to a height we've not seen in two hundred years."

Arno shook his head, voice dripping with irony. "Yes, killing everyone who disagrees with you is a brilliant way to start your rise from the ashes."

I heard a noise ahead of me and saw Bellec a second before Arno did.

"Look out," I cried as the older Assassin came lunging from the shadows with his hidden blade extended.

Arno turned, saw him and flipped to the side. He came to his feet ready to meet an attack and for a moment or so the two warriors stood facing each other. They were both bloodied and bruised from the battle, their robes tattered, almost shredded in places, but still full of fight. Each was determined that this should end here and it should end now.

From where he was, Bellec could see me at the gate

and I felt his eyes on me before his gaze returned to Arno.

"So," he began, his voice full of derision, ripe with scorn, "now we see the heart of it. It's not Mirabeau who's poisoned you. It's *her*."

Bellec had formed a bond with Arno but he had no idea of the bond that already existed between me and his pupil, and it was because of that that I didn't doubt Arno.

"Bellec . . ." warned Arno.

"Mirabeau is dead. *She* is the last piece of this lunacy. You'll thank me for this one day."

Did he mean to kill me? Or kill Arno? Or kill us both?

I didn't know. All I knew was that the church rang to the sound of steel meeting steel as their hidden blades clashed once more and they danced around one another. What Mr. Weatherall had told me all those years ago was true: most sword fights are decided in the first few seconds of engagement. But these two combatants were not "most sword fighters." They were trained Assassins. Master and pupil. And the fight continued, steel meeting steel, their robes swinging as they attacked and defended, slashed and parried, ducked and whirled; the fight carrying on until they were round-shouldered with exhaustion and Arno was able to summon hidden reserves of strength and prevail, defeating his foe with a cry of defiance and a final thrust of his hidden blade into his mentor's stomach.

And Bellec at last sank to the stone of the church floor, his hands at his belly. His eyes went to Arno.

"Do it," he implored, close to death now. "If you've

got an ounce of conviction and aren't just a love-addled milksop, you'll kill me now. Because I won't stop. I *will* kill her. To save the Brotherhood I'd see Paris burn."

"I know," said Arno, and delivered the *coup de grace*.

ix

Arno told me later what he had seen. He had seen something in a vision, he'd said, with a sideways look, as though to check I was taking him seriously.

In the vision Arno had seen two men, one in Assassin robes, the other a Templar thug, who were scuffling in the street. The Templar seemed to be triumphant but then a second Assassin entered the fray and killed the Templar.

The first Assassin was Charles Dorian, Arno's father. The second was Bellec.

Bellec had saved his father's life. From that incident Bellec had recognized the pocket watch and then, when in the Bastille, realized exactly who Arno was.

Another thing Arno had seen, a second vision: this one showing Mirabeau and Bellec talking, Mirabeau telling Bellec, "Élise de la Serre will be Grand Master one day. Having her in our debt would be a great boon."

Bellec in reply saying, "Be a greater one to kill her before she is a real threat."

"Your protégé vouches for her," Mirabeau had said. "Don't you trust him?"

"With my life," Bellec had replied. "It's the girl I don't trust. Nothing I can say to convince you?"

"I'm afraid not."

Bellec—reluctantly, Arno had said, seeing that his mentor had taken no Machiavellian satisfaction in slaying the Grand Master and had considered it a necessary evil—dropped poison into one of the glasses and handed it to Mirabeau. "Cheers."

Ironic that they should drink to each other's health. Just moments later Mirabeau was dead and Bellec was planting the Templar pin and leaving. And not long after that, of course, I had come on the scene.

We had managed to find the culprit and so prevent me from being accused of the crime. Had I done enough to ingratiate myself with them? I didn't think so.

12 SEPTEMBER 1794

i

I knew what had happened next, although it wasn't in her journal.

I leafed forward but no; instead there were pages missing, torn out at some later date, perhaps, in a fit of . . . what? Regret? Anger? Something else?

The moment I told her the truth—she had torn it from her diary.

I knew it would be difficult, of course, because I knew Élise as well as I knew myself. In many ways, she was my mirror, and I knew how I would have felt had the shoe been on the other foot. You can't blame me for putting it off and putting it off, then waiting until one evening when we had eaten well, and there was an almost empty bottle of wine on the table between us.

"I know who killed your father," I told her.

"You do? How?"

"The visions."

I gave her a sideways look to check she was taking me seriously. As before she looked bemused, not quite believing, not quite disbelieving.

"And the name you came up with is the King of Beggars?" she said.

I looked at her, realizing that she had been conducting her own investigations. Of course she had. "So you were being serious when you said you would avenge him," I said.

"If you ever thought otherwise, then you don't know me as well as you think you do."

I nodded thoughtfully. "And what did you learn?"

"That the King of Beggars was behind the attempt on my mother in '75; that the King of Beggars was inducted into the Order after the death of my family, all of which makes me think that he was inducted as a way of rewarding him for successfully killing my father."

"Do you know why?"

"It was a coup, Arno. The man who has declared himself Grand Master arranged for my father's killing because he wanted to take his position. No doubt he used my father's attempts to truce with the Assassins as leverage. Perhaps it was the final piece to the puzzle. Perhaps it finally tipped the balance in his favor. No doubt the King of Beggars was acting on his orders."

"Not just the King of Beggars. There was someone else there, too."

She nodded with an odd, gratified smile. "That makes me happy, Arno. That it took two of them to kill Father. I expect he fought like a tiger."

"A man named Sivert."

She closed her eyes. "That makes sense," she said, after a while. "They are all in on it, no doubt, the Crows."

"The who?" I'd said, because of course I had no idea whom she meant by that.

"It's a name I call my father's advisers."

"This Sivert—he was one of your father's advisers."

"Oh yes."

"François took his eye out before he died."

She chuckled. "Well done, Father."

"Sivert is dead now."

A shadow crossed her face. "I see. I would have hoped to have done the deed myself."

"The King of Beggars too," I added, swallowing.

And now she turned to me.

"Arno, what are you saying?"

I reached for her. "I loved him, Élise, as though he were my own father," but she was pulling away, standing and pulling her arms across her chest. Her cheeks colored red.

"*You* killed them?"

"Yes—and I make no apology for it, Élise."

Again I reached for her and again she stepped nimbly away, unfolding her arms to ward me off at the same time. For a second—just a second—I thought she was going to reach for her sword but if so she thought better of it. She gained a hold on her temper.

"You killed them."

"I had to," I said, without going into the matter although she wasn't interested in why, whirling around for a moment as though not quite sure what to do with herself.

"You took *my* revenge from me."

"They were mere lackeys anyway, Élise. The real culprit is out there."

Furious, she rounded on me. "Tell me you made them suffer," she spat.

"Please, Élise, this isn't you."

"Arno, I have been orphaned, beaten, deceived and betrayed — and I will have my revenge at whatever cost."

Her shoulders rose and fell. Her color was high.

"Well, no, they didn't suffer. That is not the Assassin way. We take no pleasure from killing."

"Oh? Really? So now you're an Assassin you feel qualified to lecture me on ethics, do you? Well, make no mistake, Arno, I take no pleasure from killing. I take pleasure from justice."

"So that is what I did. I brought these men to justice. I had a shot. I took it."

That appeared to calm her, and she nodded thoughtfully.

"You leave Germain to me, though," she said, not a request, a command.

"I can't promise that, Élise. If I get a shot, then . . ."

She looked at me with a half smile.

"Then you'll have me to answer to," she said.

ii

After, we did not see each other for a while though we wrote, and when at last I had some information for her, I was able to tempt her away from Île Saint-Louis and we went in search of Madame Levesque, who fell beneath my blade. It was an adventure that continued with an unexpected and unscheduled ride on Monsieur Montgolfier's hot-air balloon, though gallantry forbids I should reveal what took place during the flight.

Suffice it to say, at the conclusion of our journey, Élise and I were closer than ever.

But not close enough for me to notice what was happening to her; that the deaths of her father's advisers were a mere diversion for her. That what was concerning, maybe even eventually *consuming* her, was getting to Germain.

20 JANUARY 1793

i

In the street in Versailles was a cart I recognized. Harnessed to it a horse I knew. I dismounted, tethered Scratch to the cart, loosened his saddle, gave him water, nuzzled my head to his.

I took my time making Scratch comfortable, partly because I love Scratch and he deserves all the attention I give him and more, and partly because I was stalling, wanting to put off the moment I faced the inevitable.

The outside wall showed signs of neglect. I wondered which of our staff had been responsible for it when we all lived here. The gardeners, probably. Without them the walls ran thick with moss and ivy, the tendrils reaching up to the top of the walls like veins on the stone.

Set into the wall was an arched gate I knew well, yet which seemed unfamiliar. At the mercy of the elements the wood had begun to mottle and pale. Where once the door had looked grand, now it looked merely sad.

I opened the gate and entered the courtyard of my childhood home.

Having witnessed the devastation at the villa in Paris, I suppose I was at least mentally prepared. Yet still I found myself stifling a sob to see flower beds choked with spindly weeds, the benches overgrown. On a step by a set of drooping shutters sat Jacques, who brightened on seeing me. Jacques rarely spoke; the most animated I ever saw him was deep in hushed conversation with Helene, and he didn't need to speak now. Just indicated behind himself, into the house.

Inside were boards across the windows, the furniture mostly overturned, the same sad story I was seeing so much now, only this time it was even sadder because the house was my childhood home and each smashed pot and splintered chair held a memory for me. As I stepped through my wrecked childhood home I heard the sound of our old upright clock, a noise so familiar and redolent of my childhood that it hit me with all the strength of a slap, and for a second I stood in the empty hallway, where my boots crunched on floors that had once been polished to a high shine, and stifled a sob.

A sob of regret and nostalgia. Maybe even a little guilt.

ii

I came out onto the terrace and gazed out upon the sweeping lawns, once landscaped, now overgrown and unkempt. About two hundred yards away, Mr. Weather-all sat on the slope, his crutches splayed on either side.

"What are you doing?" I said, coming to join him.

He'd started a little as I sat but regained his composure and gave me a long, appraising look.

"I was heading for down the bottom of the south lawn, where we used to train. Trouble is, when I pictured myself being able to make it there and back, I pictured the lawns looking like they used to, but then I arrived and found them like this, and suddenly it's not so easy."

"Well, this is a nice spot."

"Depends on the company," he said with a sardonic smile.

There was a pause.

"Sneaking out like that . . ." he said.

"I'm sorry."

"I knew you were going to do it, you know. I haven't known you since you were but a child without learning something about a certain look that comes into your eyes. Well, you're alive at least. What you been up to?"

"I went for a ride in a hot-air balloon with Arno."

"Oh yes? And how did that go?"

He saw me blush. "It was very nice, thank you."

"So you and him . . ."

"I would say so."

"Well, that's something, then. Can't have you being lovelorn. What about"—he spread his hands—"everything else. You learn anything?"

"Plenty. Many of those who plotted against my father have already answered for their crimes. Plus I now know the identity of the man who ordered his murder, the new Grand Master."

"Pray tell."

"The new Grand Master, the architect of the take-over, is François Thomas Germain."

Mr. Weatherall made a hissing noise. "Of course."

"You said he was cast out of the Order . . ."

"He was. Our friend Germain was an adherent of Jacques de Molay, first-ever Grand Master. Molay died screaming at the stake in 1314, raining curses down on anyone in the near vicinity. Master de Molay is the sort of bloke nobody can decide on, but that was an argument you had to have in private back then because showing support for his ideas was heresy.

"And Germain—Germain was a heretic. He was a heretic who had the ear of the Grand Master. To end the dissension he was expelled. Your father had begged Germain to come back into line and his heart was heavy to expel Germain. The Order was told that any man standing by him would be exiled as well. Long afterward his death was announced, but by then he was just a bad memory anyway. Not so, eh? Germain had been rallying support, controlling things behind the scenes, gradually rewriting the manifesto. And now he's in charge, and the Order scratches its heads and wonders how we moved from unswerving support of the king to wanting him dead, and the answer is that it happened because there was nobody to oppose it. Checkmate." Mr. Weatherall smiled. "You've got to give it to the lad."

"I shall give him my sword in his gut."

"And how will you do that?"

"Arno has discovered that Germain intends to be present at the execution of the king tomorrow."

Mr. Weatherall looked sharply at me. "The execution of the king? Then the Assembly has reached its verdict already?"

"Indeed it has. And the verdict is death."

Mr. Weatherall shook his head. The execution of the king. How had we arrived here? As journeys go, I suppose the final leg had begun in the summer of last year when twenty thousand Parisians signed a petition calling for a return of rule by the royal family. Where once there had been talk of revolution, now the talk was of counterrevolution.

Of course the Revolution wasn't having that, so on 10 August the Assembly had decided to march on the Palace at Tuileries, where the king and Marie Antoinette had been staying ever since their undignified exile from Versailles almost three years before.

Six hundred of the king's Swiss Guard lost their lives in the battle, the final stand of the king. Six weeks later the monarchy was abolished.

Meanwhile, there were uprisings against the revolution in Brittany and Vendée, and on 2 September, the Prussians took Verdun, causing panic in Paris when stories began to circulate that the Royalist prisoners would be released from prison and take bloody revenge on members of the Revolution. I suppose you'd have to say that the massacres that followed were an attempt at pre-emption, but massacres they were, and thousands of prisoners were slaughtered.

And then, the king went on trial, and today it had

been announced that he should die by the guillotine tomorrow.

"If Germain is there, then I shall be there, too," I told Mr. Weatherall now.

"Why is that, then?"

"To kill him."

Mr. Weatherall squinted. "I don't think this is the way, Élise," he said.

"I know," I said tenderly, "but you realize I have no other choice."

"What's more important to you?" he asked, testily. "Revenge or the Order?"

I shrugged. "When I achieve the first, the second will fall into place."

"Will it? You think so, do you?"

"I do."

"Why? All you'll be doing is killing the current Grand Master. You're as likely to be tried for treachery as welcomed back into the fold. I've sent appeals all over. To Spain, Italy, even America. I've had murmurs of sympathy but not a single pledge of support in return, and do you know why that is? It's because to them the fact that the French Order is running smoothly makes your dismissal of marginal interest.

"Besides, we can be sure that Germain has used his own networks. He'll have assured our brothers overseas that the overthrow was necessary and that the French Order is in good hands.

"We can assume also that the Carrolls will be poisoning the well wherever their name bears standing. You cannot do this without support, Élise, and the fact is you have no support, yet even knowing that, you plan to carry on regardless. Which tells me that this isn't about the Order, it's about revenge. Which tells me I'm sitting next to a suicidal fool."

"I will have support," I insisted.

"And where will that come from, Élise, do you think?"

"I had hoped to form an alliance with the Assassins," I said.

He gave a start, then shook his head sadly. "Making peace with the Assassins is fanciful stuff, child. It'll never happen, no matter what your friend Haytham Kenway says in his letters. Mr. Carroll was right about that. You might as well ask a mongoose and a snake to take afternoon tea."

"You can't believe that."

"I don't just believe it, I know it, child. I love you for thinking otherwise, but you're wrong."

"My father thought otherwise."

He sighed. "Any truce your father brokered was a temporary one. He knew it, like we all do. There never will be peace."

21 JANUARY 1793

It was cold. Biting cold. And our dragon breath hung in the air in front of us as we stood on the Place de la Concorde, which was to be the site of the king's execution.

The square was full. It felt as though the whole of Paris, if not the whole of France, had gathered to watch the king die. As far as the eye could see were people who just a year ago would have sworn fealty to the monarch but were now readying their handkerchiefs to dip in his blood. They clambered onto carts to get a better view, children teetering on their fathers' shoulders, young women doing the same as they sat astride husbands or lovers.

Around the edges of the square merchants had set up stalls and were not shy about calling out to advertise them, every one an "execution special." In the air was an atmosphere I could only describe as one of celebratory lust for blood. You wondered whether they wouldn't have had enough of blood by now, these people, the people of France. Looking around, obviously not.

Meanwhile, the executioner was calling up prisoners to be beheaded. They cried and protested as they were dragged to the scaffold of the guillotine. The crowd called for their blood. They hushed in the moment before it was spilled and they cheered when it came spurting forth into a crisp January day.

ii

"Are you sure Germain will be here?" I'd said to Arno when we arrived.

"I'm sure," he'd said, and we went our separate ways, and though the plan had been for us to locate Germain, in the end the treacherous ex-lieutenant had made his presence felt, clambering onto a viewing platform, surrounded by his men.

This was him, I thought, looking at him, the crowd seeming to fall away for a moment or so.

This was François Thomas Germain.

I knew it was him. He wore the robes of the Grand Master. And I wondered what bystanders thought, seeing this robed man take such an exalted viewing position? Did they see an enemy of the Revolution? Or a friend?

Or, as their faces were turned quickly away, as though not wanting to catch Germain's eye, did they just see a man to fear? Certainly he looked fearsome. He had a cruel, turned-down mouth and eyes that even from this distance I could see were dark and penetrating. There was something about his stare that was disquieting. His graying hair was tied back in a black bow and he was clad in the dark robes of a Templar Grand Master.

I seethed. These were robes I was used to seeing on my father. They had no place adorning the back of this imposter.

Arno had seen him, too, of course, and managed to come much closer to the platform. I watched as he approached the guards stationed at the foot of the stairs, whose job involved keeping the surge of people away from the platform. He spoke to one of them. There were shouts. My eyes went to Germain, who leaned over to see Arno, then indicated to the guards to let him up.

Meanwhile, I came as close to the platform as I dared. Whether Germain would recognize me I had no idea, but there were other familiar faces around. I couldn't afford to be seen.

Arno had reached the platform, joining Germain and standing by his side, the two of them looking out over the crowd toward the guillotine, which rose and fell, rose and fell . . .

"Hello, Arno," I heard Germain say, but only just, and I risked raising my face to stare up at the platform, hoping that with a mix of reading the lips of the speakers and the wind in the right direction I could make out what they were saying.

"Germain," Arno said.

Germain indicated to him. "It's fitting you're here to

see the rebirth of the Templar Order. After all, you were there for its conception."

Arno nodded. "Mr. de la Serre," he said simply.

"I tried to make him see." Germain shrugged. "The Order had become corrupt, clutching at power and privilege for their own sake. We forgot de Molay's teachings, that our purpose is to lead humanity into an age of order and peace."

On the stage the king had been brought up. And to give him his due, he faced his tormentors with his shoulders thrown back and his chin held high, proud to the very last. He began to give a speech he had no doubt rehearsed in whatever rough surrounds he had been kept prior to his journey to the guillotine. But just as it came to delivering his final words, the drums started up, drowning them out. Brave, yes. But ineffectual to the very last.

Above me Arno and Germain continued to talk, Arno, I could see, trying to make sense of things.

"But you could set it right, is that it? All by killing the man in charge?"

The "man in charge"—my father. The surge of hatred I had experienced on first seeing Germain intensified. I longed to slide the blade of my sword between his ribs and watch him die on the cold stone, just as my father had done.

"The death of de la Serre was only the first stage," Germain said. "This is the culmination. The fall of a Church, the end of a regime . . . the death of a king."

"And what did the king do to you?" sneered Arno. "Cost you your job? Take your wife as a mistress?"

Germain was shaking his head as though disappointed with a pupil. "The king is merely a symbol. A symbol can inspire fear, and fear can inspire control—but men inevitably lose their fear of symbols. As you can see."

He was gesturing toward the scaffold, where the king, denied his final chance to recover some of his regal pride, had been forced down to his knees. His chin was fitted into the notched block, the skin of his neck was exposed for the waiting guillotine.

Germain said, "This was the truth de Molay died for: the Divine Right of Kings is nothing but the reflection of sunlight upon gold. And when Crown and Church are ground to dust, we who control the gold will decide the future."

There was a ripple of excitement around the crowd, which then fell to a hush. This was it. This was the moment. Looking over, I saw the guillotine blade shimmer, then drop with a soft *thunk*, followed by the sound of the king's head falling into the basket below the block.

There was a moment of silence in the courtyard, which was followed by a sound I would find difficult to identify at first, until, later, I recognized it for what it was. I recognized it from the Maison Royale. It was the sound a classroom full of pupils makes when they realize they've gone too far, when a collective intake of breath says there's no going back. "That's torn it, there's going to be trouble now."

Speaking almost under his breath, Germain said, "Jacques de Molay, you are avenged," and I knew I was dealing with an extremist, fanatic, a madman. A man to whom human life had no cost other than its worth in the promotion of his own ideals, which, as the man in charge of the Templar Order, made him perhaps the most dangerous man in France.

A man who had to be stopped.

On the scaffold, Germain was turning to Arno.

"And now, I must take my leave," he was saying. "A good day to you."

He looked at his guards and with an imperious wave of the hand, ordered them after Arno, with the simple, chilling words: "Kill him."

Two guards were moving forward on Arno, who swung his upper body to meet them, his sword hand reaching across his front.

His blade never cleared leather; my sword spoke once, twice: two fatal arterial slashes that had the guards pitching forward, eyes rolling up in their sockets even as their foreheads made contact with the bloody boards of the platform.

It was quick; it achieved the objective of killing the two guards. But it was bloody and not at all discreet.

Sure enough, from nearby came a scream. In all the commotion of the execution it wasn't quite urgent or loud enough to panic the crowd, but it was sufficient to alert more guards, who came running, mounting the steps of the platform to where Arno and I stood ready to meet them.

I surged forward, desperate to get to Germain, running the first of our assailants through with my blade, withdrawing and spinning at the same time in order to slash backhanded at a second guard. It was the kind of move Mr. Weatherall would have hated, an attack born more of the desire for a speedy kill than the need to maintain a defensive stance, the kind that left me vulnerable to a counter. And there was nothing Mr. Weatherall despised more than a showy, incautious attack.

But then again, I had Arno on my flank, who dealt with a third guard, and just maybe Mr. Weatherall might have forgiven me.

In the space of just a few seconds we had three bodies piled at our feet. But more guards were arriving and a few yards away I caught sight of Germain. He had seen the tide of battle turn and was making a run for it—racing toward a carriage on the thoroughfare at the perimeter of the square.

I was cut off from reaching him, but Arno . . .

"What are you doing?" I screamed at him, urging him to go after Germain.

Deflecting the first of my attackers. Seeing Germain getting away.

"I'm not leaving you to die," called Arno, and turned his attention to where more guards had appeared on the steps.

But I wasn't going to die. I had a way out. I glanced up to the thoroughfare, saw the carriage door gaping open, Germain about to climb aboard. Thrashing wildly with my sword I vaulted the barrier, landing badly in the dirt but not quite badly enough to die at the hands of a guard who thought he'd seen his chance to kill me and paid for the assumption with steel in his gut.

From somewhere I heard Arno shout, telling me to stop—*"It's not worth it!"*—seeing what he'd seen—a phalanx of guards who rounded the platform, creating a barrier between me and . . .

Germain. Who had reached the carriage, clambered in and slammed the door shut behind him. I saw as the coachman shook the reins and the horse's crests were whipped by a wind as their muzzles rose and their hocks tightened, and the carriage set off at a lick.

Damn.

I braced myself, about to take on the guards, when I felt Arno by my side, grabbing my arm. "No, Élise."

With a cry of frustration I shook him off. The squad was advancing on us, blades drawn, shoulders dropped and forward. In their eyes was the confidence of strength in numbers. I bared my teeth.

Blast him. *Blast Arno.*

But then he grabbed me by the hand, pulled me into the safety and anonymity of the crowd and began pushing his way through startled onlookers at the periphery and into the heart of the mob, the guards behind us at last.

It wasn't until we had left the scene of the execution behind—until there were no more people around—that we stopped.

I rounded on him. "He's gone, damn it, our one chance . . ."

"It's not over," he insisted, seeing I needed cooling down. "We'll find him again . . ."

I felt my blood rising. "No, we won't. You think he'll be so careless now, knowing how close at heel we are? You were given a golden opportunity to end his life, and you refused to take it."

He shook his head, not seeing it that way at all. "To save your life," he insisted.

"It isn't yours to save."

"What are you saying?"

"I'm willing to die to put Germain down. If you don't have the stomach for revenge . . . then I don't need your help."

And I meant it, dear journal. As I sit and write this, and mull over the angry words we exchanged, I remain certain that I meant it then and mean it now.

Perhaps his loyalty to my father was not as great as he had professed it to be.

No, I didn't need his help.

10 November 1793

They called it the Terror.

"Enemies of the Revolution" were being sent to the guillotine by the dozens—for opposing the Revolution, for hoarding grain, for helping foreign armies. They called the guillotine "the national razor" and it worked hard, claiming two or three heads a day in the Place de Revolution alone. France cowered beneath the threat of its dropping blade.

Meanwhile, in events even closer to my own heart, I heard that Arno had been laid low by his Order.

"He's been banished," Mr. Weatherall read from his correspondence, holding a letter, the last vestiges of his once-proud network having got in touch at last.

"Who?" I asked.

"Arno."

"I see."

He smiled. "You pretending not to care, are you?"

"There's no pretense about it, Mr. Weatherall."

"Still not forgiven him, eh?"

"He once pledged to me that if he had his chance to take a shot, then he would take it. He had his chance and didn't take it."

"He was right," said Mr. Weatherall one day. He spat it out, as though it was something that had been on his mind.

"I beg your pardon," I said.

Actually, I didn't "say" it. I "snapped" it. The truth was that Mr. Weatherall and I had been irate with one another for weeks, maybe even months. Life had been reduced to this one thing: *lying low*. And it made me howl with frustration. Each day spent worrying about finding Germain before he found us; each day spent waiting for letters to arrive from an ever-changing series of drops. Knowing that we were fighting a losing battle.

And yes, I seethed, knowing that Germain had been so close to feeling my sword. Mr. Weatherall seethed, too, but for slightly different reasons. What went left unsaid was that Mr. Weatherall believed me to be too rash and hotheaded; that I should have waited and bided my time to plot against Germain, just as Germain had done in his takeover of our Order. Mr. Weatherall said I was thinking with my sword. He tried to tell me that my parents would not have acted with such incautious haste. He used every trick he knew, and now he used Arno.

"Arno was right," he said. "You would have been cut

down. You might as well have slit your own throat for all the good it would have done you."

I made an exasperated sound, shooting a resentful look around the room of the lodge in which we sat. It was warm, homely and I should have loved it here but instead it felt small and crowded. This room and the lodge as a whole had come to symbolize my own inaction.

"What would you have me do, then?" I asked.

"If you truly loved the Order, the best thing you can is offer to make peace. Offer to serve the Order."

My mouth dropped open.

"Yield?"

"No, not yield, make peace. Negotiate."

"But they are my enemies. I cannot *negotiate* with my enemies."

"Try looking at it from another point of view, Élise," Mr. Weatherall pressed, trying to get through to me. "You're making peace with the Assassins but you don't negotiate with your own people. That's what it looks like."

"It wasn't the Assassins who killed my father," I hissed. "You think I can truce with my father's murderers?"

He threw up his hands. "Christ, and she thinks that Templars and Assassins can just make up. What if they're all like you, eh? 'I want revenge, bugger the consequences.'"

"It would take time," I admitted.

He pounced. "And that's what you can do. You can bide your time. You can do more on the inside than you can on the outside."

"And they'll know that. They'd have smiling faces and knives behind their backs."

"They won't murder a peacemaker. The Order would think it dishonorable, and what they need above all is harmony within the Order. No. If you bring diplomacy, they'll respond with diplomacy."

"You can't be sure of that."

He gave a small shrug. "No, but either way, I believe risking death that way is better than risking death your way."

I stood and glared down at him, this old man hunched over his crutches. "So that's your advice, is it? Make peace with my father's killers."

He looked up at me with eyes that were sad because we both knew there was only one way this could end.

"It is," he said. "As your adviser, that's my advice."

"Then consider yourself dismissed," I said.

He nodded. "You want me to leave?"

I shook my head. "No. I want you to stay."

It was I who left.

2 APRIL 1794

It was almost too painful to come here again, to the château in Versailles, but this was where Arno was staying, so this was where I came.

At first I thought the information I'd been given must have been wrong because inside, the château was in the same—if not worse—condition than it had been when I was last here.

Then again, something else I'd learned was that Arno had evidently taken his banishment from the Assassins badly and had gained something of a name for himself as the local drunk.

"You look like hell," I told him, when eventually I found him ensconced in my father's office.

Regarding me with tired eyes before his gaze slid away, he said, "You look like you want something from me."

"That's a fine thing to say after you up and vanished."

He made a short scoffing sound. "You made it fairly clear my services were no longer required."

I felt my anger rise. "Don't. Don't you dare talk to me like that."

"What do you want me to say, Élise? I'm sorry I didn't leave you to die? Forgive me for caring more about you than killing Germain?"

And yes, I suppose my heart did melt. Just a little. "I thought we wanted the same thing."

"What I wanted was you. It kills me knowing my carelessness got your father killed. Everything I've done has been to fix that mistake and to prevent its happening again." He dropped his eyes. "You must have come here with something in mind. What was it?"

"Paris is tearing itself apart," I told him. "Germain has driven the Revolution to new heights of depravity. The guillotines operate nearly twenty-four hours a day now."

"And what do you expect me to do about it?"

"The Arno I love wouldn't have to ask that question," I said.

I waved a hand at the mess that had once been my father's beloved office. It was in here that I had learned of my Templar destiny; in here I had been told of Arno's Assassin lineage. Now, it was a hovel. "You're better than this," I said.

"I'm going back to Paris—are you coming?"

His shoulders slumped and for a moment I thought it was the end for Arno and me. With so many secrets poisoning the lake of our relationship, how could we ever be what we were? Ours was a love thwarted by the plans made for us by other people.

But he stood, as though having made the decision. He raised his head and looked at me with bleary, hung-over eyes that were nevertheless filled with renewed purpose.

"Not yet," he told me. "I can't leave without taking care of La Touche."

Aloys La Touche was a new addition to our—or should I say "their"—Order. One of Germain's appointments, he had joined the ranks of the Crows. Besides a kind of dull, burning hatred I felt for all of those close to Germain, I had no particular feelings for the man either way. Arno could kill him for all I cared. Even so.

"Is this really necessary?" I asked him. "The longer we wait, the more likely Germain will slip through our fingers."

"He's been grinding Versailles under his boot for months; I should have done something about this a long time ago."

He had a point.

"All right. I'll go see to our transportation. Stay out of trouble."

He looked at me. I grinned and amended my fare-well. "Don't get caught."

3 APRIL 1794

"Things have changed a great deal since you left Paris," I told him the next day as we took our places on a cart back to the city.

"A great deal to be set right." He nodded.

"And we're no closer to finding Germain."

"That's not entirely true," he said. "I have a name."

I looked at him. "Who?"

"Robespierre."

Maximilien de Robespierre. Now there was a name to conjure with. The man they called "l'Incorruptible" was president of the Jacobins and the nearest France currently had to a ruler. Thus, he was a man who wielded enormous power.

I said, "I think you'd better tell me what you know, don't you?"

"I've seen everything, Élise," he said, his face crumpling as though unable to cope with the recollection.

"What do you mean, 'everything'?" I asked him carefully.

"I mean—I see things. You remember when I killed Bellec? I saw things then. It's how I was able to know what to do next."

I nodded, thinking about what my father had told me of Arno. It was as though he had believed Arno possessed special gifts. Something not quite . . . usual.

"Tell me more," I said, wanting him to open up but at the same time not wanting to speak to him.

"You remember that I killed Sivert?"

I pursed my lips, damping down a little surge of denial.

"I had a vision then," Arno continued. "I have had visions for them all, Élise. All of the targets—men and women with whom I have personal connection. I saw Sivert denied entrance to a Templar meeting by your father, the first seeds of his resentment toward your father; I saw Sivert approach the King of Beggars. I saw the pair of them attack your father."

"Two of them," I spat.

"Oh, your father fought bravely, and as I say, he managed to take out Sivert's eye; indeed, he would most definitely have prevailed were it not for the intervention of the King of Beggars . . ."

"You saw it happen?"

"In the vision, yes."

"Which is how you knew that an initiation pin was used?"

"Indeed."

I leaned into him.

"This thing you do. How do you do it?"

"Bellec said that some men are born with the ability, others can learn it over time through training."

"And you're one of those born with it."

"It would seem so."

"What else?"

"From the King of Beggars I learned that your father resisted his overtures. I saw Sivert offer him the pin, with talk of how his 'master' could help."

"His 'master'? Germain?"

"Exactly. Though I didn't know that then. All I saw was a robed figure accepting the King of Beggars into your Order."

I thought of Mr. Weatherall with a pang of regret that we had parted on such bad terms, wishing I could share with him the fact that our theories had been correct.

"The King of Beggars was rewarded for killing my father?" I said.

"It would seem so. When I killed Madame Levesque I saw behind the Templars' plans to raise the price of grain. I also witnessed your father expelling Germain from the Order. Germain invoked de Molay as they dragged him away. I saw Germain later approach Madame Levesque. I saw the Templars plotting to release information that would be damaging to the king.

"Germain said that when the king was executed like a

common criminal he could show the world the truth of Jacques de Molay.

"I saw something else, too. I saw Germain introduce his Templar confederates to none other than Maximilien de Robespierre."

8 JUNE 1794

i

I could barely remember a time when the streets of Paris weren't thronged with people. I had seen so many uprisings and executions, so much blood spilled on the streets. Now, on the Champ de Mars, the city had gathered again. But there was a different feeling in the air this time.

Before, Parisians had come ready for battle, certainly prepared to kill, and prepared to die if need be; where before they had gathered to fill their nostrils with the smell of guillotine blood, now they came to celebrate.

They were arranged in columns, with the men on one side, the women on the other. Many carried flowers, bouquets and branches of oak, and those who didn't held flags aloft, and they filled the Champ de Mars, this huge park space, looking toward the man-made mountain at its center, on which they hoped to see their new leader.

This, then, was the Festival of the Supreme Being, one of Robespierre's ideas. While the other revolutionary factions wanted to dispense with religion altogether, Robespierre understood its power. He knew that the common man was attached to the idea of belief. How they wanted to believe in *something*.

With many Republicans supporting what they were now calling "de-Christianisation," Robespierre had had an idea. He had come up with the creation of a new creed. He had put forward the idea of a new, non-Christian deity: the Supreme Being. And last month announced the birth of a new state religion, with a decree that the "French people recognizes the existence of the Supreme Being and the immortality of the soul . . ."

To convince the people what a great idea it was, he had come up with the idea of festivals. The Festival of the Supreme Being was the first one.

What his *real* motives were, I had no idea. All I knew was that Arno had discovered something. Arno had discovered that Robespierre was Germain's puppet. Whatever was happening here today had less to do with the needs of the general populace and more to do with furthering the aims of my former Templar associates.

"We'll never get close to him in the middle of all this," observed Arno. "We had best retire and wait for a better opportunity."

"You're still thinking like an Assassin," I chided him. "This time, I have the plan."

He looked at me with raised eyebrows and I ignored his attempts at humorous disbelief.

"Oh? And what plan is that?"

"Think like a Templar."

There came the sound of artillery in the distance. The babble of the crowd died, then rose again as they readied themselves, and solemnly the two columns of people began moving toward the mount.

There were thousands of them. They sang songs and called, "Viva Robespierre," as they advanced on the mount. Everywhere the tricolor was held aloft, fluttering in a gentle breeze.

As we approached I saw more and more of the white breeches and buttoned double-breasted jackets of the National Guard. Every one of them had a sword at his hip, most with muskets and bayonets too. They formed a barrier between the crowds and the mount from which Robespierre would deliver his address. We drew to a halt before them, waiting for the great speech to begin.

"All right, what now?" asked Arno, appearing at my side.

"Robespierre is unassailable, he's got half the Guard out in force," I said, indicating the men. "We'll never get within yards of him."

Arno shot me a look. "Which is what I said."

Not far away from where we stood was a large tent, ringed by vigilant-looking National Guard. In there would be Robespierre.

In there, Robespierre would no doubt be preparing himself for his great speech, like an actor before the show, ready to appear before the people as regal and presidential.

Indeed, there was no doubt in anyone's minds to whom the Supreme Being referred; I'd heard mumbles of it as we made our way inside the main arena. True, there was a celebratory mood in the air, with the singing, the laughter, the branches and bouquets we all held, but there was no shortage of dissension either, even if it was delivered at far lower volume.

And that gave me an idea . . .

"But he's not as popular as he was," I said to Arno. "The purges, this Supreme Being cult . . . All we have to do is discredit him."

Arno agreed. "And a massive public spectacle is the perfect venue."

"Exactly. Paint him as a dangerous lunatic and his power will evaporate like snow in April. All we need is some convincing evidence."

ii

From the mount, Robespierre gave his speech. "The eternally happy day which the French people consecrates to the Supreme Being has finally arrived . . ." he began. The crowd lapped up his every word, and as I moved through the crowd I thought, *He's really doing it*. He was really inventing a new God, and he meant for us all to worship it.

"He did not create kings to devour the human species," Robespierre said. "Neither did he create priests to harness us like brute beasts to the carriages of kings."

Truly this new God was a God fit for a revolution.

Then he was finished and the crowd was roaring, perhaps even those naysayers caught up in the communal joy of the occasion. You had to hand it to Robespierre. For a country so divided we were at last calling with one voice.

Arno, meanwhile, had found his way into Robespierre's tent, looking for something we could use to incriminate our supreme leader. He reappeared bearing gifts, a letter I read, proving beyond a doubt Robespierre's link to Germain.

Monsieur Robespierre,

Take care that you do not allow your personal ambitions to come before the Great Work. That which we do, we do not for our own glory, but to remake the world in de Molay's image.

G

There was also a list. "A list of names—about fifty or so deputies of the National Convention," said Arno. "All written in Robespierre's hand and all opposed to him."

I chuckled. "I imagine those good gentlemen would be quite interested to know they're on that list. But first . . ."

I indicated a short distance away. "Monsieur Robespierre brought his own refreshments. Distract the guards for me. I have an idea."

iii

We performed our tasks well. Arno had ensured that the list grabbed the attention of some of Robespierre's fiercest critics; I, meanwhile, had drugged his wine.

"What exactly was in that wine?" said Arno as we stood and waited for the show to begin—for Robespierre to make a speech under the influence of what I had slipped in his drink, which was . . .

"Powdered ergot. In small doses it causes mania, slurred speech, even hallucinations."

Arno grinned. "Well, this should be interesting."

Indeed it had been. Robespierre had rambled and slurred his way through his speech, and when his adversaries challenged him about the list, he had no sensible answer.

We left as Robespierre was clambering down from the mount accompanied by the boos and jeers of the crowd, probably confused by how the Festival could start so well and end quite so catastrophically.

I wondered if he could sense the presence of hands behind the scenes, manipulating events. If he was Templar, he should be accustomed to it. Either way, the process of discrediting him had well and truly begun. We only needed to wait.

27 JULY 1794

i

Reading that last entry back. "We only needed to wait."

Well, pah! A pox on it, as Mr. Weatherall would have said. It was the waiting that drove me insane.

Alone, I whirled across the bare floors of the empty villa, sword in hand, practicing my swordplay, and I found myself looking for Mr. Weatherall, who would be sitting watching me with his crutches close to hand, telling me my stance was wrong, my footwork overcomplicated—"And will you stop bloody showing off"—only he wasn't there. I was alone. And I should know better, really, because alone was no good for me. Alone I pondered. I had too much time to wallow in my own thoughts and dwell on things.

Alone I festered like an infected wound.

All of which was part of the reason that today I lost sight of myself.

ii
___

It began with news that spurred me into action, then a meeting with Arno. Robespierre had been arrested, I told him. "Apparently he made vague threats about a purge against 'enemies of the state' and the Committee turned on him. He's scheduled for execution in the morning."

We needed to see him before that, of course, but at the For-l'Évêque prison we found a scene of carnage. Dead men were everywhere, Robespierre's escort slaughtered, but there was no sign of Robespierre himself. From a corner came a groan and Arno scrambled to kneel with a guard who lay half–sitting up against the wall, his chest sticky with blood. He reached to loosen the soldier's clothes, find the wound and stop the bleeding. "What happened here?" he asked.

I stepped closer, craning to hear the answer. As Arno struggled to help him live, I stepped over a puddle of his blood to bring my ear closer to his mouth.

"Warden refused to take the prisoners," coughed the dying man. "While we were waiting for orders, troops from the Paris Commune ambushed us. They took Robespierre and the other prisoners."

"Where?"

"That way." He pointed. "Can't be going far. Half the city's turned out against Robespierre."

"Merci."

And of course I should have helped tend to the man's wounds. I should not have hastened away to find Robespierre. It was the wrong thing to do. It was bad.

Even so, it was not as bad as what happened next.

iii

Robespierre had tried to escape, but as with many of his plans lately, it was thwarted by me and Arno. We reached him at the Hôtel de Ville, with the Convention troops moments away from bursting through the door.

"Where's Germain?" I had demanded to know.

"I'll never talk."

And I did it. This terrible thing. This thing that is proof I've arrived at the edge of what it means to be me, which I can't stop, because to get here, I've come too far.

What I did was pull my pistol from my belt and even as Arno was raising his hand to try to stop me, I was pointing my pistol at Robespierre, seeing him through a veil of hatred, and firing.

The shot was like cannon fire in the room. The ball slapped into his lower jaw, which cracked and hung limp at the same time as a blood began gushing from his lips and gums, splattering to the floor.

He screamed and writhed, his eyes wide with terror and pain, his hands at his shattered and bleeding mouth.

"Write," I snapped.

He tried to form words but could not, scribbling on a piece of paper, blood pouring from his face.

"The Temple," I said, snatching up the paper and ignoring the horrified look Arno was giving me. "I should have known."

The boots of the Convention troops were close now.

I looked at Robespierre. "I hope you enjoy revolutionary justice, monsieur," I said, and we departed, and behind us we left a weeping, wounded Robespierre, holding his mouth together with hands that were soaked in blood . . . and a little bit of my humanity.

iv

These things. It's as though I'm imagining them being done by another person—"another me" over whom I have no control, whose actions I can only watch with a kind of detached interest.

And I suppose that all of this is evidence, not only that I know I have failed to heed the warnings of Mr. Weatherall and perhaps most egregiously failed to act upon the teachings of my mother and father, but that I have reached some place of mental infection and it is too late to stop it. There is no choice but to cut it away and hope that I survive the amputation a cleansed person.

But if I do not survive . . .

I must now conclude my journal, at least for tonight. I have some letters to write.

12 SEPTEMBER 1794

i

I suppose here is where I should take up the story. I should take it up by saying that when I met her at the Temple the following day she looked pale and drawn, and I now know why.

Over a hundred years ago the Temple du Marais had been modeled on the Roman Pantheon. Rising behind an arched frontage, with its own version of the famed dome, were high walls. The only traffic in and out was the occasional wagon full of hay passing in through a postern gate.

Straightaway Élise wanted to split up, but I wasn't sure; there was something about the look in her eyes, as though there was something missing, as if a part of her were absent somehow.

Which in a way, I suppose, was right. I took it then to

be determination and focus and I've read nothing in her journals to suggest it was anything more than just that, writ large. Élise may have been determined to reach Germain but I don't think she believed she would be killed, only that she was going to kill Germain that day or die in the process.

And perhaps she allowed that serenity of the soul to swallow her fear, forgetting that sometimes, however determined you are, however advanced your skills in combat, it's fear that keeps you alive.

As we'd split up to find a way into the Temple's inner sanctum, she'd fixed me with a meaningful look. "If you get a shot at Germain," she said, "you take it."

ii

And I did. I had found him inside the Temple, dark within the dank gray stone, a lone figure among the pillars inside the church.

And there I had my shot.

He was too quick for me. He produced a sword of uncanny powers. This sword was the kind of thing I would have once laughed off and said must be a trick. These days, of course, I knew better than to scoff at things I didn't understand, and anyway, as Germain wielded the strange glowing thing, it appeared to harness and unleash great bolts of energy as though converting them from the air around him. It appeared to glow and spark. No, there was nothing laughable whatsoever about this sword.

Now I wonder: had I been a quarter of a second faster

then, would Élise still be alive? I wonder about the fantastical sword that had given him the edge over me—even as it spoke again, sparking and throwing out a bolt of energy that seemed to leap for me as though it had a mind of its own.

"So, the prodigal Assassin returns," called Germain. "I suspected as much when La Touche stopped sending his tax revenues. You've become quite the thorn in my side."

I dashed from out of my hiding place from behind a column, my hidden blade extended and glowing dully in the half-light.

"I assume Robespierre was your doing as well?" he said as we squared up.

I grinned agreement.

"No matter." He smiled. "His Reign of Terror served its purpose. The metal has been fired and shaped. Quenching it will only set its form."

I darted forward and struck out at his sword, aiming not to deflect it but damage it, knowing that if I could somehow disarm him, I might swing the battle in my favor.

"Why so persistent?" he taunted. "Is it revenge? Did Bellec indoctrinate you so thoroughly that you do his bidding even now? Or is it love? Has de la Serre's daughter turned your head?"

My hidden blade came down hard on the shaft of his sword and the weapon seemed to give out a hurt, angry glow, as though it was wounded.

Even so, Germain, on the back foot now, was somehow able to harness its power again, this time in a way even I had difficulty believing. With a burst of energy that threw me backward and left a scorch mark on the floor, the Grand Master simply disappeared.

From deep within the recesses of the Temple came an answering bang that seemed to ripple around the stone walls and I pulled myself to my feet to head in that direction, scrambling down a set of damp steps until I reached the crypt.

From my left Élise emerged from the dark of the catacombs. Clever. Just a few moments earlier and we would have had Germain cut off in both directions.

(These moments, I realize now—a few seconds here, a few seconds there. They were tiny heartbreaking quirks in time that decided Élise's fate.)

"What happened here?" she said, studying what had once been the gate to the crypt, but which was now blackened and twisted.

I shook my head. "Germain's got some kind of weapon . . . I've never seen its like before. He got away from me."

She barely glanced my way. "He didn't come past me. He must be down there."

I shot her a doubtful look. Even so, with our swords ready we took the few remaining steps down to the crypt.

Empty. But there had to be a secret door. I began to feel for one and my fingertips found a lever between the stones, pulled it, stood back as a door slid open with a deep, grinding sound and a large vault stretched ahead, lined with pillars and Templar sarcophagi.

Inside stood Germain. He had his back to us, and I had just realized that his sword had somehow recovered its power and that he was waiting for us, when from by my side Élise leapt forward with a shout of rage.

"Élise!"

Sure enough, as Élise bore down upon him, Germain swung around, wielding the bright glowing sword, a snakelike bolt of energy surging from it and forcing us to dive for cover.

He laughed. "Ah, and Mademoiselle de la Serre as well. This is quite the reunion."

"Stay hidden," I whispered to Élise. "Keep him talking."

She nodded and crouched behind a sarcophagus, waving me away and calling to Germain at the same time.

"Did you think this day would never come," she said, "that because François de la Serre had no sons to avenge him, your crime would go unanswered?"

"Revenge, is it?" He laughed. "Your vision is as narrow as your father's."

She shouted, "You're one to talk. How wide of vision was your grab for power?"

"Power? No, no, no, you're smarter than that. This was never about power. It's always been about control. Did your father teach you nothing? The Order has grown complacent. For centuries we've focused our attentions on the trappings of power: the titles of nobility, the offices of Church and State. Caught in the very lie we crafted to shepherd the masses."

"I'll kill you," she called.

"You're not listening. Killing me won't stop anything. When our brother Templars see the old institutions crumble, they will adapt. They will retreat to the shadows and we will, at last, be the Secret Masters we were meant to be. So come—kill me if you can. Unless you can miracle up a new king and halt the Revolution in its tracks, it does not matter."

I sprung my trap, coming up on Germain's blind side, and was unlucky not to finish him with my blade; instead, his sword crackled angrily and an orb of blue-white energy came shooting out of it with the velocity of a cannonball, inflicting a similar kind of damage on the vault around us. In a moment I was engulfed by dust as masonry fell down around me—and in the next moment was trapped beneath a fallen pillar.

"Arno," she called.

"I'm stuck."

Whatever the great ball of energy had been, Germain hadn't been in full command of it. He was picking himself up now, coughing as he squinted through the swirling dust at us, stumbling on masonry littering the stone floor as he dragged himself to his feet.

Hunched over, he stood and wondered whether to finish us off but evidently decided against it, and instead he spun and fled farther into the depths of the vault, his sword spitting angry blacksmiths' sparks.

I watched as Élise's desperate eyes went from me, trapped and in need of help, to the retreating figure of Germain, then back to me.

"He's getting away," she said, her eyes blazing with frustration, and when she looked back at me I could see the indecision written all over her face: the two choices. stay and let Germain escape, or go after him.

There was never any doubt, really, which option she'd choose.

"I can take him," she said, deciding.

"You can't," I said. "Not alone. Wait for me. *Élise*."

But she had disappeared. With a howl of effort I freed myself from the stone, scrambled to my feet and set off after her.

And if I had been just a few seconds earlier (as I say— each step of the way toward her death, decided by just a few seconds) I could have tipped the battle, because Germain was defending furiously, the effort written all over those cruel features, and perhaps his sword—this thing I've decided was almost alive—somehow sensed that its owner faced defeat . . . and with a great explosion of sound, light and a huge, indiscriminate burst of energy, it shattered.

The force rocked me on my feet but my first thought was for Élise. Both she and Germain had been at the very center of the blast.

Through the dust I saw her red hair where she lay crumpled beneath a column. I ran to her, went to my knees, took her head in my hands.

In her eyes was a bright light. Élise saw me, I think, in the second before she died. She saw me and the light came into her eyes one final time—and then was winked out.

iii

I ignored Germain's coughing for a while, and then gently laid Élise's head down on the stone, closed her eyes and stood, walking across the debris-strewn chamber to where he lay, blood bubbling at his mouth, watching me, almost dead.

I knelt. Without taking my eyes off his, I brought my blade to bear and finished the job.

12 SEPTEMBER 1794

I saw the vision when Germain died.

(And let me pause to imagine the sideways look on Élise's face when I told her about the visions. Not quite belief, not quite doubt.)

This vision was different from the others. I was somehow present within it, in a way that I never had been before.

I found myself in Germain's workshop, watching as Germain, looking like he once had, in the clothes of a silversmith, sat crafting a pin.

As I gazed at him, he clutched as his temples and began to mutter to himself, as though assailed by something in his head.

What was it? I wondered, just as a voice came from behind me, startling me.

"Bravo. You've slain the villain. That is how you've cast this little morality play in your mind, isn't it?"

Still in the vision I turned to see the source of the voice, only to find another Germain—this one much older, the Germain I knew—standing behind me.

"Oh, I'm not really here," he explained. "I'm not really there either. At the moment I'm bleeding out on the floor of the Temple. But it seems the father of understanding has seen fit to give us this time to talk."

All of a sudden the scene shifted and we were in the secret vault beneath the Temple where they had been fighting, only the vault was unscathed, and there was no sign of Élise, no rubble all over the ground. What I saw were scenes from another, earlier time as the younger Germain approached the altar where de Molay's texts were laid out.

"Ah," came the voice of the guide-Germain from behind me. "A particular favorite of mine. I did not understand the visions that haunted my mind, you see. Images of great golden towers, of cities shining white as silver. I thought I was going mad. Then I found this place—Jacques de Molay's vault. Through his writings, I understood."

"Understood what?"

"That somehow, through the centuries, I was connected to Grand Master de Molay. That I had been chosen to purge the Order of the decadence and corruption that had set in like rot. To wash clean the world and restore it to the truth the father of understanding intended."

And once again the scene shifted. This time I found

myself in a room, where high-ranking Templars passed judgment on Germain and banished him from the Order.

"Prophets are seldom appreciated in their own time," he explained from behind me. "Exile and abasement forced me to reexamine my strategies, to find new avenues for the realization of my purpose."

Once more the scene shifted and I found myself being assaulted with images of the Terror, the guillotine rising and falling like the inexorable ticking of a clock.

"No matter the cost?" I said.

"New order never comes without the destruction of the old. And if men are made to fear untrammeled liberty, so much the better. A brief taste of chaos will remind them why they crave obedience."

And then the scene warped again and once more we were in the vault. This time it was moments before the explosion that had claimed her life, and I saw in her face the effort of making what had been the battle's decisive blow, and I hoped that she knew her father had been avenged and that it had brought her some peace.

"It appears we part ways here," said Germain. "Think on this: the march of progress is slow, but it is inevitable as a glacier. All you have accomplished here is to delay the inevitable. One death cannot stop the tide. Perhaps it will not be my hand that shepherds mankind back into its proper place—but it will be someone's. Think on this when you remember her."

I would.

12 SEPTEMBER 1794

Something puzzled me in the weeks after her death. How was it possible that I had known Élise better than any other person, had spent more time with her than anybody else, and that it had counted for nothing in the end because I didn't really know her?

The girl, yes, but not the woman she became. Having watched her grow, I never really got the chance to admire the beauty of Élise in bloom.

And now I never will. Gone is the future we had together. My heart aches for her. My chest feels heavy. I weep for love lost, for yesterdays gone, for tomorrows that will never be.

I weep for Élise, who for all her flaws, is the best person I will ever know.

12 September 1794

Not long after her death, a man called Ruddock came to see me at Versailles. Smelling of perfume that barely masked an almost overpowering body odor, he came bearing a letter marked, "To be opened in the event of my death."

The seal was broken.

"You've read it?" I said.

"Indeed, sir. With a heavy heart I did as instructed."

"It was to be opened in the event of her death," I said, feeling a little betrayed by the shake of emotion in my voice.

"That's right, sir. Upon receipt of the letter I placed it in a dresser, hoping never to see it again, if I'm honest with you."

I fixed him with a stare. "Tell me the truth, did you

read it *before* she died? Because if you did, then you could have done something about it."

Ruddock gave a slightly sad, airy smile. "Could I? I rather think not, Mr. Dorian. Soldiers write such letters before battle, sir. The mere fact of them contemplating their own mortality does not a postponement make."

He'd read it, I could tell. He'd read it before she died.

I frowned, unfolded the paper and began to read Élise's words for myself.

Ruddock,

Forgive the lack of pleasantries but I'm afraid I have reconciled my feelings toward you, and they are this: I don't much like you. I'm sorry about this, and I appreciate you may consider it a rather rude thing to announce, but if you're reading this then either you have ignored my instruction or I am dead and in either case neither of us should be concerned with matters of etiquette.

Now, notwithstanding the fact of my feelings toward you, I appreciate your attempts to make recompense for your actions, and I have been touched by your loyalty. It is for this reason that I would ask you to show this letter to my beloved Arno Dorian, himself an Assassin, and trust that he will take it as my testimonial to your changed ways. However, since I very much doubt the word of a deceased Templar will be enough to ingratiate yourself with the Brotherhood, I have something else for you, too.

Arno, I would ask that you pass the letters I am about to discuss to Monsieur Ruddock, in order that he may use them to curry favor with the Assassins in the hope of being accepted back in the Creed. Monsieur Ruddock will be aware that this deed illustrates my trust in him and my faith that the task will be completed sooner rather than later, and for this reason will require no monitoring whatsoever.

Arno, the remainder of my letter is for you. I pray I will return from my confrontation with Germain and can retrieve this letter from Ruddock, tear it up and not think of its contents again. But if you're reading it, it means, firstly, that my trust in Ruddock has been repaid, and secondly that I am dead.

There is much I have to tell you from beyond the grave, and to this end, I bequeath to you my journals, the most recent of which you will find in my satchel, the preceding ones being kept in a cache with the letters of which I speak. If, when inspecting the trunk, you reach the sad conclusion that I had not been treasuring letters you sent to me, please know that the reason why may be found with the pages of my journals. You will also find a necklace, given to me by Jennifer Scott.

The next page was missing.

"Where's the rest?" I demanded to know.

Ruddock held out calm-down hands. "Ah, well now. The second page includes a special message regarding the location of the letters the mademoiselle says may prove my redemption. And, well, um, forgive the seeming rudeness, but it strikes me that if I give you this letter I have no 'bargaining chip' as it were, and no guarantee that you won't simply take the letters and use them to further your own standing within the Brotherhood."

I looked at him, gesturing with the letter. "Élise asks me to trust you and I ask you do the same in return for me. You have my word of honor that the letters will be yours."

"Then that is enough for me." He bowed and handed me the second page of the letter. I read it through until I reached the end.

> . . . *now, of course, I lie at the Cimetière des Innocents, and I am with my parents, close to those I love.*
>
> *Who I love most of all, though, Arno, is you. I hope you understand how much I love you. And I hope you love me too. And for allowing me the honor of knowing such a fulfilling emotion, I thank you.*
>
> *Your beloved,*
> *Élise*

"Does she say where the letters are?" asked Ruddock hopefully.

"She does," I told him,

"And where is that, sir?"

I looked at him, saw him through Élise's eyes and could see that there were some things too important to be left to newly won trust.

"You've read it; you already know."

"She called it *Le Palais de la Misère*. And that means something to you, does it?"

"Yes, thank you, Ruddock, it means something. I know where to go. Please, leave your current address with me. I shall be in touch as soon as I have recovered the letters. Know that to thank you for what you have done, I shall be endorsing any effort you make to win favor with the Assassins."

He drew himself up little, squared his shoulders.

"For that I thank you . . . Brother."

12 SEPTEMBER 1794

i

There was a young man on a cart in the road. He sat with one leg up and his arms folded, squinting at me beneath a wide-brimmed straw hat, mottled by sunlight that found its way through a canopy of leafy branches overhead. He was waiting—waiting, it turned out, for me.

"Are you Arno Dorian, monsieur?" he said, sitting up.

"I am."

His eyes darted. "Do you wear a hidden blade?"

"You think me an Assassin?"

"Are you?"

With a snick it was out, glinting in the sunlight. Just as quickly I retracted it.

The boy nodded. "My name is Jacques. Élise was a friend to me, a good mistress to my wife, Helene, and the close confidante of . . . a man who also lives with us."

"An Italian man?" I said, testing him.

"No, sir." The young man grinned. "An Englishman who goes by the name of Mr. Weatherall."

I smiled at him. "I think you'd better take me to him, don't you?"

On his cart, Jacques led the way, and we took a path that led us along one side of a river. On the other bank was a stretch of manicured lawn that led up to a wing of the Maison Royale, and I looked at it with a mixture of sadness and bemusement—sadness because the mere sight of it reminded me of her. Bemusement because it was nothing like I had imagined from the Satanic picture she had painted in her letters all those years ago.

We continued, as though we were skirting the school, which I supposed we were. Élise had mentioned a lodge.

Sure enough, we came upon a large-based, low building in a clearing, with a couple of ramshackle outbuildings not far away. Standing on step of a porch was an older man on crutches.

The crutches were new, of course, but I half recognized the gray beard from having seen him around the château when I was growing up. He had been someone who belonged to Élise's "other" life, her François and Julie life. Not someone I had ever concerned myself with then. Nor him with me.

And yet, of course, I write this entry having read Élise's journals, and can now appreciate the position he held in her life, and again I marvel at how little I really knew of her; again I mourn the chance to have discovered the "real" Élise, the Élise free of secrets to keep and a destiny to fulfill. I sometimes think that with all of that on her shoulders, we were doomed from the start, she and I.

"Hello, son," he growled at me from the porch. "It's been a long time. Look at you. I hardly recognize you."

"Hello, Mr. Weatherall," I said, dismounting and tethering my horse. I approached him, and had I known then what I know now, I would have greeted him the French way, with an embrace, and we would have shared the solidarity of bereavement, we who were the two men closest to Élise. But I didn't; he was merely a face from the past.

Inside the lodge the décor was simple, the furniture spartan. Mr. Weatherall leaned on his crutches and ushered me to a table, requesting coffee from a girl I took to be Helene, at whom I smiled and received a curtsy in return.

Again, I paid her less mind than I would have done had I read the journals. I was just taking the first steps into Élise's other life, feeling like an interloper, like I shouldn't be there.

Jacques entered, too, doffing an imaginary cap, greeting Helene with a kiss. The atmosphere in the kitchen was bustling. Homely. No wonder Élise liked it here.

"Was I expected?" I said, with a nod at Jacques.

Mr. Weatherall settled before he nodded thoughtfully. "Élise wrote to say Arno Dorian might be collecting her trunk. A couple of days ago Madame Levene brought the news that she'd been killed."

I raised an eyebrow. "She wrote to you? And you didn't suspect there was anything wrong."

"Son, I may have wood beneath my armpits but don't go thinking I've got it in my head. What I *suspected* was that she was still angry with me, not that she was making plans."

"She was angry with you?"

"We'd had words. We parted on bad terms. The not-on-speaking-terms sort of terms."

"I see. I have been on the receiving end of a number of Élise's tempers myself. It's never very pleasant."

We looked at one another, smiles appearing. Mr. Weatherall tucked his chin into his chest as he nodded with bittersweet remembrance. "Oh yes, indeed. Quite a will on that one." He looked at me. "I expect that's what got her killed, is it?"

"What did you hear about it?"

"That the noblewoman Élise de la Serre was somehow involved in an altercation with the renowned silversmith François Thomas Germain, and that swords were drawn and the pair of them fought a battle that ended in their mutual death at each other's hands. That about how you saw it, was it?"

I nodded. "She went after him. She could have exercised more caution."

He shook his head. "She never was one for exercising caution. She give him a good battle, did she?"

"She fought like a tiger, Mr. Weatherall, a true credit to her sparring partner."

The older man gave a short, mirthless laugh. "There was a time when I was sparring partner to François Thomas Germain as well, you know. Yes, you may make that face. The treacherous Germain honed his own skills on a wooden blade wielded by Freddie Weatherall. Back then, when it was unthinkable that a Templar might turn on a Templar."

"Unthinkable? Why? Were Templars less ambitious when you were younger? Was the process of backstabbing in the name of advancement less developed?"

"No." Mr. Weatherall smiled. "Just that we were younger, and that bit more idealistic when it came to our fellow man."

ii

Perhaps we would have more to say to one another if we ever met again. As it was, we two men who were closest to Élise had precious little in common, and when the conversation had at last withered and dried like an autumn leaf, I asked to see the trunk.

He took me to it, and I carried it to the kitchen table, set it down, running my hands over the monogram EDLS, then opening it. Inside, just as she'd said, were the letters, her journals and the necklace.

"Something else," said Mr. Weatherall, and left, returning some moments later with a short sword. "Her first sword," he explained, adding it to the trunk with a disdainful look, as though I should have known instantly. As though I had a lot to learn about Élise.

Which of course, I did. And now I understand that, and realize that I may have appeared a little haughty during my visit, as though these people were not worthy of Élise, when in reality it was the other way around.

I went to fill my saddlebags with Élise's keepsakes, ready to transport them back to Versailles, stepping out into a clear and still moonlit night and going top my horse. I stood in the clearing, the buckle of a bag in my hand, when I smelled something. Something unmistakable. It was perfume.

iii

Thinking we were on our way, my mare snorted and pawed at the ground but I steadied her, patting her neck and sniffing the air at the same time. I licked a finger, held it up and verified the wind was coming from behind me. I searched the perimeter of the clearing. Perhaps it was one of the girls from school who had made her way down here for some reason. Perhaps it was Jacques's mother . . .

Or perhaps I recognized the scent of the perfume and knew exactly who it was.

I came upon him hiding behind a tree, his white hair almost luminous in the moon.

"What are you doing here?" I asked him. Ruddock.

He pulled a face. "Ah, well, you see, I . . . well, you could say I was just wanting to safeguard my prize."

I shook my head with irritation. "So you don't trust me, after all?"

"Well, do *you* trust *me*? Did Élise trust me? Do any of us trust each other, we who live our lives in secret societies?"

"Come on," I said, "inside."

iv

"Who's this?"

The occupants of the lodge, having turned in for bed just moments ago, reappeared: Helene in a nightdress, Jacques in just his breeches, Mr. Weatherall still fully dressed.

"His name is Ruddock."

I don't think I've ever seen such a remarkable transformation as the one that came over Weatherall then. His face colored, a look of fury crossing it as his glare descended on Ruddock.

"Mr. Ruddock plans to collect his letters, then be on his way," I continued.

"You didn't tell me they were going to him," said Weatherall with a growl.

I cast him a look, thinking that I was growing tired of Weatherall, and that the sooner my business was concluded, the better.

"There is bad blood between the two of you, I take it."

Mr. Weatherall merely glowered; Ruddock simpered.

"Élise vouched for him," I told Weatherall. "He is by all accounts a changed man, and has been forgiven for past misdemeanors."

"Please," Ruddock implored me, his eyes darting, clearly unnerved by the thunder that rolled across the face of Weatherall, "just hand me the letters and I will go."

"I'll get you your letters, if that's what you want," said Weatherall, moving over to the trunk, "but believe you me, if it wasn't Élise's wish, you'd be picking them out your throat."

"I loved her too in my own way," protested Ruddock. "She saved my life twice."

By the trunk Weatherall paused. "Saved your life twice, did she?"

Ruddock wrung his hands. "She did. She saved me from the hangman's noose and from the Carrolls before that."

Standing by the trunk, Mr. Weatherall nodded thoughtfully. "Yeah, I remember she saved you from the hangman's noose. But the Carrolls . . ."

A guilty shadow passed across Ruddock's face. "Well, she told me at the time that the Carrolls were coming for me."

"You knew them did you, the Carrolls?" asked Weatherall innocently.

Ruddock swallowed. "I knew *of* them, of course I did."

"And you scarpered?"

He bristled. "As anybody in my position would have done."

"Exactly." Weatherall nodded. "You did the right thing, missing all of the fun. Fact remains, though, they weren't going to kill you."

"Well, then I suppose you'd have to say that Élise saved my life once. I hardly think it matters and after all, once is enough."

"Unless they *were* going to kill you."

Ruddock gave a nervous laugh, his eyes still flitting around the room. "Well, you've just said yourself they weren't."

"But what if they were?" pressed Weatherall. I wondered, what on earth was he getting at?

"Well, they weren't," said Ruddock with a wheedling note in his voice.

"How do you know?"

"I beg your pardon."

Sweat glistened on Ruddock's brow and the smile on his face was lopsided and queasy. His gaze found mine as though searching for support, but he found none. I was just watching. Watching carefully.

"See," continued Weatherall, "I think you were working for the Carrolls back then, and you thought they were on their way to silence you—which they might well have been. I think that either you gave us false information about the King of Beggars or he was working on behalf of the Carrolls when they hired you to kill Julie de la Serre. That's what I think."

Ruddock was shaking his head. He'd tried a look of nonchalant bemusement; he'd tried a look of "this is outrageous" indignation and settled on a look of panic.

"No," he said. "Now this has gone far enough. I work for myself."

"But have ambitions to rejoin the Assassins?" I prompted.

"No." He shook his head furiously. "I'm cured of all that. And you know who finally cured me? Why, the fragrant Élise. She hated both of your Orders, you know that? Two ticks fighting for control of the cat, was what she called you. Futile and deluded, she called you, and she was right. She told me I'd be better off without you, and she was right." He sneered at us. "Templars? Assassins? I

piss on you all for a bunch of worthless old women squabbling over ancient dogma."

"So you have no interest in rejoining the Assassins,
and thus no interest in the letters?" I asked him.

"None at all," he insisted.

"Then what are you doing here?" I said.

The knowledge that the hole he'd dug was too deep
flashed across his face, then he whirled and in one movement drew a brace of pistols. Before I could react he had
grabbed Helene, pointed one of the pistols at her head
and covered the room with the other one.

"The Carrolls say hello," he said.

v

As a new kind of tension settled over the room, Helene
whimpered. The flesh at her temple whitened where the
barrel of the pistol pointed hard and she looked imploringly over Ruddock's forearm to where Jacques stood
coiled and ready to strike, fighting the need to get over
there, free Helene and take Ruddock apart with the
need not to spook him into shooting her.

"Perhaps," I said, after a silence, "you might like to
tell me who these Carrolls are."

"The Carroll family of London," said Ruddock, one
eye on Jacques, who stood tensed, his face in furious
knots. "At first they hoped to influence the path of the
French Templars, but then Élise upset them by killing
their daughter, which gave it a somewhat 'personal'
dimension.

"And of course they did what any good doting parents with a lot of money and a network of killers at their disposal would do, they ordered revenge. Not just on her but on her protector, oh, and I'm sure they'll pay handsomely for these letters into the bargain."

"Élise was right," said Weatherall to himself. "She never believed the Crows tried to kill her mother. She was right."

"She was," said Ruddock, almost sadly, as though he wished Élise could be here to appreciate the moment. I wished she was here, too. I'd have enjoyed watching her take Ruddock apart.

"Then it's over," I told Ruddock, simply. "You know as well as we do that you can't possibly kill Mr. Weatherall and leave here alive."

"We shall see about that," said Ruddock. "Now open the door, then step away from it."

I stayed where I was until he cast me a warning look at the same time as eliciting a shout of pain from Helene with the barrel of the pistol. And then I opened the door and moved a few steps to the side.

"I can offer you a trade," said Ruddock, pulling Helene around and backing toward the black rectangle of the entrance.

Jacques, still tensed, dying to get a shot at Ruddock; Weatherall, furious but thinking, thinking; and me, watching, waiting, fingers flexing on the hidden blade.

"His life for hers," continued Ruddock, indicating Weatherall. "You allow me to kill him now, and I free the girl when I'm clear."

Weatherall's face was very, very dark. The fury seemed

to roll off him in waves. "I would sooner take my own life than allow you to take it, boy."

"That's your choice. Either way your corpse is on the floor when I leave or the girl dies."

"And what about the girl?"

"She lives," he said. "I take her with me, then let her go when I'm clear and sure you're not trying to double-cross me."

"How do we know you won't kill her?"

"Why would I?"

"Mr. Weatherall," I began, "there's no way we're letting him take Helene. We're not . . ."

Weatherall interrupted me. "I beg your pardon, Mr. Dorian, let me just hear it from Ruddock here. Let me just hear the lie from his mouth, because the bounty isn't just for Élise's protector, is it, Ruddock? It's for her protector *and* her lady's maid, Ruddock. You've no intention of letting Helene go."

Ruddock's shoulders rose and fell as his breathing became heavier, his options narrowing by the second.

"I'm not leaving here empty-handed," he said, "just so you can hunt me down and kill me another time."

"What other choice do you have? Either people die and one of them is you, or you leave and spend the rest of your life as a marked man."

"I'm taking the letters," he said, finally. "Hand me the letters, and I'll let the girl go when I'm clear."

"You're not taking Helene," I said. "You can take the letters, but Helene never leaves this lodge."

I wonder if he appreciated the irony that had he not

followed me, had he just waited in Versailles, I would have brought him the letters.

"You'll come after me," he said, uncertainly. "As soon as I let go of her."

"I won't," I said. "You have my word of honor. You may have your letters and leave."

He seemed to decide. "Give me the letters," he demanded.

Weatherall reached into the trunk, took the sheaf of letters and held them up.

"*You*," Ruddock told Jacques, "lover boy. Put the letters in my bag on my horse and bring it around, then shoo away the Assassin's mount. Be fast and get back here or she dies."

Jacques looked from me to Weatherall. We both nodded and he darted out into the moonlight.

The seconds passed and we waited, Helene quiet now, watching us over Ruddock's forearm as Ruddock covered me with the pistol, his eyes on me, not paying much attention to Weatherall, thinking he posed no threat.

Jacques returned, sidling inside with his eyes on Helene, waiting to collect her.

"Right, is everything ready?" said Ruddock.

I saw Ruddock's plan flash across his eyes. I saw it so clearly he might as well have said it out loud. His plan was to kill me with the first shot, Jacques with the second, deal with Helene and Weatherall by blade.

Perhaps Weatherall saw it, too. Perhaps Weatherall had been planning his move all along. Whatever the truth, I don't know, but in the same moment as Ruddock shoved Helene away from himself and swung his gun arm toward me, Weatherall's hand appeared from within the trunk, the sheath to Élise's short sword flipped up and away, and the sword itself appeared in his fingers.

And it was so much larger than a throwing knife that I thought he couldn't possibly find his target, but of course, his knife-throwing skills were at their honed best and the sword twirled and I dived at the same time, hearing the shot and the ball zip past my ear as one sound, regaining my balance and springing my hidden blade, ready to leap and plunge it into Ruddock before he loosed his second shot.

But Ruddock had a sword in his face, his eyes swiveling in opposite directions as his head snapped back and he staggered, his second shot going safely into the ceiling, as his body teetered back, then he fell, dead before he hit the floor.

On Weatherall's face was a look of grim satisfaction, as though he had laid a ghost to rest.

Helen ran to Jacques and then for some while we just stood, the four of us, looking at one another, then at Ruddock's prone body, barely able to believe it was all over and that we had survived.

And then, once we had carried Ruddock outside for burial the next day, I collected my horse and went to continue loading my saddlebags. As I did so I felt Helene's hand on my arm and gazed into eyes that were bloodshot from crying, but no less sincere for that.

"Mr. Dorian, we'd love you stay," she said. "You could take Élise's bedchamber."

12 September 1794

I've stayed here ever since, out of sight and, perhaps even where the Assassins are concerned, out of mind.

I've read Élise's journals, of course, and realized that though we didn't know enough of each other in our adult lives, I still knew her better than anyone else, because we were the same, she and I, kindred spirits sharing mutual experiences, our paths through life virtually identical.

Except, as I said before, Élise had got there first, and it was she who had come to the conclusion that there could be unity between Assassin and Templar. Finally, from her journal had slipped a letter. It read . . .

Dearest Arno,

If you are reading this then either my trust in Ruddock has been justified, or his greed has prevailed. In either case, if you are reading this, then you have my journals.

I trust having read them you may understand me a little more and be more sympathetic to the choices I have made. I hope you can see now that I shared your hopes for a truce between Assassin and Templar, and to that end have one final request of you, my darling. I ask that you take these principles back to your Brothers in the Creed and make good on them. And when they tell you that your ideas are fanciful and naïve, remind them how you and I proved that differences of doctrine can be overcome.

Please do this for me, Arno. And think of me. Just as I shall think of you, until we are together again.

Your beloved,
Élise

"Please do this for me, Arno."

Sitting here now, I wonder if I have the strength. I wonder if I could ever be as strong as she was. I hope so.

LIST OF CHARACTERS

Albertine, Lucio: scholar
Albertine, Monica: Lucio's mother
Bellec, Pierre: Assassin
Bernard: informant
Birch, Reginald: Templar Grand Master
Burnel, Jean: young Templar
Calvert, Jean-Jacques: Templar
Carroll, Madame: Templar
Carroll, May: Templar, daughter of Madame and
  Mr. Carroll
Carroll, Mr.: Templar
Christian: shoemaker
de Calonne, Vicomte: French controller-general
  of finances

de Flesselles, Jacques: French provost of the merchants

de Kilmister, Marquis: Templar

de la Serre, Élise: Templar Grand Master

de la Serre, François: Templar Grand Master, father of Élise

de la Serre, Julie: Templar, mother of Élise

de Launay: governor of the Bastille

de Molay, Jacques: Templar Grand Master

de Pimôdan, Marquis: Templar

de Robespierre, Maximilien: president of the Jacobins

de Simonon, Marquis: Templar

Dorian, Arno: ward of the de la Serre family

Dorian, Charles: Assassin, father of Arno Dorian

Emanuel: the de la Serre family's gardener

Germain, François Thomas: Templar

Harvey, Mr.: Templar hit man

Helene: Élise's lady's maid

Henri: gardener

Hook, Mr.: Templar hit man

Jackson, Captain Byron: ship's captain, smuggler

Jacques: school groundskeeper

Jean: the de la Serre family's coachman

Justine: Julie de la Serre's lady's maid

Kenway, Edward: Assassin

Kenway, Haytham: Templar Grand Master

La Touche, Aloys: Templar, a Crow

Lafrenière, Chretien: Templar, a Crow

Le Fanu, Claire: wife of Monsieur Le Fanu

Le Fanu, Monsieur: Templar

Le Peletier: Templar, a Crow

Levene, Madame: school's headmistress

Levesque, Madame: Templar, a Crow

Louis XVI, King: king of France

Marat, Jean Paul: doctor and scientist

Marie Antoinette: queen of France

Mills: Jennifer Scott's footman

Mirabeau: Master Assassin

Mother Superior: head of Élise's convent

Olivier: the de la Serre family's head butler

Poulou, Judith: Élise's schoolmate

Ruddock: Assassin

Ruth: Élise's nursemaid

Scott, Miss Jennifer: daughter of Edward Kenway, sister to Haytham

Selene: servingwoman

Sivert, Charles Gabriel: Templar, a Crow

Smith: Jennifer Scott's butler

Valerie: Élise's schoolmate

Weatherall, Freddie: Élise's confidant and protector

Acknowledgements

Special thanks to

Yves Guillemot

Aymar Azaizia

Anouk Bachman

Travis Stout

And also

Alain Corre

Laurent Detoc

Sébastien Puel

Geoffroy Sardin

Xavier Guilbert

Tommy François

Christopher Dormoy

Mark Kinkelin

Ceri Young

Russell Lees

James Nadiger

Alexandre Amancio

Mohamed Gambouz

Gilles Beloeil

Vincent Pontbriand

Cecile Russeil

Joshua Meyer

The Ubisoft Legal

Department

Etienne Allonier

Antoine Ceszynski

Clément Prevosto

Damien Guillotin

Gwenn Berhault

Alex Clarke

Hana Osman

Andrew Holmes

Chris Marcus

Virginie Sergent

Clémence Deleuze

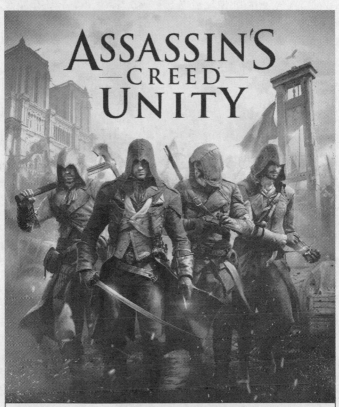